PRAISE FOR R

"I would follow Robert Dugoni a

—Lisa Gardner, #1 *New York Times* bestselling author

"Dugoni is a superb storyteller."

—*Boston Globe*

"Dugoni is every bit the equal of Lisa Gardner and Harlan Coben when it comes to psychological suspense."

—*Providence Journal*

"Dugoni has become one of the best crime novelists in the business."

—*Romantic Times*, Top Pick

"A writer at the top of his game."

—Authorlink

"An author who seems like he hasn't met a genre he can't conquer."

—Bookreporter

"Dugoni's writing is compellingly quick, simple, and evocative."

—Seattle Book Review

Praise for the Tracy Crosswhite series

"Tracy Crosswhite is one of the best protagonists in the realm of crime fiction today, and there is nothing cold about *A Cold Trail*."

—Associated Press

"Crime writing of the absolute highest order."

—*Providence Journal*

Praise for the Charles Jenkins series

"Reviving all that was tense during the Cold War, Dugoni has fashioned a wonderful series around sleeper agents and one American's duty to protect those involved."

—*Mystery and Suspense Magazine*

"*The Eighth Sister* is a great mix of spycraft and classic adventure, with a map of Moscow in hand."

—Martin Cruz Smith, international bestselling author

A KILLING ON THE HILL

ALSO BY ROBERT DUGONI

Her Deadly Game
The World Played Chess
The Extraordinary Life of Sam Hell
The 7th Canon
Damage Control

The Tracy Crosswhite Series

My Sister's Grave
Her Final Breath
In the Clearing
The Trapped Girl
Close to Home
A Steep Price
A Cold Trail
In Her Tracks
What She Found
One Last Kill
"The Last Line" (a short story)
"The Academy" (a short story)
"Third Watch" (a short story)

The Charles Jenkins Series

The Eighth Sister
The Last Agent
The Silent Sisters

The David Sloane Series

The Jury Master
Wrongful Death
Bodily Harm
Murder One
The Conviction

Nonfiction with Joseph Hilldorfer

The Cyanide Canary

A KILLING ON THE HILL

A THRILLER

ROBERT DUGONI

THOMAS & MERCER

This is a work of fiction. Names, characters, organizations, places, events, and incidents are either products of the author's imagination or are used fictitiously. Otherwise, any resemblance to actual persons, living or dead, is purely coincidental.

Published by Thomas & Mercer, Seattle

www.apub.com

ISBN-13: 9781662500268 (hardcover)
ISBN-13: 9781662500251 (paperback)
ISBN-13: 9781662500244 (digital)

Cover design by Will Staehle
Cover images: © ClassicStock / Alamy Stock Photo / Alamy; © Ihor Nebesnyi / Shutterstock; © Claudio Gennari / Shutterstock; © Paul Popper/Popperfoto / Contributor / Getty Images; © RetroClipArt / Shutterstock

Printed in the United States of America

First edition

To the Glendale boys: James, Johnson, Jim, Jeff, Tim, Mark, Kevin, Alan, Doug, and Dr. Dan. From eastern Washington to Ireland, Mexico, and everywhere in between. It's been a lot of fun.

There can be no higher law in journalism than to tell the truth and shame the devil.

—Walter Lippmann

Part I

Chapter 1

Mrs. Alderbrook shouted as she banged on my door, giving little consideration to either the early morning hour or the sleeping schedules of the other occupants of her twelve-room boardinghouse, where I rented a room for five dollars a month.

"William? William! You have a telephone call on the house phone!"

I shot out of bed fearing the worst—a call from my mother that my father had become another Depression statistic, like my uncle Ted.

It had been almost a year to the day, June 11, 1932, that I graduated from high school and my father informed me he could no longer provide me room and board. As moths danced around the bare bulb lighting our porch in Kansas City, Missouri, my father expressed his regret and his frustration. "I'm sorry, son. I don't have the money to send you to college, and, well, your aunt Ida lost Uncle Ted and is coming to live with us. We can't put her out on the street."

My uncle Ted wasn't lost. He'd committed suicide and had to be buried in a nondenominational cemetery.

It made me nervous knowing my father also hung by a financial and emotional thread. "The unemployed don't need an accountant," he told me just before he handed me an armed forces recruitment brochure and asked, "Have you thought about the military?"

I had. Every boy in my high school had given the military thought.

"William?" Mrs. Alderbrook persisted. "I can't tie up the line all morning."

"I'm coming," I shouted and struggled to pull on trousers and make myself presentable.

When I yanked the door open, I found the hallway empty of Mrs. Alderbrook's hulking figure and hightailed it down two flights of stairs in my bare feet, fearing she would indeed hang up. She hadn't. The receiver to the upright candlestick telephone lay on the scuffed reception desk. I glanced at the grandfather clock in the lobby—7:10 a.m.

Mrs. Alderbrook glared at me, then lowered her gaze back to the *Seattle Post-Intelligencer*. Having a reporter for the *Seattle Daily Star* living in her boardinghouse didn't influence her choice of newspapers. Politics did. The *Post-Intelligencer* was the Republican voice, conservative, respectable, and a little prudish. The *Seattle Daily Times* backed the Democrats and was splashy, bold, and a bit vulgar. Between these two extremes, Howard Phishbaum, the *Daily Star* owner and my boss, sought to establish a secure foothold publishing the city's only afternoon newspaper. How did he intend to do this?

Pizzazz, Shoe! Get me some pizzazz!

Short for Shumacher, "Shoe" had become my nickname at the newspaper, and on the city beat I covered.

"Don't tie up the line," Mrs. Alderbrook huffed.

I placed the receiver to my ear and lifted the mouthpiece to my mouth. My hand quivered. "Hello?" I said, fearing the worst.

"William Shumacher?" The voice was male.

"Yes," I said, relieved.

"No need to shout, son. My hearing is just fine. This is Chief Detective Ernie Blunt."

After a year hustling stories—from the mayor's recall for graft and corruption, and his reelection just six months later, to best-in-class kennel dog shows—I'd finally received my hard-earned press badge from the chief of police. The badge accorded me access to crime scenes, though I had yet to be contacted by a detective, and certainly not one as esteemed as Ernie Blunt, the chief detective of Seattle's famed homicide squad. I moved the speaker away from my mouth. "Yes, Chief Detective."

"I've just received a call to hurry to the Pom Pom Club. Might be a gangster shooting. You know it?"

My adrenaline spiked. A gangster shooting. *Pizzazz!*

"If you want the story, meet me there in fifteen minutes. Top of Profanity Hill at Tenth and Yesler. Can't miss it. Big white house."

"Profanity Hill. Tenth and Yesler. A gangster shooting, you said. Yes."

"Try not holding the mouthpiece so close to your mouth," Blunt said. "I'm liable to go deaf."

I moved the mouthpiece away another few inches. "I'll find it," I said.

The perch clicked. Mrs. Alderbrook's meaty hand had reached across the counter and ended my call.

I raced up the stairs to my room. In no time I had finished dressing, grabbed my jacket and knit cap, and stocked my leather satchel with pencils and notebook paper before slinging it over my shoulder and hurrying back downstairs. I handed Mrs. Alderbrook the key to my room, which she kept on a hook below my mail slot, then rushed out the door to catch the Second Avenue streetcar at Pike Street for the ten block ride south to Yesler Way. At Yesler, I transferred to the streetcar that took me up Profanity Hill. My timing was impeccable and fortuitous. I didn't want to walk up First Hill. The city courthouse had once loomed large atop the hill, and stories were told of red-faced lawyers, judges, and litigants lugging heavy briefcases and uttering profanities when the streetcars broke down, which was often, giving First Hill its nickname.

I arrived at Tenth Avenue in just twelve minutes. The silence that precedes dawn still hung heavily over Profanity Hill. The white house did indeed stand out, as Blunt had said it would, but not as I had imagined. Blunt's use of the term "gangster killing" had caused me to imagine a back-alley dive rather than the elegant, two-story home I encountered. The house was nearly a quarter of a block long. Its fresh coat of paint; expansive, sloping lawn; and ornate flower beds were both a sharp contrast to the homes around it and an indication money flowed freely within the club's walls. It had no doubt been one of the many mansions the wealthy built atop the 366-foot slope. First Hill was peppered with Georgian Revivals, and Italianate and Queen Anne Victorians with slate roofs, gabled bays, teakwood furnishings, mosaic tile floors, Oriental carpets, stained-glass windows, and half a dozen fireplaces. As business and industry had expanded, and the necessary waterfront workforce moved to First Hill, the wealthy, loath to mix, fled. Their mansions had become low-rent boardinghouses, hotels, and disorderly houses of prostitution.

I noted a patrol car parked at the curb, and a Cadillac just around the corner from the club's front entrance. My nerves tingled with anticipation as I approached a police officer in his navy-blue uniform and peaked hat standing in front of a heavy-looking entrance door. The door was one of two. The second, an interior door, had a grated "peephole" such as I had seen at Chinatown speakeasies. Club members either showed a pass or uttered a password. And if the police came by the establishment, the person manning the interior door flipped a switch to flicker the lights, a sign to the staff to hide alcohol and evidence of gambling.

Getting closer, I recognized the officer's grim expression and large form. "Officer Lutz," I said, adjusting the press badge on my lapel.

Lutz was a stout man of German descent, which seemed to give us common ground, though I was just five foot nine and 140 pounds.

"Shoe. How did you get here so fast?" Lutz asked, his voice gravelly from the early morning hour. Lutz was close to retirement. His gray hair had receded in a horseshoe pattern, and his blue eyes had become clouded with age, like my Oma's.

"Got a call of a shooting," I said, having learned from Phish—which is what everyone called Howard Phishbaum—to never reveal a source.

We beat reporters had an unwritten agreement with the police department, especially the brass. The police provided us with story tips and access to crime scenes, police investigations, witnesses, and, ultimately, the prosecutor who would try the case. In return, we wrote favorable articles about the police department. Step out of line, and the chief of police would pull your press badge. The relationship was incestuous, even to me, just a year on the job, but in a depression, most people were a paycheck away from moving to one of the city's Hoovervilles, shantytowns named after the former president that housed Seattle's homeless and down-and-out. "Hmm," Lutz grunted. "Well, you can't go in. Not yet. Waiting on the detectives."

"You been in?" I asked.

"Found the body," he said. "Called it in."

"What time was that?"

"Call came in at six thirty this morning. I got here as quick as I could."

"How many shots were fired?"

"Can't be certain."

"Anyone inside when you arrived?"

Another nod. "George Miller, the owner, and his partner, Syd Brunn. A waiter and the bartender too. Also the caretaker who cleans the place was asleep in the back."

"Who got shot?"

"Frankie Ray."

"The prizefighter?"

Lutz's eyes narrowed. "Before your time; ain't he?"

As a boy I had listened to the fights on the radio with my father. Ray, a lightweight boxer, had made his way up the ranks in Washington State. He had a knockout combination that included two right hands. "Right, Right Ray" they had called him. If he hit you, you went down and stayed down—if you knew what was good for you. Had a shot at Tony Canzoneri, the lightweight champ, but lost a preliminary to Barney Ross. Some said Ray took a dive.

"Shame. Guy like that," Lutz said. "Had a chance to be somebody, and instead he's just a punk."

"A punk?"

"A hanger-on, more or less, at least as far as the underworld is concerned. Not a fellow you'd expect to be killed by some gangster."

"George Miller?" I asked.

Lutz nodded once and looked up at the white house dwarfing us. "Owns a number of clubs, though not like this. This is his crown jewel. The others are much smaller—roadside taverns and other such establishments. And a few disreputable houses too."

As Lutz talked, his gaze shifted to behind me. Ernie Blunt and King County prosecutor Laurence McKinley approached. The prosecuting attorney's office and the police also had a symbiotic relationship. A prosecuting attorney often accompanied detectives to crime scenes. The office claimed the cooperation helped bring criminals to justice.

"Shoe," Blunt said, hand extended. He approached like a battlefield tank. Square and sturdy, from his jaw to his shoulders. When I shook his hand, it was like shaking a catcher's mitt. He had a five-o'clock shadow but otherwise dressed as if for a night on the town in a well-made, three-piece, dark-brown suit and oxford shoes.

"Detective Blunt," I said. "Mr. McKinley." I used their formal names out of deference. I knew McKinley from covering two superior court trials he had prosecuted. In his late thirties, McKinley had a serious look about him. His prematurely gray hair aged him. Whereas Blunt was a brick, McKinley was a reed, over six feet. His suit hung from his shoulders like he'd recently lost weight.

Blunt's use of my nickname made me feel like I belonged and relieved some of my nerves. "So this is the Pom Pom Club?" My comment sounded simple, and I rushed to explain. "I expected some basement hole-in-the-wall at the end of an alley. Gangsters here?"

"Just the underworld putting out a little honey to attract bigger flies," Blunt said, then started toward Lutz atop the steps. Everything about Blunt exuded confidence. He acted like he was entering the club as a customer anticipating a good meal and a show.

"Chief Detective," Lutz said. "I'm glad you got here."

"What do you got, Walter?"

"Call came in to the radio operator. Shots fired at six thirty this morning. I was first on scene."

Blunt nodded to the two doors. "Doors open or closed?"

"Open."

"Anybody at the door?"

Lutz shook his head.

"They expected us, then. What next?"

"Next, I stepped inside the club and stopped short."

Blunt gave Lutz a perplexed look.

"Four men in suits and hats stood with their backs against the bar as if on their way out. Hats on, coats draped over their arms. The caretaker too. They stared at me but not one uttered a word."

"Where was the victim?"

"Found him in the adjacent room, face down on the dance floor in a pool of blood."

"Dead?" Blunt asked.

"That's what I asked." He shook his head as if disgusted. "Not one word spoken. They remained silent as statues. I moved to the victim and bent to a knee. I heard gurgling sounds coming from the man's throat and saw pinkish foam on his lips."

"Alive, then."

"When they took him away, he was."

"Who called for an ambulance?"

"I did. Used the telephone in the hallway on the wall. Asked that they send a doc to the Pom Pom Club and gave them the address. Told them to hurry. Ambulance arrived in under five minutes. Took the victim to the city hospital."

"None of the men at the bar has said anything?" McKinley asked.

"Not a word," Lutz reiterated.

"We'll see." Blunt moved past Lutz, McKinley following. I took that as my cue to also enter. I was anxious to see the inside of a swanky nightclub. From the entryway, we stepped down into a barroom that smelled of beer and leftover food.

Five men at a modernistic bar did indeed stand as rigid as Medusa's victims turned to stone, but I was struck more by the luxurious mahogany bar lined with glasses and beer bottles—as beer was now legal—and a cash register with its tray open, as if it had just rung up another sale. I didn't see liquor bottles, but liquor was here. A place like this, you could bet on it. Behind the bar, a large mirror reflected the room, making it look twice as large. Beneath the bar sat an iron safe, the door cracked open, a handgun atop it. Down a narrow hall from the bar was a lavatory and the wall phone Lutz had mentioned. The hall looked to open onto a polished wood dance floor, of which I could only see a portion.

One of the men at the bar said, "Hello, Ernie. It's about time somebody with some authority got here to let us go." The man, clad in immaculate tropical flannels, spoke calmly, without urgency. As Lutz had described, the men had hats on, and light topcoats draped over their arms.

"Hello, George," Blunt said, his tone also casual, but his gaze roamed over the barroom and the hallway beyond it.

"Nasty business to have happen in a guy's place, huh?" the man, whom I now assumed to be George Miller, said. A gangster, Officer Lutz had said, part of the underworld. Miller looked and sounded like a guy on his way to work downtown, not someone who had just killed another man. "It'll keep business away for a while, I would guess. Seems a guy can't make an honest living no more without someone trying to take advantage."

"Save the gab, George," Blunt said, clearly not buying whatever Miller was selling. "You'll need it."

Blunt walked toward the dance hall. I followed. Private dining rooms and wall booths with luxurious overstuffed seats surrounded tables with partly filled liquor glasses, champagne bottles, and plates of half-eaten dinners—what looked like scrumptious steaks, pork chops, chicken, baked potatoes, vegetables, and slices of pie—enough food to feed half of Hooverville. Mounds of cigarette stubs littered ashtrays on the tables, and stale smoke permeated the air. The room's focal point was a mural on the wall behind the private booths, a three-masted schooner in a winter storm.

The windows had been blackened to provide the guests privacy. I could imagine men dressed in their finest worsted-wool suits and tuxedos escorting bejeweled women wearing sequined gowns and furs onto the dance floor to hear the orchestra, or playing dice at craps tables at the back of the room—living as if the Depression was something to avoid catching, like consumption or whooping cough.

I asked Blunt, "That was George Miller?"

"He's a slick one," Blunt said quietly. "He owns and manages this joint."

Lutz and McKinley stood beside us in the large dance hall. "Everything is just as we found it, Chief Detective, except the guy who was shot," Lutz said. "But I marked the floor here with chalk where he was lying."

"Good man," Blunt said.

The faint chalk lines on the dance floor were just inside the entryway from the barroom and circled a puddle of blood.

"Who got shot?" Blunt asked.

"Frankie Ray," Lutz said.

"The boxer?" Blunt sounded surprised.

"One and the same," Lutz said.

"I think we better go over to the hospital, see if he's still alive and what tale he'll tell," Blunt said to McKinley. As he spoke, more police officers entered the club. Blunt spoke to Lutz. "Keep our gentlemen friends at the bar entertained while we're gone. Don't let them, or any of you, touch anything."

Outside, Blunt, McKinley, and I walked toward a black Ford Model B two-door sedan parked among several patrol cars. Blunt said, "Nice little weapon. Luger semiautomatic. You catch it atop the safe?"

"I did," McKinley said.

“Looks like two shots. Both went through Ray,” Blunt said.

“How could you know?” I asked.

Blunt smiled.

“I suppose you noticed the handgun,” I said. “But, I mean, how could you know it was the gun used or the number of shots fired?”

“The safe was dusty and some of the dust had been recently disturbed, meaning the gun was placed there but didn’t start out there. So we can presume the killer used the Luger. As for the number of shots, two ejected casings were lying just inside the dancing room. And two bullets are embedded in the wall on the other side of the room, above the wainscoting. That’s where I may be wrong. One shot may have missed Ray. But from the position of the holes—close together—I judged if one bullet struck Ray, the other must have also.”

McKinley smiled as if he’d witnessed this type of deduction before and got a kick out of my amazed expression.

Chapter 2

We arrived at the City Emergency Hospital inside the Yesler Building. In my year working as a reporter, I had become a fixture at the building in Pioneer Square as well as the newly constructed courthouse on Third Avenue. Nathan Kawolski, my predecessor on the police and court beats, had given me a brief introduction to the city beat when I started. Seattle politics, he said, were more than a little incestuous, particularly within the walls of the Yesler Building.

"The mayor appoints the chief of police, and both keep an office, along with some King County Superior Court judges, in the Yesler Building." He pointed to the trapezoid-shaped structure that resembled a battleship with its prow steaming down First Hill toward the waterfront. "On the top floor is the city jail. The emergency hospital is on the third floor, and the Seattle Police Department on the second. You'll spend most of your time there. You don't even have to be ambitious," Kawolski emphasized. "If you hang around the lobby long enough, a story will hit you on the head like a brick falling from one of the buildings in Pioneer Square, which happens, so be careful."

That had been the extent of my introduction to my beat as a *Daily Star* reporter. Kawolski, I would learn soon enough, didn't have the time or the inclination to help. He came to work promptly at seven and left even more promptly after the *Daily Star*'s afternoon publication. He ate lunch sitting at his desk, usually a cheese sandwich, and drank a cup of black coffee.

I'd had just one year of high school journalism, and my initial articles took Phish more time to correct than they took me to type. Fearing I might get fired during Phish's imposed probationary period, I had devoted my evenings to studying the articles written in the two established morning newspapers, the *Seattle Daily Times* and the *Seattle Post-Intelligencer*. The *Post-Intelligencer*, the city's oldest newspaper, had survived the 1889 Great Fire; the Panic of 1893; and, so far, the Depression. Its city beat reporter was Archibald Greer, a well-seasoned newsman. The *Seattle Daily Times* emphasized crime and scandal, what its detractors called "yellow journalism," after the comic strip character the Yellow Kid. Its city beat reporter was Emmet Winn, who'd earned the nickname "Early" because he'd once always been first to a story. I studied how each reporter opened his articles stating the most important facts first, then filled in the story with quotes—a strategy that soon became my best friend. Quotes lengthened my articles, and since Phish paid me a penny for every inch of printable news, the more quotes I used, the more money I made.

I had no choice but to survive. Things had turned for the worse for my family. My father's accounting income dried up completely. My mother and her sister brought in some money doing odd sewing jobs, though not much. I sent home what money I could, which didn't amount to more than a couple dollars a month. Not that I could afford it. The first six months, dinners at the boardinghouse were often my only meal of the day. I cinched my belt two additional notches and still had trouble keeping my pants up. My shoes had holes in the bottoms that I fixed with cardboard, and my face had become gaunt.

As we walked the hospital hallway, Blunt encountered a doctor.

"Dr. Hartley," Blunt said.

"Detective," Dr. Hartley said. It seemed everyone knew Blunt. Dr. Hartley wore a long white coat and grim expression. "I assume you're here about Frankie Ray?"

"How is he?"

Dr. Hartley slowly shook his head. "He's badly wounded," he said. "Two bullets shot clear through him." Blunt glanced knowingly at McKinley. Hartley continued: "One fired at close range through the right side of his body. The other through his left arm and left side."

"Conscious?"

"Just barely. I doubt he can talk. We're just about to move him into surgery."

"Will it matter?"

"Not a chance, I'm afraid. He may die any minute." He nodded over his shoulder. "You want to go in, I assume?"

"Before he dies."

"Better be quick."

Again, I followed Blunt and McKinley, this time into a sterile room. Frankie Ray, his face pain-racked and pale, lay on a table.

"Hello, Frankie," Blunt said.

Ray turned his head ever so slightly. His eyes showed signs of recognition, but he said nothing.

"You're going to die," Blunt said. "You might as well tell us who got you."

Ray's head rolled further toward the detective. His chest oozed blood from the two bullet wounds. He heaved, and for a second, he held his breath, as if to gain the strength to utter the words he was about to say. Blunt leaned down and put his ear within an inch of Ray's lips. Ray spoke, though it was inaudible to me.

Blunt straightened, seemingly perplexed. He whispered something close to Ray's ear, but I heard him. "Tell me."

Ray grinned. Odd.

"Tell me, Frankie."

Ray responded, this time loud enough for me to hear. "That's for you to find out, Ernie. Do me a favor? Tell George Miller to go to hell."

Pink bubbles of foam appeared on Ray's lips. He gasped once and his eyes swept the room as if in an appeal, then closed for good. Though I did not know the man, the finality of the moment made me nauseous.

I'd never watched a man die. I fought to keep my empty stomach down and my pride intact. An acidic taste burned at the back of my throat.

Dr. Hartley put the ends of his stethoscope in his ears and held the bell to the four segments of Ray's chest, then removed the earpieces and shook his head.

Blunt turned from the hospital bed seemingly unfazed. "Give him credit. He wasn't a rat. He stuck to the underworld code. He didn't squeal." Then Blunt spoke to Hartley. "Where are his clothes and the stuff you found in his pockets?"

The doctor led us down a corridor to the receiving room. Frankie Ray's possessions had been laid out on a table. A billfold, a handkerchief, a pencil and a pen, a package of cigarettes, some small change, and some matches.

"Not much here," I said.

"Look again," Blunt said.

I did, but I didn't see anything significant.

"The handkerchief," Blunt said. He didn't elaborate, but I knew somehow this dirty piece of linen taken from Ray's pocket had some strange significance. Blunt turned to Dr. Hartley. "I want you to send a piece of the bloody cloth from Ray's shirt downstairs to headquarters, care of Luke May. You can attend to that?"

"I can," the doctor said.

Blunt turned and left. McKinley and I followed, though I had the good sense not to question Blunt about his statements. He'd tell me the significance of the pieces of bloody cloth when and if he wanted me to know.

I sensed, however, that I was on the verge of a big story, and I didn't want to blow this opportunity.

◆ ◆ ◆

Back at the Pom Pom Club, Blunt ordered the men at the bar into separate booths in the dance hall, with police officers standing close by. The men begrudgingly did as he asked, though Miller voiced his complaint on behalf of all. Blunt followed them into the room, stooped to retrieve the two ejected casings, then jingled them in his hand like spare change, eyeing the men.

"Frankie Ray is dead," Blunt said. "I'm sorry to detain you gentlemen, but you are all held as material witnesses to his shooting." Miller and a man I assumed to be Syd Brunn grumbled audibly. Blunt ignored their protests. "I'm going to talk to each of you in a few minutes. Wait here, please." He turned to the police officers. "No chatting between them." With that, he slid the casings into the pocket of his trousers and went back to the barroom.

Carefully, Blunt lifted the Luger semiautomatic from its place atop the safe, wrapped it in a linen napkin he took from behind the bar, and set it beside him on a table in the far corner of the room. Then he sat.

"Bring in George Miller," he instructed Officer Lutz. He spoke to me and McKinley in a quiet voice: "When I ask for a handkerchief, fumble for yours, but don't find it."

Puzzled, I nodded my assent. McKinley also looked confused.

Lutz walked in behind Miller. The underworld club owner had soured by this time. "What's the idea of keeping us all here so long?" he whined.

"Take a seat," Blunt said. Miller complied. Blunt leaned across the table. "Listen, George," he said, voice calm. "All I want is your story of what happened here this morning. You'll tell me, of course."

It was not a question. Miller considered McKinley, then me. "Who's the kid?"

"Never you mind that," Blunt said. "Just tell me your story."

Miller shifted his attention back to Blunt. "Sure thing, Ernie. There's nothing to hide. It was a stickup, and the stickup man got it, and that's all there is to it."

"Stickup, huh?" Blunt did not look or sound impressed.

"That's right. Ray came in late . . . or early, depending on how you look at it," Miller said. "Maybe around five o'clock. Just a few patrons left. I think maybe two or three over at the gambling tables and maybe a couple or two in the dance hall. The orchestra had wrapped up and left, and we were shutting it down."

I was surprised Miller admitted the club had gambling tables, which were illegal.

"Anybody with Ray?" Blunt asked.

"Nah. He was alone. So getting on here . . ."

Something about the way Miller said Ray had been alone struck me as rushed, a topic Miller didn't want to dwell on.

"Frankie goes into the dance hall and orders two or three drinks. Before that he'd sat at a booth drinking until everyone was gone—except for the five of us. We were all in here around the bar, except for the caretaker. He was off asleep. I was counting out the cash—the night's take, see. When all of a sudden, Ray comes and stands in the doorway over there between the barroom and the dance hall." Miller turned and motioned with his finger. "I turned and just then he reaches into his pocket and pulls out the semiautomatic." Miller's gaze shifted to the safe, then to the table. "I guess you got the gun," he said.

"I got it," Blunt said.

"Well, so Ray says, 'This is a stickup.' He was kind of wild and unsteady."

"A stickup, huh?" Blunt said again. He managed to say it without any judgment in his voice this time, as if reciting a fact, but I thought it odd he repeated the phrase.

"That's right. I came out from behind the bar and said, 'Frankie, what is this?' And he started for me. I thought he'd gone screwy, that he was drunk or something. So when the opportunity presented itself, I took a chance. I jumped at him and we wrestled for the gun."

I noticed Blunt was looking skeptically at the distance between the bar and the doorway leading to the dance floor, which had to be eight to ten feet. A heck of a jump.

"And I got ahold of the gun, see. Frankie, he twisted my arm, and the gun turned toward him, and I guess my finger closed on the trigger because there was a shot, see, and Frankie, he stumbled backward through the doorway and fell. I thought he was done. But after a moment or two he starts to get up, and he raises his hands over his head. Like this." Miller demonstrated. "I thought he was coming for me again. So, I let him have another and he fell. And that's all there is to it."

Miller told the story as if discussing a change in the weather.

For a long moment the detective stared at Miller.

"Ask the others. They'll tell you," Miller said.

Blunt spoke, as quiet as a whisper. "I will, but would you mind acting it out for me, George? I'd like to get it a little clearer in my mind."

Miller stood and did so, but this time McKinley and Blunt interrupted him frequently, asking him to reenact certain motions and answer additional questions. Miller moved behind the bar, then out into the room, demonstrating what happened. He stepped closer to the doorway where he said he leapt upon Ray before the gun went off. He moved closer to the bar and said he pulled the trigger a second time. Despite the persistent questioning, he stuck to his story, which sounded like a fable, even to me, but Blunt and McKinley seemed content to let Miller affirm it.

As Miller completed the demonstration, Blunt began a fit of coughing. His face reddened and he fumbled through his pockets. Then, with eyes watering, he asked me, "Got a handkerchief?"

His performance was so convincing I had my handkerchief halfway out of my pocket before I recalled Blunt telling me to say I didn't have one. Luckily, McKinley reminded me. "I must have left mine in my other suit," he said.

I inched my hand from my pocket and displayed my empty palm. "I must have left mine in my room," I said.

Miller pulled out his handkerchief and handed it to Blunt, who placed it before his mouth to stifle another cough. Then Blunt walked to the bar and poured himself a glass of water. "I'm sorry, can you repeat what happened one more time, George?" As Miller recounted his story yet again, Blunt shoved the handkerchief into his left pants pocket.

When Blunt and McKinley finished with Miller, Blunt instructed Lutz to bring Miller back to the dance hall and to escort in the other witnesses one by one. He asked each to explain what they saw and heard, then to act it out, playing the role of George Miller.

First was Syd Brunn, a bail bond broker who was also Miller's partner in the club. I thought he looked a bit like Clark Gable, who'd recently burst onto the Hollywood scene in the movie *Red Dust*, which I'd taken in at the Green Parrot Theatre. He had Gable's big ears and neatly combed dark hair. But he also had a withering gaze and serious expression. I would not have wanted to owe him money. He didn't seem the least bit intimidated to have Seattle's best detective questioning him.

Brunn, unlike Miller, was reticent. He responded with one-word answers and rarely expounded, even when Blunt asked him to do so. He also declined to act out the shooting, saying, "I ain't no actor. You should ask George these questions."

"I'm asking you," Blunt said.

"And I'm telling you to ask George what he did."

"So you didn't see what happened?" Blunt said.

"I didn't say that."

"So you did see."

"I saw whatever George told you happened," Brunn said, this time with a smug expression. He and Blunt engaged in a staring contest that seemed to last minutes. Blunt broke it off and told Lutz to take Brunn back and to bring in the bartender, Billy Vahle.

Vahle and Archie Brown, a waiter, offered stories identical to Miller's, which was interesting only because Vahle said he had gone into a back room to get his coat to go home and didn't really see the shooting or what had led to it. And Brown said he'd been busy bussing tables. The last interview was Sandy Allen, who said he was asleep in the back room, heard the shots, but by the time he dashed into the barroom, it was over. He didn't see or hear what had happened. To me, Allen was the only one who sounded credible.

Blunt asked each man, "If you didn't see what happened, why'd you stay put?"

Each said Miller told them to stay, that the police would have questions about what had happened.

As each man told Blunt his version of the story, Blunt repeatedly engaged in coughing fits, like a man who had a critical case of consumption. He managed to obtain each man's handkerchief, except for Allen, who didn't have one. Blunt slipped each handkerchief in a different pocket of his trousers and his jacket, in a clockwise fashion, which, I deduced, was to better remember which handkerchief belonged to which man.

After questioning, Blunt ordered the uniformed officers to take the five men to headquarters for further questioning, despite Miller's persistent protests.

"What are you trying to do, Blunt? I told you what happened, and these men confirmed my story. What do you want us for?"

I wondered the same thing, as well as the purpose of all those handkerchiefs. The story Miller told might have been a fable, but if so, the others had corroborated it, even the two who claimed not to have seen what had happened. Outside, I told Blunt as much. McKinley again smiled, as if I was the most naïve person on the planet.

"It's not even a good lie," Blunt said. "But I'm hungry. It's way past breakfast time. Let's get something to eat and let them cool their heels in jail cells until we get back to question them again."

We left the Pom Pom Club and drove to a reserved spot at the Yesler Building, then walked down the hill to Manning's Cafeteria on Third Avenue. Just outside the door, a young boy hawked the *Seattle Daily Times*. At the end of the block, another boy hawked the *Post-Intelligencer*. I took pride knowing only the *Daily Star* had been privy to what had happened at the Pom Pom Club. My story would be in the afternoon paper, well ahead of the other newspapers. Initially, I had wondered why Blunt called me and not Greer or Winn, but Winn and Greer had become complacent and lazy. Based on the articles I read each day, neither reporter did much investigating. I had not seen either at the Yesler Building or at the new courthouse on Third Avenue but once or twice. Their articles had become rote and lacked pizzazz.

By contrast, I had been at the Yesler Building and courthouse hustling every day, for pennies on the inches, asking questions, doing interviews, digging in files. I didn't have a choice. I couldn't lose this job. My family was depending on me. So maybe people like Detective Blunt had taken notice of my hard work and given me a chance?

The cafeteria owners greeted Blunt like a celebrity. They seated us at a booth close to a long buffet. I didn't have money to spend on breakfast and was content to sip a cup of coffee, but Blunt handed me a platter from the buffet. When I deftly declined, he said, "They won't charge you. They like having a detective and a prosecuting attorney in their establishment; don't they, Larry?"

McKinley smiled.

I was almost always hungry since moving to Seattle and needed no further encouragement. The smells from the buffet made my mouth water. I tried to be judicious, but Blunt encouraged me to fill my plate with crisp bacon, a slice of ham, scrambled eggs, diced potatoes, and toast. At the table, the waitress poured each of us a cup of steaming black coffee while bantering with Blunt.

I slid out a notebook and a couple pencils from my leather satchel and set them on the table beside my plate and utensils. Blunt was about to speak when I asked, "What did Ray say to you in the hospital room?"

Blunt sipped his coffee. "You didn't hear him?" he asked over the rim. McKinley and I both shook our heads. Blunt set down his cup. "Said he wasn't a squealer. It was for me to find out who shot him."

"Wow," I said softly. "Even while dying."

"'Thieves are never rogues amongst themselves,'" Blunt said. "*Don Quixote*. Have you read it?"

"No," I said. I only brought one book out from Kansas City, *The Count of Monte Cristo*. I kept meaning to get to the library, but I never seemed to find the time.

"Getting back to your question outside the Pom Pom Club about Miller's story . . ." He glanced down at my notepad and pencils.

I set my fork and napkin on the table, picked up a pencil, and opened the notepad.

"In the first place," Blunt said, "Ray isn't a stickup man. He's never carried a gun in his life."

"But," McKinley said, shoveling eggs into his mouth. "That isn't evidence, Ernie. That wouldn't even get to a jury."

"I know," Blunt said. "I'm merely explaining for Shoe's benefit." He redirected his attention to me and nibbled a piece of bacon. "Remember I picked up the two ejected casings just inside the door to the dance hall?"

"Sure."

"Does that mean anything to you?"

I wasn't sure where this was headed, but Blunt didn't give me a chance to guess.

"With a semiautomatic, shell casings fly backward when they're ejected. If Miller fired those shots from where he said he stood, the shell casings would have landed close to the bar—not in another room some twenty feet away. That's evidence he's lying," Blunt said.

"You'll need more than that," McKinley said and sipped his coffee.

"No. *You'll* need more than that." Blunt gave me a wry grin, then bit off another piece of bacon. "That first shot might have been fired the way Miller said, even if we disregard the ejected shell casings, but the second shot could not have been." Blunt watched my face for a moment before continuing. "Remember what the doctor said?"

"One shot was fired at close range. The other shot wasn't."

"That's right. If we accept Miller's story, it was the second shot that tore through Ray's arm and then into his body," Blunt said. "Miller said Ray's hands were raised over his head when he fired the second shot."

"That's right. He did say that," I said, a little too animated.

Blunt then stated what he'd made obvious. "You can't shoot a man through the arm *and* his body with one bullet if his arms are raised."

McKinley said to Blunt, "Hell, Ernie, that's not enough evidence to hold these fellows on if they fight us with a writ." Then for my benefit he said, "Trying to hold five men in jail as material witnesses without a charge isn't a job I relish. At the moment, convinced as I might be George Miller is a liar, I have no proof to charge him as a killer."

"How long before they can obtain a hearing on a writ?" Blunt asked.

"Forty-eight hours."

"That's about time enough."

"What do you mean?" McKinley asked.

Blunt continued eating. "I think George Miller lied in every detail," he said finally. "And I think someone else went with Ray to the club."

I felt good, having reached the same conclusion.

"And I think George Miller had a reason to kill Ray," Blunt said. "I don't know what it is yet, but we'll know soon enough."

"Someone else with him?" McKinley said. "What evidence exists of that?"

I had an epiphany. "The handkerchiefs."

Blunt slid his plate to the side and gave me a nod. "I wanted to finish breakfast before I showed you this." He drew from his pocket a dirty and bloodstained handkerchief, holding it gingerly between his fingers. He twirled it once. "Frankie Ray's handkerchief was in his pants pocket at the hospital, so it isn't this bloody one I found near the bar," Blunt said. "And the rest of them had their handkerchiefs on them when I asked for one, except for the caretaker, who was sleeping in the back and wouldn't have had one given he was sleeping in his boxers and a T-shirt. I established that, haven't I?" He didn't wait for an answer. He provided it by laying the collection of handkerchiefs he'd commandeered on the table beside the one soaked with blood.

"I wanted to make sure the bloody one wasn't one of theirs, first," he said. "I'm sure now it wasn't. Not many men carry two handkerchiefs. I thought maybe Miller, or one of the others, might have used their handkerchief to try and stop the flow of blood from Ray's wounds.

That didn't seem likely given Lutz's recounting that the men didn't help Ray, but it was a possibility. Not anymore. Now I'm sure this handkerchief belongs to someone else. Someone in the room when Ray was shot, but who fled before the police arrived."

"But Ernie, that handkerchief could belong to anyone." McKinley sounded like he was trying to regain some semblance of composure for missing Blunt's deduction. "A guest at the club with a bloody nose. A bartender who cut his hand. Anyone."

Even as McKinley spoke, however, I wondered if the bloody handkerchief's owner had murdered Frankie Ray. I wondered if it was this person George Miller's lies were protecting.

"I think we can rule out this handkerchief belonging to your mythical guest with a bloody nose," Blunt said calmly, and he slid from the booth without elaborating.

Chapter 3

A few minutes later, we were back at headquarters inside the Yesler Building. The police department was hopping. The five men had been processed, then given separate cells on the fourth floor. McKinley went down the hall to the smoking room in the northeast corner to have a cigarette. Afterward, he'd take a private passage along the building's south side and fill in corporate counsel/city attorney Anton Van Soelen about the murder. I commandeered a telephone in the hallway and dictated the lede of my article to Monte Kravitz, the *Daily Star*'s apprentice. I deliberately did not call Phish, concerned he'd send out Nathan Kawolski, who had more experience and could hijack the story. This was the chance I had waited for to prove to Phish I could handle a big story. It was coming up on a year since my arrival, and I hoped my competence would be rewarded with a weekly salary.

I used what I'd learned from Blunt as the lede to my article.

> Frankie Ray was not a big shot in the underworld. He was not a leader, not even a lieutenant or a good henchman. The former lightweight boxer was more of a hanger-on, gleaning here and there what others dropped in their hustles. Why then was he shot dead this morning, found lying in a pool of his own blood on

the polished oak dance floor of the luxurious Pom Pom Club on Yesler Hill?

Two gunshots cracked the serenity of Yesler Hill at approximately 6:30 this morning, followed by the screeching sound of police cars converging on the nightclub run by Seattle's underworld. Cocktail glasses with banned alcohol and plates of unfinished meals and desserts littered the tables and booths surrounding the dance floor. Blacked-out and curtained windows hid empty gambling tables, and chalk outlined where Ray lay dying.

Clinging to life in the City Emergency Hospital in the Yesler Building, Ray wouldn't tell Chief Detective Ernie Blunt who'd pulled the trigger of a Luger semiautomatic pistol and put two projectiles of lead in his body. He'd adhered to the code amongst thieves not to rat, not even on the man who had twice pulled the trigger and murdered him.

Who was that man?

The secret belongs to those who are not in the habit of confiding in the police. Blunt and prosecuting attorney Laurence McKinley are holding five material witnesses in the King County Jail, but based on Blunt's initial interviews at the Pom Pom Club, they will have to fight to get the answers to Ray's killing.

I added as much as I could without revealing anything about the handkerchiefs or other sensitive information that could possibly jeopardize my press pass. I had also become more attuned to Phish's desire for pizzazz in my articles, and of course, I fought for every article inch and the pennies each inch paid.

After I'd hung up the phone, I found Blunt in the detective room snapping orders at his staff sitting at cluttered desks. The detectives wore vests and ties, some already loosened, and talked over one another on their desk telephones, while secretaries buzzed in and out to deliver messages or files or to clear desk boxes.

Blunt handed a junior detective the gun in the napkin. "Take this to Luke May and have him examine it for fingerprints, inside and out. Tell him not to miss a beat. If he finds prints, have him compare them with the prints we have on record of Miller and any other man present at the club."

May was an internationally known criminologist. He had one of the best-equipped crime laboratories in the US, and his scientific skill had helped many police departments across the country solve baffling crimes, making him a bit of a celebrity, like Blunt.

Blunt pulled out the bloody handkerchief and told another detective, "I want the blood on this handkerchief analyzed and compared with the blood on a piece of shirt the hospital is sending down, and I want the results by two o'clock this afternoon."

Blunt then turned to Detective Richard F. O'Leary, one of his most brilliant assistants. "Dick, there's a car parked in front of the Pom Pom Club. A big Cadillac." In all the excitement, I had forgotten about the car. "Here is the license number." Blunt handed O'Leary a sheet of notepaper with some figures scrawled on it. "There's a tire cover on the rear of the car with the name Clark Cadillac Company. Call the dealer. Find out who owns that car. And pronto."

Once more I was astounded by Blunt's powers of observation. I had noticed the big car, but I couldn't recall a single license plate number, much less the name on its tire cover.

"We're working against time," Blunt commented to no one in particular. "I want quick action. Now—the rest of you—get busy on the telephones. Call every cleaning and dyeing place in town, no matter how small. Tell them to telephone headquarters the minute someone brings in clothes with blood on them." Blunt smiled at me. "We'll get quite a few calls. There are always people with nosebleeds, cut fingers, or jam that looks like blood," he said with a playful grin. To his detectives he said, "But tell these cleaners to call us just the same—jam or blood. When we get a hit, have the clothing brought in—I want the blood tested and compared to the blood on the handkerchief and on the piece of shirt from the hospital. See if it's the same blood type."

I'd read of an Austrian scientist who three years earlier had won the Nobel Prize in Physiology or Medicine for his discovery of three human blood groups, A, B, and O.

Blunt's assistants looked curious, but I knew what Blunt was thinking. He hoped the man who owned the bloody handkerchief also had splatters of blood on his clothing. He hoped the blood spots under microscopic and chemical examination would trap the man. It was a long shot, but I thought a brilliant one.

McKinley returned without his jacket and sat in one of two chairs across from Blunt.

"We'll question the gang again," Blunt said. "See if they can still remember the yarn they're spinning."

"Why go through it again?" McKinley said. "We have what they said."

"To see if we can trip them up. Someone is bound to forget what they've been told is the truth."

One by one the men were brought into a small room and questioned, then returned to their cells. All told the same story that they'd told at the Pom Pom Club.

When the last of the men had been questioned, Blunt said, "Just what I expected. It's the one story that puts them all in the clear. But it's phony."

"How can you tell? They each told the same story. No deviations," McKinley said.

Blunt spoke to me. "What do you think?"

"The prosecutor is right. They each did, separately, tell the same story. No deviations."

"That's right. No deviations." Blunt slapped his palm on the table. "Which makes their story more accurate than Matthew, Mark, Luke, and John's recounting in the Bible."

"Meaning what?" McKinley asked.

"Meaning, if the four Gospels were exactly the same, we could assume the four apostles rehearsed what they wrote down. The fact that their stories are not identical, not scripted, is evidence each apostle told it truthfully from his perspective. These men at the Pom Pom Club are not the four apostles."

"What do you think happened?" I asked.

"I don't know for certain, yet. But I do know Frankie Ray did not try to rob George Miller." He spoke to McKinley. "In the first place, Miller and Ray knew each other as well as I know you. In the second place, I've known Ray for ten years, and as I've said, he has never packed a gun or been mixed up in armed-robbery scrapes. It just doesn't fit."

"Times are hard now," McKinley said. "Men are desperate."

His comment made me think of my uncle Ted and of my own father, hanging on by a thread. My mother always said things were fine when we spoke by phone Sunday afternoons, but I knew things were a long way from fine. For one, she never turned me down when I told her I would have Western Union wire home the few dollars I could spare.

"Maybe, but Frankie Ray was certainly smart enough to realize he couldn't get away with a robbery in a place everybody knew him."

"But if you don't know what happened, how are you going to make anyone believe their story isn't true?" I asked.

"Simple," Blunt said. "I gotta prove what really happened."

"We can only hold them on an open charge for forty-eight hours, Ernie," McKinley reiterated. "And the clock is ticking. If you're going to prove it, you're going to have to hurry. I couldn't charge them based on what we know at present."

Blunt said, "Which is why you and I are going to pay a visit to George Miller's home while he's locked up. You want to come, Shoe?"

With my afternoon deadline at three, I still had plenty of time, but that wasn't my reason for wanting to go. I was excited to be invited, thought of as part of an emerging story, and I remained even more anxious to see how the underworld lived, having observed a bit of how the wealthy dined and entertained themselves when they ventured out at night. "You bet," I said.

We piled into Blunt's Ford for the long ride to Seward Park's residential section, where the dapper George Miller maintained his home in a quiet and peaceful neighborhood on the shores of Lake Washington.

Blunt remained silent behind the wheel, seemingly relaxed, but once he stepped from the car, he became alert and attentive.

McKinley and I accompanied him to a cathedral entrance of the largest home I'd ever seen. A redheaded woman answered the door, dressed as if she might be on her way out, in a red sequined dress, a strand of pearls draped around her neck, and enough makeup that my mother would have said she looked like "a woman of the night."

Blunt held up his detective's badge. "Seattle Police. We'd like to take a look around."

The woman never glanced at the badge. "You got a warrant, Detective?" She didn't act or sound the least bit intimidated, as if SPD showing up at the home was a regular occurrence.

Blunt looked at McKinley. "I don't recall George Miller being married; do you, Laurence?"

"No. I don't believe he is," McKinley said.

"Meaning you have no ownership interest in the property," Blunt said to the woman.

"And no legal grounds to deny us admittance," McKinley said in what sounded like rehearsed lines in a play.

"Who are you?" the woman asked.

"Laurence McKinley. Prosecuting attorney of King County. And you would be?"

"Not pleased to meet you," she said.

"How about a name?" Blunt said.

"Katheryn Conner."

"And your relationship to George Miller?" McKinley asked.

"Friend," she said.

"Friend? But you live here?" McKinley asked.

"Good friend."

"Well, Miss Conner. Unless you'd like to be arrested and taken to headquarters for obstructing a police investigation, I'd suggest you step aside," Blunt said. "What's it going to be?"

"I was just stepping out to have a smoke anyway." She grabbed a silver cigarette case off an entry table and moved out of the way.

Blunt entered, then McKinley. I followed the attorney, but Conner put a hand on my chest, stopping me. "And who would you be?" I could smell her perfume mixed with the aroma of tobacco.

"He's my assistant," Blunt said.

She raised her eyebrows. "Assistant? He doesn't look old enough to shave."

"You a connoisseur of young men, Miss Conner?" McKinley said.

She smiled and gave me a sidelong glance. "I'm a connoisseur of all men, Mr. McKinley." She stepped past me, letting her hand slide down the front of my shirt to the belt buckle of my pants, where it paused, briefly, before she chuckled and went out onto the porch. Heat emanated from my face, and I knew I was as red as an apple, but thankfully neither Blunt nor McKinley commented.

We moved from room to room, Blunt still not revealing the purpose of this trip, what he hoped to find. His eyes probed every nook and corner of every room. His trained fingers rummaged through drawers of clothing without leaving a trace they had been disturbed. In an upstairs closet of a large bedroom, he removed suitcases, opening and closing them, then poked behind some books on a shelf overhead. He pulled down an empty holster, turning it over in his hands, inspecting it. He smiled. "Figured it would be here, someplace."

"What do you mean?" McKinley said.

"It's a holster for a Luger semiautomatic."

"Okay, but there are a lot of Luger semiautomatics out there, Ernie. Miller will say he lost the gun or sold it and forgot to sell the holster with it. It's not worth a darn unless we can connect it directly to the gun in the Pom Pom Club."

Blunt smiled again. "Laurence, you'd make a swell defense attorney," he said. "And damn it, if every detective had someone like you along on a case questioning him, he wouldn't leave any loose ends dangling. You wouldn't let him. I think, however, there may be a way of connecting the gun from the Pom Pom Club to this little holster here."

Blunt walked through the remaining rooms and continued looking under beds, in dresser drawers, and in closets, opening any suitcases and hatboxes he found. He even went into the basement and walked the concrete floor.

After an hour, we returned to headquarters and listened to the reports of the detectives Blunt had put to work.

"We've completed telephoning all the cleaners in town," O'Leary said. "They're all looking for blood."

Blunt stepped past me to his desk and shuffled through papers in a wooden in-box. "No report back from the lab yet on the blood type on that shirt or handkerchief?" he asked O'Leary.

"We'll have the results soon, Chief," O'Leary said. "We turned it and the Luger over to Luke May."

Blunt held out the holster he'd taken from Miller's home. "Have May examine this also. Ask him to see what it reveals, if anything, regarding whether the gun from the Pom Pom Club was once in there. And ask him, politely, to hurry. The clock is ticking, and we have limited time to complete the work." Blunt turned to me and McKinley. "Let's go talk to the coroner."

Otto Schmidt, the King County coroner, kept an office in the Yesler Building basement. Tall and thin with sinewy arms and hands, he told us he had examined Frankie Ray's body and confirmed one bullet had entered the right side of his chest and the other the left. Both bullets had nicked the heart as they passed through.

After meeting with Schmidt, we returned to the Pom Pom Club, this time with additional detectives equipped with drawing boards and rulers to diagram the interior to scale. Blunt told them the things he deemed important—the location of blood spots and of the two ejected shells, where the body had lain, the bullet holes in the woodwork, the exact places where the men at the bar said they stood when the shooting occurred. Blunt carefully checked the distances, figuring out at what angles the bullets had been fired to make the marks in the wainscoting. In the barroom we stepped closer to several knockdown dice tables.

"See here." Blunt showed me dice he'd picked from the cash register. "The numbers have been altered to increase the likelihood of rolling a seven. And these," he said holding up a second pair, "are what are called 'percentage' dice because they've had the edges shaved."

"But the people rolling them don't notice?" I asked, though I had to admit it was tough to see the dice had been shaved.

"They pull these dice out late in the evening, after first giving the rollers a chance to win and to quench their thirst," Blunt said. "By the time they're rolling these dice, the patrons are three sheets to the wind, and just happy to be out on the town and having a good time—things being as they are at present. You don't get the experienced gamblers in here. They go to the gambling clubs in town where there's more action and money."

Had Frankie Ray gotten into a gambling argument? Had he lost money at the craps table, then learned the dice were crooked and become angry? Was he shot to ensure his silence?

I thought it an angle to work and asked Blunt.

He dismissed me. "As I said, this racket is for suckers. Ray would have never fallen for it. He was certainly wise to the nightclub's tricks."

Upstairs we found more intimate and private dining rooms. We also found what appeared to be an office. Blunt opened and closed desk drawers. "What do we have here?" He pulled out a black book and flipped through the pages. "A list of the club's patrons." He smiled as his eyes scanned the entries. "As I suspected, the club members include names I know well, prominent civic and business leaders. Quite a few people in Seattle will shiver when they read your story in the afternoon paper. They'll wonder if their names might be mentioned."

"I don't suppose I could take a look," I said.

"You can't," Blunt said. "It might cost me my job." Again, he smiled. "Off the record?"

"Sure."

Blunt licked a thumb and continued flipping the pages. "The mayor, some city council members, and the chief of police have all been rumored to have attended this nightclub . . . more to keep their spouses happy. So I've been told." He said it with sarcasm, then slipped the black book into the inside pocket of his suit coat without further elaboration.

When my three o'clock deadline approached, I called in the remainder of my story on the phone in the hallway. The apprentice, Kravitz, told me Phish wanted to speak to me.

"Tell him I'm working another angle. I'll talk to him in the morning," I said.

"He isn't going to like that."

"A lot happening. More to come soon." I hung up.

When the diagrams had been completed, it was well past midnight, and I was exhausted and hungry. I'd missed my boardinghouse meal.

"We'll bring George Miller up here tomorrow," Blunt said. "If he sticks to his initial story, we can call him on his lies and use the diagrams to prove it." He turned. "I'll drop you off, Shoe. Where do you live?"

His offer surprised me, but I was glad for the ride.

Blunt dropped me off at my boardinghouse on Pike Street. When I went inside, I was surprised to find Mrs. Alderbrook seated behind her desk. She kept a room behind the counter and must have heard me enter. Her hair was up beneath a nightcap, and she wore a long night coat tied around her waist.

"Mrs. Alderbrook," I said. "I hope I didn't wake—"

"Phone's been ringing off the hook for you. And I've been taking messages." She picked up a cluster of message slips, holding them in her hand.

"I'm sorry," I said. "I've been out all day investigating the murder at the Pom Pom Club."

"I know." She smiled. "I read your article."

"You read the *Star*?" I asked.

"I did when your publisher called trying to track you down and said you'd made the front page!"

She held up the *Daily Star*. Across the top, just below the banner, Phish ran my story with an intriguing headline.

Mystery in Yesler

Nightclub Killing

Witnesses to Tragedy

Held in County Jail.

George Miller Admits Shooting,

Tells Police Victim Attempted Holdup

of Pom Pom Nightclub.

I felt my chest swell with pride.

"Your editor wants you to call him as soon as you get in. I suppose at this point that means in the morning."

"I'll get to my office early and talk to him so I don't encumber the line," I said.

"Nonsense," she said. "I didn't know we had a celebrity living here. Use the house phone, by all means."

"Thank you," I said, cautious of her sudden generosity. I held up the afternoon edition. "Can I keep this?" I thought my mom and dad would like to know I was making my way in Seattle just fine.

"Of course," she said. I tucked it under my arm and started for the staircase.

"Aren't you forgetting something?"

I turned back. "What's that?"

She reached behind her and held up a plate of food and my room key. "You can't afford to miss a meal. You're skin and bones as it is and shrinking by the day."

I didn't know what to say. "Thank you, Mrs. Alderbrook."

"I kept it warm in the oven, so be careful. The plate is a bit hot."

On the plate were two slabs of meat loaf, mashed potatoes, green beans, and a bread roll. "It looks wonderful, and I'm starved," I said.

I took the plate and room key, thanked Mrs. Alderbrook, and again started for the stairs.

"William?"

"Huh?"

She held out her hand. "Money doesn't grow on trees. That newspaper cost two cents."

Like most people in a depression, Mrs. Alderbrook's generosity only extended so far.

Chapter 4

I awoke the following morning before the crack of dawn, not a streak of sunlight through the thin curtain covering my eastern-facing window. I hadn't slept much. My mind kept replaying the prior day's events. I had gone from a junior beat reporter to the center of the biggest story in Seattle.

My mind churned over what we had learned, and what we still did not know.

The positions of the spent casings and the wound made by the second bullet indicated Miller was lying. But whom was he protecting? A Luger semiautomatic was used in the killing. Miller said Ray pulled the gun from his pocket. Yet Blunt found a holster for a Luger in Miller's home. According to McKinley, the holster was circumstantial evidence, not enough to hold Miller or the others. Miller had also said Ray came into the club alone, but an unaccounted-for bloody handkerchief indicated someone else had been there.

McKinley's mantra had been "I hate to say this, Ernie, but the case is still too thin. An alibi or a smart attorney will free Miller and his cronies, and we can count on him having both."

I got out of bed and went down the hall to the washroom to clean up, then returned and dressed. I slid my cap onto my head, grabbed my leather satchel, and went down the staircase. Mrs. Alderbrook had undoubtedly slept in following her late night, the desk vacant. I returned the dinner plate and fork, which I had cleaned in the sink upstairs. I didn't want to appear ungrateful. The dinner had killed my hunger pangs. I'd learned to drink a lot of water to quell those pangs when I missed meals, but real food was so much better.

I put my room key on the hook beneath my mail slot and slid outside. A morning chill and a marine layer, thinning from the breeze blowing up Pine Street from Elliott Bay, gave the awakening city an eerie feel and brought the briny smell of salt water and fish. I loved peaceful mornings like this, before the clang of the trolleys and rumble of car engines disturbed it. When I wasn't working or studying the structure of articles in the other newspapers, I had been determined to learn the city's fabric down to its most minute thread. What I found was not always a pretty suit. I fell in love with the vast natural beauty of a city built on the shores of Elliott Bay's crystal-blue waters and ringed by rugged, snowcapped mountain ranges with enough trees to build every person in America a decent home. But the streets, especially around the waterfront, were just as rugged and steeped in Old West debauchery and vice—disorderly houses, gambling establishments, speakeasies, and social clubs. Liquor had flowed and crime soared to record heights in 1932. So had the number of suicides. Nearly two hundred men, despondent over financial losses, took their own lives.

Seattle, I had learned, was also a city of ambition—the 484-foot Smith Tower stood taller than any building west of the Mississippi—as well as a city of rain.

A lot of rain.

Which didn't bode well when you'd worn out the soles of your shoes.

Along my route to work I walked past Mr. Neversleeps, which was the name the fellow who hawked newspapers day and night at the entrance to the Pike Place Market told me to call him. This morning, he called out to me by my nickname. "Hey, Shoe! Nice article. Selling like hotcakes at the Bread of Life Mission. Going fast. You got another one coming?"

I smiled and gave him a wave. "What kind of reporter would I be if I didn't have another story?" I called back, cocky, though still worried Phish would pull me in favor of Kawolski.

"Unemployed," Mr. Neversleeps responded.

He was right about that. I hoped I wasn't just some flash in the pan, a one-article wonder.

I cut through the Pike Place Market. I loved to hear the Italian phrases hurled by the vendors who drove up from Garlic Gulch in Rainier Valley to sell homegrown vegetables, fresh bread, pastries, and meats—including horsemeat. During a depression, one could not be choosy. The fish vendors sold salmon, halibut, oysters, and other fresh fish. As the shoppers passed their booths, the vendors snapped open brown paper bags to attract the attention of housewives in hats, furs, and opera gloves, and men in fedoras and suits, some old and worn, but an indication they still had dignity. Only upon closer inspection did one notice their hollow eyes and the sunken cheeks sporting stubble and nicks from dull razors.

A vendor yelled "Oopla," and I turned in time to watch a large salmon get tossed from the top of a banked stall to an aproned man waiting below. He caught the salmon, which had to weigh thirty pounds, with great fanfare for the few enjoying the early morning show.

I made my way down First Avenue to Giovacchini's Bakery, bypassing Manning's Cafeteria. At Giovacchini's, if you purchased a bread roll, pastry, or doughnut for a nickel, black coffee was complimentary. But that wasn't what attracted me to spend a hard-earned nickel when I couldn't really afford it.

I stepped inside to the warmth of the ovens and the smells of baking dough and spices. Customers stood in a horseshoe-shaped line that started at the door, bent past the pastry shop's occupied booths and barstools, and ended at the pastry-counter cash register. Mr. Giovacchini worked behind the counter, hurriedly filling orders while imploring those of us waiting to "Move down the line, please!" so more people could enter. His Italian accent was thick, and his Mediterranean skin coloring made him look tanned compared to his white apron flecked with dough and flour.

This morning, I was disappointed to find his wife ringing up purchases at the cash register, smiling and thanking the customers and asking them to come again soon. Mr. Giovacchini's daughter, Amara, often worked the pastry counter or the cash register, and though she rarely had time for any conversation beyond "What will you have?" it made my heart soar to hear her voice and glimpse her long, brown hair beneath the red bandana that matched the color of her apron. Her brown eyes sparkled, and her smile, warm like her mother's, could melt butter.

As the line snaked along the counter, I caught site of Amara's profile in the rectangular hole in the wall separating the kitchen from the shop. She had flour along the side of her nose, and though I could not see below her shoulders, I imagined her hands in dough, kneading the flour and yeast to make the rolls and the pastries.

"Next," Mr. Giovacchini called out, his face and tone serious.

"Good morning, Mr. Giovacchini," I said, deliberately loud, while glancing past his shoulder at his daughter.

"What will you have?" he asked.

"Cinnamon-raisin pastry and a cup of coffee," I said. The cinnamon-raisin pastry was the largest in the display case and would help get me through the morning.

Amara turned at the sound of my voice, and her gaze found me for just a moment before she returned her attention to her job, but not before a smile creased her lips.

"Five cents. Pay at the register. Next," Mr. Giovacchini said, setting my pastry on a waxed sheet.

I moved down the line to pay when Amara came around the wall to the counter. "They need you in the kitchen, Mama," she said.

Mrs. Giovacchini departed, and Amara helped the customer ahead of me, glancing at me as she did. When I reached the register, I became tongue-tied, but Amara solved that problem for me.

"I read your article in the newspaper, William. The top of the page," she said.

"Did you?" I managed, focused on the way she had said my name, with the hint of an Italian accent.

"It is you, right? William Shumacher."

"Yes," I said.

"That's an important story. Will you be writing more about it?" Her voice was whimsical and light.

"I will," I said. "I'm heading back to police headquarters this morning." I thought that sounded important.

"Move down the line, please," Mr. Giovacchini shouted. "Amara, the customers." He raised his hands to emphasize the line behind me.

"Mr. Shumacher wrote the article you read yesterday afternoon in the *Daily Star*, Papa. The one about the shooting at the Pom Pom Club."

With Amara's pronouncement, those in line turned to look at me, and some engaged in animated conversation about the shooting and complimented me on my story.

Mr. Giovacchini looked from his daughter to me. "Did you?" he asked.

"I did," I said with pride, hoping he'd see me as someone with a steady job.

"Do you want a medal to pin on your chest to go with your pastry and coffee? Amara, we have customers waiting to pay."

She grabbed a paper cup, which you could now take with you from the restaurant and throw away. "He is singularly focused in the morning," she said under her breath. "He read your article. And I thought it brilliant."

My new celebrity status gave me a confidence I had not felt before in her presence. "They're showing *The Picture Snatcher* at the Green Parrot Theatre. I heard James Cagney is terrific."

"Was the killing at the Pom Pom Club really by the underworld?" she asked, deliberately pouring the coffee into the cup slowly.

I deflated at her disinterest in my reference to the latest picture show but was glad she'd read my article. "I'm going to find out soon," I said.

Just then Mr. Giovacchini appeared at Amara's side. "You're holding up my line, Mr. Front Page."

"I had to pour his coffee, Papa," Amara said.

"Now you have it. Move along. Or they'll be writing a different banner in the obituaries with your name in it."

"Yes, Mr. Giovacchini." I took my pastry and my coffee cup, which was hot to the touch, and moved toward the door.

"William," Amara said.

I turned back.

"I'd like to see *The Picture Snatcher*," she said.

I smiled, then put my finger to the side of my nose. "You have some flour," I said.

She quickly moved her apron to the smudge, and her face turned the most beautiful shade of red I had ever seen. I hurried out the door before Mr. Giovacchini threw something at me, my feet not touching the pavement on my walk to the *Daily Star*.

The day after my graduation, and my father's suggestion that I join the military, my mother, stubborn, practical, and pragmatic, had been up before the sun making phone calls. She'd taken one look at the armed forces brochure and had forbidden me from enlisting. "Not with the shenanigans happening in Europe at the moment," she'd said. Adolf Hitler had been named chancellor in Germany and had begun rearmament. My mother worked the phone line tirelessly and eventually found a relative with a relative who might have a job for me—Howard Phishbaum, publisher of the *Daily Star* in Seattle, Washington. I had never been outside of the state of Missouri, never seen a body of water larger than a lake, or a mountain taller than a hill.

When I spoke to Mr. Phishbaum on the candlestick phone in our kitchen the following afternoon, he said he had an apprentice's position available. I had no idea what an apprentice at a newspaper did, but I wasn't about to tell him that. He said I would work ten hours a day, six days a week, and he'd decide if I was up to the task before offering me employment. That was not negotiable.

"If you want the position, be here next Monday morning at seven a.m."

I arrived on a Saturday at the Union Station in Seattle's famed Pioneer Square carrying my hard suitcase stuffed with what clothes I could fit and my favorite novel, *The Count of Monte Cristo*. I made my way to Seventh Avenue and the freestanding, two-story building with the plate-glass windows and the words "*The Daily Star*, Publisher Howard Phishbaum" stenciled in black block letters.

I had pushed open the door that first day uncertain what to expect, and I grew more concerned when no one so much as greeted me. A man and a woman, both considerably older than me, glanced up from their typewriters on cluttered desks, then reburied their heads in their work, their fingers hunting and pecking the keys. Deciding neither would be of much help, I walked toward a glass enclosed office at the back of the building where a man—presumably Howard Phishbaum, since his name was stenciled on the glass portion of the door—sat behind a desk, his gaze fixed on papers, pencil in hand. He spoke before I'd knocked. "Whatever you're selling, we aren't buying."

"I'm not selling anything," I said. "I'm William Shumacher, from Kansas City. We spoke on the telephone about a job."

"A job?" He looked up. "What job?"

"An apprentice, you said."

"When did I say that?"

"On the telephone. Last week. I'm Maddie Shumacher's son."

Mr. Phishbaum removed round spectacles and reached into a back pocket, pulling out a handkerchief and feverishly polishing the lenses while staring at me. The spectacles had left a red impression on each side of his pointed nose. He resembled a Midwestern scarecrow—his face narrow with high cheekbones, his hair unkempt, and his limbs long and gangly.

"I told you to start Monday morning."

"The train arrived early."

"And you thought you'd stop by and get the lay of the land."

That sounded good, so I said, "Yes, sir."

"You sounded older on the phone."

I didn't know how to respond.

"You have experience writing news stories?"

I didn't. Not really. My senior year I had written for the Central High School newspaper, the *Daily Eagle*. But in a depression, desperate for a job, I wasn't about to say no. "Yes, sir."

"Good. We've had a change of plans."

"A change of plans?"

"The *Daily Star* has always had two reporters and an apprentice. You see the woman seated at the desk out there?" He pointed out his window.

She was hard to miss. She looked very old.

"That's Grace Mary Altobelli. She covers flower shows, charitable functions, and gossip. The other reporter is Nathan Kawolski. He covers the mayor's office, the city's administrative offices, the police, the fire department, and the courts, as well as any other news fit to print. At least he did."

From Kawolski's appearance I concluded he was a fastidious man in his mid to late forties. He had a harried demeanor, like he was two steps behind wherever he needed to be.

"He has a wife and six children," Mr. Phishbaum said, as if to explain. "And he's Catholic, so only God knows how many more mouths he'll have to feed when he and his wife are finished. Seattle is growing. Fast. There's too much news for one reporter. I need another reporter more than I need another apprentice, which is where you come in."

"Where I come in?"

"That's right. Your beat, if you don't screw up this magnanimous opportunity, will be to cover the police and fire departments, and the courthouse. Kawolski will cover everything else. You'll start on a trial basis, so you won't make a weekly wage."

"I won't?"

"You'll earn a penny for every inch of copy I deem worthy to print. You do well and we'll discuss a weekly salary."

I sensed no room for negotiation and made no attempt to do so.

"Come back Monday morning," Mr. Phishbaum said. "Kawolski will show you around the Yesler Building and introduce you. After he does, you'll have to pull your own weight." He lowered his gaze to what he'd been working on before I had interrupted him.

I lingered, uncertain where to go.

Phishbaum raised his head. "What did you say your name was?"

"Shumacher. William Shumacher."

"Uh-huh. Have you found a place to stay?"

"No, sir."

Mr. Phishbaum grunted, ripped a piece of paper off a pad, and scribbled with a pencil. Then he held out the paper to me. "This is a boardinghouse on Pike Street. Ask for Mrs. Alderbrook. Tell her Howard Phishbaum sent you. The rooms are clean. The price is reasonable, and it includes dinner six days a week. Breakfast and lunch you're on your own."

Beggars having no right to be choosy, I took the slip of paper with thanks.

This morning, following the publication of my Pom Pom Club scoop, I expected some acknowledgment, but when I entered the office, Kawolski and Altobelli had not yet arrived, and Kravitz sat at his small desk pushed up against the masonry wall in between filing cabinets. He gave me no more than a passing glance. Kravitz was just two years older, but he had never warmed to me. I deduced he had wanted the reporter's job Phish had given to me. Kravitz's job was to track down sources and locations for reporters, confirm our facts, and take dictation if either I or Kawolski needed to call in a story by the afternoon deadline.

I had no sooner set my Danish and coffee on my desk than Phish spotted me from inside his glass office. Above him, on the wall behind his desk, hung a bat autographed by Seattle Indians baseball manager George Henry Burns. I didn't know much about baseball, but Burns, called "Tioga George," was the Indians' player coach and a former Major League Most Valuable Player. Phish purchased the bat for five dollars at a charitable auction to raise money for children suffering from smallpox.

Phish strode from his office to the newsroom in a robotic, gangly flow of elbows and knees. Tall and painfully thin, he constantly adjusted his suspenders onto his shoulders or the garters he wore on his shirtsleeves to keep from getting ink stains on the cuffs of his shirts. If I had first met him on the street, I would have mistaken him for one of Hooverville's many hungry.

"What are you doing here?" he asked.

"I thought I would stop in to tell you what is happening."

"What is happening, I presume, is happening at police headquarters," he said.

I felt deflated. Kawolski was not at his desk, and I concluded that Phish had assigned him to cover the story. When I said nothing, Phish removed his spectacles, along with the handkerchief from his back pocket, and polished the lenses. He again asked, "What are you doing standing here?"

I was a little dull, but you didn't have to hit me with a Tioga George baseball bat twice. "Right," I said. "Just came in to check if anything important had transpired overnight."

"That's your job, Shoe. Get crackin'."

He didn't smile, nor did he compliment me on the article I'd written the day before, but his acknowledgment that this would be my story was better than praise. I hurried for the door.

"Shoe?"

I turned back.

He pointed to the pastry and coffee.

I hurried back to my desk and picked them up. "And remember what I told you about saving those cups. Waste not, want not," he said, scrupulously frugal.

I rushed down Seventh Avenue and then made my way to the Yesler Building's westernmost side entrance to the police department. I finished my pastry and coffee before going inside. The marbled floor was abuzz with uniformed and plain-clothed officers on the move. Ernie Blunt stepped into the hallway from his office with Laurence McKinley trailing.

"Ah, young Shumacher," Blunt said. "Back for more?"

"Of course," I said.

"Then you can ride with us. We're off."

"Where are we going?" I asked.

"You'll know soon enough, my boy. I want to get there when it opens."

We drove to an auto dealership on Queen Anne hill, and I deduced this had to do with the Cadillac parked at the curb on Tenth Avenue. Inside the dealership, Blunt explained to a heavyset man in an ill-fitting suit what he wanted to know, and the man pulled a file from a cabinet.

"The car belongs to Frankie Ray." The man used a handkerchief to blot his face and the top of his balding head, though it wasn't particularly hot yet.

"Ray must have been bigger than you thought, Ernie," McKinley said. "You can't buy a car like that with chicken feed."

"He didn't," the car dealer said. "Buy it, I mean. He was making monthly payments on a financing agreement. Though not him, exactly."

"Who, then, exactly?" Blunt asked.

The man pulled spectacles from the top pocket of his suit and fastened them behind his ears. "It seems a gal named Joan Daley. She missed the last two payments though. There's a $550 balance to be paid at $55 a month. We were about to repossess the car."

Which might have explained the man's nervous perspiration. The expensive car was currently in the police impound yard, and the police certainly weren't about to make the monthly payments.

"Joan Daley?" Blunt said.

"That's what the paperwork says." The man turned the file for Blunt to read the contract.

Blunt said the name again, this time smiling. He turned to McKinley. "I'll have the vice squad get us everything they know about Joan Daley. She fits into this somehow."

"You know her?" I asked.

"She's an underworld dame," Blunt said. "Works at a disorderly house and has her hands in the pockets of just about everyone prominent in Seattle. Rumor is she also keeps a little black book with the names of her clientele and the dates of their visits—to protect herself."

"Blackmail?" I said.

"Or a smart business operator. Depends on your perspective. She's tough as nails."

"What was she doing buying a car for someone like Frankie Ray if he was a nobody in the underworld?" I asked.

"Good question." Blunt smiled. "Very good question. And I think I know the answer, and why the last two payments haven't been made."

We went back to police headquarters. McKinley moved down the hall for his nicotine fix. Blunt went into his office, removed his suit coat, and hung it on the coat tree near the door. He instructed O'Leary to get in touch with the vice squad and to find Joan Daley.

"Will do," O'Leary said, handing Blunt a freshly typed sheet of paper.

"What's this?" he asked.

"The report from the laboratory on the bloody handkerchief you found near the bar and on the piece of Ray's shirt. The two are the same blood type."

Blunt grunted as if he'd known that was likely and drew nonsensical designs on a desk pad, a habit when he was thinking. "Wait," he said to me. "Just wait."

I did not have to wait long. Within fifteen minutes, O'Leary returned to the office grinning like the cat that swallowed the canary.

"Joan Daley," O'Leary said to me, Blunt, and McKinley, who'd returned from his smoking break, "was Frankie Ray's girlfriend."

Blunt smiled.

"But . . . get this," O'Leary added. "She also worked for Miller, running one of his disorderly houses on Profanity Hill. Federal agents conducted a raid there a few months ago, and Daley apparently jumped from a second-story window to get away, broke her leg, and hurt her back."

"Where is she now?" Blunt asked.

"Harborview," O'Leary said, meaning the large, charitable hospital atop Yesler Hill.

"Her income stopped," Blunt said, glancing over at me. "It's why she missed the two payments on the car."

"But what could Daley have to do with the shooting?" McKinley asked. It was clear he had doubts.

"No sense speculating," Blunt said. "Let's go get some answers."

As Blunt stood, L. L. Norton, chief of police, walked in the office door. He was a small man in stature with thick, dark eyebrows on a serious face and salt-and-pepper hair.

"Got a press conference I'd like you to handle," he said, then noticed me. "Who's the kid?"

"William Shumacher, *Daily Star*." I stood and extended my hand.

Norton ignored it. "You wrote the article that ran yesterday afternoon," he said.

"Young Shoe got a call about the shooting and beat us to the Pom Pom Club," Blunt said, not adding that he had been the one to call. "Thought it would be friendly to let him come along, seeing as he was already there."

Norton eyed me up and down. I hoped he didn't ask me the name of my source. He didn't.

"I talked to Van Soelen," Norton said to McKinley, meaning the city attorney. "The press knows clubs like the Pom Pom have member rolls, and those members aren't coming from Hooverville." Norton directed his gaze to me. "Before speculation runs rampant, we're going to let you newspapermen know we have the names of the Pom Pom nightclub members and that the roll includes prominent Seattle financiers, doctors, insurance and railroad executives, and jewelers. Our hope is the threat of exposing these men will get those present the night before the shooting to come forward. At the same time, we expect you to proceed with discretion since those individuals didn't have anything to do with the murder."

Norton didn't mention the names Blunt said were also within the book, which included the mayor, some city council members, and possibly Norton himself. The mayor and the chief were clearly protecting their own interests.

"Handle it," Norton said to Blunt, then left the office.

"Best you go out the side exit and come back in, Shoe," Blunt said to me. "To keep it official police business."

I understood. I left the building through the exit onto Terrace Street, walked around the back, and came in through the Yesler Way entrance. A cluster of reporters stood in the conference room, including Emmet Winn and Archibald Greer, who had left their desks, indicating the potential magnitude of the story.

"How the hell did you get the story?" Winn asked, blowing a puff of cigar smoke in my face.

"What gives, Shoe? You have a contact?" Greer asked.

"Something like that," I said, reveling in my sudden celebrity.

Blunt and McKinley came into the room and garnered everyone's attention.

"Can you tell us what happened, Ernie?" Greer asked.

"Shooting at the Pom Pom Club. You can read all about the details in the *Daily Star*," Blunt said, needling the other reporters.

The heads in the room turned to me, then back to Blunt and McKinley.

"Who shot Frankie Ray?" Winn asked.

"We've made no arrests yet," Blunt said.

"You have the owner, George Miller, in custody on the fourth floor," Greer said. "Syd Brunn, and a couple of others as well." Someone was providing Greer information.

"Only those we believe were material witnesses to the shooting," Blunt said.

"What are they saying?" Winn asked.

McKinley and Blunt told the newspapermen George Miller's story and said they weren't satisfied with Miller's version that he wrestled the gun from Ray, who was attempting a stickup.

"We haven't yet been able to establish who owned the pistol," Blunt said. "But Ray was never known to own or carry a pistol, and George Miller admitted he owned such a pistol. There is more to this killing than appears on the surface, boys. Miller and Ray have known each other since at least 1926. It doesn't look reasonable to me that Ray would hang around the club all night getting soused, then try to hold up an old friend like Miller at six thirty in the morning."

"How will you find out the truth? I heard the five men are all telling the same story," Greer said.

"Indeed," Blunt said, then added they were preparing to question "a few more men and one Seattle girl supposed to have been a friend of Ray's who might have information on a grudge between the two men."

I knew that tidbit would generate considerable interest, which was why Blunt had said it. He wanted the press to think he was giving them something juicy to run with—a quarrel between two men over one gal ends in murder.

"We believe these witnesses will throw light on Ray's life and solve the mystery of his death in the Pom Pom Club," Blunt said.

"How will you find them?" Winn asked.

"We are in possession of the names of the Pom Pom nightclub's members," Blunt said, "which reads like a chapter from the city's social register. Millionaires and prominent professional men are listed as the club's habitués. I don't have to tell you learned men that the Pom Pom Club was known as the brightest spot in Seattle's nightlife. We'll go through the list member by member, if we have to, looking for other witnesses there last night."

Blunt and McKinley left to the sound of shouted questions. Blunt had dropped another hand grenade. He wanted the reporters to spread the word wide that anyone who knew anything had better step forward voluntarily or risk being hauled into the police station and having their name and mug in the papers.

The reporters turned to me with their questions, and I answered them, without answering them. A good reporter, Phish had counseled me, never revealed his sources, especially to other beat reporters seeking the same story. When the coast was clear, I slipped from the building and hurriedly turned the corner. A hand to my chest stopped me. Winn.

"Where are you off to in such a hurry, young William?" Winn chewed on the end of his cigar, clouds of smoke escaping his mouth like puffs from a train engine.

"Chasing stories, just like you," I said.

"That's the problem," Winn said. The remnants of his hair were pasted on his balding pate with pomade. Phish had told me that when Winn had been a young and hungry reporter, he'd chased stories all over Seattle. I knew my beating him to this scoop was eating at his enormous ego.

"None of my contacts knew about the murder, least not as quickly as you. How'd you manage it?" Winn asked.

"Just got lucky," I said.

"Hmm," Winn said. He flicked the ashes of his cigar, and they fell in a clump close to my shoe. Then he put an arm around my shoulder.

"Here's the deal, Shumacher. If you help me out, I'll help you out. That way we both win. What do you say?"

"Sounds good," I said.

"Good. So, who's your source?"

"Promised I wouldn't tell, but if I get another lead, I'll let you know. You'll be sitting at the city desk, I assume?"

Winn handed me a business card with his name on it and a telephone number. I took it and walked, this time slowly, as if in no hurry, up the street, feeling Winn's eyes boring into the back of my head.

Chapter 5

I took the trolley headed east up Yesler to Harborview, then hurried to the hospital reception counter and told the nurse behind the desk I was looking for Joan Daley's room. The nurse scowled at me. "Visiting hours don't start until noon."

"Did you let in two men, a detective and a prosecuting attorney?"

"What of it?"

"I'm with them." I pulled my press badge from my pocket. "They're expecting me."

She studied my badge and considered the likely ramifications of denying me admittance. "Third floor. The nurse on duty can decide what to do with you."

I took the elevator to the third floor and went through the same interrogation with the nurse at the duty desk. Luckily, Blunt and McKinley huddled outside a room down the hall.

"Detective?" I called out.

Blunt waved me forward. "Thought you weren't going to make it. Laurence and I were just discussing how to handle this interview. As I said, Daley is a tough customer and not likely to talk. I might be able to surprise her with the news Ray is dead, get her to say something before she thinks twice about it."

Blunt wasn't awaiting my thoughts on the matter. He pushed open the door and stepped inside.

Joan Daley lay in a hospital bed, her leg elevated and in a cast. Despite her circumstances, she reminded me of Jean Harlow, the platinum blonde and Hollywood's bad-girl movie star. A blue bandana covered Daley's hair, and she wore makeup. She looked like she was lounging poolside during a break in filming, but with a cunning gleam in her eyes that seemed to quickly size up all three of us.

"Detective Blunt," she said, her voice husky. "To what do I owe the pleasure."

"Joan," Blunt said. "They got Frankie Ray."

Blunt hadn't been kidding when he said he'd hit Daley hard with the news. But Daley didn't so much as flinch.

"And I suppose you thought by popping it to me like that, you'd catch me off my guard, huh, Ernie?" I glanced at Blunt, surprised by Daley's use of his first name and the familiarity with which it rolled from her tongue. She lay back, languid, and smiled. "Well, copper, try those tricks on someone else. I don't know a thing about it." She directed her gaze to McKinley.

"Laurence McKinley," he said. "Homicide prosecutor."

"It was a murder, then?" she said.

"That's what we're trying to find out, Joan," Blunt said.

She eyed me from my shoes to the top of my carefully combed hair as she lifted a silver cigarette case from the table beside her bed. "Who's the kid?" She flipped the case open and removed a cigarette, a Chesterfield. At twenty cents a pack during a depression, it was a luxury. "They run out of adults at the police station?"

"Go easy on him, Joan," Blunt said. "His first homicide. William Shumacher."

She gave a subtle nod. Then held out the case. We all declined. She flicked a silver Zippo lighter, the first I had seen anyone use, and seemed to take joy in our watching her. She held the flame to the cigarette tip, inhaled, and snapped the Zippo closed, then blew smoke at the ceiling.

"You married, Billy the kid?"

"Billy the kid. I like that," Blunt said. "He's wise beyond his age."

"Not that wise," Daley said. "Billy the Kid got shot at twenty-one." She smiled at me. "Why don't you come up sometime and see me?" She sounded just like Mae West speaking to Cary Grant in the movie *She Done Him Wrong*, which I'd recently seen at the Green Parrot Theatre. "I might not look like much now"—she winked—"but in a few days I'll look like a million bucks."

"Few days?" Blunt asked.

"Finally getting out of this joint. The food has been divine." Her voice dripped sarcasm.

"Like I said, Joan. Frankie's dead. Body's going cold at the morgue as we speak. Someone shot him, twice."

"Can't help you, Ernie." She motioned to the cast on her leg. "Wasn't there. I'm psychic about matters of a man's heart . . . and other organs, but not much else."

"Heard anything?"

"About the shooting? This place is locked up tighter than Fort Knox. Don't even get the newspaper delivered." She shook her head as she blew another puff of smoke.

"What was your and Frankie's relationship?"

"Close friends."

"How close?" Blunt prodded.

"A nice girl doesn't answer those kinds of questions, Ernie. You should know better."

"Close enough you bought him a car. A Cadillac," Blunt said.

She gave him a sidelong glance. "There a crime in buying a man a car, Ernie?"

"Expensive token of one's friendship."

"I'm extravagant. What can I say? It's always been my downfall. That and falling for the wrong guy." She gave me a sly grin.

"You missed the last two car payments. Company is going to repossess," Blunt said.

She shrugged. "Couldn't be helped, under the circumstances." She blew out more smoke. "I don't think Frankie is going to mind; do you?"

"Nah, I guess he won't. Have you seen George Miller?"

"Is he laid up here in the hospital?"

"Don't get smart, Joan. You know who I mean. Owner of the Pom Pom Club."

"Not exactly ready to go dancing, Ernie. I'll take you up on it when the doc removes this cast though." She motioned to an ashtray on the table beside her bed. "Would you mind, Kid? All this moving around has exhausted me."

Blunt gave me a subtle nod. I stepped forward to hand her the ashtray. Her eyes roamed again, and she smiled at me the way one smiles when holding a secret. "No ring," she said. "So, the kid ain't married."

I stepped back. My face flushed.

Her smile broadened but she broke off her stare. "So, who shot Frankie?" she said to Blunt.

"Don't know yet," Blunt said, already moving toward the door. "We'll talk again, Joan."

"Looking forward to it, Ernie."

I started for the door.

"Bye, Kid."

I turned back, and she gave me that look again, undressing me with her eyes.

Outside Daley's room, I hurried to catch up to Blunt and McKinley and said, "You know her?"

"You do this job long enough, you know who just about everyone is and what they aren't. Daley's living in an F. Scott Fitzgerald novel. She sees herself as Daisy Buchanan and ignores that the Roaring Twenties have ended and we're in a depression. But don't let appearances fool you. She's struggling like the rest of us. Especially being in a hospital for weeks and likely out of commission a few more."

We left Harborview and stopped on the way back to headquarters for Blunt and McKinley to eat breakfast. This wasn't a freebie, like before. Not wanting to spend money needlessly, I ordered black coffee and listened to Blunt and McKinley discuss the case and the dwindling forty-eight hours they had to hold Miller and the others. It was nearly noon when Blunt and I arrived back at Blunt's office. The detective sat at his desk, pensive, a cigarette in an ashtray emitting a snaking trail of smoke.

O'Leary came in with another typed sheet of paper. "Four cleaners found blood spots on clothes brought in yesterday. The laboratory has them now, and Luke May's on his way down."

"Call McKinley. Let him know."

McKinley arrived a minute before Luke May, the lanky criminologist. I got up from my seat across the desk from Blunt, and May sat down beside McKinley. I stood off to the side. May held a sheaf of papers and a few photographs in his hands. He showed us the photographs first. They were odd looking, remotely resembling topographical maps showing mountains and rivers. "These are microphotographs of the pistol and the holster," he explained. Blunt leaned across the desk. "See these scratches on the holster? They look like valleys under the microscope, but they're only tiny scratches." May pointed. "Now, here's a composite photograph matching the holster and the pistol. It depicts what I have done. It shows the ridges on the handgun and the scratches made on the holster line up exactly, meaning that Luger belongs in that holster. No other gun would make identical scratches."

Blunt's smile broadened. He had told me it might be possible to connect the Luger with the holster, though not how.

"I also found Miller's fingerprints on the gun," May announced.

That was not unexpected, given Miller's story, and McKinley pointed this out.

"Okay," May said, seemingly unperturbed by McKinley's pessimism. "But I also found Miller's fingerprints only on the gun's magazine and on the bullets. The man who loaded it left his prints. And that man was George Miller."

Blunt glanced at McKinley, as if daring him to question that piece of evidence. When McKinley didn't, Blunt said, "Well now. That is going to be tough to argue. Wouldn't you say, Larry?"

"Ernie, if you say so, I'll charge George Miller with murder," McKinley said. "I don't say we can convict him yet, but I'll certainly try. And if you give me a motive, I promise I'll send him to the penitentiary for a long time."

Blunt didn't immediately answer. After a moment, he said, "We still have some of that forty-eight hours left. Maybe I can get a motive by then."

Blunt let me use a phone in an unoccupied office, and I called in the story I had so far to Kravitz. I laid out what the evidence had revealed, including what Joan Daley had said, and what Luke May's science had uncovered. Kravitz would get the typesetter going, but I told him to leave space for a lede until I knew what else Blunt and McKinley might uncover, their investigation picking up steam. I had another couple of hours to get my lede. As I was finishing up with Kravitz, Blunt stuck his head in the office.

"Got back a report from a dry cleaner on Pike Street, said a suit came in with blood on the sleeves."

I felt a rush of adrenaline. We were on the trail of the man who was in the club but had left after the shooting—maybe someone who could tell us what really happened. Maybe the killer.

We took a drive up to the cleaner on Pike Street. Men and women walked the sidewalks beside sailors in uniform from a recently docked ship. Vendors called out their goods, and shoeshine boys sold shines for a nickel. Bells rang atop the door of the dry cleaners as we entered. The shop owner looked nervous when Blunt showed him his badge. He said the suit belonged to an Albert Smith and provided a cleaning slip with Smith's address at a nearby hotel.

Blunt thanked him and we exited.

The three-story hotel didn't have an elevator. Blunt, in his mid to late fifties, stopped to catch his breath on the second-floor landing. Luckily, Smith was home, because I don't think Blunt would have climbed back up the steps a second time.

Smith opened his door and stepped back, hands raised, looking more than concerned. He looked frightened. "I don't want no trouble." He was tall. I'd bet six foot three, with broad shoulders. He wore slacks cinched tight at the waist with a black belt, a T-shirt that showed off a thick chest and meaty arms. A square jaw dominated his face, along with stitch lines over his left eye, the kind that scarred from being reopened and restitched multiple times. I guessed Smith to be a pugilist, like Frankie Ray, though likely in a heavier weight class—light heavyweight or heavyweight.

When Blunt lifted his shiny gold badge, Smith gave a sigh of relief. He had clearly been expecting another kind of trouble. Underworld trouble. "I was coming to see you fellows," Smith said.

"Were you?" Blunt asked. He didn't sound convinced.

"Absolutely, but I know what happens to guys who want to tell the cops the truth," Smith said.

"The truth would be a welcome change," Blunt said.

"How'd you find me?"

"You left a bloody suit at the cleaners."

"My only suit. I had to get it cleaned."

"Can we come in?" Blunt said.

Smith stepped back. We entered a small room that looked like my boarding room—a bed, a table, one chair. A radio. The bathroom was down the hall.

"I take it you and Ray were friends?" Blunt asked.

"Not friends so much. Acquaintances," Smith said.

"How so?" Blunt asked.

"We boxed for a time on the same cards in town. Frankie was older than me and backed me for a while."

"Any good?" Blunt said.

"Held my own. Thirty-eight wins, twenty-four by knockout."

"How many losses?" Blunt said.

"Forty-three," Smith said.

Which meant Smith was what my dad called a "palooka," a punching bag. A fighter who filled the undercard to prepare the audience for the main event. Nobody cared if they won or lost, including the fighters, who were well past "up and coming" and just looking for a payday—win, lose, or draw.

"What do you do when you aren't boxing?" Blunt asked.

"I was a salesman."

"Not anymore?"

"The joint closed. Times being what they are, I haven't been able to get another job."

"Yet you were at the Pom Pom Club the morning Ray got shot."

"That's right."

I was both startled and amazed Blunt had been correct that the handkerchief indicated another man had been present at the club.

"Why? You a regular there?"

"Never been," Smith said, shaking his head. "First time."

"What prompted the occasion?"

"Frankie called me out of the blue. Asked me if I'd go with him, have a few drinks, roll the dice, and maybe meet a dame or two. I'd never been but had always wanted to go. I'm not much for dancing, but I like to play the dice."

"The dice games were rigged for suckers," Blunt said.

"No. Really?"

"Really," Blunt said, and again it sounded like he didn't believe Smith's story. "So you went with Ray?"

"That's right."

"Anyone else go with you?"

"Just Frankie."

"What happened?" Blunt asked.

"Frankie was in a bad mood when we piled into his car."

"Did he say why?"

"Well, I commented about how nice the car was; you know? About the interior being so clean and the car running smooth. A Cadillac.

Frankie said his sweetheart, Joan Daley, bought it for him, that she'd been working in a disorderly house. He said he wanted her to quit, but she'd been paying for Frankie's car, see."

"Been paying?" Blunt asked.

"Frankie said there was an unexpected raid—by federal agents—at the disorderly house, and Daley jumped from a window to avoid arrest and injured herself and was in the hospital. He said Miller had agreed to take care of her expenses."

"Miller? Why would Miller pay her hospital bill?"

"He owned the disorderly house, according to Frankie, though the deed was in Miller's sweetheart's name."

"Katheryn Conner?" McKinley said.

"Maybe. I don't remember if he said the name. Anyway, Frankie said Miller had reneged on paying an eighty-dollar hospital bill, so they shipped Daley to the county hospital at Harborview. Frankie was upset about it because Daley now has these expenses and couldn't pay for his Cadillac. But I think there was more to the beef."

"Let me guess," Blunt said. "You think Miller was sweet on Joan Daley?"

Smith nodded.

"You know George Miller?" Blunt asked.

"Who doesn't around here?"

Blunt didn't respond.

"Anyway, I didn't know we were headed to the Pom Pom Club to try to recover the debt until I got in the car and Frankie said so."

Blunt looked Smith up and down. "And Ray brought you as what, his muscle?"

"I didn't know it at the time. Not until I got in the car and Frankie told me he wanted to collect on the debt. I said I didn't want no part of George Miller. He's known to have a bad temper and to fly off the handle. But Ray said I didn't have to say or do nothing. Just stand there with my hands in my pockets. He offered me ten bucks of the take we'd get from Miller. Times are tough, and ten bucks is a month's rent. That's it. I was just an innocent bystander."

"Uh-huh," Blunt said. "I take it Miller wasn't intimidated."

Smith shook his head. "He laughed at Frankie. Then Frankie followed Miller into the bathroom to talk about his promise to pay the debt, but it obviously didn't go well because when they came out, they were arguing. Miller called Frankie a bum and said the only way he'd pay Daley's bill was if she swore to never see Frankie again."

"Which is why you think Miller was sweet on her?"

"Well, he has a bit of a reputation for the ladies."

"I take it Frankie refused."

"Frankie's got a temper too. He got angry, so I ushered him to the door to leave, but then Frankie, he says he left his smokes on the bar and goes back inside."

"You go with him?" Blunt asked.

"Not me. I stayed back."

"And things escalated from there?"

"I heard them arguing again, so then I went back in. Miller and Frankie were jawing about the money and about the dame, and then Miller pulls a gun."

"You said, 'the money.' For the hospital or for the Cadillac?" McKinley asked.

"I figured it was the money for Joan Daley's debt, like Frankie said, but . . . I mean, without Miller paying the hospital bill, Frankie was going to lose his Cadillac. So . . ."

"Six of one, half dozen the other," Blunt said. "What happened next?"

"Like I said. Miller's a known hothead, and Frankie had gotten under his skin. Miller pulls the trigger and Frankie gets hit in the side and goes down. Miller walks up to him and says, 'You got no respect. You should have stayed out of matters over your head,' and he lets him have it a second time."

"Then what?" Blunt asked.

"Well, I didn't know what to do. I mean, the guy's bleeding to death on the floor. So, I took out my handkerchief and tried to stop the bleeding, but then Miller says, 'Leave him be and get the hell out of my club.' I stood and Miller points the gun at me. I told him I didn't want no trouble. I was only there because Frankie promised me ten bucks. Miller says, 'You'll get ten slugs if you don't get out of here and keep your mouth shut.' So I scrammed and beat it back here."

Blunt turned to McKinley. "And that," he said, "is your motive."

Blunt told Smith to stick around town or he'd bring him in to jail and hold him as a material witness. Smith said he had no place to go, but he feared maybe Miller might have guys looking for him.

As we descended the stairs, I thought it odd Miller would have the men at the bar stay to back up the story he had concocted but allow Smith to leave. Seemed to me Smith had a justifiable reason to be scared that Miller would recognize the risk and have someone pay Smith a visit. I asked Blunt this, but he dismissed it.

"Miller ain't as big as he thinks he is. He isn't backed by any of the East Coast or Chicago families, and he doesn't have guys at his beck and call to do his bidding for him. If he did, he never would have pulled the trigger himself with witnesses around. Smith's right about one thing though. Miller's known to have a temper and to fly off the handle. I think this is one of those times."

When we arrived back at headquarters, McKinley disappeared to his office to draw up the charging document against George Miller, and another pleading to hold the others in jail as material witnesses. I went back to the *Daily Star*. I'd scoop Early Winn and Archibald Greer again with my afternoon article, and it had the pizzazz Phish craved.

Phish was like a cat on a hot tin roof with the paper's deadline for the afternoon fast approaching. He was also enthralled by what I had already dictated to Kravitz. Phish questioned me about what more I had, and I told him I was thinking of leading with Luke May and the fingerprint and holster evidence. Phish shook his head and told me to lead with Joan Daley. "Sex trumps science selling newspapers, Shoe. It's pizzazz on top of pizzazz."

Phish sent Richard Kneip, the *Daily Star*'s photographer, to get pictures inside the Pom Pom Club to accompany the article. Then he stood over my shoulder as I typed the lede, throwing out words like "underworld," "gangster," "beautiful," and "bloody trail."

When we had finished, just minutes before deadline, the front page was awash in pizzazz.

4 Jailed in Pom Pom

Club Killing

Police Work Quickly.

Discover Murder Weapon

Owned by George Miller.

Witness in Hiding Says Dispute

Relates to Victim's Sweetheart

and $80 Debt.

The nightclub slaying of Frankie Ray has brought several startling new bits of sensational evidence to light overnight and called into question the story told by the shooter.

George Miller, Pom Pom nightclub proprietor, has admitted to the killing, but insists he wrestled the gun away from the victim, Frankie Ray, a 34-year-old former lightweight boxing contender.

Startling new evidence uncovered by Chief Detective Ernie Blunt and King County prosecutor Laurence McKinley, however, puts Miller's story in question. Blunt and McKinley recovered a holster in George Miller's home that famed Seattle criminologist Luke May confirms held the murder weapon. May also determined the magazine and the bullets inside the murder weapon bore the fingerprints of George Miller.

What precipitated this tragic shooting? Blunt and McKinley say the shooting may relate to a beautiful young woman who runs a disorderly house owned by Miller, and a dispute over an $80 hospital bill.

That's the story told by an eyewitness to the shooting who had been in hiding. Blunt tracked this witness down following a bloody trail to a cleaner on Pike Street.

When we had finished, I checked the clock on the wall. "I got to run," I told Phish. "There's another press conference starting."

"Give my regards to Early Winn and Greer," Phish said. The *Daily Star* would be in the hands of every person downtown and headed for home. "Ask them how they like coming in second, again."

Chapter 6

I arrived at police headquarters just a minute or two after the press conference had started and stood at the back. Other reporters glanced over their shoulders at me, as if they'd been looking for me. I must admit I liked the attention.

McKinley addressed the crowded room, and this time he and Blunt were joined by the district attorney, Robert Burgunder. As McKinley spoke, sheets of paper were being handed out. "This afternoon, the King County prosecuting attorney's office has charged George Miller with the first-degree murder of Frankie Ray. We have also requested Miller's business partner and bail bondsman, Sydney Brunn, be held as a material witness under a fifty-thousand-dollar bond."

A significant sum of money for sure, and the crowd reacted to it with surprised looks and a few whistles. McKinley said the charges were filed to forestall any attempt to obtain the release of Miller and Brunn by habeas corpus proceedings, which had apparently already been threatened by Miller's personal attorney, Arnie Chevas.

I received a copy of the complaint. A quick review revealed it did not provide details, merely alleging, in customary legal verbiage, Ray was shot with a "premeditated design to effect his death."

"We can't yet discuss specifics," McKinley said. "But we are satisfied Miller didn't shoot Ray resisting an attempted holdup, as he claims. Until we get through the tangle of conflicting stories, it is essential both

Miller and Brunn be held in custody, and we will oppose any effort to have bail for either man."

"Do you agree, Detective?" Greer called out.

Blunt cleared his throat. "There is no longer any doubt in our minds Miller owned the gun that killed Ray, a German Luger semiautomatic. We found a holster in Miller's home yesterday, and criminologist Luke May has confirmed the recovered Luger is a direct match to the impressions in that holster. He also found George Miller's fingerprints on the murder weapon and on bullets in the magazine."

It sounded to me like this conference was not intended for the reporters as much as it was to let the lawyers for George Miller and Syd Brunn know their clients were in the soup. Blunt and the prosecuting attorney's office were using the press to get out their message.

"When the witnesses talk, and they will talk, I think we'll have more answers to this mystery," Blunt said.

The reporters called out additional questions, speaking over one another and making it difficult to hear. By the time the questions stopped, the *Daily Star* had hit the streets. A reporter had left the conference, purchased several copies, and brought them into the conference room for others to read.

I wanted to leave, especially when Winn approached, but others had now cornered me, asking me where I was getting my information. I smiled and reasserted that I would not reveal my sources. The article indicated I had already spoken with Joan Daley and Luke May, as well as the witness in hiding, meaning anything my colleagues would write would be old news.

Winn approached me once more after the crowd had thinned.

"I don't know what you're playing at, son, but you're playing with fire," Winn said, his face flushed.

"I can tell," I said. "Your face looks like it's burning up."

"You're the one who's going to get burned," he said. "You don't have the experience for a story this big."

"How am I doing so far?" I said, defiant.

"Mark my words." Winn rotated like a globe and stormed down the hall.

His comment gave me pause. I knew he was right, to a certain extent. I didn't have the experience he or Greer had, but I had ambition and initiative. I also wasn't naïve. Phish told me the police used us in the press, and my job was to be careful to write factual stories and not press releases.

A benefit of working for an afternoon newspaper was that meeting my deadline gave me the night off, and I had plans to put it to good use. I walked up First Avenue, listening to the newspaper boys hawking my story on every street corner. I stopped near a shoeshine stand to watch passersby stop to buy copies. Some stopped right on the sidewalk to read my article.

"Shine for a nickel, mister," a shoeshine boy asked.

I didn't have money for such luxuries. I shined my one pair of dress shoes myself. "No thanks," I said.

He lowered his voice. "Twenty-five cents and I can find you a girl."

He looked no more than twelve or thirteen. "A girl?"

"A nice lady to spend the evening with."

This caught me off guard. "What's in it for you?" I asked, curious.

"Same as what's in it for everybody," he said, and moved to another man.

Money, I thought. That's what was in it for everybody, and that's what everyone needed during a depression. I thought of Joan Daley. I couldn't help but wonder what a woman that beautiful would cost, and what the experience would be like. I'd never know, even if I had the courage. If I didn't have a quarter for the introduction, I certainly didn't have the money for a Joan Daley.

I walked on. As I approached the Pike Place Market, Mr. Neversleeps called out from his newsstand booth. "You a man of his word, William Shumacher. You had another story the whole time, and in time for the commute home too! Been selling out. Sending boys running all over to find me more copies. This might be a bestseller, just behind our entry into World War I, April 6, 1917; the stock market crash, October 1929; and legal beer, April this year."

My chest puffed with pride. I would send a copy of the paper to my parents. They'd be relieved their son was not destined for Hooverville. I was so puffed up I decided that tomorrow I would ask Phish for a raise to a salaried position. It had been a year.

I stopped at a flower stand in the market and purchased a bouquet, then I bought a box of chocolates from a second stand. It cost me a half dollar, or fifty column inches, what I'd earned that day, but I didn't care. Now was not the time to be frugal on matters of the heart. Now was the time to be bold.

With my newfound confidence and courage, I made my way down First Avenue to Giovacchini's pastry shop. I pushed open the door, causing the bells to ring. The interior was much more subdued than during the morning rush. Two people on barstools at the counter turned and looked at me like I had two heads. A woman seated in a booth and eating chocolate pastries with her two small children smiled like I was twelve.

Mr. Giovacchini came around the counter at the sound of the bells. He looked confused. He approached as if the flowers and the chocolate might bite. "You're the reporter who was holding up my line this morning."

"I'm sorry," I said. Out of the corner of my eye, I caught Amara peeking around the wall separating the counter from the kitchen. Her mother stepped out, rubbing her hands on her apron.

"What is this?" Mr. Giovacchini gestured to the flowers and the box of chocolates.

"I wanted to ask your permission to take Amara to the picture show at the Green Parrot Theatre," I said. I hadn't actually, but now that the opportunity presented itself, I thought it would make a good impression with Mr. Giovacchini. "I will ensure she is well cared for and bring her home safely."

Mr. Giovacchini's eyes widened, then narrowed. He said, "Shumacher?"

"Yes," I said. "William Shumacher."

"German," he said.

"Yes," I said. "Both my parents are German. They—"

He cut me off with a raised hand and shook his head. "No. My daughter will not go out with a German sympathizer."

"I'm . . . I'm not a German sympathizer," I stuttered.

"No," he said again. This time his voice louder and gruffer. "Get out of my pastry shop."

"Papa," Amara said.

"Do not question me," Mr. Giovacchini said. "My daughter will not go out with a German sympathizer."

"Arturo," Amara's mother said, stepping forward.

"No!" he said again, more adamant. Then to me, "Out! Get out!"

I stepped back. I was so humiliated I was momentarily paralyzed. It felt like an hour. I turned and left. Outside the shop I saw Amara through the window. She dropped her head in her hands, and her mother took her behind the wall. I walked up the street with the flowers at my side. A young woman holding the arm of a sailor walked toward me. I handed them the flowers and the chocolates and walked off before they could question me.

When I reached my boardinghouse, Mrs. Alderbrook waited with her newspaper. "The banner headline again," she said with a joyous smile. "You're becoming famous, William Shumacher. People are starting to know your name."

I was, at the moment, painfully aware of that.

Chapter 7

Thursday morning, I came downstairs to an interrogation by Mrs. Alderbrook. She seemed to believe we had a connection through the news. In a sense we did. While crotchety, she could be motherly, and at times, I missed my mother. Last night was one of those moments. I missed not being able to talk to her about what had happened with Mr. Giovacchini. My mother would have had words of wisdom. She always had, when it came to relationships, not that I'd had many. I'd dated in high school but never anyone serious. I remained a virgin, and I didn't see that changing soon.

"Did you know George Miller changed his story overnight?" Mrs. Alderbrook sounded like the newsboys hawking papers on the street corners.

"He did?" I snapped from my self-pity.

"You didn't know it?" she said.

"I haven't read the paper yet." It had become my habit to read the morning *Post-Intelligencer* and the *Daily Times* unless I was rushing to court or the police station.

"It's right here in the *Times*." She held up the paper. "George Miller admits he owned the gun that shot Frankie Ray."

I read the article written by Emmet Winn as she continued speaking.

Winn got the scoop he wanted.

Brunn and Miller had changed their story in what the *Times* was calling an exclusive. Miller had not yet commented, waiting to be questioned by police in the presence of a stenographer. Brunn, however, had clearly set the stage for how Miller would plead in a portion of the article.

> "Ray wanted $80 but his credit was no good, and when it was refused, he got tough and attacked Miller," Syd Brunn said. "Ray had been drinking and Miller knew Ray was a prizefighter. In self-defense, Miller pulled the pistol out and shot Ray as Ray kept coming toward him."
>
> Asked why he and Miller told Detective Ernie Blunt that Ray attempted a holdup, Brunn said, "Well, Miller naturally was nervous and excited after the shooting, and when he said it wasn't his gun and Ray tried to rob him, I felt nothing could be gained by my saying otherwise, so I simply said nothing, except to show the police where I was sitting when the shooting occurred."
>
> Brunn's change in his story came at the behest of famed Seattle defense attorney John Sullivan, who will defend Miller.
>
> "I told Miller and Brunn I didn't believe the first story—that the gun was Ray's, and Miller took it from Ray and killed him when Ray tried to hold him up," Sullivan said. "I advised both to come clean and tell the truth. It was a case of self-defense. Miller knew Ray was a tough customer."
>
> Sullivan also named a mystery witness, Al Smith, a known prizefighter who accompanied Ray to the club.

"I expect to surrender Smith," Sullivan said. "I understand he's left town. He probably got frightened and didn't want to get mixed up in it, especially after the *Daily Star* irresponsibly printed what Miller and Brunn first told the police."

Prosecutor McKinley, reached for comment, said he would not comment until after Miller told his new story to a court stenographer later this morning.

Chief Homicide Detective Ernie Blunt is said to have gone into conference today to determine a new course of action, but he did say he believed powerful interests were at work on behalf of Miller and Brunn, especially the socially prominent. In addition to Brunn, bartender Billy Vahle is also being held in jail as a material witness. Two other witnesses, originally held, have been released, Archie Brown, a waiter, and Sandy Allen, the club caretaker. Police are convinced neither had any connection to the shooting.

I nearly laughed. "Irresponsible"? "Powerful interests"? Indeed.

The powerful interest was Emmet Winn, eager for a front-page story for which he likely never had to leave his desk, who didn't care Sullivan was using him to sway public opinion. *Miller simply told a fib in the heat of the moment.* Poppycock, as my mother liked to say. Sullivan clearly had convinced Miller his lies didn't hold water, and if he wanted to get away with murder, he needed a better story. Self-defense was a relatively new tactic in criminal law to justify the killing of another human being.

The story also did a good job of what Winn did best. It rehashed old news with a spin to make it sound new and important. Blunt and

McKinley already knew Miller and Brunn had lied, but now they could prepare for Miller's self-defense argument.

"How come you didn't get that story?" Mrs. Alderbrook asked.

I almost defended myself, told her the story came after the *Daily Star* had gone to print and offered nothing new, but what was the point? I smiled and handed her my room key. "I can't get them all," I said.

"I guess not." She sounded pleased with herself.

I didn't dare walk down First Avenue to work, my humiliation from the prior afternoon still as fresh as the morning air. I walked Pike Street to Seventh Avenue, then to the *Daily Star*. Phish sat behind his desk but rose when the bells sounded above the door, came into the newsroom, and wasted no time telling me the number of newspapers my story had sold the prior two afternoons. I took his good mood as an opportunity.

"About that," I said. "I've been here a year, and we discussed a raise after I'd worked a year."

Phish froze. Then, as was his habit when stalling, he removed his spectacles, blew a breath on each lens, and alternately rubbed them furiously with his handkerchief. He held the lenses up to the light streaming through the windows.

"You read Early Winn's article?" he asked.

"Typical Winn, Phish. It's a rehash of old news. Blunt and McKinley knew Miller and Brunn lied. John Sullivan used Winn to disseminate his client's self-defense claim and to try to reduce Brunn's bail."

"What have you got for me today?"

"I just got in, Phish. I'll make a couple of phone calls and find out what's what."

"About Sullivan using Winn . . . Be careful you don't fall into the same boat with Blunt and McKinley. I want pizzazz, but I want facts to back it up. I don't need the expense of a lawsuit."

"I'll be careful," I said.

We both stood like statues.

Phish slipped his spectacles back around his ears. "A raise, huh?"

"It's been a year."

"Has it?" He turned his head to look at the calendar hanging on the wall. "What did you have in mind?"

"A weekly salary, like Altobelli and Kawolski."

"Grace Mary Altobelli makes three dollars and thirty cents a week—"

"Writing gardening tips and covering flower shows. Not hard news," I said.

"I can go as high as four dollars a week," Phish said.

"Six dollars a week."

"Five."

"Five fifty," I said.

"Five forty. But I expect an article every day, Monday through Friday."

I was already meeting that requirement, but a salaried position would mean more money and allow me to budget and send a bit more home to my struggling parents. "Deal," I said, and stuck out my hand.

Phish shook it reluctantly. At nearly the same moment, my desk phone rang. Phish and I separated, and I answered the phone. Blunt.

"Miller is coming in to give his statement this morning with his attorney and a court stenographer."

"Just read about it in the *Daily Times*," I said, my tone intimating my displeasure at being scooped.

"If I could have, I would have let you know," he said.

"Miller's going to plead self-defense," I said.

"We've always suspected it. The general public hasn't heard directly from Miller. But if you're not interested . . ."

And that was the reason for Blunt's call. "I'm interested. When is he coming in?"

"Fifteen minutes, but no way I can get you into the interview."

I didn't think he could. "You won't allow Winn; will you?"

"Not a chance. Meet me at the Central Cafe at half past eleven, and I'll tell you what Miller has to say."

I hung up the receiver and wondered how the man was not twice his size given how much and how regularly he ate his meals. Phish stared at me.

"Hold the front page," I said. He gave me a curt nod. While I waited to meet with Blunt, I got curious. Recently the licensing board had approved the sale of beer in certain establishments, which Phish said meant the owner had paid a bribe to a board member. I researched whether the Pom Pom Club had a license to sell beer. It took a few minutes to find the number for the licensing board and then to explain to the person what I sought. He told me the club did not have permission, then hurriedly added, "Though an application has been submitted and is expected to be approved in the upcoming weeks."

"How is it the club was selling not just beer but hard alcohol?" I asked.

The clerk cleared his throat. "We don't enforce the laws," he said. "We just grant or deny licenses."

I decided to visit the licensing board in person, which was in an administrative building across the street from the new courthouse on Third Avenue, and dig a little deeper into the Pom Pom Club's application for a liquor license. Again, it took a bit of time, but I eventually received a file and learned the club had used the name "the Flamingo" on a May 27 application, which initially seemed odd. A police lieutenant in a report to the city council, which Police Chief L. L. Norton approved, had also provided a statement. "So far as complaints or reports are concerned, this place is conducted in an orderly manner."

On a hunch, I asked for any files the board had for the Pom Pom Club, George Miller, or Syd Brunn. What I found inside a second file revealed why the Pom Pom Club had applied for its license as the Flamingo. Several complaints had been lodged by neighbors against the Pom Pom Club for drunk and disorderly conduct and loud disturbances by its patrons, and for illegal parking, which had led to opposition to the beer license. Federal abatement proceedings had also been instituted against the Pom Pom Club for failure to pay taxes. In other words, the police, including the chief, knew the complaints would be problematic to the Pom Pom Club being granted a beer license and told Miller and Brunn to apply for the license under a different name so they could push the application through the board, no doubt for a hefty fee.

An interesting story for certain, but also a good way to get Norton to pull my press pass if I pursued it.

At eleven fifteen, I headed out to meet Blunt. I loved the bustle of First Avenue in Pioneer Square. A ship was in town, and sailors walked the streets in their bright-white uniforms and Dixie Cup hats. They were looking for a good time, and the shoeshine boys seemed to be shouting "Shine!" a little louder. The newspaper boys on the corners were also busy shouting out the morning headlines. "Miller changes story. Read it in the *Daily Times*!" I wondered if they, too, were selling more than news. Farther along, a woman rang a bell for the Salvation Army and tried in vain to outshout the boys and the clatter made by the passing trolley cars to gain the attention of men in suits and fedoras or boaters and women wearing dresses and cloche hats hurrying along the sidewalks.

The Central Cafe was across the street from the steel-and-glass pergola erected at the corner of James Street to shelter passengers from rain and wind while awaiting streetcars. On this bright and clear day, rain was not a problem. Behind the pergola rose a sixty-foot totem pole. I'd once suggested a news story to Phish on the pole's history and learned that prominent and wealthy Seattle citizens serving on the chamber of commerce had it chopped down and shipped it to Seattle from a Tlingit Indian village in Alaska while the villagers were away fishing. When confronted, the guilty quietly paid the village, then created the story that the pole was a testament to Seattle's celebration of the Indian way of life.

I crossed Yesler to the Central Cafe. The interior was long, narrow, and smelled of greasy food. Several sailors, who looked no older than me, sat in booths with their arms around young women. No doubt arranged dates the shoeshine boy had spoken of. I wondered if that was the way most sailors lost their virginity.

Blunt sat in the last booth, facing the door. I slid onto the seat across from him, and after greetings, he ordered half a chicken with potatoes and a salad. I ordered a cup of coffee. My ill-fated purchase of flowers and chocolate had already set me back, and I was running low on funds.

"You don't eat lunch?" Blunt asked.

"I had a pastry earlier," I said. I hadn't.

"That's no lunch. Betty?" He regained the attention of a tall, brunette waitress. She returned to the table but looked unhappy.

"It's okay," I said. I only had two nickels in my pocket that Phish had given me to make the daily calls to the apprentice, Kravitz, while covering the investigation.

"My friend here would like a hamburger, potatoes, and a Coke. Can we do that?"

Betty gave me a pained smile, like I was one of Hooverville's downtrodden, which made me realize Blunt would not be paying for this meal either. I doubted any restaurant in these times could afford to be so generous.

"Really," I said, feeling guilty. "It's okay."

"On the house," Blunt said. "Isn't that right, Betty?"

"Whatever you say, Ernie."

"You see," Blunt said to me. "They're happy to have a big-shot reporter like you in their fine establishment. William Shumacher here is the reporter who broke the Pom Pom nightclub killing for the *Daily Star*."

I was horrified. Receiving unnecessary charity was bad enough; getting a meal under false pretenses was worse.

"Is that right," Betty said. She smiled, but without any trace of humor. I was thankful when she departed.

"You ready?" Blunt asked. He nodded to my reporter's satchel, which made me think of Early Winn being used by Miller and his lawyers. At the moment, Blunt was calling the shots, and if I wanted any more front-page stories, I needed to go along with what he had to say. I told myself I could use other sources to verify any facts I might question, though I knew Blunt would control the flow of information. I reached into my leather satchel and removed a pencil and my notebook.

"Miller was questioned by King County prosecutor Laurence McKinley and Chief Detective Ernie Blunt in the presence of a stenographer," Blunt said. "After Sullivan announced his client would tell the truth, Miller gave a statement. He said, 'Ray came for me with his left hand raised. He had his right hand at his hip pocket, and I thought he was going to pull a knife. So I shot him. When he didn't go down and kept coming, I shot him again.'"

Blunt had just dictated what he hoped would be the lede to my article, which made me feel the way I felt about getting a lunch for free. "Why didn't he just tell the truth when you first interviewed him at the Pom Pom Club?" I asked.

"Which is what McKinley asked," Blunt said.

"What was Miller's response?"

"He said he told a different story because he hadn't had a chance to talk it over with his attorney."

"He had to talk to an attorney to tell the truth?"

"That's good," Blunt said. "I like that. Work that into your article somewhere."

I resisted squirming in my seat.

"Miller said when he told his attorney what happened, Sullivan told him the killing was self-defense," Blunt said.

"Why did he carry a gun?"

"I asked the same question. Miller said he carried the gun because the nightclub was a target for a stickup due to its popularity and all the money coming in each evening."

"Nobody is going to rob an underworld club," I said.

"Another good point you can attribute to me," Blunt said.

"Did he say why Ray came at him?"

"Said Ray got ugly when he refused to give him an eighty-dollar loan."

"I read in the *Times* that Syd Brunn said the loan was to pay for the Cadillac, not Joan Daley's hospital bill."

"Miller, or rather Sullivan, is likely trying to make Ray look bad and not like a Good Samaritan. This will no doubt be a character assassination of Ray by the defense. Also, we're releasing Vahle, the bartender, today. We're convinced he didn't see the shooting, just the aftermath."

"I read Brunn is trying to get his bail reduced from fifty thousand dollars to one thousand dollars," I said.

Blunt smiled. "Remember when I told the press some powerful forces were at work? Well, this morning acting police judge Jacob Kalina walked into my department. He said he came, at the mayor's direction, to determine why Brunn's bail was set so high, which means Sullivan made a phone call or a visit to the mayor."

"Sullivan has access to the mayor?" I asked.

"Sullivan is a Rainier Club member. So is the mayor. They both run in some high-society circles." The Rainier Club was a respite social haven for Seattle's capitalist bourgeoisie.

"What did you tell Kalina?"

"I told him Brunn was being held because another material witness in the case had disappeared, and without Brunn, the State's case might be seriously handicapped. I asked Kalina if he wanted that in an election year." Blunt smiled. "After he left my office, I called up Sullivan and struck a deal. Brunn is going to be let out this afternoon."

"Why?"

"Because he was likely going to get out anyway. I got Sullivan to convince Brunn to help us find Al Smith."

"The witness with the blood on his clothes?"

"He disappeared after we spoke to him at the hotel, but I'm sure Sullivan knows where he is."

"How are you so sure?"

"Because Sullivan agreed to the deal. That isn't public knowledge, so if you just happened to be around the Yesler Building when Brunn is released, you'll get the story first and might get a chance to talk to him."

The waitress returned with our meals on large porcelain plates. She didn't ask if we needed anything else. One bite of the greasy hamburger made me forget my guilt and satisfied my hunger pangs. I never recalled being hungry in Kansas City, but I'd been hungry often in Seattle.

After our meal, Blunt and I walked up the block to the Yesler Building. Blunt went in the Yesler Way entrance. I entered on the other side of the building and waited, which was my habit. Within half an hour, Syd Brunn walked down the corridor.

"Mr. Brunn?" I flashed my police press pass. "William Shumacher with the *Daily Star*."

"You were at the club the other morning with Detective Blunt."

"I understand your bail was lowered after you agreed to help the police find a witness."

Brunn eyed me with curiosity. Then he said, "I don't know nothing about no deal and no witness. Talk to my lawyer." He started off, then turned back. "Oh, and I'm sticking to my story. I didn't see George Miller shoot Ray."

"The article in the *Times* said you admitted seeing the shooting. You said the shooting was self-defense."

Brunn flashed a wicked smile. "Did I? Well, the shooting was self-defense for certain. But I only saw the gun in George Miller's hand. Not the shooting."

"Then how do you know it was self-defense?"

"Talk to my lawyer, kid." He scurried down the steps and out the building door.

About that same time, McKinley came down the hallway and I hurried over to him. "I understand Brunn has offered to help find Al Smith."

"He agreed to do much more than that." McKinley sounded animated. "I had a talk with Brunn yesterday in jail. He told me there was no need for Miller to shoot Ray. He said Miller could have pushed Ray away, gotten out of Ray's way, or hit him on the head, if necessary, with the butt of his gun." He smiled. "His new statement will blast Miller's claim of self-defense out of the water."

Which wasn't what Brunn had just told me, but it wasn't my job to tell McKinley the discrepancies. My job was to report the news. "Can I quote you?"

"You can. And you can add the prosecuting attorney will seek to have Miller tried for first-degree murder during the last two weeks of July, when a special term of court will be held."

I had my story: "Miller to Be Tried for First-Degree Murder."

Phish would be ecstatic. I went to a public phone and inserted one of the two nickels. Phish got on the phone, and I dictated my lede, then Miller's first words since the shooting, as relayed to me by Blunt. I added in the information about Syd Brunn's bail being reduced in exchange for his cooperation finding a missing witness, and my conflicting conversations with Brunn and McKinley. McKinley might be upset, but with Brunn, not me. He'd also be glad to know Brunn was not a man of his word.

I did not talk about the police judge trying to free Brunn, or that the mayor had likely been involved behind the scenes. It made me wonder again about the black book Blunt had found at the Pom Pom Club with the patrons' names, and what it could be used for in the wrong hands. Then I amended that thought and wondered what it could be used for in Blunt's hands.

As I spoke on the phone, I watched a man enter the Yesler Building in a double-breasted, tan, chalk-striped summer suit with a matching fedora pulled low on his forehead. He walked to the police counter. I'd seen this man before, but it took a moment to realize it was Al Smith, the witness who'd turned his bloodstained, *only* suit over to the dry cleaner. It looked like he'd managed to get another suit, an expensive one from the looks of it, as well as an expensive hat.

"I'd like to speak with Detective Ernie Blunt," Smith said.

"Who are you?" the officer asked.

"Al Smith. I was in the Pom Pom Club the morning of the shooting."

"Shoe?" Phish said.

"I'll call you back. Something interesting is developing," I said. "Clear the front page for a second article."

Chapter 8

Missing Witness in Pom Pom Killing Walks into Police Headquarters

Al Smith Claims He Didn't See Shooting.
Fled in Fear.

While police conducted a statewide search for Al Smith, "missing witness" in the fatal shooting of Frankie Ray at the Pom Pom Club on June 13, Smith walked into police headquarters today to volunteer his story. Smith came to the Yesler Building in style, wearing a double-breasted, tan, chalk-striped summer suit with a matching fedora and black-and-tan saddle shoes.

A half hour later, he was locked in the city jail on an open charge and held on a $10,000 bond. Smith told Chief Detective Ernie Blunt he was outside the Pom Pom Club when the shots were fired, and upon running back inside, he saw Ray dying on the floor.

> Smith said he didn't see the shooting and therefore didn't think there was any need to stick around.
>
> "We aren't accepting his story that he simply took a vacation," Blunt added. "I had told him not to leave town or I'd lock him up as a material witness. He also maintains he hasn't talked to anybody about the case since it happened, but Miller's attorney, John Sullivan, notified us Smith would surrender himself before Smith walked into headquarters."

The article ran on the front page in the left-hand column, the newspaper's power position. Phish had outdone himself with respect to the headline broadcasting my second front-page article beneath the *Daily Star* banner, though it wasn't exactly accurate.

> **Witness Turns Against**
>
> **Pom Pom Killer**
>
> *Brunn Claims Miller Fired*
>
> *Shots Without Need*

I left the *Star*'s office with the telephone ringing off the hook, the publishers for the *Daily Times* and the *Post-Intelligencer* questioning Phish about how I was getting the stories nobody else was getting. McKinley and Blunt both also telephoned, but I made myself scarce, at Phish's suggestion. Phish answered the calls like a man who'd just eaten a large piece of apple pie topped with a big scoop of vanilla ice cream. He told the others the stories were a result of good old-fashioned boots-on-the-ground reporting. Each time he hung up the phone, about to congratulate me, the phone would ring again, and he'd snap up the receiver. I finally gave up hanging around for a few scraps of gratitude and started for home.

Out of habit, and with my mind preoccupied with all the attention, I marched right up First Avenue. The men in the newspaper stands acknowledged me by name.

"Hey, Shoe, practically selling themselves."

"Keep those stories coming, Shoe. You're like an Alaskan gold mine."

I basked in the attention and failed to notice I had walked past Giovacchini's stenciled window, now empty of the pastries that filled the space each morning.

"Are you too big now to come into our little shop?"

I turned. Amara stood outside the door to the pastry shop, arms crossed, head tilted in expectation of an answer. Instinctively I looked toward the shop windows.

"My father isn't here. He's buying supplies for the morning."

I walked back toward her.

"I read the paper," she said. "Two stories on the front page. I guess you go to a different bakery now that you're famous."

"I'm . . . I'm not . . . famous, and I didn't . . . I didn't think . . ."

"Clearly," she said. Then she added, "You ask me to go to a movie and then you don't come back?"

"I did come back. Your father—"

"My father lost his father in the world war. He was shot and killed by German forces. He thinks anyone who is German is the enemy. But I don't. And my mother doesn't either. Tell me, do you run and hide when your news sources slam a door in your face?"

"No," I said.

"So then, I'm just not important?"

"No. I mean yes." I felt like I'd been lit on fire and my hair was ablaze. Amara's eyebrows arched. "Yes, you are important," I said. "I'm sorry I haven't been back. I didn't want to cause you any trouble with your father."

"I'm twenty-one years old. My father still treats me like I'm sixteen. All fathers treat their daughters like they're sixteen. But I'm old enough to make my own decisions. And I would like to see *The Picture Snatcher* with you. It's still playing at the Green Parrot; is it not?"

"It is. But what will you tell your father?"

"My mother will tell my father what I have told you. I'm old enough to make my own decisions. Hopefully not my own mistakes. Am I making a mistake, William Shumacher?"

I smiled. "No," I said. "I promise you."

"Because you don't want to get my mother angry. She makes my father look like a pussycat."

"No," I said. "I don't want that."

"The matinee is at one p.m. on Saturday. I'll meet you outside the theater at twelve thirty after the morning rush at the shop. After the show, you will take me home and have dinner with my family, like a gentleman."

I felt the butterflies already stirring in my stomach. "I don't have a car, Amara."

"Of course you don't. I don't either. Who has a car? We'll ride the bus. We catch it a block down on First Avenue. The bus will take you home."

"Okay," I said.

"Okay," she said, and for the first time she smiled, just a bit with her lips, but her eyes glowed as bright as a Christmas window in the Frederick & Nelson department store during the holidays.

I rushed up the street and hurried into the boardinghouse. Mrs. Alderbrook came out from behind the counter and held up a folded newspaper. I stepped past it, grabbed her outstretched arm, and put my other hand on her ample hip. I waltzed with her, at least the few steps my mother had taught me. I spun her with a flourish.

She squealed like someone with the hiccups. I bowed low. "I'm sorry, Mrs. Alderbrook. I guess I got carried away."

"I guess you did," she said. "But under the circumstances I can forgive you."

"The circumstances?"

"Two articles on the front page. I suppose that's worth dancing about."

I had completely forgotten about the articles. "Yes. It is cause for celebration," I said.

"I've kept a copy for you to send to your parents," she said. "Two cents."

I reached into my pocket and realized a new dilemma. How was I supposed to take Amara to the picture show? I had no money to spare and wouldn't be paid for a few more days.

"What's wrong?"

"I asked a girl to the picture show, but I'm afraid I don't have the money to go."

"That is a dilemma. Who is this young lady?"

"Amara Giovacchini from the pastry shop on First Avenue."

"Arturo's daughter? She's very beautiful, William. Do you like this girl?"

I nodded but no words came.

"Hmm . . . I've seen that look before on the faces of young men."

I felt horrible, for myself certainly, but more so for Amara. I didn't want to disappoint her and go back to tell her I couldn't afford to take her to the movie. "I'll have to tell her I can't take her," I said.

"Nonsense." Mrs. Alderbrook went into her room, returned, and handed me two quarters. "That should be enough for you to pay for the picture show and a box of popcorn. After the show, walk over to the soda counter at Frederick & Nelson. You can share a milkshake, but let her pick the flavor."

"I can't accept your charity, Mrs. Alderbrook."

"Charity? Ha! What do you think this is, the Bread of Life Mission? You can pay me back when you pay the month's rent."

"Thank you." I picked up my newspaper, started for the stairs, then turned back. I reached into my pocket for two pennies. "Here you go," I said.

She shook her head. "I just remembered; Mr. Willis brought the paper in. I asked him for it when he'd finished."

I knew she was not telling me the truth. But I also needed those two pennies.

Saturday morning, I fretted over my clothing. I didn't have a clean shirt. Both were well worn, as were my trousers. I did my best to look presentable, then hurried down the stairs at a quarter after twelve.

Mrs. Alderbrook looked up from the newspaper as I approached the entryway.

"How do I look?" I asked.

"Like you're missing something."

"What?" I asked, alarmed.

"These." She produced flowers from behind the counter. "Every girl loves flowers."

"I don't know what to say," I said.

"Don't say anything," she said. "Save it for the young lady. You seem to have precious few words as it is."

"I guess I'm nervous. I've never taken a girl to the picture show."

"Just ask her about herself and the pastry shop until the picture starts. And remember, the usher will try to seat you on the side. Tell him you want center-aisle seats. It will make you look worldly."

"Right," I said. "Thank you."

"Go. You don't want to be late."

As I hurried down First Avenue, Amara stepped from the pastry shop and turned in the direction of the theater. The sight of her nearly took my breath away. She wore a red dress and black shoes with white ankle socks. Her hair, which was usually beneath a scarf, flowed to her shoulders in curls, a red hat pinned atop her head. I stood dumbfounded.

She walked toward me. "Close your mouth," she said laughing. "You'll catch a fly."

"You look beautiful, Amara."

"And you look handsome."

I handed her the flowers, then realized they weren't very practical since we were going to a theater.

"It's good you met me here as I was leaving so I can quickly put these in water inside the shop. We don't want to miss the shorts, and we want to get good seats." She hurried back inside and emerged moments later. She took my arm, and we walked down First Avenue to the Green Parrot.

Inside the ornate theater, I could smell the buttery popcorn and watched it popping behind orange glass. I paid for two tickets and a box of popcorn, and an usher walked us down the aisle. He offered us two seats on the side.

"We'd like to sit in the center," I said. He took us down another row to the center aisle. We stepped past others to the two unoccupied seats.

"Good seats," Amara said, impressed. I was about to ask her about her morning, when she said, "You're not from Seattle. Where are you from?"

"Kansas City," I said. "Missouri."

"What brought you here? The newspaper?"

"Yes and no." I told her how my father and mother had fallen on hard times, and my father suggested I join the military, but my mother had intervened. I didn't tell her my father could no longer afford to have me live at home.

"Times are hard for everyone," Amara said. "We're lucky to have jobs. How do you like Seattle?"

"I'm getting used to the rain," I said.

"No one ever gets used to the rain; we just learn to live with it. A good pair of shoes is a start." She laughed and it was warm and rich, like saltwater taffy.

I moved my shoes with the holes in the soles beneath my seat. "How did your family end up in Seattle?"

She said her grandfather had been a baker in a small Italian town outside of Bologna called Rio Saliceto. "When he was drafted, my father's older brothers took over the business, but there wasn't room for my father. After my grandfather died in the war and hard times came, my grandmother told my father he would need to find his own way. My father came to America for the opportunity of a better life. He immigrated to Ellis Island, then to San Francisco, where he had a cousin, but found too much bakery competition. He moved to Seattle, took out a loan, and opened the bakery. He still wires money home to his mother."

I wanted to tell Amara her father and I had much in common, but the shorts started with a newsclip of trouble brewing in Europe with the rise of the German Nationalist People's Party. It made me uncomfortable, given my heritage, another black strike against me in Mr. Giovacchini's book.

We shared the box of popcorn and watched the movie. When it ended, the entire theater clapped. We stepped back outside. "Would you like to share a milkshake at Frederick & Nelson?" I asked.

Amara smiled. "I would. But not today. No reason to spend needlessly. Today my mother is cooking, and you better be hungry. She'll keep feeding you until you explode."

Which is what I thought might happen when her father opened the door of their house and saw me with his daughter.

We took the 10 Mount Baker bus from downtown Seattle to Rainier Valley. On the ride, I remembered what Mrs. Alderbrook had said and asked Amara more questions about herself and her job. She told me her father paid her a fair wage but with a deduction for room and board. Her family lived on a farm in Rainier Valley. On the bus, we passed Italian grocery stores, a pharmacy, barbershop, meat market, bakery, and a macaroni factory. "The Vacca brothers sell their fresh produce at their produce stand," Amara pointed out. "My brothers do also. The rest they sell at the Pike Place Market. And that's our church." She pointed to Our Lady of Mount Virgin Catholic Church on a rise that overlooked the neighborhood.

We got off the bus at the intersection of Rainier Avenue and Empire Way. I was so nervous when we stepped from the bus, I thought my legs had fallen asleep. Amara continued to play tour guide. "That used to be Dugdale Field." She pointed to an empty lot. "It burned down last year. My father was heartbroken. He's a big Seattle Rainiers fan, and now the games are on the other side of Seattle at Civic Stadium just below Queen Anne."

"My boss has an autographed baseball bat from George Burns," I said.

Amara stopped walking. "Tioga George?" she said, her voice rising. "He's my father's favorite player."

I heard the enthusiasm in her voice as she pointed out neighbors' homes and gardens we passed. "You like living here," I said.

"I love living here. It's like a small Italian village. Everybody knows everyone."

Meaning no one would know me. Again, the butterflies returned.

The stores and residences gave way to farmland, lots of it. Vegetable gardens were everywhere, and I saw small vineyards.

"Families grow their own food and make their own wine," Amara said. "My brothers have a vineyard on the farm."

"Do they sell the wine too?" I asked.

She smiled. "Not during Prohibition. I think most families drink it. My brothers certainly."

The modest house was at the end of a dirt drive, a two-story, clapboard-sided structure with a wraparound porch and a flower garden. Flowers in pots overflowed on the porch, and a white swing hung silent in the still, warm air. The house was surrounded by fields. A tractor and other equipment had been left unattended. Amara pointed out lettuce, zucchini, cauliflower, eggplant, and other vegetables.

"We have chickens also and sell the eggs at the market," she said. "And one very fat pig to eat whatever we don't finish during meals, but with two older brothers that isn't much."

"Older brothers," I said, now more alarmed. "Will they be home?"

"They'll be home," she said. "But don't let them intimidate you. They're very tall. More than six feet. So stand up straight."

Mr. Giovacchini was no taller than me. Five feet nine inches. "Where do they get their height?"

"My grandfather, apparently. My father was the shortest of six children. Come on," she said. "If we stand on the porch, they'll think we're necking."

I blushed, which caused Amara to smile. She opened the front door and pulled me inside a narrow hallway with a coatrack and mirror over an entry table. Amara put her coat on the rack and her handbag on the table and called out that she was home. I removed my cap, holding it in my hand.

Two tall, lean, dark-haired men came down the hall. "Amara," they said joyously. "You made it home. We were worried."

She swatted her two brothers, then gestured to me. "This is Mr. William Shumacher."

I put out my hand to greet them. They stepped past it, one on each side, then lifted me off the ground by my elbows and carried me down the hallway. "Come in, Mr. Shumacher. Welcome to our quiet and uneventful home."

Amara and her mother were both aghast and entertained. They told the brothers to put me down. They dropped me in the living room, where Mr. Giovacchini stood looking less than amused. We faced one another like two boxers sizing up our opponent before the fight. "Thank you for having me, Mr. Giovacchini."

"Hmm," he said. "Let's eat."

Amara's brothers were just as entertaining at the table, seemingly trying to one-up each other with each story. They sat across from Amara and me and loudly talked about everything from their day's events to the world news. Her mother and father sat at the table ends. Her mother occasionally chimed in, but her father remained silent.

"William had two stories on the front page of his newspaper the other day, Papa. One under the banner," Amara said.

Her father did not respond.

"And he received a raise. He's now a salaried reporter. Isn't that right, William?"

"That's right." I lowered my fork.

Mrs. Giovacchini congratulated me and asked if I'd be coming back to the pastry shop. "Yes," I said. "You can't get the raisin-and-cinnamon pastries anywhere else that are close to as good."

"That's because it was my father's recipe. He had a pastry shop in Italy before he went off to the war," Mr. Giovacchini said with a sharp bite.

"Amara told me," I said. "I'm very sorry for your loss."

Mrs. Giovacchini blessed herself and looked to the ceiling.

Amara had not been kidding about the amount of food. Her mother put a large platter, what she called an antipasto plate, on the table. It contained sliced meats, cheese, eggplant, olives, and peppers.

"Shall we say grace?" Mrs. Giovacchini said. She held out her hands to her son Arthur on her left and to me on her right.

"Are you Catholic?" Mr. Giovacchini said. "I understand Germans are Protestant."

"I'm Catholic," I said. "My mother and father are both Catholic, as is about thirty percent of the German population."

Mr. Giovacchini held out his hands. After grace, the plates clattered with the sound of silverware, and her brothers kept filling my glass with wine from a jug.

"Ernesto makes the wine," Mrs. Giovacchini said, referring to the younger of her two sons. "From the grapes growing on the hillside at the back of the farm."

"It's very good," I said.

Mrs. Giovacchini served homemade ravioli, salad, and fried eggplant. Each time I cleared my plate, she refilled it. After going hungry so often, my stomach wasn't used to so much food. This wasn't a problem for the brothers, but I felt like I couldn't eat another bite.

After dinner, Ernesto and Arthur excused themselves. "Have to get the chickens and farm equipment put away," Arthur said. Each said it was nice to have met me.

"I hope you weren't offended by our picking you up," Ernesto said. "Amara told us to slump, so we didn't hover over you."

"It's fine," I said. "I thought it was funny."

"Come again," Arthur said and finished his glass of wine. "Amara. Give William eggs before he leaves."

They excused themselves and left the house. Amara and her mother stood and cleared plates. I started to help, but Mrs. Giovacchini was adamant I not touch a thing on the table. "I'll serve coffee in the living room."

Mr. Giovacchini moved to the adjacent room. I followed, more than a little intimidated, and a little intoxicated. I waited until he took his seat, so I didn't inadvertently take his chair, which was near the radio. I sat on the couch in an uncomfortable silence. Periodically I could hear Mrs. Giovacchini and Amara whispering in the kitchen.

"Amara said after you lost your father, your mother suggested you come to America for a fresh start."

"Something like that," Mr. Giovacchini said.

"My father told me the same thing. My uncle took his life because of the Depression, and my aunt came to live with us. My father couldn't afford to keep me at home. It's why I came to Seattle, for a job. I send money home each month, though it isn't much."

"I'm sorry about your uncle," Mr. Giovacchini said. "You came by train? By yourself?"

"Yes, sir."

"How old are you?"

"I'm nearly twenty," I said.

"I was just about your age when I took the boat to Ellis Island," he said.

"That had to take some courage," I said.

"Not sure courage had much to do with it. I didn't have another choice."

"I know what you mean," I said.

"Do you?" he asked with skepticism.

"Well, I certainly didn't come as far, but when I arrived at Union Station, I still felt like I'd landed on the moon. Everything here is so much different than in Kansas City. The landscape, the people, the demographics. The politics."

"Seattle politics are corrupt," Mr. Giovacchini said. "The police are corrupt. But at least it keeps away most of the underworld. In Sicily my brothers pay a portion of what they make to the Cosa Nostra. Here we take care of the police and the politicians—but it's a coffee and a pastry." I thought of Ernie Blunt eating for free. "And the police and the politicians take care of us. It's the way things are."

I nodded. After several seconds Mr. Giovacchini said, "Good for you to send money home to your parents."

Amara and her mother came out from the kitchen with coffee and biscotti, then departed again. Mr. Giovacchini dipped his cookie in his coffee, and I imitated him. Unfortunately, I left my cookie in my coffee too long, and when I pulled it out, it broke off on the way to my mouth and dropped into my cup. The hot coffee tipped over the rim onto my crotch.

I swallowed the pain, my face as hot as my crotch. Then I heard a snicker. Mr. Giovacchini was red in the face, unsuccessfully stifling a laugh.

When I laughed, he let loose with a guffaw, and then a burst of laughter. Amara and Mrs. Giovacchini rushed back into the room, alarmed.

"You didn't tell me William was so funny," Mr. Giovacchini said, covering for me.

Amara looked at me and I shrugged, the cup hiding the stain on my crotch. She smiled nervously.

After coffee and cookies, I needed to catch the bus home. I grabbed my coat and my cap, and Amara walked me to the front door with her mother and father.

"Thank you for the dinner. I don't think I've ever eaten so well."

"You'll have to come again," Mrs. Giovacchini said. "Won't he, Arturo." She jabbed her husband in the ribs.

"You are welcome here," he said, then opened the door for me to leave.

"Thank you, again." I stepped onto the porch and turned back to say good night to Amara, but she came out the front door with me and closed it behind her.

"You can make it back to the bus stop?"

"I think I can manage," I said.

"Thank you for the movie and the popcorn."

"Thank you for the wonderful dinner. You weren't kidding about the amount of food. I might not eat for a week."

We laughed, mostly nerves.

The windows were curtained, and I didn't see her mother or father watching us. "Can I kiss you good night?"

Amara smiled. “Do you intend to see me again?”

“I would like to, very much.”

“Then yes.”

I stepped forward and tilted my head. Her lips were soft and moist.

I felt hands grasp each of my elbows and lift me off the ground. “They say a kiss from an Italian girl can make you levitate,” Ernesto said.

“As light as a feather,” Arthur added, the two brothers laughing.

Part II

Chapter 9

The trial of George Miller was pushed back several times during the summer. The defense filed motions for extended time, the State opposed, and the court granted the motions. McKinley explained that, given the stakes, appointed King County Superior Court judge Peter Kincaid would not rush the defense to trial and possibly give them something to appeal. The big news was the State's decision to seek the death penalty when trying Miller for first-degree murder.

Throughout the summer, I made my Sunday calls home. My mother and father were eager to talk about the stories I had sent, but I sensed there was more they were not telling me. My mother eventually called when my father was not home and explained that things had become dire. My father had lost the remainder of his clients. He now walked downtown every day to a soup kitchen with the other unemployed. Since Phish had agreed to a regular weekly salary, I had increased the amount I sent home once a month, but I knew it didn't go far with two children still living at home, along with my aunt.

My mother said they were struggling to pay the property taxes on the home but had reached a compromise with the bank, at least for now.

Late one night I received a call from my younger brother, Thomas, which was highly unusual given the expense of calling long distance. Thomas said it was important and confirmed my suspicion that things were worse than my mother had let on. "Mom sold all her jewelry but the wedding ring on her finger, and Dad is coughing all the time. He only eats the one meal a day so there's more for the rest of us. I'm worried he's going to end up like Uncle Ted."

"He won't do that," I said. "Not with a family."

"No? The other day he said he was worth more dead than alive, whatever that means."

I knew what it meant. My mother and father had a life insurance policy that paid out if my father died. I didn't tell Thomas this.

Amara and I continued our courtship, though on a budget. Neither of us felt right about spending money freely when so many were struggling. We went to the newest picture shows each month but only to the Sunday matinee, which was half-price, and Amara showed me the sights around Seattle, with her brothers chaperoning. We hiked the mountains, and I learned the details of fly-fishing, though I wasn't very good at it. Mr. and Mrs. Giovacchini even chaperoned an overnight ferry trip to the San Juan Islands, where we spent the night at the Hotel de Haro, my first time staying in a hotel and a real luxury, though I had to share a room with Amara's father, who snored. With each passing week, her father's icy exterior melted a little more, and from beneath the frost emerged a man with a strong sense of family, humor, and a quick wit.

I was in love with Amara and could think of nothing else, except of course the plight of my family. Phish would catch me sitting at the typewriter with a vacant stare and yell to get my attention. "Shoe! I'm not paying you five dollars and forty cents to think. I'm paying you to report. We have a deadline to meet."

Phish wanted every angle on the George Miller story. He even used the term "the Trial of the Century" to describe the upcoming battle. The phrase generated an excitement Seattleites usually reserved for championship prizefights. The *Daily Times* and the *Post-Intelligencer* eagerly adopted the phrase, and all three newspapers were selling record numbers of papers. People read the news in cafeterias and coffee shops, while walking the streets and riding the trolleys each morning and afternoon.

I ran a profile on McKinley. Speculation swirled around the Yesler Building that the district attorney, Robert Burgunder, would try the case, but Burgunder had a medical issue and ultimately decided on McKinley, who had obtained convictions in half a dozen murder trials. The prosecutor would try the case alone, sort of a David against Miller's Goliath defense team that included trial attorney John J. Sullivan; Arnie Chevas, Miller's personal attorney; and a number of different research attorneys who sat in the first pew behind counsel's table. The State hoped that McKinley standing alone would create empathy from the jury.

I also ran a profile on Sullivan, though he was guarded in his answers to my questions, perhaps considering me, or the *Daily Star*, to favor the State due to my early access to the story. Or maybe he was just protecting his client. Sullivan reiterated Miller had acted in self-defense, and that he would call an astounding fifty-nine witnesses, including men serving federal prison sentences, as well as prominent Seattleites.

The State would call just fourteen witnesses.

Phish loved it. He said the trial would expose Seattle's working class and downtrodden to the city's underbelly—the underworld and the prominent citizenry who spoke out against the sins of alcohol, prostitution, and gambling during the day, but at night donned their tuxedoes and three-piece suits, their sequined dresses, furs, and jewelry, and made their way to the speakeasies and the dinner clubs. At Police Chief L. L. Norton's order, Blunt had provided the press a list of Pom Pom Club members, though I noted it omitted certain people, like Norton and the mayor. Phish did not publish the list, nor had the *Daily Times* or the *Post-Intelligencer*. I rationalized that the publishers of those two dailies, which catered to the Democrats and Republicans respectively, had received considerable pressure from prominent citizens—perhaps even threats about what would happen were they to publish the names, but it seemed like the kind of information Phish thrived on. He steadfastly maintained the *Daily Star*'s independence from such politics. When I asked him about it, Phish had a ready answer.

"You and I both know what we received isn't the full list," Phish said. "We're being partially fed with the hope our curiosity will be satisfied. If we publish some but not all the names, the impact—were we to later obtain the full list—would be diluted. By not publishing the list, we maintain leverage—the fear that we know all the names on the list, and we won't be hand-fed by the police or the politicians. We remain independent."

Phish scrupulously edited my articles, and he didn't hesitate to change a word here or there to add "pizzazz!"

Defense to Call Prisoners

Prominent in Pom Pom Case

State Prosecutor Warns Defense Will

Conduct Character Assassination of Victim

The defense will marshal as disorderly a crew of witnesses as ever were paraded before a Seattle jury to support its unusual defense technique that George Miller (36) shot and killed Frankie Ray (34) in self-defense. From the city's dives and brothels will come friends of the defendant, former friends of his victim. Witness testimony, the State argued in court today, will be less about Miller and more about the man he had rubbed out in the Pom Pom Club on the morning of June 13th.

> King County Superior Court judge Peter Kincaid smoked a pipe and leaned back in his plush leather chair listening to lengthy and, at times, heated arguments between defense attorney John Sullivan and prosecutor Laurence McKinley about witnesses who will defile Frankie Ray's character as drunk and disease ridden, while few will say a bad word against the defendant, George Miller.
>
> Sullivan, for his part, tried desperately to prevent the State from referring to George Miller as an "underworld" member, a request soundly rejected by Judge Kincaid. "The nature of Mr. Miller's establishment speaks for itself. The jury can decide what that makes him. We will not, however, take an apple and attempt to turn it into a pear. Not in my courtroom."

Mr. Neversleeps had picked up on the growing divide between the *Daily Star* and the other papers and started hawking his papers with sayings like "*Star*'s Shumacher says Miller looks cool as a cucumber in court."

People knowing my name was emboldening, especially when Amara or her brothers were with me, or on occasion when Mr. Giovacchini swept the sidewalk in front of his pastry shop, though I couldn't help but think of one of my mother's frequent adages to me and my siblings: "Pride goes before a fall."

I had hoped just this one time she was wrong, but of course, mothers are never wrong. As Amara and I walked arm in arm down First Avenue on a weeknight to watch the sunset at the pier, I heard my name being called, and the voice sent a tingling chill down my spine.

"If it isn't Billy the kid."

Joan Daley walked behind us, arm interlocked with a sailor, though not an ordinary seaman. This sailor was in a khaki-colored shirt and pants with colorful bars across his chest. Joan looked again like the Hollywood starlet Jean Harlow in *Hell's Angels* or *Red Dust.* Her platinum-blonde hair was tucked beneath a red jaunty hat with black netting extended over her left eye. Her face was made up, and she had dressed to the nines in a red summer dress, a green scarf, and red pumps.

Amara and I stopped.

"Hi, Joan," I said, trying to sound casual.

Daley looked at Amara with an inquisitive gaze. "Is this your gal?" she asked.

"Yes," I said, feeling my face flush.

"Well, ain't you going to introduce us, Kid?"

"Yes. Of course. Amara, this is Joan Daley. She's . . . She's, uh . . ."

"Pleased to meet you," Daley said. "You and the kid heading for dinner?"

Amara looked and sounded uncertain, the way one might approach a stray dog. "William is taking me to watch the sunset," she said.

Joan looked at her sailor. "Now that is a romantic thing to do," she said. "Don't you think so?"

The officer smiled. "We don't have that much time," he said.

"Pity," Joan said. Then she turned back to me. "Don't lose your sense of romance, Kid."

"Your leg is healed," I said, stumbling to change the subject.

"A girl has to make a living," she said. "Can't exactly go back to my former place of employment with everything going on; can I?"

She couldn't, of course. Not given what had happened between Miller and Frankie Ray.

"I suppose not," I said.

The captain tugged at Joan's arm. "We should be going."

Joan gave him a withering glare that set the officer on the heels of his black wing-tip shoes. "Be a good boy," she said, and he stood still like a dog told to stay. She said to me, "You and your lady have a good evening, Kid. And remember. The offer still stands." She chuckled as she strode off, stepping in a way that her hips swayed slowly. I had to fight not to turn around and watch her go.

Amara was looking at me with a wrinkled and questioning brow. “Who was that?”

“‘That’?”

“Yes,” Amara said. “The woman.”

“That was Joan Daley. She was Frankie Ray’s girl. Detective Blunt and I . . . and the prosecutor paid her a visit when she was in the hospital with a broken leg.”

“How did she break her leg?”

“She was trying to get out of a hotel too quickly,” I heard myself say. It wasn’t a lie. Not exactly.

“Why does she call you ‘kid’?”

“Billy the Kid was from Kansas City,” I said. “Well . . . Missouri. And I guess I look young.”

“What does she do?” Amara asked.

“She . . . she worked for George Miller.” Again, that part was true, but I couldn’t bring myself to tell Amara the rest.

“It’s no wonder she can’t go back to work. What did she mean, ‘The offer still stands’?”

“She said if I wanted an interview, I could speak to her.”

“Are you?”

“What?”

“Interested in an interview?”

“Not at the moment, but things can change. Come on, we’ll miss the sunset.” I hurried Amara down to the pier.

Chapter 10

The Trial of the Century finally started Monday morning, October 2, in Judge Kincaid's courtroom on the eighth floor of the King County Courthouse.

Before I left the *Daily Star* offices that morning for court, Phish had a piece of advice. "Remember, this isn't about the facts, Shoe. Facts don't sell newspapers. Pizzazz sells newspapers! The public wants to know who's in the gallery and what they're wearing. Are they part of Miller's underworld? What's his attitude? How's he dressed? The public is curious about the underworld, as well as the wealthy who cross over at night and cross back again in the morning. It's an altogether different world than the one in which they're living. They will live it vicariously through the *Star*, Shoe. They'll live it through you."

With that insight, I left for court. The weather was uncomfortably warm for Seattle, what they were calling an Indian summer. If the pretrial battles between the litigants over various motions were any indication, I expected the trial to be a grueling slog. It seemed Sullivan and McKinley could not agree on the time of day if they were staring at the same clock.

The new courthouse had been the subject of much public intrigue, and Phish wanted me to mention it in my articles. I noted the interior was both elegant and modern, with a grand staircase of green-and-white marble, and a vaulted ceiling with acorn-shaped pendant lights. The walls, floor, and columns contained two and one-half acres of Alaskan marble. This morning the lobby hummed as if there was an electric charge. I stepped onto an elevator and felt butterflies when the doors closed and the car lifted, which confirmed the county's claim the elevators traveled 450 feet per minute.

I stepped from the elevator onto the eighth floor and encountered a crowd so large, police officers stood in the lobby calling for order. The crowd of hopefuls seeking a seat in the gallery snaked from the tall exterior courtroom doors, down the corridor, and around the building corner. They came dressed as if for opening night at the opera or symphony. With my pay raise, and at Amara's urging, I'd splurged on a pair of gray, double-pleated wool trousers, two striped dress shirts, and a tweed jacket with elbow patches, all on sale at Bon Marche.

"We can't have Seattle's most prominent reporter showing up on the first day of trial looking like a ragamuffin," Amara had said as she held shirts to my face to find something to "match my complexion." "Blue and gray bring out the color of your eyes and accentuate your hair coloring. Avoid browns," she concluded.

The final ensemble set me back almost two weeks' pay, and spending that much made me uncomfortable, as did Phish's repeated statements that the facts didn't matter. I kept thinking my job wasn't to be a part of the unfolding show. It was to report the news, wasn't it? That's what I had always thought. With each passing day, however, between Blunt feeding me information he wanted to disseminate to the public and Phish making changes to my articles to add "pizzazz," I felt like the newspaper boys hawking the sensational simply to sell papers, with little regard for the truth.

I cut to the front of the line, garnering dirty looks from those in the crowd pushing forward, until I flashed my press badge to an officer turning away spectators at the door. He checked for my name on a list attached to his clipboard. Then he said, "Mr. Shumacher. The *Daily Star*. You've been busy cracking cases and writing about them." His tone dripped sarcasm.

At the mention of my name and occupation, those standing near the front of the line grew silent.

"There should be a spot reserved for me." I felt my cheeks flush and thought I should have warned Amara about my propensity to change complexions when we had been buying clothing.

The officer scanned his clipboard. "There should be; you say? I don't know. It's awfully crowded in there, and room for just a few more."

I looked down. He had his hand open. I looked at the others in line closest to the courtroom door. Some held bills in their hands. He was selling the seats in the gallery. My God. It upset and emboldened me. "If you want, I can have Detective Blunt come over and vouch for me . . ." I paused. "What's your name again?"

"Officer Olsson." He gave me a sharp look. "Don't get bent out of shape. I see your name here, Mr. Shumacher, a perfect spot, front and center in the press section. Second row behind the State's counsel table. Will that be sufficient for a man of your stature?"

"Thank you," I said.

"No, Mr. Shumacher. Thank *you*," the officer said. More sarcasm. He nodded to the court bailiff just inside the second set of tall doors.

I removed my cap as I was ushered to a seat in the second row behind the State's table. Seated behind me in the third row were Early Winn and Archibald Greer. Neither reporter looked happy to be taking a back seat to me.

"Nice jacket," Winn said after I'd been seated for a minute or two. "It must be new."

I felt his breath on my neck and turned in my seat, uncertain if his compliment had been sincere. "Thank you," I said. "It is."

"We know." Winn smiled. "You might want to remove the Bon Marche price tag."

I reached back and felt the price tag. Those seated behind me snickered. I wanted to crawl under the pew, then I felt another hand on my shoulder, looked up, and was surprised to see Joan Daley. She looked resplendent, tall and lean in a light-green dress cinched tightly at the waist with a black belt that displayed the curves in her figure and turned every head in the gallery.

"Let me help, Kid." I felt her gently remove the price tag. She bent down to hand it to me, her lips so close to my ear I could feel her warm breath and smell her rose perfume. "Don't let these stooges bother you, Kid. They're just jealous because you're seated in front of them." She ran her fingers across my neck, and the chill created goose bumps all over my body. "And women appreciate a well-dressed man."

The snickering stopped cold.

Joan added, loudly, and in her Brooklynese accent, "What's the matter, boys? Haven't you ever seen a woman help a young man get dressed?" Then she laughed.

I sighed and focused on my job, as defined by Phish. I removed my notebook from my reporter's satchel, drew sketches and scribbled notes to paint a vivid picture. The attorneys were dressed in three-piece worsted-wool suits and sat at two tables facing the elevated judicial bench adorned with the Washington State seal, flags on each side. Sullivan sat closest to the jury box. He sported a bow tie. His dark, heavy eyebrows reminded me of Groucho Marx. Arnie Chevas sat beside Miller, whispering into a small ear trumpet Miller held to his ear. Blunt had told me Miller claimed hearing loss from childhood measles made the trumpet a necessity, not an attempt to elicit juror sympathy.

Miller was the most dapper man in the room in a brown pinstriped suit and a light-brown tie. He didn't look like a murderer. He looked like Gary Cooper in *A Farewell to Arms*. Handsome, debonair, and self-confident, he turned frequently to smile at acquaintances who were well represented in the courtroom's packed gallery. No doubt because they had money to pay the admission fee. Each time Miller turned, newspaper photographers' flashbulbs exploded. He seemed to revel in the attention.

Blunt sat directly across the gap in the tables and kept his back to Miller, whispering to McKinley, an indication, perhaps, he didn't buy Miller's claim to be hard of hearing.

I spotted Richard Kneip, Phish's prize *Daily Star* photographer, and motioned him forward. Together we approached an officer beside the swinging gate in the railing. "Can we get a picture of the attorneys and the defendant for the *Daily Star*?" I asked, keeping my voice low.

The officer turned to the empty bench before he reengaged me. "Do it now before Judge Kincaid takes the bench. He won't take kindly to such nonsense in his courtroom when we're underway."

Kneip and I stepped through the railing, and Kneip said, "How about a photo for the *Star*, boys?"

The attorneys sat up, and Kneip quickly knelt and snapped the picture. When the bulb flashed, the other reporters and photographers, realizing what we had done, quickly stood and tried to get through the gate, but Chevas destroyed the tableau when he left the table and walked to the door.

A moment later, Chevas escorted Katheryn Conner, Miller's red-headed and sharp-tongued sweetheart, into the courtroom and seated her in the front row alongside the several research attorneys. Again, heeding Phish's admonition, I scribbled down Conner's silver fox-fur piece and neat gray ensemble with a light-gray turban and snakeskin pumps. As photographers snapped Conner's picture, she smiled and blew a kiss to Miller. I was suddenly struck by the percentage of fur-clad blondes, brunettes, and redheads seated in the gallery. Their immaculate appearances betrayed them as habitués of nightclubs, or perhaps the disorderly lodgings Miller was said to also own. They appeared tired, as if unaccustomed to rising so early. Miller was stocking the gallery with sympathizers.

Contrary to the popular adage, crime did pay, and it paid well.

I heard a murmur and turned to see the court bailiff enter from behind the bench. "All rise. The King County Superior Court is now in session. The Honorable Peter Kincaid presiding."

Kincaid ascended three steps in his flowing black robe that, in keeping with the morning theme, seemed more dramatic theater than court proceeding. He looked to me like Wyatt Earp, the famed lawman—tall and lean with thick silver hair and a handlebar mustache, the ends of which he waxed to points as sharp as his well-documented temper. McKinley had told me the State was thrilled at Kincaid's appointment to try the case. A conservative Republican, Kincaid was perceived to be tough on crime, particularly graft and vice crimes, and had publicly favored Prohibition. He had gained a seat on the King County bench largely with the support of Seattle Presbyterian Church's influential minister Mark Matthews and his congregation. They wanted Seattle "closed" to immoral conduct. Notwithstanding Kincaid's public position, Phish told me the judge was known to partake in a glass of whiskey in the privacy of the Rainier Club.

Kincaid's gaze swept over the crowd like a teacher looking to expel troublemakers. He sat and took his time packing a pipe with tobacco. "Quite a crowd we have this morning," he said to his bailiff. "Quite a crowd. Of course, the public has a right to be here. We wouldn't have bench seats if they didn't," he said, which elicited a few polite chuckles. He turned his attention to the gallery. "However, let me remind you all that you are guests of the King County Superior Court. Specifically, you are guests in my courtroom. That means I can ask any one of you, or the entire lot of you, to leave if I am so inclined. I'm not . . . at the moment, so inclined, so let me welcome you."

Kincaid directed his gaze to counsel. "Gentlemen, this morning we are going to pick a jury. That's not a request. It's a fact. Now, who will conduct voir dire for the State?"

McKinley rose. "I will. Laurence McKinley."

"Very well. And for the defense?"

Sullivan rose. "Your Honor, we—"

"Now, let me stop you right there, Mr. Sullivan. There will be no 'we,' despite this gaggle of attorneys sitting in the first row behind you. Not this morning. Not during voir dire. There will be only 'I' or 'me.' Would that 'I' or 'me' be you?"

"It would, Your Honor."

"Very well. You can be seated."

With that, the first thirty citizens were led into the courtroom by Kincaid's bailiff. They were men and women, some young, some old. Some looked eager, some bored, some curious, some disgruntled.

Kincaid turned to McKinley. "Mr. McKinley, the State may voir dire the panel."

McKinley rose, and I quickly noted he was the most conservatively dressed lawyer in the room. He wore a three-piece, well-worn blue suit. He asked the panel about their occupations, relatives, and professional acquaintances, including whether they had any relationship to the defendant. Then he said, "Now, good citizens of King County. Mr. George Miller, the defendant, has been accused of murder in the first degree. A ramification of that charge is, should the State obtain a finding of guilt, the State may seek the death penalty. How many of you, by a show of hands, have a moral or a religious belief that would prevent you, under any circumstance, from imposing capital punishment?"

Though I tried to quickly count the hands, it appeared to be more than half the panel.

Kincaid growled, took another puff on his pipe, and said to the jury, "I'm going to accept your responses as truthful, and not an excuse to skirt your civic duty, for which you will be paid a dollar a day. I hope my faith in your integrity is well founded."

A juror raised his hand.

"Yes, young man?"

"I'd like to change my answer, Judge. I don't have a moral or a religious conviction that would prevent me from so finding."

Another man raised his hand, as did a woman. Whether it was guilt, or whether each needed the dollar a day, they, too, recanted their previous answer. Kincaid excused the remainder who had raised their hands.

McKinley then asked if any of the jurors had ever attended the Pom Pom Club on Tenth Avenue on Yesler Hill.

Two jurors raised their hands, and Kincaid had them recused. Whether liars remained among the panel, I couldn't tell.

McKinley then asked, "Would the fact that Mr. Miller ran a nightclub where liquor was served and gambling permitted influence anyone's verdict?"

Sullivan shot from his chair. "Objection, Your Honor. State's counsel intimates it is illegal to sell liquor, but the Congress of these United States has deemed otherwise. Modifications to the Volstead Act permit the sale of beer with up to 3.2 percent alcohol. Since Washington has already repealed Prohibition in the state, beer is no longer illegal."

McKinley scoffed. "Your Honor, the State will prove the Pom Pom Club is a bootlegging and gambling club."

"And you, Counsel, are deliberately attempting to taint this jury without the introduction of any evidence," Sullivan shot back.

"We'll introduce evidence. You can count on it," McKinley retorted.

Kincaid rapped his gavel three times, the sound of wood on wood like the crack of a whip. Deliberately, he removed his pipe. Smoke filtered from his nostrils like he was an angry bull. "Gentlemen," he said. "I warned you during motion practice that if you persisted in these types of dialogues without addressing me, I would feel left out of these proceedings in my own courtroom. I will, therefore, find each of you in contempt and fine you twenty-five dollars. Let me also point out, these good people sitting in the jury box have given up their time to be here. Waste it, and you will pay an additional price. Mr. McKinley, ask your question without reference to liquor or gambling, since there is no evidence of either . . . yet."

Half an hour later, McKinley sat. Sullivan strode quickly to the railing. "Juror number six," he said to a midthirties housewife. "Ma'am, would you consider in your deliberations the state of mind of a man who shoots someone as that person is about to attack him, and the shooter fears for his life?"

This time it was McKinley's turn to jump to his feet. "Objection. It is up to the defense to prove it was self-defense. It is not up to the State to prove it was not self-defense."

Sullivan said in reply, "It is always the law for the State to prove a man guilty, not for him to prove his innocence."

Judge Kincaid again admonished counsel to cease bickering.

By the lunch hour, five women and eight men had been agreed upon, with one juror being an alternate. Outside the courtroom doors, a pack of reporters surrounded Sullivan. "Do you think the State will seek the death penalty?" Archibald Greer asked.

"The death penalty threat is all bosh," Sullivan said. "I believe the State is charging first-degree murder in hopes of getting a manslaughter conviction."

I hurried down the hall to where McKinley and Blunt were holding a separate interview, and when told what Sullivan had said, McKinley gave a dismissive laugh. "I can't see manslaughter in this case. Not for a crime so blatant. It is either murder or self-defense."

I left the courthouse and rushed back to my office to type up my notes. Phish immediately approached me, but I told him I didn't have a lot of time to get back, and he largely left me alone. We both knew the advantage and disadvantage to being Seattle's only afternoon newspaper. I would be first with stories on the day's proceedings. However, should there be fireworks after my 3:00 p.m. deadline, I'd be out of luck, and the morning newspapers would beat me to that punch. Still, it was like my father said when describing the prizefights we used to watch together.

"It isn't who hits who first. It's who hits who first with the stiffest punch."

I planned to deliver the stiffest punch and to do so before three o'clock every day.

Chapter 11

I returned to the courthouse after lunch, cognizant time would be tight. On the eighth floor I stepped from the elevator and rushed down the hall as the officer turned his back on those who had not obtained an afternoon seat.

"Wait," I said.

The officer turned. "Well, if it isn't Scoop Shumacher. And just in time. Judge Kincaid has issued orders this door be locked at one p.m. sharp. I'd hate to have to lock you out of these proceedings, but it is the judge's orders." He smiled.

I ignored him and stepped past to my pew, excusing myself as I maneuvered by those already seated. Winn gave me a smile like he'd discovered another price tag on my clothing. I ignored him also, but Joan Daley's penetrating gaze dared me to ignore her. She winked, and I again felt it over every inch of my body.

As I took my seat, Judge Kincaid returned to the bench, and I couldn't help but think his nose looked redder than it had that morning. He instructed the bailiff to bring in the agreed-upon jury, read to them a statement about the case, then turned his gaze to the State's table.

"Mr. McKinley, you may give your opening statement."

Using maps, McKinley detailed for the jury the club's location as well as its interior layout, including where the elaborate bar "served its illicit drinks."

Sullivan rose. "Objection, Your Honor, to counsel's inappropriate use of 'illicit.'"

"Your Honor," McKinley said, "the State will gladly avoid any reference to liquor if the defense will stipulate liquor played no part in what transpired at the Pom Pom Club on the morning of June thirteenth."

I thought it a brilliant move by McKinley. Sullivan couldn't very well make such a concession since his self-defense theory relied on the jury believing Ray was a violent and dangerous drunk and had been drinking that morning.

"Will you make the concession?" Kincaid asked Sullivan.

"The defense will not," Sullivan said.

"Then the objection is overruled. Continue, Counsel."

The jurors gave him their rapt attention. McKinley used drawings as well as photographs to show the gambling tables, the booths with plates of food on the tables, and the polished dance floor where the social elite rubbed elbows with the underworld. The jurors' expressions revealed they had never imagined a place so luxurious existing in a depression, let alone having been to one.

"The blare of a jazz orchestra," McKinley said. "Dancers whirling on the polished hardwood floors. Waiters in white coats dashing about, carrying trays laden with drinks and plates of food. Laughter and the clinking of coins at a craps table in a room adjoining the dance floor. The Pom Pom Club at two a.m."

McKinley gave a dramatic pause. "And four hours later. Two shots ring out from a Luger semiautomatic. A shot hits Frankie Ray on the left side of his chest. A second shot strikes the right side, beneath his armpit." McKinley raised his arms to give the jurors a visual of a man surrendering, not a man attacking. "Both bullets touched the heart as they passed through the body. The defendant"—McKinley pointed and stared at Miller, who showed no emotion—"claimed in a statement to the police that he was counting the night's receipts when Ray came in with the Luger to rob the joint. Miller said the two struggled, and he managed to somehow, heroically, wrestle the gun from Ray and, in the process, shot Ray." McKinley gave the jury a knowing look.

Then he slapped the jury rail with his palm. "A lie. A blatant lie. One that others in the bar who gave statements that night had all agreed upon or been told to tell, as preposterous as the made-up story was. But . . ." McKinley raised a finger and strode several paces before turning back to the jury. "Detectives learned another witness to the shooting had fled the Pom Pom Club before their arrival. Police found that witness, Al Smith, in a Seattle hotel room, and he told a different, unrehearsed, and honest account of what happened the morning of June 13, 1933. The defendant knew the jig was up. So did his business partner.

"What did they do?" McKinley's eyes widened.

"*After* consulting with their counsel"—this time McKinley's finger pointed at Sullivan—"they changed their story. Miller admitted Ray didn't try to rob him. This time, he said Ray demanded money to pay an installment on his automobile to keep it from being repossessed." McKinley raised a sheet of paper and read from it. "'I refused to give him any money. Ray had been drinking, and when Ray started toward me, his left hand raised, I feared he wanted to kill me. When he reached for his pocket, I shot him.'"

I was a little surprised McKinley would tell the jury Miller's self-serving statement, and my surprise was confirmed when Sullivan rose from his seat.

"Your Honor, the defense will stipulate Mr. Miller did not tell the truth in his original story to the police, and he does not deny he shot Mr. Ray in self-defense, so we can move matters along."

McKinley, realizing perhaps his error, turned away from the jury so they would not see his surprise, but quickly recovered. "Your Honor, the State does not agree the second story Mr. Miller told the police was any more truthful than the first. The State does not believe the shooting was in self-defense. I am simply informing the jury of the array of lies Miller told the police."

"Objection," Sullivan said. "Counsel offers his opinion, which is outrageous in an opening statement."

"It wasn't in my opening statement," McKinley shot back. "It was in response to your objection."

Kincaid rapped his gavel to regain order, denied the objection, and told McKinley to continue.

"The true story, the State will prove, is that the decedent, Frankie Ray, went to the Pom Pom Club in the company of Al Smith at about four thirty in the morning and proceeded to finish a night of drinking. During his last hours on Earth, Ray drank nine shots of whiskey. Drunk, yes, but in no condition to endanger anyone. Yet, Miller took his pistol out of the safe shortly after Ray's arrival and put it in his pocket.

"Witnesses will tell you Ray was trying to get money, but not for a car payment. In fact, Ray had a sweetheart who had worked for Miller in the New Cecil Hotel."

I was aware of Joan Daley seated behind me.

"Ray's sweetheart had incurred hospital bills when the hotel where she worked was raided and she jumped out a window. Miller had promised to pay her hospital bill, then reneged." McKinley then ended with a punch. "Underworld character though he was, Frankie Ray died on an errand of mercy.

"Miller didn't say anything about self-defense when confronted by police because he had no such justification for shooting Frankie Ray. There was no attack, and he had no reason, other than a spirit of ill will, to arm himself more than an hour before he shot and killed Frankie Ray. That, ladies and gentlemen, is premeditation. That is first-degree murder." He paused, taking in each juror. "Thank you for your attention to these grim details."

McKinley returned to counsel table and sat.

"Mr. Sullivan, do you wish to give your opening statement or reserve until the defense presents its case?"

Sullivan rose. "Despite the fabrications just uttered, the defense reserves until its case in chief."

"Without the soliloquy, please, Counsel."

"The defense reserves," Sullivan said.

The clock on the wall read 2:37 p.m. I didn't dare get up and leave the courtroom, and I couldn't very well do so if the officer had locked the door as instructed, but I caught a break when Kincaid called for a recess until 3:00 p.m. I was first in line for the door. "Keep your pants on, kid. Maybe don't drink so much at lunch next time," the guard said.

When the door opened, I hurried to a public phone booth along the far wall and dictated the rest of my story, mindful of the limited time. At two minutes to three I rushed back to the courtroom.

McKinley called Officer Lutz, the first policeman on the scene. Lutz arrived in his dress blue uniform with his cap under his right arm. He looked seasoned and serious, a good first witness, I thought, for the State to parade before the jury. After establishing his credentials and what brought him to the nightclub, McKinley asked, "Who met you when you arrived inside the club?"

"Nobody," Lutz said in his gravelly voice. "The door was open, and when I stepped in, nobody said a word."

"Did you speak to the defendant, George Miller?"

"Later I did. He told me Ray attempted to rob him of the night's receipts."

McKinley walked to a table and picked up a napkin. With deliberation, he unwrapped its folds and revealed the Luger semiautomatic pistol, walking it up and down the jury box. The jurors were mesmerized.

Lutz identified the gun as the one Miller said he took from Frankie Ray. "He showed me where he put it on the safe behind the bar."

McKinley sought to introduce photographs of Ray's body, but Sullivan objected.

"The prosecutor is seeking to inflame the minds of the jury."

"Denied," Kincaid said. "Proceed."

The jurors passed the photographs quickly. Then McKinley asked, "Officer Lutz, when you arrived at the club and found the body, who was attending to Mr. Ray?"

"Nobody."

"Not one man was helping him?"

"They were all standing at the bar like blocks of ice."

"Who amongst them called the ambulance?"

"No one. I had to do that myself. On the pay phone on the wall."

"How long was it before the ambulance arrived?"

"About four minutes," Lutz said.

"You arrived at approximately six forty-five in the morning?"

"Thereabouts. Call came in of shots fired about six thirty."

"And the ambulance arrived at around when?"

"Just about six fifty or so," Lutz said.

"That's an awful lot of blood for a body to lose in those minutes between the time Ray was shot and abandoned on the floor and the time the ambulance arrived; isn't it?" McKinley said.

Sullivan shot from his seat. "Objection, Your Honor. That is not a question, but another statement intended to inflame the jurors."

"Sustained," Kincaid said. "Mr. McKinley, refrain from statements and ask questions."

"The State has no more questions of this witness."

Sullivan rose and strode to the witness chair. "Officer Lutz, did Mr. Miller seem panicky to you?"

"Well," Lutz said. "I did have to ask him questions twice."

"Because he was panicky," Sullivan said more to the jury than the witness.

"Not exactly," Lutz said, causing Sullivan to return his gaze to the officer. "You see, Mr. Brunn said Mr. Miller was hard of hearing, and I needed to raise my voice. After I did so, Miller didn't have any trouble hearing me and answering my questions."

Several jurors concealed smiles, as did many in the gallery.

As Judge Kincaid adjourned for the day, it felt like opening night had come to an end, and with it, so, too, did the thrill and anticipation such an event generates. The adrenaline had subsided. The attorneys' shoulders slumped as they stood and waited for Kincaid to leave his bench. I wondered how they would withstand at least two weeks of similarly grueling days.

I hurried up Seventh Avenue and filled in Phish on the afternoon's events. He showed me the afternoon edition. For Phish, the headline was bland, situated beneath the banner and just above the photograph Kneip took of defense counsel and Miller seated at counsel's table.

Death Trial Lawyers Clash

Miller Looks Calm In Court for

Slaying at Pom Pom Nightclub

Five women and seven men who had disavowed any prejudice against capital punishment were seated this morning on the jury that will try George A. Miller, debonair proprietor of the Pom Pom Club, on a first-degree murder charge for killing Frankie Ray, one of his nightlife intimates.

Prosecuting attorney Laurence McKinley concentrated on female jurors, obviously concerned those more genteel jurors would be unable to sentence Miller to death, were his alleged actions to be proven, but deemed five such persons up to the task.

Miller, a symphony in brown—brown-striped suit, dark-brown shoes, contrasting brown socks, and brown tie—was easily the best-dressed man in court.

> He appeared suave and self-possessed, as though he were back in the Pom Pom Club instead of being on trial for his life.
>
> His sweetheart, Katheryn Conner, was present for moral support, resplendent in a silver fox-fur piece and neat gray ensemble with a light-gray turban, along with snakeskin pumps. There were a few other people in the audience whose pallid faces and too-immaculate appearances betrayed them as habitués of the nightlife clubs like Miller's.

Phish loved the last line of the opening and so did I.

I checked the clock on the wall. It was after five p.m. If I hurried, I might meet Amara before she caught her bus. I raced along Seattle streets with my reporter's satchel banging against my hip, dodging commuters headed for home. When I arrived at Giovacchini's Bakery, the lights in the windows were turned off and a "Closed" sign hung inside the glass. Out of breath, I leaned my head against the door, gasping and quietly uttering profanities.

"You look like a man in need of a strawberry milkshake at the Bon Marche."

I turned. Amara stood on the sidewalk dressed in a plain brown dress, her hair clipped on the side beneath a hat, her makeup simple. But she was more beautiful than all the fur-clad society women in the courtroom.

"You are a sight for tired eyes," I said.

"Tired body from the looks of you. I'm glad you didn't pass out before you reached the door."

"You waited for me," I said.

"Don't flatter yourself, William Shumacher. I just locked the door. But I will say timing is everything in life, and you, William Shumacher, have great timing."

"Timing isn't everything," I said.

"No?"

"I'd much prefer to levitate." I stepped forward and kissed her right there on the sidewalk, nearly knocking off her hat, which she grabbed with her hand. The trolley cars clanked and clamored, car horns blared, and afternoon commuters stepped around us on their way home.

I could not have cared less.

Chapter 12

Tuesday morning, the crowd on the eighth floor was smaller and much more subdued than opening day, but the courtroom still had all the hallmarks of a spectacle. The gallery was standing room only. Katheryn Conner entered on her own this day, and I noted her appearance for Phish's sake. Her red hair was framed in a black hat, set off by a mustard-yellow knit suit, white gloves, and a thick gold bracelet.

As George Miller entered the court, he made a point of turning to the newspaper reporters in the gallery, maintaining his carefree attitude. "Say, I understand the newspapers published something about my brown suit. I hope my tailors see it. It's a good boost for their business. I used to buy suits from two tailors to keep them from fighting. It's too bad I'm kept in jail during this trial, or I'd get a pair of shoes with Cuban heels. Then I would be in style."

Kincaid took the bench, and McKinley called Jimmy Powers to the stand.

"You were a craps dealer at the Pom Pom Club; is that right?" McKinley asked.

"That's right," Powers said.

"Was there gambling paraphernalia, like dice?"

"Sure," he said with a wry smile. "You got to use dice. You can't play craps without dice."

The jurors smiled along with Powers.

"When you left the club on June thirteenth, who remained in the Pom Pom Club?"

"Mr. Miller let me out the door to go home. The only other occupants were a few waiters and fellas from the orchestra, and Frankie Ray and a man with Frankie. They were at the bar along with Mr. Brunn and the bartender, Billy Vahle."

"How much had they had to drink?"

"I don't know, but they had glasses in front of them."

"What kind of glasses?"

"Cocktail glasses."

"And they were drinking liquor?"

"That's what most people drink in cocktail glasses; ain't it?" he said, now working the room for smiles.

McKinley obliged him. "They weren't drinking beer?"

"No, sir. It was liquor."

"Did the club use loaded or shaved dice?"

Powers paused, caught off guard by the question. "Well, I can't really say anything about that."

McKinley went to the exhibit table and picked up several sets of dice, showing them to the jury, then to Powers. "The police found these dice in the club's cash register. This set appears to have the edges shaved, and this set, well, it appears a couple numbers are the same, doesn't it?"

"I don't know anything about that," Powers said.

"You never used these dice at your craps table?" McKinley walked toward the jurors, who leaned forward to get a closer look at the dice. "And before you answer, Mr. Powers, let me remind you that you are under oath to tell the truth, the whole truth, and nothing but the truth, so help you God."

Powers squirmed in his seat. "You're fixin' to get me in trouble, sir."

"Just answer the questions asked," Judge Kincaid said, "and no one will be fixin' to do anything."

"Well, we don't start out using 'em, see. We wait a while, let the folks win some money, have a good time."

"Why do you wait?"

"People having a good time, well, they tend to stay longer and drink more, and that's where the club really makes its money, see. Then after the people have been drinking awhile, that's when I slip in the other dice, and the house wins back most of the money it shelled out."

"The game is fixed?"

"I don't know about that."

"It's a sucker's game; isn't it?"

"The people, see, they play to have a good time. They aren't as concerned about the money as, say, everyday folks."

McKinley let that sink in with the jury. Then he asked, "Who taught you how to cheat the people playing the game at the Pom Pom Club?"

Powers squirmed again.

"Answer the question," Kincaid said.

"Well. I guess that would have been Mr. Brunn and Mr. Miller. They're the ones who gave me the instructions and told me when to use these here other dice."

McKinley sat.

Sullivan stood. "You said the people playing craps were having a good time?"

"They sure seemed to be."

"Laughing and smiling and getting along all right."

"Sure."

"So, this was just a form of entertainment, like dancing and listening to the orchestra?"

"I guess you could say that, sure."

Sullivan sat and McKinley stood.

"The orchestra announces songs they play, don't they?"

"At times they do, sure."

"Did you announce to the people playing craps when you were going to start using crooked dice?"

"Now why would I go and do something so stupid? I'd be fired for sure," Powers said.

McKinley smiled. "For sure," he repeated, then dismissed the witness.

Following Powers, McKinley called Billy Vahle. The Pom Pom Club's bartender wasn't a big man, but he carried himself as if he'd been in a fair number of scrapes and usually came out on top, or at least got his licks in. He wore his hair neatly combed—the color darkened from a liberal amount of pomade. He had a high-pitched voice that contrasted with his rugged appearance.

"On the night of June twelfth and the morning of June thirteenth, where were you?" McKinley asked.

"I was working the Pom Pom Club up on Profanity Hill."

"And what was your job at the Pom Pom Club?"

"I was the bartender."

"Were you busy?"

"As a one-armed paperhanger, as they say." Vahle sounded displeased and disinterested.

"The State is pleased to note you have full use of both your arms," McKinley said, drawing chuckles from the courtroom. "Did you know Frankie Ray?"

"Well, that's why we're all here; ain't it?" Vahle raised his eyebrows to accentuate his question.

"What time did Mr. Ray come into the Pom Pom Club?"

"It was right around five in the morning. At least that's when I first seen him. He walked in with another guy."

"Did you know the guy who walked in with Frankie Ray?"

Vahle shook his head. "I didn't. Big guy though. Had a nose like he boxed and got smacked a few times."

"Can you name the men remaining in the club?"

"I can try," he said and repeated Powers's testimony.

"Were these men at the bar?"

"There's always men at the bar."

"What were these men talking about?"

"A good bartender doesn't snoop on his customers' conversations. Besides, I was getting ready to go home."

"Was there some conversation at the bar about girls?" McKinley asked.

"That's sort of expected when guys get together and have a few drinks; ain't it?" Vahle said. "One of those universal truths, is what they call it."

"Any girls in particular?"

"Like I said, I can't be certain."

"Who bought drinks that night and morning?"

"They all bought rounds, taking turns paying for them."

"How many rounds?"

"I'd say like nine or ten."

"And what was these men's demeanor?"

"They started out friendly. I recall Ray and Brunn had their arms on each other's shoulders, like old chums, but then, later on, Ray started hollering and gnashing his teeth. And he pounded the bar with his fist, like this." Vahle proceeded to stand and pound on Judge Kincaid's desk.

Kincaid raised his eyebrows in surprise.

"What was Mr. Ray hollering about?" McKinley asked.

"I think he was shouting at Mr. Miller. I heard him say, 'Why in hell don't you talk about my girl in the hospital?'"

"No profanities, please," Kincaid said.

"Right," Vahle said. "Then Ray's pal got Ray to leave, but Ray, he came back in."

"Did you witness the shooting?"

"Nah. I was in the back and was putting on my coat to go home. I heard a scuffle and a thump against the wall. Then one shot."

"You sure you heard only one shot?"

"That's what I heard."

"You didn't hear anything before the shot?"

"I heard Mr. Miller say, 'Don't do that. What the hell's the matter with you? Have you blown your topper?'" Vahle's eyes shifted from McKinley to Miller.

"Mr. Vahle," Judge Kincaid said, "I won't remind you again to watch your language."

Vahle nodded.

"What did you do when you heard the shot?" McKinley asked.

"I wanted to scram," Vahle said. "Somebody starts shooting, I don't want no part of that, but Mr. Miller, he asked me and Archie Brown, a waiter, to stick around, in the event the police had questions."

"And did Mr. Miller tell you what to say when the police arrived?"

"Nah. Just said, 'Stick around. The police will likely have questions.'"

Again, Sullivan kept his cross-examination brief.

"You said Frankie Ray drank as much as nine shots of liquor?"

"Thereabouts. I didn't keep count."

"And you said his demeanor changed from initially being happy to becoming angry."

"That's right."

"And then, when you were in the back, you heard Mr. Miller say 'Don't do that. What the hell's the matter with you? Have you blown your topper?'" He glanced at Judge Kincaid. "With respect, Your Honor."

"That's it."

"Did Mr. Miller sound angry?"

"Not angry. Just questioning, you know? Surprised."

When Sullivan sat, McKinley dismissed Vahle and called Al Smith. Again, I thought it a good call by McKinley to contrast what the men in the bar had been coached to say with what Smith would say actually happened.

Smith appeared on the witness stand sleekly dressed in a black suit with a red-dotted tie. His shoes shone like a bridegroom's. Well dressed for a man who in his hotel room had professed to owning just the one brown suit. I had a feeling his testimony was going to bring more fireworks.

McKinley seemed to think the same thing and started out cautious, like a prizefighter circling the ring and sizing up his opponent. "The morning of June 13, 1933, did you go to the Pom Pom Club?"

"That's right. I got a call from Frankie Ray, and he asked me to go with him."

"Did Ray say why he was going?"

"Not until I got in his Cadillac, and we were driving over there. Then he said we were going to the Pom Pom Club because he needed some money to make his car payments."

The response looked like it surprised McKinley. "Did he say anything about collecting money George Miller had agreed to reimburse Joan Daley for her hospital bill, but then had reneged?"

"Frankie might have said something about her having made the payments on the Cadillac, but then she got hurt and racked up a hospital bill and couldn't make the payments."

"And is Frankie Ray's sweetheart in the courtroom?"

"That would be Joan Daley." Smith pointed directly at me, though not at me, to Joan Daley, who was once more seated in the row behind me. People in the gallery murmured, unaware of her identity before this moment.

"Did Mr. Ray mention Joan Daley having a hospital bill that George Miller agreed to pay?"

Smith made a face like he was thinking. "I don't recall that; no."

The testimony was 180 degrees different from the story Smith had told in his hotel room.

McKinley stepped closer to the witness stand. "Did Ray seem nervous?"

"Nervous? No. He seemed angry."

"Angry?" McKinley asked. Again, he sounded surprised by Smith's response.

"Yeah, he was angry Miller hadn't paid Joan Daley's hospital bills so she couldn't make the car payment on Frankie's car."

McKinley paused. "So he did mention Miller having agreed to pay Joan Daley's hospital bill."

"What?" Smith realized his mistake. "He didn't say anything about paying the hospital bill, just said Joan Daley had these bills, see, and therefore couldn't make the car payment."

"Did Mr. Ray say what Joan Daley did for a living, specifically?"

"Well, a gentleman doesn't say or talk about those things. Let's just say I understood she worked in a disorderly house Mr. Miller owned."

The murmurs in the gallery grew louder. Judge Kincaid gazed at the crowd like a father looking over his unruly children in the church pew, and the gallery settled without him so much as picking up his gavel.

"What happened next, after Ray told you this was the purpose for his going to the Pom Pom Club?"

"I told Frankie I didn't want no part of any dispute with George Miller, but Ray said it was no big thing."

"Did you know George Miller?"

"Never met him, but I knew he owned the club."

"Did you know him to be a gangster?"

Sullivan shot to his feet. "Objection, Your Honor."

"Sustained."

"Why did you go with Frankie Ray to the Pom Pom Club if you wanted no part of George Miller?" McKinley asked.

"Well, Frankie said he'd give me ten bucks to just stand there with my mouth shut. I'd never seen the Pom Pom Club, and I guess I was curious to see what all the fuss was about."

"And what happened when you arrived?"

"We took a booth in the back, and Ray was sort of brooding; you know? We had a couple drinks, and he was just sort of gnashing his teeth."

I lifted my head from my notes. This was the second witness to use that exact term, "gnashing his teeth," which seemed a peculiar phrase.

"'Gnashing his teeth'? What exactly does that mean?" McKinley asked, making sure the jurors also caught the repetition by the different witnesses; the implication being they had been coached in their testimony.

"I don't know. You know, like in a frenzy."

"Did you try to calm him?"

"No. Not me."

"Was there any animosity you sensed between Mr. Ray and Mr. Miller?"

"Well, yeah. I heard Ray say, 'I'm going to kill Miller.'"

The courtroom gave a collective gasp, then a silence so profound you could have heard a pin drop.

McKinley blanched. Clearly, he had not expected Smith to tell a story that helped Miller's self-defense argument.

Miller glanced at Sullivan, and though he didn't smile, the edges of Miller's mouth lifted.

"What did you do then?" McKinley asked, now sounding tentative.

"I got Ray to leave the club, but then Ray said he forgot his cigarettes and went back in."

"But you did not?"

"No. I waited by the door."

"Then what happened?"

"I heard a scuffle, followed by two shots about this far apart." Smith clapped his hands once, then paused, and in dramatic silence waited about seven seconds and clapped his hands a second time. The jurors were riveted.

The testimony clearly amazed McKinley as much as the jury. Smith had changed his story. The question was, who got to him?

McKinley said, rather testily, "Mr. Smith, do you recall talking to Chief Detective Ernie Blunt the morning after the shooting in your hotel room in Seattle?"

"Yeah. We spoke."

"But you didn't tell him any of this, did you?"

Sullivan rose. "Your Honor, the question is leading. This is a State's witness, not an adverse witness."

McKinley, red in the face, turned to Judge Kincaid. "May it please the court, Your Honor, the State is surprised by the testimony of this witness. I'd like to introduce the witness's police statement to dispute his testimony here this afternoon."

Sullivan remained standing. "Objection, Your Honor. Mr. Smith has been called by the State as its witness. The State cannot now impeach its own witness. And, the statement is hearsay," Sullivan added. "Beyond those objections, the defense has never seen the statement. We demand the prosecutor McKinley produce it forthwith."

McKinley paused, the way someone might pause when struck by an idea. Then he moved to his desk and held up the statement. "Your Honor, the State will gladly produce this statement to the defense, and suggest it be offered into evidence."

"Does the defense object?" Judge Kincaid asked.

"The defense does not object to it being offered into evidence so we can receive a copy and review what the witness allegedly said," Sullivan said.

With that, Judge Kincaid admitted the statement, and as the clock neared day's end, he abruptly adjourned.

I had called in my story at the afternoon recess, but it would not contain the Al Smith fireworks, which occurred after my 3:00 p.m. deadline. The *Daily Times* and the *Post-Intelligencer*'s headlines in the morning would no doubt scream that the key witness in the trial had changed his story and testified Frankie Ray had said he "was going to kill George Miller." I went back to the office and told Phish what had happened.

"Don't sweat it. We can't get them all," Phish said.

"If I didn't know better, I'd say McKinley has something cooking."

"Cooking?" Phish asked.

"Like when that light bulb in the Fritzi Ritz comics goes off over a character's head. McKinley looked like a light bulb popped over his head."

"You said he looked angry."

"This was after. When the attorneys were arguing over his use of Al Smith's statement. I got the impression he was up to something."

"Type up what you have and what happened, and I'll get it typeset," Phish said. "That way, if there are any fireworks in the morning, we'll have a way to salvage this."

That was all well and good, but I was supposed to have dinner with Amara before she headed home. I called her at the bakery and told her I'd be late, but I'd get there as soon as I could.

As I typed up the story, Phish appeared at my desk. "Thought of a sidebar. I want you to talk to Joan Daley, find out what her take is on all this."

I felt anxious the moment Phish said Joan Daley's name, but also intrigued. "Blunt tried speaking to her. She wouldn't say anything."

"Blunt is the police. You're not. Just ask her for a few minutes of her time."

I could imagine what Daley would think I meant if I asked for a few minutes of her time, and about what I might say to her if she did indeed invite me again to come up and see her sometime.

I'd say no, of course. I mean, I was seeing Amara. But a part of me couldn't be so sure. It was like the time my buddy Danny Pearson brought his dad's *Spicy Stories* magazine to school with pictures of scantily clad women. I knew I'd get in trouble if caught looking, but the temptation to look was stronger than the fear of being caught.

"What's wrong with you?" Phish said. "You're as red as a fire engine."

I feigned something about it being hot in the room, quickly finished my story, then hurried out the door. On my rush to the bakery, I couldn't help but remember my meetings with Joan Daley, first in her hospital room, the encounter on the pier, then the incident in the courtroom when I felt her breath warm on my neck. I wasn't going to lie: the woman intimidated me, though she wasn't much bigger than a minute, and if I was being honest, she aroused me. I found myself wondering what a woman like her could teach me.

When I reached the bakery, a faint, flickering light inside reflected in the window. I went to knock, but a sign on the door said to enter and to lock the door behind me. When I stepped inside, a single red candle flickered on a table set for two with a white tablecloth, napkins, cutlery, two plates, wineglasses, and a jug of Giovacchini family wine. In the background soft music played, and I recognized Bing Crosby's voice and his hit "Did You Ever See a Dream Walking?"

"Hello?"

Amara came out from the room behind the counter. She was elegantly dressed in a long, formfitting blue dress with a slit up the leg. She wore black heels and a gold necklace with a cross. Her hair rested atop her head. As Bing sang, I had my answer. I had seen a dream walking.

"What's all this?" I asked.

"When you said you were going to be late, I thought we could eat here and save our money."

"I'm sorry," I said.

"Are you, really?"

I smiled. "No. Not really."

"Sit down," she said. I did, but not before I kissed her once and then again. I wanted her badly. We'd had a couple of evenings where things got hot and heavy, but Amara had always stopped us. She wanted to wait until we were married. I respected her wishes, but I'd had some long nights when I returned home alone to my boardinghouse.

She poured me a glass of wine and one for herself. I smelled something cooking in the kitchen, but it wasn't cinnamon or roasted raisins or almonds. It wasn't pastries.

"What smells so good?"

"I made ravioli," she said. "That's the sauce you're smelling."

"You made ravioli?"

"And the sauce." She arched her eyebrows. "You have doubts."

"No. None. I just . . . your mother always cooks when I come over."

"At home, yes. It's Mama's kitchen. But I've learned a lot watching her and hope to one day open a restaurant."

"I didn't know that."

"I don't want to work in a pastry shop the rest of my life."

"Does your father know this?"

"We reached a compromise. I told him my restaurant would serve the farm's vegetables and his pastries—the best in the city. My father just wants me to be happy."

"Are you happy?" I asked.

"The happiest I've ever been," she said.

Her face was aglow in candlelight as Russ Columbo sang "Prisoner of Love" in the background. I couldn't think of a more ideal setting, or a more ideal person to spend my life with. Rash, certainly. I could hardly afford to care for someone other than myself, and Amara and I had not discussed marriage to this point, but I loved her, and I was certain she loved me. That's what was important, wasn't it? Just as I was about to drop to a knee and take her hand she said, "No."

"No?"

"I know what you're thinking and what you're going to do, William Shumacher, but you have to do it the right way. You have to ask my father's permission."

She was correct, of course. I smiled at the thought of going to the Giovacchini home to ask Mr. Giovacchini for Amara's hand in marriage. "Will your brothers be there as well?"

She smiled. "I don't know. Why do you ask?"

"I'm afraid they'd carry me in by the elbows to get your father's permission."

Chapter 13

Early the next morning, before I left for court, I used the phone at the boardinghouse to call my parents, with Mrs. Alderbrook's permission, of course. She remained in a good mood, impressed with my daily articles. She stood at the counter while I made my call. When I told my mother and father of my intent to ask Amara to marry me, I'm not sure who squealed louder, my mother or Mrs. Alderbrook. So much for a family moment.

My father, always practical, asked, "Do you have a ring?" He sounded down, depressed.

I didn't, of course, nor did I have the money to buy one. That presented a problem I hadn't considered. "No," I said.

My mother asked more about Amara, but I didn't have time to fill them in, with the trial that morning. They had received the newspapers I'd sent home with my articles, and my mother was keeping a growing scrapbook. She hoped the articles would get me a full-time job at the *Kansas City Star*. I deftly deflected the subject. I told her I was too busy to think of anything except doing well at my current job. I didn't blame her, though. I knew every mother hoped her children would live close by.

After I hung up, Mrs. Alderbrook wanted every detail and told me I had to plan the evening when I would ask Amara, but I didn't see that happening until I could afford a ring. As I spoke, the phone rang, and Mrs. Alderbrook snatched the receiver from the cradle. My mother, calling back.

"I had to wait until your father left the room," she said. "I have Oma's ring." Her mother had passed of cancer at a young age, and my mother, as the eldest daughter, inherited the ring. "It's perfect," she said. "I'll send it by post."

"No, Mom," I told her. "Sell it and keep the money."

"I'll die a thousand deaths before I sell my mother's ring, William. And we're getting by."

"How's Dad? He doesn't sound well, Mom."

"Physically he's fine. We've all lost a little weight, but we had a few inches to spare."

"Is he still eating just one meal a day?"

"We have some seeds, and we've tilled the backyard. I traded some sewing for manure. We'll plant vegetables in the garden."

"Mom, that won't be until spring."

"We're fine, William. You just concentrate on your job and that young woman of yours. The ring will be in the post."

One problem solved, but likely not the biggest. The bigger problem would be getting Mr. Giovacchini's permission, but that was for another day. I thanked my mother, and we said our goodbyes, then I handed the receiver to Mrs. Alderbrook and dashed out the door.

When I arrived at the courthouse, it seemed the crowd outside Judge Kincaid's courtroom had swelled, perhaps because both the *Daily Times* and the *Post-Intelligencer* had run articles on Al Smith's change in testimony and the furor it had caused. The trial was unfolding like an episode told by the Shadow, more and more compelling and mysterious by the minute.

But this trial wasn't fictitious. These *were* real people, and there had been a real crime—a murder. A man had lost his life. I tried not to forget that. I didn't agree with Phish that pizzazz and selling newspapers was more important than reporting the news accurately, and I decided I wasn't going to comment anymore on what everyone was wearing. Damn what they were wearing. I'd focus on what they were saying.

Once inside the courtroom I looked for but didn't see Joan Daley seated in her customary seat, or anywhere in the gallery. I felt disappointed by her absence. Some first timers sat in the last row and stood against the back wall, looking excited.

Minutes after I'd sketched the scene in my notebook, the bailiff announced Judge Kincaid's arrival. The judge wasted no time getting to his seat. He did not look happy and directed his displeasure at defense counsel.

"Mr. Sullivan, you've sent word you wish to bring a motion outside the presence of the jury impaneled this morning?"

Sullivan rose. "Yes, Your Honor. The defense objects to the State's use of Mr. Smith's statements to the police as hearsay and without any judicially recognized exception. We therefore move to have the statement barred."

McKinley rose, the hint of a smile on his lips. I wondered anew what he was playing at. "Your Honor, the defense cannot now object. The statement has already been admitted into evidence. It was admitted yesterday, *without* objection."

Which had been the reason for McKinley's light-bulb moment at the close of trial. He'd baited Sullivan, taken advantage of Sullivan's curiosity about what Smith had told the police, and defense counsel took the bait. Now he was like the trout I'd recently learned to catch, desperately struggling to spit the hook and avoid being netted.

Sullivan flushed red. "We agreed to admit the statement for the limited purpose of allowing the defense to see the statement."

"The defense's reason for agreeing to the statement's admittance is irrelevant," McKinley calmly replied. "What matters is the defense did not object. An admitted statement cannot now be unadmitted. The proverbial cat is out of the proverbial bag. Beyond all that, the State did not admit the statement to establish the witness told the truth, but to establish the witness's courtroom testimony was unreliable. Therefore, while hearsay, it falls within a recognized exception."

"But, Your Honor, the State is attempting to discredit its own witness," Sullivan said.

"A witness who has clearly become hostile," McKinley responded. "I wonder how he could have such a dramatic change in his testimony?"

"I object to your insinuation of wrongdoing," Sullivan shot back.

"And I think you do protest too much . . ."

Kincaid closed his eyes and let out a long sigh. "Counsel, I have a jury waiting, and it is eleven minutes after nine o'clock. I do not intend to keep them waiting another minute to listen to your bickering. The statement has been admitted and shall remain admitted. I am not going to unadmit it or tell the jury to disregard it. The motion is denied." He pulled out his pipe and his bag of tobacco. "Bailiff, you may bring in the jury. Mr. Prosecutor, please have Mr. Smith return to the witness stand."

After the jury was seated, Al Smith reentered the courtroom, and though I wasn't going to focus on attire, I couldn't help but notice he wore yet another suit, this one a symphony of tan, from his shoes and socks to his necktie. With Smith back on the witness stand McKinley rose at Judge Kincaid's invitation to resume his questioning.

"Mr. Smith, I have here before me the statement you made to Chief Detective Ernie Blunt when he questioned you the day after the shooting of Frankie Ray, in your hotel room. A copy of your statement is on the railing. Will you turn to page three?"

Sullivan stood and made an objection to the use of the statement for the record, meaning it could be an appealable issue, if he needed one.

Smith turned the pages of the statement.

"Feel free to review the statement and tell me if, anywhere in that statement, which you gave willingly, you ever told Detective Blunt about any threat Frankie Ray made about killing George Miller?"

Smith glanced at the statement hardly long enough to read a word. "I don't see it typed up here, but I believe I did make that statement."

"And in that written statement, you also said Mr. Ray and Mr. Miller were arguing about money and a woman, and Mr. Miller shot Mr. Ray twice. Do you see that?"

"Yeah, I see it."

"You told Detective Blunt that you tried to help Frankie Ray, but Mr. Miller threatened you and said, 'Leave him be and get the hell out of my club.'"

"Well, I don't know what to tell you."

McKinley pounced on the response. "The truth, Mr. Smith. You are to tell this jury what you've been sworn to tell. The truth."

"Objection," Sullivan said.

"Sustained. Mr. McKinley, you are treading on my job," Kincaid said.

"Yesterday you testified that, after you heard the shots, you fled to your hotel room. But the day after the shooting you told Detective Blunt that you were present when the shooting occurred." McKinley then read Smith's statement about using his handkerchief to try to stop the bleeding and Miller threatening him with ten slugs. "Do you recall saying that to Chief Detective Blunt?"

"I don't recall how I could have, since I had scrammed," Smith said.

"So let me see if I understand this strange code of ethics. You're now telling this jury you left your dying friend on a club floor without even inquiring about who shot him, and without knowing if he had lived or died?"

Smith said, "I didn't see there being anything more I could have done."

"I see," McKinley said. "Tell me, Mr. Smith, if you left when you heard the shots, how did you get blood on the sleeves of your only suit, which you turned in to the cleaners on Pike Street to have cleaned?"

Again, Smith paused, caught in the web of his own deceit. "I guess . . . maybe . . . I didn't leave right away. Something like that, you know, the shock of it . . . well, maybe I don't recall the details too good."

"So you lied here today?"

"Well . . ."

"Lies are difficult to remember, aren't they, as opposed to the truth?"

Sullivan bolted to his feet. "Objection, Your Honor. Counsel offers an opinion."

"Sustained."

"And if you are going to quote Mark Twain, at least get it right," Sullivan said. "'If you tell the truth, you don't have to remember anything.'"

McKinley smiled. "Indeed," he said. "A poignant and applicable observation by counsel. Mr. Smith, were you employed the night you went to the Pom Pom Club?"

"No. Like a lot of people, I was unemployed."

"Are you still unemployed?"

"No."

"Where do you work now?"

"I manage the Oasis Roadhouse Café."

"Seems an odd transition for a salesman."

"Well, times are tough. You take what you can get."

"And from whom you can get it?"

"I suppose."

"Tell me, who owns the Oasis Roadhouse Café?"

"A company is what I was told."

"Would that company be the Musketeers?"

"I think that's the name on my checks."

"And do you know the names of the men who are members of the Musketeers?"

"Members?" Smith said.

McKinley went to his desk. "Your Honor, the defense would like to introduce the incorporation articles for the Musketeers Company."

Sullivan objected. "I don't see the relevance."

"Mr. McKinley?" Kincaid said.

"Counsel knows the relevance, Your Honor, and it will be readily known by this court and this jury."

"I'll tentatively admit the document, pending counsel's objection as to relevance."

The clerk stamped the document and handed it back to McKinley, who handed the document to Smith. "Mr. Smith, can you read for the jury the names of the members of the Musketeers Company. It's on page two."

Smith flipped the page. "It says here Mr. George Miller and Mr. Sydney Brunn, but I don't know nothing about 'members.'"

"So you work for Mr. Miller and Mr. Brunn," McKinley said, which explained how Smith could afford new suits.

Sullivan stood. "Objection, Your Honor. The document speaks for itself."

McKinley smiled at the jury. "It most certainly does. No further questions."

As McKinley sat, Sullivan practically rushed to the witness stand like a bull released from its chute. Even Smith pulled back from the hard-charging attorney. "Did you tell the police Mr. Miller was trying to protect himself from Ray?"

"I thought I did, but I'm confused now."

"Did you not tell the police Mr. Ray was 'gnashing his teeth' and in a fury?"

"That's right," Smith said, though it was clear to me Smith was not remembering what had happened, but what he'd been coached to say.

Sullivan asked Smith for details about Ray and Miller's conversation. Smith just shook his head. "I guess I was too dense to know an argument was going on. I had too much liquor."

"And Mr. Ray. How much did he have to drink?"

"A lot," Smith said, the first answer he gave with conviction.

"How much is 'a lot'?"

"We was drinking at a table in the club, and then again taking shots at the bar. I'm not sure how many he had, but it was more than half a dozen, I'd say."

Sullivan concluded, and McKinley dismissed Smith without further questioning.

When we broke for lunch, I rushed to the phone booth, closing the retractable door, to dictate my current story. After I had done so, I told Phish I'd heard murmurings that Syd Brunn was going to testify that afternoon and I was expecting more fireworks. More pizzazz!

I just hoped Brunn testified before my 3:00 p.m. deadline.

◆ ◆ ◆

Back in the courtroom, McKinley rose and wasted little time.

"The State calls Syd Brunn," he said.

I felt a twinge of excitement, like when I was a kid and opened a wrapped present on Christmas morning. Those of us in the gallery turned to the courtroom doors as the officer stepped out and, moments later, returned with Brunn.

If Brunn were a Christmas present, he'd have been the kind that disappointed when the wrapping was removed. He'd slicked his thinning hair back off his forehead and had a thin Clark Gable mustache, but in a dark-blue suit and silver tie, he didn't look like Hollywood's new leading man. He looked like someone trying and failing to look like Hollywood's new leading man. There was something dishonest about his appearance and, I sensed, about the man. McKinley established Brunn was a bail bond broker and part owner of the Pom Pom Club, present the morning of June 13.

"Did you see Mr. Ray and Mr. Al Smith in the Pom Pom Club that morning?"

"Yep."

"Did you drink any liquor at the Pom Pom Club that night and the following morning?"

"I drank ginger ale." If true, it made Brunn the only sober man in the club. But it was also at odds with the testimony of Billy Vahle, the bartender, who as far as I could tell had no reason to lie.

"Was Mr. Ray quarrelsome with you?"

Brunn gave McKinley a thin, sardonic smile. "Not with me. He said I was the best friend he had in the world."

"Hmm . . ." McKinley paused, I suppose, for the jury to absorb his reaction. "Did he seem sore at anyone?"

"He seemed sore at himself and the whole world," Brunn said, his tone becoming derisive. "And he quarreled with George Miller."

"Do you know what the quarrel was about?"

"Something about a car payment. Ray needed a loan to pay for a car."

"Did Ray talk about his girl, Joan Daley, being in the hospital and George Miller having reneged on a promise to pay her hospital bill?"

"I don't recall."

McKinley asked, "Where were you when the shooting occurred?"

"In the dance hall turning off the lights on the tables in the booths."

"What time was that?"

"Around six in the morning."

"What happened?"

"I don't know. I wasn't in the room."

McKinley narrowed his gaze. The testimony appeared to be headed in the same direction as Al Smith's testimony. Nothing like what Brunn had told McKinley at police headquarters. "What did you hear, if anything?"

Brunn sighed. "I heard a scuffle, some indistinguishable shouting, and then two shots. When I ran into the dance hall, Ray was lying wounded on the floor. Miller might have had his pistol in hand but I'm not sure."

"You didn't see the shooting?"

"No."

McKinley scratched the back of his neck and made a face like he was confused, his way of letting the jury know he didn't believe Brunn was telling the truth. "You saw Frankie Ray's body in the dance hall?"

"That's where the police found him; ain't it?"

"Yes, it is. And you just testified, under oath, that you were in the dance hall turning out the lights on the tables in the booths. So, if that is true, I'm wondering how you didn't see or hear the shooting in the dance hall?"

Brunn seemed to swallow what he had been prepared to say.

"I must have finished turning off the lights by then and went into the bar. Things are fuzzy."

"I'll bet. Did you see Al Smith?"

"I don't believe so."

"Wasn't Al Smith alongside Ray's body on the floor, using his handkerchief to try to stop the bleeding?"

"No one was by Ray on the floor."

"No one?"

"It was like this." Brunn turned to the jurors. "I was turning out the lights. I turned around and saw the back of Miller's coat as he backed into the dance hall. I heard voices, a scuffle, and two shots; it all happened so quickly. I thought Miller and I were alone in the club. I didn't see Smith."

"You weren't at the bar with Mr. Smith and Frankie Ray drinking shots?"

"Not me."

"So, if Mr. Vahle, *your* bartender at the Pom Pom Club, testified you had been at the bar drinking with Frankie Ray and Al Smith, even taking turns buying rounds, that would be a lie?"

"Like I said, I had one ginger ale."

"So you're saying your bartender lied when he testified you were there?" McKinley's questions were becoming more animated.

"I don't know what he said. Maybe you got him all confused, too, with your slick questions. I can only tell you what was."

"Did you do anything after the shooting to help Frankie Ray?"

"I called for an ambulance."

"Didn't Patrolman Lutz use the phone on the wall to call for an ambulance?"

"It might have happened that way."

"So you did nothing?"

"I guess not."

"You just let Mr. Ray who, you testified, had just told you that very morning that you were his best friend in the world, die alone on the dance floor?"

"He was drunk when he said it. I didn't give it no never mind."

"So you just let him die?"

Sullivan objected that the question was asked and answered and McKinley was badgering the witness. Kincaid agreed.

McKinley then asked Brunn about his lies at the bar the morning of the shooting. "Why would you inform the authorities of something that didn't happen? A lie?"

"Well, like I said, I heard Mr. Miller saying it, and I didn't see the point of saying something else."

"Mr. Miller was telling everyone what to say; wasn't he?"

"I didn't say that."

"Mr. Miller wasn't agitated. He was cold and calculating. And after he shot Frankie Ray, he concocted a story and told you what to say; didn't he?" McKinley's voice rose. "Then he enlisted Vahle, the waiter, and the caretaker and told them what to say also; didn't he? To corroborate his made-up version of the events."

"Objection," Sullivan said. "Again, counsel is cross-examining his own witness and using leading questions."

"A witness we all can agree is hostile," Kincaid said. "Overruled."

"I didn't say he was cold and calculating," Brunn said.

"Mr. Ray never said he had a quarrel with Mr. Miller, did he?"

"I don't know if he said it, but he'd been like a wild man in a frenzy every time Miller's name was mentioned."

McKinley went back to counsel table and picked up typewritten pages. He handed Brunn a copy. For the next hour, McKinley read statements Brunn had given, first to Blunt at the Pom Pom Club, then in the presence of his counsel with a stenographer present. The man seemed to have no conscience. He repeatedly said, "I don't remember saying that." Or "Must have been someone else." Or "Maybe the transcriber got it wrong."

After it was apparent to the jury, and everyone else in the courtroom, that Brunn couldn't or wouldn't tell the truth if he were standing at the pearly gates being questioned by Saint Peter, McKinley simply shook his head, disgusted, and passed the witness.

Sullivan stood and approached, but his examination already compromised, he asked questions for just a few minutes before he walked back to counsel table and sat.

After McKinley said he had no further questions, Judge Kincaid rapped his gavel. "Then we are adjourned."

Chapter 14

I returned to the *Daily Star* to type up the afternoon's events. It would, at Phish's discretion, run at the end of whatever story tomorrow might bring. I checked in with Phish, who was always eager to hear the courtroom shenanigans. We debated exactly what the defense was trying to accomplish.

"It looks to me like the defense attorneys orchestrated every witness's testimony, but each was too thick to remember his lines without it sounding rehearsed," I said in Phish's office. "It's backfiring, in my opinion. The jurors don't appear to be buying a word the defense is selling. They look frustrated."

"Throwing mud on the wall and hoping something sticks," Phish said to me. "Sometimes if you don't have a good defense, you just try to confuse the jury as much as possible. Unless you can get to a juror."

"You think that could really happen?"

"Someone got to the witnesses; didn't they?"

Someone clearly had. It made me wonder if that was why George Miller appeared so calm, cool, and collected. Maybe he already knew the outcome, and the trial was just one big charade he had to go through. Maybe he already knew he'd be back at the Pom Pom Club greeting his clientele in no time, regardless of how much evidence McKinley put before the jury.

"Listen," Phish said, his look and tone becoming serious. "You're doing a great job covering this trial. Just be certain you don't get sucked in by either the State or the defense."

"Sucked in?"

"Our job is to report the events of the day, not to analyze them. We all know the relationships aren't exactly symbiotic. The police and the politicians pull the strings, and we in the press play nice so as not to get aced out of stories altogether, but that doesn't mean we become anybody's stooge. I don't want you to compromise your integrity. We'll call a spade a spade if we need to."

Phish had given me the same admonition several times during my year working for him. "I won't." I stood to leave.

"One more thing."

I turned and Phish handed me a sheet of notebook paper across his desk. "Kravitz found Joan Daley," he said.

"I didn't know he was looking for her."

"At my suggestion. Get to her before Early Winn does. What she has to say could sell a lot of newspapers."

Which was true, but it did nothing to calm my sudden nerves. "I'll need to call someone first. Let her know I'm working late."

"'Her'?"

I couldn't hide the smile stretching my face. "Amara from the bakery on First Avenue."

"Giovacchini's Bakery? I've seen her working. She's a beautiful young lady. Is it serious?"

"I'm going to ask her to marry me."

Phish's eyes widened. "Tonight?"

"No. Not tonight. I'm waiting to get my Oma's ring."

"Have you asked her father?"

"Well, no. Not yet."

"You can't do anything without her father's permission and his blessing. He's Italian, for God's sake."

"I guess I better think more about it," I said.

"You only get married the first time once, Shoe. My wife and I have been married for thirty-five years. I was a reporter here at the *Star*, just like you, when I asked her. We were in love. And I can tell by the silly look on your face that you are also."

"I guess I am," I said.

"Well," Phish said, removing his glasses and cleaning the lenses. "I guess when you get married, you'll need to make more money. You'll have a wife to support and children."

"Children?" I said. I hadn't thought about children, and more importantly what they would cost.

"You want to have children; don't you?"

"I guess so. I mean, I do. Just not right away." I wanted to build up my savings, maybe buy a home.

"That's not always up to you to decide, my boy. God has a hand in it, as well as the woman. When the time comes, we'll discuss a raise. You've earned it."

I thought I'd misheard Phish, since I'd just become a salaried reporter. "A raise? Thank you, Phish. I appreciate everything you've done for me."

"My publisher was my wife's father. He did the same for me, and more, though he did have a vested interest."

"Your wife's father owned the paper?"

"And the building. And a lot of other buildings. His sons didn't want the paper, so when it came time for him to retire, he wanted to give it to me, but I wouldn't take it for free. My father told me, 'Never be beholden to anyone.' I put together a payment plan. I had to scrape for a few years, but I bought the paper and the building, on my own. You can do a lot more than you think with a good woman at your side." He smiled, pensive. "You remind me of myself at your age. Eager. Looking to make a name for yourself. Maybe someday you'll own this paper."

"Me?"

"My two boys think of it as an albatross around my neck. I've missed too many birthdays, family holidays, and celebrations, covering breaking stories. It isn't for everyone. You have to have ink in your veins! You have to bleed ink! I think you just might."

I wasn't sure I had ink in my veins. Maybe not yet. But working at the paper did get me up in the morning—a good sign. I called Amara at the bakery and told her the good news, but also that I had to work late. I said I'd stop by in the morning for a Danish and coffee. She sounded disappointed but said she understood. "Work comes first, but I'll expect double the attention next time I see you."

Already missing her, I set out to catch a trolley up Profanity Hill to Joan Daley's address on Jackson Street. The evening was warm, and I ran through various scenarios of what might happen. I contemplated calling Daley, but as Phish liked to say, it was easy to hang up the phone, not so easy to slam a door in someone's face.

I got off the trolley and walked the last couple of blocks past grand mansions built by Seattle's early settlers—Yesler, Boren, Hanford, and Denny. I wondered who had the kind of money to walk away from such grand homes and simply build new ones. The homes, once the finest in Seattle, looked tired and worn. Stucco had cracked, shutters needed painting, gardens had become weed patches.

I stopped before a three-story building with multiple chimneys protruding from the slate rooftops. Grand columns wrapped a front porch. The beige stucco had discolored in places, cracked in others, and there were patches with nonmatching paint. They looked like scars. The paint peeled around the windows and the doors, the yard needed a good mowing, and the flower boxes needed weeding. But all in all, it didn't look like a bad place to live.

I pulled open the solid oak door and stepped inside an entry of dark-wood floors and paneled walls. As with my building, a countertop had been added, along with a series of mail slots and hooks on which to hang the occupants' room keys.

No one sat at the desk. I deduced the person who staffed it might be eating dinner. I almost rang the bell on the counter, then decided it could generate a lot of questions regarding whom I was visiting and the nature of my visit, which I really didn't want to answer. The butterflies were already beating their wings.

I moved through the entry to a wide, grand staircase with a worn red carpet runner, and climbed to the first landing. Rooms were located off the hallway running north and south, the room numbers on the doors. The first-floor room numbers went from one to six. I ascended the staircase another level and found fewer rooms on a smaller floor plan. The door numbers ascended from seven to ten. According to the address Kravitz provided, Joan Daley lived in room nine. I was momentarily confused when I passed from door eight to the adjacent room. The number on the door was a bronze six. Then I realized a nail had come loose at the top and the nine hung upside down.

Outside Joan Daley's door, alone in the hall, I felt self-conscious and was relieved no one saw me loitering—yet. I again imagined what awaited me inside her room, and when I did, I swore I felt Daley's breath on my neck and smelled her fragrance. I quickly knocked twice, softly. Too softly. I knocked a second time, with more force, three sharp raps, and looked left and right.

"Hold your horses," came the reply, Daley's Brooklynese accent pronounced. I no longer thought it sounded gruff. She sounded just like Mae West.

The door momentarily stuck in the jamb, then pulled open with a shudder. For a second, I thought Kravitz had given me the wrong room number. The disheveled woman standing in the doorway with one hand cocked on her hip looked nothing like the put-together woman in the courtroom the first two days of trial, or whom I'd run into on the street, nor even like the woman I'd first seen lounging in a hospital bed. Her hair was ratted atop her head and partially hidden beneath her blue bandana. I could see gray hairs peeking out the sides. She wore a blue-gray sweater over a flannel nightgown, the bottom of which dragged on the carpeted floor. Her face was free of makeup, and she looked much older without it.

Her voice, however, was unmistakable, though a bit slow and her words slurred.

"Well, if it isn't Billy the kid. You really did come up and see me sometime; didn't you?"

Momentarily stunned, I managed to say, "I'm sorry to bother you unannounced in your home."

"A little notice and I would have made myself more presentable." She gave me that wicked smile that hinted at pleasures I could only imagine, then stepped aside, stumbling a bit when she did, and holding tightly to the door with her left hand. She'd clearly been drinking.

I entered and she closed the door behind me.

I removed my cap from my head, holding it in my hands, which helped conceal a tremor. The room smelled of whiskey and rose perfume.

Daley walked to a table between two plush maroon chairs. A radio rested on the table along with a bottle of caramel-colored liquor, less than half-full, and a glass. She clicked off the volume on the radio—she'd been listening to George Burns and Gracie Allen—and picked up the glass. She dangled it. "Can I offer you a drink, Kid?"

I thought about it. A drink would no doubt take the edge off my nerves and maybe give me a little courage. "No. Thank you," I said.

"Are you looking for something else, then?" She put her hand to the side of her head as if to push her hair like Mae West might and said, "When I'm good, I'm very good. When I'm bad, I'm better."

I felt my face flush and could do little to hide it. I stared at her bed behind a beaded curtain for what felt like a long time and imagined what might happen there.

"Relax, Kid. I don't bite. Unless you want me to." She ran a hand across my cheek, stepped away from the radio, and sipped her drink, her movements languid. "What is it I can do for you?"

"You weren't in court today," I said.

"And you were worried about me? Sweet."

"I was hoping to ask you a few questions."

"For a newspaper article?"

"Yes."

She shook her head. Her eyelids drooped. She was more drunk than I initially thought. When she spoke, she sounded disappointed. "And here I hoped this was a social visit. Not going to happen, Kid."

"Your name is already in the newspapers, Miss Daley."

"Joan," she said firmly. "You make me sound like your schoolmarm when you call me 'Miss Daley.' And my name in the papers isn't of my doing."

"Still, the papers are reporting Frankie Ray was killed because he went to the Pom Pom Club to recover a debt you had incurred."

"Is that so?" She sounded disinterested, or maybe disappointed. I didn't have much experience with the latter, so it was hard to tell.

"It's come out in court, as you know. This is your chance to tell your side of the story."

She wobbled over to one of the two chairs, almost tipping over sideways before finally sitting. She motioned to the other chair. I removed my satchel and sat. "What makes you think I want to tell my side of the story?"

I thought I'd try a different tack. "Why weren't you in court today?"

"I'm sick," she said. "Don't worry. It isn't consumption. Just a bug."

"Have you been to a doctor?"

She lifted the bottle. "I got Doc Thompson right here. Fixing me right up. Hardly feel a thing. Sure I can't interest you in . . . a drink, Kid?" The drugstores sold Sam Thompson whiskey as medicinal to get around the law still forbidding the sale of liquor.

I didn't answer right away. I sensed the rumpled bed behind me. I could get rid of all my inexperience at once. Become a man. Then I thought of Amara and what a breach of trust that would be. I turned to address Joan, but when I did, her eyes were closed. Then her eyelids fluttered open and she sat up, as if startled.

"Are you okay?" I asked.

"My side of the story, huh? What do you think is my side of the story, Kid?"

"Well, I'd say your story is you were working for Mr. Miller in one of his . . . businesses, and you jumped out a second-story window to avoid getting caught in a raid. You got hurt and Mr. Miller, your employer, promised to pay your hospital bill, then reneged. Frankie Ray went to collect the debt, but Miller turned ugly."

She smiled, but it was patronizing. "Sounds like a good story, Kid. My daddy used to say the best stories are those not constrained by the truth."

"So that story isn't true?"

She smiled but didn't answer me.

"Was it an argument about you? I heard George was sweet on you."

"Could have been. A part of it anyway. George has flirted with me a number of times. Frankie knows. It makes him angry, but is that why George shot Frankie? Not likely. George has a temper, and Frankie got him mad. When George gets mad, he's no longer rational."

"Did he get mad about you?"

She set her glass on the table. "I read in the paper you spoke to the Cadillac salesman."

"I was with Detective Blunt and the deputy district attorney when they spoke to the salesman."

"Detective Blunt." She scoffed. Then she said, "So you know who was making the monthly payments for Ray's car."

"You were."

"That's right. A luxury item. Does that sound like someone who couldn't pay an eighty-dollar hospital bill?"

It didn't. "But you were . . . out of work," I remembered.

"Was I?" She gave me another wicked smile. "A girl can always work, Kid. Don't need to stand on a leg to be at my best."

"Well, I mean, if you weren't out of work, why didn't you just pay the bill?"

"Couldn't."

"I don't understand."

"No, you don't." She paused as if contemplating whether to say more. Then she did. "If I made the payments on the Cadillac while I was supposedly laid up and not working . . . Or if Frankie had made the payments, well, people would become suspicious about where the money was coming from; wouldn't they?" She gave a loud sigh. "I told Ray not to drive that Cadillac to the club that morning. But he wanted to be the big shot. I told him George Miller was at the club, and if he saw the car, he'd start to wonder."

So it *was* Miller she was referring to. "Why would George Miller care if Frankie drove a Cadillac?"

She didn't answer.

Then an answer popped into my head. "Miller would wonder why Frankie couldn't pay your hospital bill himself if he was paying for a Cadillac. He'd wonder where Ray was getting the money to make the monthly payments for the car, but not your hospital bill?" Then something more hit me. "Which is why the car was in your name. Frankie Ray didn't want Miller to know he'd bought the car. Why not? Was it George Miller's money?"

She smiled and went to touch her index finger to the tip of her nose, but she missed and hit her cheek instead. The light bulb must have flashed over my head because Daley said, "Now you're starting to get it."

"So, Ray asking for money to pay your hospital bill was . . . what, then . . . Just a ruse to make George Miller think neither of you had any money."

"Which is why I told Frankie not to drive the Cadillac."

"That's what caused the dispute," I said. "Miller was asking Ray where he got the money to pay for a Cadillac if he couldn't pay an eighty-dollar hospital bill. Frankie was stealing from George Miller?"

"You're catching on, Kid. But be careful. Finding out those answers might get you killed."

That last word hung in the air between us. I couldn't tell from Daley's drunken condition if she was worried or just trying to get another rise out of me. "But George Miller is in jail," I said. "Syd Brunn? Al Smith? Vahle, the bartender? Do I have to worry about one of them?"

"Not Syd," Daley said, her voice softening, and her eyes nearly closed. "He's never carried a gun a day in his life."

"Someone else, then."

Her final words were whispered. Too soft for me to hear what she'd said. I had another recollection, and I flashed back to the emergency hospital in the Yesler Building, to Frankie Ray lying on the table like a slab of already-cold meat. But he hadn't been cold. He'd still been alive. He, too, had whispered something, something so softly Ernie Blunt had to bend down and put his ear near Ray's lips, obscuring them. In my mind I saw Blunt's coat open, revealing his shoulder holster and his gun.

I felt my blood run cold.

Blunt had given the dying man a curious look, as if whatever Ray had said had been unexpected.

"Tell me," Blunt had said.

But Frankie Ray defiantly looked at the ceiling.

"Tell me, Frankie," Blunt had said a second time.

Ray's final words came slowly, but this time they had been loud enough for me to hear. *"That's for you to find out, Ernie. Do me a favor? Tell George Miller to go to hell."*

Pink foam then appeared on Ray's lips and he gasped, but he died with a wry smile on his face, the smile of a man who held a secret he would take to his grave.

"Ernie Blunt," I said, but Joan Daley had fallen asleep in her chair, glass in her hand.

I stared at her a moment. She no longer looked like Jean Harlow, the glamorous Hollywood movie star lounging poolside. She looked sad. She looked like the men and women I'd seen on the street, not far from Hooverville. I no longer thought of her the way I once had. Reality is often a harsh reminder our fantasies are just that. Fantasy.

I felt sorry for Joan Daley, alone in a rooming house, losing her youth, and likely afraid she was losing her sex appeal and would end up in Hooverville, which was maybe why she toyed with me, to see if she could still entice a young man into her bed.

She could. I wasn't going to lie to myself. But I also wasn't going to be that young man. Like George Miller and so many in the gallery, Joan had been in costume, but I'd had the chance to see into the greenroom—the place where actors waited before going onstage. I'd seen Joan Daley out of character and out of costume.

I stood and placed my cap on my head, then adjusted the satchel at my waist. I removed the glass from Daley's hand—she stirred but didn't wake—and I set it on the table. I contemplated lifting her from the chair and placing her on her bed, but I didn't want to linger a moment longer in her room.

Something wasn't right.

I didn't know what exactly, but I could feel it. A premonition. I shouldn't be there, alone in that room. Something else was going on, something that had led to Frankie Ray's death but hadn't yet come out at trial.

I moved to the door and pulled it open, searching the hall in both directions to ensure it was vacant before I stepped out. I initially moved toward the staircase, then turned and walked to a door at the far end of the hall. The door opened to narrow stairs, like at my boardinghouse, no doubt used by servants to enter and exit rooms unobtrusively when the house had belonged to one of Seattle's grand families.

I followed the stairs down two flights to the ground level and pushed open a door to an alley behind the house. The murky light indicated dusk. I hurried down the alley listening to my breath, the leather satchel rubbing on my hip. Then I heard a car engine. I turned. Headlights appeared at the opposite end of the alley, too far for me to tell the car's make or model. The headlights moved toward me. I jogged down the alley in the opposite direction, to the intersection. The car kept coming. I spotted a trolley headed down the hill and chased after it, managing to grab the outside bar at the back and pull myself up. The car had reached the intersection. I still couldn't tell the model or see the person sitting behind the wheel, but the car was black.

Minutes later, at First Avenue, I stepped off the moving trolley and grabbed another headed north up First Avenue, getting off at Pike Street. Looking left, I saw a black car, which wasn't exactly unusual. This time it was close enough for me to determine the make and model. A 1932 Ford Model B, the same make and model Ernie Blunt drove. Blunt had also dropped me off at my boardinghouse the first night of the investigation, so he knew where I lived.

I hurried into my boardinghouse. Thankfully, Mrs. Alderbrook was not at her desk. I grabbed my key and shuffled up four steps.

"Shoe?"

I turned back. "Mrs. Alderbrook. I didn't want to disturb you. I have my key."

She stepped around the desk to just below the stairs. "Do you feel all right? You're white as a sheet and you're perspiring."

"I hurried here. I'm a little out of breath."

She eyed me. "Maybe you're working too many hours."

"Maybe," I said. "I'm going to try to get a good night's sleep." I turned.

"Your mother called," Mrs. Alderbrook said.

"My mother? But it isn't Sunday."

When Mrs. Alderbrook didn't respond, I said, "Did she say why?" I thought maybe she'd called to tell me she'd put my Oma's ring in the post.

"She just asked that you call her when you got in."

I went back down the stairs. Mrs. Alderbrook gave me a thin smile and handed me the phone. Then she left the counter for her room. Odd. With growing trepidation, I called home.

My aunt Ida, my mother's sister, answered. "William. We've been waiting for your call."

"What do you mean? Where's my mother? Why didn't she answer the phone?" I had another thought—of my uncle Ted.

"She's at the hospital, William."

My knees went weak. "What happened?"

"Your father's had a heart attack," she said. "From all the stress."

"Is he alive?"

"He's alive. Your mother told me to tell you—"

"I'll catch a train home tomorrow," I said. I needed to be home with my family. My father needed me.

"No," my aunt said.

"No?"

"No. Your mother told me to tell you not to do anything that could jeopardize your employment covering the Trial of the Century."

"I don't care about any of that."

"You have to care, William. We can't survive with the sewing and laundry jobs we have. We need your help. We all need your help. We need the money you send her every month."

"But my dad—"

"Is in the hospital getting the best care. You coming home won't change his circumstances. It will just hurt the rest of us."

I felt like I should get on a train, my aunt be damned, that I should be there in Kansas City with my family, but my aunt Ida was correct. It would only make my mother's situation worse, not better. I couldn't do that to her or to my brother and sister. I couldn't be that selfish.

"You'll have my mother call me," I said.

"In the morning," Aunt Ida said.

I hung up the receiver. When I did, Mrs. Alderbrook appeared. "Is everything all right, William?"

I shook my head, then I broke down in tears, stepped forward, and lowered my head onto Mrs. Alderbrook's shoulder and cried. After a moment, when she was likely trying to decide how to respond, she put her arms around me and gave me a hug. Other than Amara, it was the first hug I had received from anyone since leaving my family in Kansas City.

It made me cry all the more.

Chapter 15

The following morning, Thursday, I again awoke to Mrs. Alderbrook knocking on my door; her voice, soft at first, grew in volume. "William? William?"

I pushed my head from my pillow, disoriented. I'd fallen asleep in my clothes and atop the bedcovers. I didn't even remember going to bed or dreaming. My sorrow had knocked me out. A breeze through my window tickled the back of my neck. I didn't remember opening the window. Getting my bearings, I rolled my feet to the floor and sat on the edge of the bed to give my head a chance to catch up so I wouldn't fall over when I stood. "Just a minute."

"There's a call for you," she said, and I thought immediately it was my mother. Then she said through the door, "Your editor, Howard Phishbaum. He said it's urgent."

Phish?

I hurried to the door and reached to pull it open. The doorknob slipped from my hand. I had locked the door before going to bed. The remainder of my night came back to me. I had left Mrs. Alderbrook's consoling arms and hurried to my room. I inserted the key and, just about to step inside, had a thought. The key was readily accessible to anyone when Mrs. Alderbrook wasn't guarding the lobby. I remembered what Joan Daley had said, about asking the wrong people too many questions and maybe getting killed.

But she had been drunk.

And yet, her words had a ring of truth to them.

I had pushed open the door and clicked on the lamp near my lone chair. The yellow light had illuminated my empty room. Not satisfied, I had checked the armoire in which I stored my meager belongings. No one.

Paranoid maybe, but I wasn't going to also be stupid.

"Shoe?"

I retrieved my room key from the table, unlocked the door, and pulled it open.

"He said he needed to speak to you right away," Mrs. Alderbrook said, following me down the hall as I adjusted my suspenders onto my shoulders. "Do you think something has happened in the Pom Pom Club trial?"

I didn't know. I was still trying to get my wits about me. In the lobby, I picked up the receiver and spoke into the phone. "Phish?"

"Shoe. I need you to get over to Profanity Hill before you come into the office this morning."

The grandfather clock chimed, 6:15 a.m. "What's going on?"

"Remember that address I gave you last night, for Joan Daley?" I reached into my pocket and pulled out the slip of paper. "You can forget about talking to her."

"Did Early Winn beat me to the story?"

"No one beat you to anything. Joan Daley is dead."

I felt the floor come out from beneath my legs and would have collapsed but for leaning against the counter. Instinctively, I looked for the wastebasket, so queasy I thought I might vomit. I managed to ask, "What?"

"I just got a call from one of my contacts on the police force. They found Joan Daley in an alley behind her building. Looks like she jumped from the second floor and landed on her head. The police are there now."

I didn't know what to say, whether to say anything. My stomach roiled.

"Shoe? Are you still there?"

"Yeah. Yeah, I'm still here."

"Get going."

"Where?"

"What do you mean, where? Profanity Hill. This is going to be big news. I've got the headline already written. 'Mystery Woman in Nightclub Shooting Found Dead.' How's that for pizzazz?"

"Who called you, Phish?"

"A patrolman first on the scene. Now get moving. Then get in here and we'll type up the story together before you head to court."

Phish disconnected and for a long minute I stared at the phone.

"It's related to the Pom Pom Club; isn't it?" Mrs. Alderbrook said. "I can tell by the look on your face."

I hung up the receiver without responding. I felt numb. Joan Daley was dead. How? I'd just spoken to her.

"William, are you all right? It's not your father; is it?"

"What?"

"You look like someone died. Your father didn't die; did he?"

"No. I mean . . . no," I said, and I thought about what Phish had told me. Joan Daley jumped from the second-story window, just like she'd jumped to avoid the raid at her place of work. She'd done it before. That's what someone wanted people to believe. Joan Daley had jumped before, so this was not completely unexpected, except this time she'd landed on her head, not her feet.

I made my way up the stairs to grab my satchel off the floor, but when I bent down, I again felt queasy. Knowing what was to come, I stumbled down the hall and into the bathroom, which was, thankfully, unoccupied. I fell to my knees on the terrazzo tiles by the toilet and retched, followed by dry heaves.

◆ ◆ ◆

After cleaning myself up, I retraced my route back to Profanity Hill with my mind racing between my father's heart attack and Joan Daley's death.

When I arrived at the boardinghouse, police cars lined the street and the alley. Uniformed officers milled about the lawn and the porch, some smoking cigarettes. I climbed the steps to the front door and showed an officer my press pass. "Where's the body?" I asked.

"Gone," he said. "Taken to the morgue."

"What have you heard?"

"Aren't you the reporter for the *Daily Star*? The one covering the Pom Pom Club trial?"

"Yes," I said. "William Shumacher."

"I've read all your articles. They're good."

"Thank you. Have you been told anything?"

"Well, you know as much as I do about this one, Mr. Shumacher."

"Who knows more?"

"The detectives, I would guess. They're in the room now." He pointed to the stairs inside.

"Which detectives?"

"Chief Detective Ernie Blunt and Luke May. Deputy Prosecutor McKinley is also up there. I shouldn't let you up, but I can make an exception given your credentials and all."

I stepped past him.

"Don't you want to know her room number?" the officer asked.

I stopped. "How's that?"

"It's room nine. Top floor."

"Right. Thanks."

I felt a pit in my stomach the size of a watermelon as I crossed the lobby to the staircase and climbed the steps to the second floor. I went down the hall to room number nine. Half a dozen police officers roamed the hallway. The door to Joan Daley's room was open.

A hand stopped me. "Crime scene," a uniformed officer said. "You'll have to wait out here."

Inside the room, Blunt spoke with McKinley.

"Detective Blunt," I said.

Blunt looked surprised to see me. We locked gazes for what seemed a long moment. Then he walked to the door. "It's all right," he said to the uniform at the door. "He's with me."

The officer stepped aside, and I stepped into a mess. My eyes swept over Joan Daley's belongings strewn across the floor, including her bedding. The armoire doors were open, the contents spilled, clothing and shoes and two suitcases. The chair had been toppled. So had the bed frame. Someone looking under the bed? For what?

"How'd you find out?" Blunt asked.

"Phish called me on the house phone," I said.

"How did he find out?"

"I don't know. A contact. What happened?"

"Looks like she went on a binge and leapt out the window. There's a lot of that going around now."

There was, but almost all of the two hundred who had taken their lives in Seattle were out-of-work men. I found it hard to believe the woman I had left the night before leapt out the window. She was in no condition to stand, let alone tear apart her room and jump out the window. But each time I contemplated saying as much to Blunt, the image of Blunt, bent over a dying Frankie Ray, gun in his holster, stopped me.

"Intentional?" I asked.

"That's how it appears," Blunt said.

"Why would she have torn through her belongings?"

"Who knows."

"Looks like someone was looking for something?" I said it off-the-cuff, without thinking.

"Yeah?" Blunt gave me a curious look. "What would that be?"

Blunt's question startled me and alerted me. I needed to be cautious. "I don't know. It's just . . . everything is . . . everywhere, and the suitcases are open like someone was searching for something."

His gaze swept over several empty bottles I hadn't seen the night before. "Based on the number of empties, she'd been on a hell of a bender."

"Maybe it was Miller's men," I said.

Blunt gave me another sharp look. "Miller's men? Who are Miller's men?"

"I don't know. You said he was in the underworld, so I thought . . ."

"That someone pushed her out the window?"

"Maybe?"

"This isn't the first time she's jumped," Blunt said.

No, it wasn't. "You said she jumped the first time to avoid a raid. This is different."

"That's what she said, but who knows why she jumped the first time. Besides, why would Miller have any reason to kill her?"

"I don't know. Maybe she knew something, and he wanted to be sure she couldn't testify."

"Something like what?"

"I don't know. Or maybe she had something. It would explain the room's condition."

Blunt gave me a queer look, but whatever he was going to ask me, he didn't get the chance. A uniformed officer entered. "Chief Detective? Call on the house phone in the lobby. The chief of police. Wants to talk to you."

Blunt left the room. McKinley rubbed a hand over his unshaven face. "Will this impact the case?" I asked the prosecutor.

"I don't see how," he said quietly. "Neither side had her listed as a witness."

"I wondered about that. Didn't you need her to testify she made payments on Frankie Ray's car?"

"The Cadillac salesman can testify. He had the contract."

"What about the hospital bill. The eighty dollars?"

"The defense is willing to stipulate to the hospital bill."

"She could have testified Miller promised to pay the bill," I said.

"And Miller would deny it. She was a hooker. Nobody was going to believe what she had to say. It's why I didn't list her as a witness. Besides, it's irrelevant what led to the argument that ended Frankie Ray's life. Miller shot Ray. That's all that matters. I don't want to complicate things and play into the defense's hand of confusing the jury until they don't know what's up and what's down. The two men quarreled—over car payments or a hospital bill. Doesn't matter. It was over money. And Miller shot him. Simple as that."

But I knew now, or at least believed I knew, it wasn't that simple. Again, I almost told McKinley I had been in the room just the night before, but again something held my tongue. Truth was, I feared I'd become a suspect, which sounded crazy, even to me. "Don't you think it's a bit of a . . . I don't know . . ."

"Coincidence that the woman at the center of the controversy ends up dead?" McKinley said, finishing my thought.

"Well, yeah."

"No. I don't. Her name was smeared all over *your* articles in *your* paper along with the fact that she worked at a disorderly house. She was out of a job, and her boyfriend was just killed. A lot of people have killed themselves for a lot less these past few years. She's just another in a long line of down-and-out who chose *out*, permanently." McKinley pulled a watch from his pocket. "I have to get home, shave, and get to court."

He stepped past me. My question stopped him at the door. "Why'd you come?"

He turned. "What?"

"With the trial and all . . . Why'd you come here?"

McKinley didn't answer. He just turned and left.

I took a mental picture of what I was seeing, scribbled some notes, and went back downstairs. Blunt stood in the lobby talking with Luke May, the criminologist. He waved me over and introduced me. May and I shook hands. "May was just telling me he'll run a blood test and confirm Joan Daley was drunk," Blunt said. "Is that right, Luke?"

"We'll know more soon," May said. "And we'll dust the room for fingerprints to try to determine who was here, just in case."

"Just in case?" I asked.

"Like you said upstairs," Blunt said. "Just in case she didn't jump."

"Right," I said, but my mind was thinking of the prior night, what I might have touched and where I possibly might have left my fingerprints.

May went up the steps.

"You better get going so you can get to court on time . . . before the guard locks the door," Blunt said.

"You as well."

Blunt smirked. "Nobody locks the door on me."

I went past Blunt toward the front door. He called out to me. "Shoe?" I turned back. "Got something for your story." He walked toward me. "A uniformed officer says a witness across the alley told him she was tending to her chickens in the backyard at dusk last night and saw a man come out the back door of this boardinghouse into the alley."

I felt my pulse quicken but recovered enough to say, "Why does that matter—if Joan Daley took her own life?"

"Thought it might add a little intrigue. Help you to sell newspapers."

"Right," I said.

"We'll talk to the neighbor," Blunt said. "Get a description of the person she saw in the alley. Who knows, maybe your intuition is correct. Maybe Joan Daley didn't jump. Maybe you're more detective than reporter."

"I don't think so." I turned to go, then turned back. "This witness. Did you get a name or an address?"

"Not yet," Blunt said. "When I do, I'll let you know."

I departed. On the front lawn no one paid any attention to me. I went around to the back of the house and walked down the alley. As I did, I peered over a wooden fence into backyards. I didn't see any chicken coops or chickens. During a depression, chickens would have been a luxury most couldn't afford and others would have stolen.

Blunt had lied to me. Why?

Chapter 16

Though I had to get to the office, I couldn't go straight there, not in my current emotional state. I needed to think things through, what to do. I walked to the bakery, and when I opened the door, Mr. Giovacchini took one look at me and stopped his daily instruction in midsentence.

"Move down the—" He came toward me with a look of concern. "William. Are you all right?"

I shook my head. "No," I managed. "I'm sorry to interrupt your morning rush. I know how busy you are, but . . . Is Amara here?"

A dumb question, certainly. Where else would she be?

Amara came out from the kitchen behind the counter. "Can we talk for a minute?" I asked.

Mr. Giovacchini directed us to a storage room off the kitchen. When Amara closed the door, I lost it. Everything came spilling out at once. My father's heart attack. My desire to be with my family, but my duty to stay here and provide for them. My conversation with my aunt Ida. My failed attempt to interview Joan Daley the previous evening, and Phish's call that morning.

Amara massaged the back of my head. "William. I'm so sorry. First things first. Have you spoken yet to your mother this morning?"

I shook my head. "She's at the hospital with my father."

"Well, of course she is," Amara said. "So maybe it isn't too bad."

"'Isn't too bad'?" I said, raising my eyes.

"I mean, there are many types of heart attacks. My uncle in Italy had one and he was back to normal in no time."

"But what if he's not?" I said. "I should be there, with my family. My mother needs me."

"Your aunt is right, William. Right now, your mother needs you here, working. She's going to have a lot of expenses."

"I know," I said. "Which is why I can't say anything about being in Joan Daley's room last night."

"What do you mean?"

"I can't tell Detective Blunt I was there last night. If I do, he'll bring me in as a material witness. Maybe hold me in jail. My name and photograph will be in all the newspapers. I could lose my job. Then what would my family do?"

"But you didn't do anything."

"Yes, but Blunt can't be sure of that. And even if I'm ultimately found innocent, I might not have a job to go back to. At the very least Phish will pull me from covering the trial. He'll say I'm too close to the story to be impartial. He'll have Nathan Kawolski cover it."

"You need your job, William. Your family needs the money."

"I know."

"I don't mean to add to your worries, but what if they find your fingerprints in Joan Daley's room? You said a criminologist was there."

"I thought that through. I don't remember touching anything. I wasn't there long. And even if they found my prints, they couldn't identify them as mine. They'd likely think they belonged to a man Joan Daley had in her room."

Which made me think of my fascination with Joan Daley, imagining having sex with her, and that made me feel more guilty for having run to Amara's arms for comfort. I'd been an idiot to even contemplate throwing away something so beautiful with Amara.

"Maybe she jumped. So many people have seen the hopelessness of their situation," Amara said.

"She didn't jump, Amara. The woman I left was passed out drunk, and someone went through her things. They were looking for something. I'm sure of it."

"So you're not going to say anything?"

"I don't think I have any other choice. At least until I find out what is really going on."

"How are you going to do that?"

"I don't know. Not exactly. But I feel like I owe it to Joan Daley to find out what happened to her."

"Owe it to her? You hardly knew her."

"I know what she was, Amara, but she was kind to me in the courtroom." I told Amara about leaving the tag on my jacket. "And she confided something in me. Something to let me know things are not as they seem." I stopped myself, not wanting to tell Amara Joan Daley's warning. I didn't want to scare her any more than I already had.

"William, do you think it could be dangerous? I mean, George Miller is part of the underworld."

"George Miller isn't going anywhere anytime soon, except back to his cell each night. And no one knows I was in Joan Daley's room. Not even Phish." But even as I said it, I thought about the black car following me down the alley.

"Be careful, William," she said and hugged me tight.

I said I would be.

She pulled back. "When will you speak to your mother? Do you want to call her now?"

"She won't be home now. She'll be at the hospital with my father. I'll call her tonight, after I get off work."

Amara dried my tears with her apron.

"Do I look like I've been crying?" I asked, embarrassed.

She smiled. "If anyone asks, just tell them you have allergies."

I returned her smile. "Thank you, Amara. I don't know what I would do without you."

Mr. Giovacchini shouted, "Move down the line, please. Move down the line."

"And I'm not sure what my father will do without me. I better get back out there."

When we went back into the pastry shop, Mr. Giovacchini asked if I was all right.

"I'm fine," I said. "Better now."

"You look pale. You're not sick; are you? You've got to be careful about burning the candle at both ends."

"I'm not sick," I said. "And I will be careful."

He reached into the pastry counter with tongs and grabbed a cinnamon-and-raisin pastry, putting it on wax paper. "Amara, pour him a coffee."

It was a small gesture, but it meant the world to me, and it made me miss home just a little bit less. I gave Mr. Giovacchini a hug, which I know surprised him.

At the counter, I said to Amara, "I'll try to come by after court this afternoon, after trial, but I may be working late again."

"Let me know about your father and the other thing as well."

"Are you covering the trial?" a woman in line asked. "What newspaper?"

"The *Star*," I said, before returning my attention to Amara. "I'll let you know. But don't worry."

"I've read all your articles. You're very good."

"Thanks," I said. Then to Amara, "Maybe we can have dinner?"

"I can't tonight," Amara said. "My aunt and cousins are visiting. Why don't you come to the house? You can meet them."

"I still don't think George Miller did it," the woman said. "He looks like such a nice young man in the photographs."

"I won't be able to come tonight. Maybe tomorrow?" I said.

"I'll let you know," she said. "But I'm here if you need me."

"Do you think he'll get off?" the woman asked.

"I don't know," I said.

The woman paid and exited.

"You better go before Phish gets angry," Amara said.

Outside, the woman had waited for me. "It sounds so glamorous," she said. "Everyone in court is so dressed up. It must be so interesting."

Dressed up like wolves in sheep's clothing, I thought, *and maybe not just the underworld. A lot of people, it seemed, were wearing costumes.* I hurried down the street, not giving the woman time to ask any more questions.

As I made my way down First Avenue to the *Daily Star* offices, the morning breeze made me feel better and helped me to think. Part of me wondered if I had somehow been responsible for Joan Daley's death; if going to her boardinghouse had made someone think she'd told me something, something they didn't want her talking about. But why then had they searched her room? Clearly someone was looking for something tangible. Thinking back to the black car in the alley, I wondered if perhaps that had just been my overactive imagination.

But I hadn't imagined Joan Daley, passed out and in no condition to tear apart her room and jump out a window.

What exactly had she meant when she warned me that asking questions could get me killed?

At the office Phish didn't ask me what was wrong or if I had been crying, a good thing since I felt like the smallest thing could put me over the emotional edge. We put together a story on the death of Joan Daley with little detail and lots of speculation. While I named Blunt and McKinley as being at the scene and quoted them, the quotes were bland and noncommittal. I quoted McKinley as saying Daley's death wouldn't impact the trial, and I quoted Luke May that blood work and an autopsy would provide more answers. I left Phish to finish the story so I could get to court on time.

The courtroom seemed empty without Joan Daley smiling at me, and I stared for a moment at where she had regularly sat.

"She's not here," Winn said, smiling. "If you'd like, I could look to see if you left any tags on your clothes."

Those sitting close by chuckled.

I'd had enough of Winn. I leaned over the back of the pew until my nose was inches from his. "That would entail you getting off your ass and doing some work, which, as far as I can tell, you haven't done in years. You missed another story this morning, Early. An important one, but you'll know soon, when the *Star* is published this afternoon."

Winn nearly swallowed the stub of cigar in the corner of his mouth.

I sat. Moments later Judge Kincaid entered, and we were again underway.

McKinley called Dr. P. C. West, county autopsy surgeon. He appeared in a tweed sport coat with elbow patches and described the nature of Frankie Ray's wounds.

Sullivan's cross-examination was just one question. "Was an autopsy performed of Ray's brain to ascertain if the former boxer suffered a mental ailment?"

West said one was not.

Sullivan made a face, clearly for the jury's benefit, then sat.

Next, McKinley called Ernie Blunt. I felt the gallery and jurors sit up, clearly intrigued by the famed chief detective and what he might say. Blunt slid back his chair and took the stand in a well-worn blue suit, and I couldn't help but think his choice was by design. The State no doubt wanted to continue to paint a contrast between a hardworking, everyday cop and the high-rolling, tailored underworld.

Blunt, who I imagined had testified dozens of times in his career, looked poised and confident. McKinley established Blunt's impressive credentials, then got down to business. He had Blunt go over the crime scene meticulously and provide his conclusions based on the evidence. He used photographs as Blunt testified about the chalked outline Officer Lutz drew on the dance floor around Ray's body, and the statements made shortly after the shooting by the various persons who remained in the bar. He also testified as to where the shell casings were found on the floor and the locations of the bullet holes in the wall, which were depicted in photographs also shown to the jury.

Blunt then testified as to what the Cadillac salesman told him about payments being made by Joan Daley. Each time her name was mentioned I felt tears well in my eyes, but neither Blunt nor McKinley flinched. The subject of her death was not brought up, and I knew it wouldn't be. If the State raised Daley's death, it would be potential grounds for a mistrial, because the jury could speculate that Miller was somehow involved in her death to keep her from testifying.

The detective discussed how he had located Al Smith using the bloody handkerchief found at the scene. I deduced much of this testimony was intended to impress the jury with the chief detective's ingenuity, and to show that Smith and Brunn had lied on the stand.

Blunt detailed what Miller told him had happened.

"Did Miller tell you Ray was drunk?"

"He did say Ray was drunk, and because Ray was drunk, he said Ray wasn't pointing the gun directly at him but rather off to the side."

Blunt recounted Miller's story of how he disarmed Ray, then shot him, twice.

"And did you determine whether that account was true or false?"

"It was false."

"Did Miller say who called an ambulance?"

"He said Syd Brunn called for an ambulance."

"And was that statement true or false?"

"False. Patrolman Lutz said Ray was alone in the ballroom on the floor. No one was with him. He said Ray was still breathing so he, Patrolman Lutz, called the ambulance."

Which made me wonder whether Miller and Brunn didn't help Frankie Ray because they wanted him to die. What was that saying about dead men telling no tales? Or secrets perhaps?

"Did Miller ever tell you he was afraid of Frankie Ray?"

"In fact, I asked Miller if he was afraid of Ray, and Miller said, no, he was not."

Blunt testified about searching Miller's house and finding the gun holster, then turning the holster over to Luke May. "I think it best to let Detective May explain his tests and what they mean."

Blunt testified on direct examination until well into the afternoon. When McKinley sat, everyone in the courtroom seemed to lean forward as Sullivan approached the witness stand, expecting a heavyweight fight between a seasoned detective and a seasoned defense attorney.

But again, Sullivan pulled his punches and kept his cross-examination short. Perhaps he had concluded he wouldn't be able to rattle Blunt, and it was therefore best to get him off the stand quickly rather than have him reiterate why George Miller was guilty. In any event, I could sense the disappointment in the courtroom as Blunt returned to his seat at counsel's table.

Following Blunt, McKinley called Luke May. May used science to poke more holes in Miller's story. As he explained how he matched the gun to the holster, Sullivan rose. "Your Honor, the defense does not dispute the gun belonged to Mr. Miller, nor does it dispute the gun fit within the holster. This testimony is unnecessary and irrelevant."

"Your Honor, it establishes Mr. May's credentials," McKinley said.

"And the defense stipulates Mr. May is the leading criminologist in the state," Sullivan said. "If not the entire country, which, again, makes this line of questioning unnecessary."

"Sustained. Move on, Mr. McKinley," Kincaid said.

It was a good move by Sullivan, preventing the State from further impressing the jury.

McKinley regrouped and asked May whether the location of Ray's wounds supported Miller's statement he shot Ray as Ray rushed at him with his left hand raised.

"Certainly not," May said. "Given the damage to Ray's left arm, his arm was not raised when the first bullet entered the body. If anything, Ray was turning away from Miller."

"Do you have an opinion, therefore, whether Miller shot in self-defense?"

Sullivan rose and objected that May's opinion was irrelevant, but Kincaid allowed May to answer.

"I do not believe he shot in self-defense, not the first or the second bullet. Mr. Ray could not have been going forward in a crouched position given the height at which the two bullets embedded in the wall. It's much more likely, in my expert opinion, that Ray had put his hands up after he was initially shot and spun around, exposing his right side when Miller shot a second time."

"So we can also rule out a second shooter, or a mystery bullet?" McKinley asked.

"We most certainly can. There's no mystery here. Mr. Ray was shot twice from the same gun, while standing."

Sullivan again kept his cross-examination brief. "You're speculating about what happened when the first bullet hit Mr. Ray; aren't you?"

"I don't speculate, sir. My opinions are based in science."

"Isn't it possible Ray approached crouched, like a wrestler, but when he saw the gun, he pulled up and spun, exposing his left arm?" Sullivan demonstrated.

"It could have happened that way, but that's my point. If the gun stopped Mr. Ray's advance, and made him turn, as you speculate, then Mr. Miller did not need to fire his weapon, and certainly not twice."

"Unless Mr. Ray stopped to grab a knife or a gun of his own."

"He did not have a knife or a gun in his possession," May said. "They were not in the belongings catalogued during the autopsy or found at the Pom Pom Club."

"But you learned that after you took inventory of Mr. Ray's possessions while in the hospital; didn't you?"

"That's correct."

"Mr. Miller did not have the same luxury of hindsight; did he?"

"I don't know."

"He didn't know, in that split second that he had to make a decision, whether Mr. Ray was or was not armed, or reaching for a weapon; did he?"

"I don't suppose he could have known. Not with certainty."

Sullivan sat. He'd scored his best points against the State's most acclaimed witness, and for the first time several jurors leaned back, looking duly impressed.

As Judge Kincaid prepared to slam his gavel and end the day, advising the courtroom the defense would begin its case in the morning, Sullivan rose. "Your Honor, the defense has submitted a motion for the jury to view the crime scene prior to the defense giving their opening statement. We think it would be most beneficial to the jurors to view the premises in person, rather than making decisions based on scaled drawings."

From the smiles on the jurors' faces, this was a field trip they were looking forward to—getting to see a famed nightclub where the rich and the powerful ventured late at night.

Kincaid asked McKinley if he had any objection. The deputy prosecutor was intelligent enough not to deny the jurors this respite after the long hours they'd sat in the courtroom.

"The State is in full agreement these jurors see the scene of this crime," he said, sounding magnanimous.

"Then we will so proceed. Ladies and gentlemen, a bus will be arranged for you to be transported to and from the club. We shall meet here in the courtroom tomorrow morning at nine a.m. and proceed from here. Though you will not be in the courtroom, the same rules apply on the bus and at the Pom Pom Club as apply here in court with respect to the attorneys and yourselves."

I left the courtroom and returned to the *Star*, telling Phish there had been nothing more exciting than Joan Daley's death. The day, given the anticipation, had been a letdown.

Phish went with the death of Joan Daley as the lead, then ran a sidebar down the right side recounting Blunt's and May's testimonies.

"Sullivan is up to something," I said. "He hardly conducted any cross-examination of Blunt or May."

"Maybe he didn't see the point . . . Knew he wouldn't be able to rattle two experienced and well-versed detectives."

"That's what I thought, but I still think he has something up his sleeve. He's taking the jury to the Pom Pom Club, though I'm not exactly sure what they will see. It's been closed down since the shooting."

"If Sullivan's up to something, we'll find out soon enough," Phish said.

At my desk I tried to keep my mind on my work. I thought through the day's events and what Joan Daley had told me the previous night. Ray had not gone to Miller seeking money. Rather, Miller had likely called Ray into the club to question him about how he was paying for the Cadillac. Why would Miller care? Unless Ray was flashing money he shouldn't have been—meaning money that Miller didn't want others to know about. I wondered again, was it possible Ray was somehow cheating Miller? Was that the reason Ray brought Al Smith to be his muscle? Had Ray anticipated a confrontation with Miller that had nothing to do with Miller reneging on a promise?

I then thought back to Frankie Ray dying in the hospital while Blunt questioned him. Whatever Frankie Ray had said, Blunt had twice responded, *"Tell me."* I had assumed Blunt meant *Tell me who shot you.* But Blunt had also asked Ray *"Where?"* That didn't make any sense *if* Blunt had been asking Ray, *Tell me who shot you.* He knew full well *where* Ray had been shot. Blunt's question did, however, make sense if Ray had told Blunt he'd hidden money, and Blunt was asking him, *Tell me where.* Ray's response also made sense. *"That's your job to find out, Ernie. Tell George Miller to go to hell."*

That's your job, Ernie . . . *to find the money.* Tell George Miller to go to hell . . . *He's never going to find it.*

It also made me think about the search of Miller's home. Blunt found the holster, but he hadn't stopped there. He'd searched dressers, closets, and suitcases, just as someone had searched Joan Daley's suitcases. He'd even gone down into the basement and walked the concrete floor.

With Ray dead, and Miller in prison, Blunt would have unfettered time to try to find hidden money, if it existed. It also made sense for him to search Miller's address for clues, and to question Frankie Ray's sweetheart, Joan Daley. I mean, if anyone besides Ray knew where the money was hidden, it would be her, wouldn't it?

And Blunt's motivation?

Where to start? The Depression. Looming retirement. Meager pay compared to the luxurious life led by the criminals he put away. No more free meals after he'd retired.

Maybe Blunt had had enough. Maybe he saw this as his opportunity to set himself up for the rest of his life. One thing I had learned during my year on the job was everyone in Seattle was scamming for a nickel or a quarter or more—from the shoeshine boys to the mayor.

Why would Blunt be immune to such temptation? Heck, he used his position to get free meals, though the businesses had to be hurting and could ill afford to be giving away food.

But taking free food was a far cry from killing Joan Daley. Would Blunt go so far?

Maybe Blunt thought, after decades on the job with little to show for it, that this was his last chance to get what he believed he was due. And Blunt could have been the person in the black Ford that followed me down the alley behind Daley's boardinghouse. He had a similar car, though everyone seemed to have a black Ford. Could Blunt fear Joan Daley had told me something last night in her room? Like where to find the money?

I recognized this as speculation, my mind running wild. I needed facts to prove or disprove my burgeoning theory. I needed to know if Miller and Ray had been sitting on a brick of money.

That's where I would start.

The next question was whether I would have any competition from the other papers, but I doubted I would. Did I want any? Winn had said he would like to share information, but I didn't believe that for a second. He wanted my stories, the ones I worked so hard to get. And neither Greer nor Winn would find this story—if there was a story to be found. In addition to being lazy, they would have no impetus to investigate. They hadn't been in the hospital and heard Frankie Ray's dying words or seen Blunt's odd response. They hadn't gone to Miller's home and watched Blunt go through Miller's belongings, closets, and suitcases, and they hadn't spoken to Joan Daley, and thus didn't know there was more to the story and it revolved around money. They also hadn't been in her room shortly after Daley had died and didn't know someone had gone through her belongings searching for something—at least that's how it had looked to me.

They might question why Miller shot Ray, and what had been his motivation, but that had been answered by Smith when Blunt first interviewed him. Miller was a hothead with an explosive temper. He also had a thing for Joan Daley and had told Ray as much. Things got heated, then got out of hand. Miller lost his temper and killed Ray. Was that the whole story? I didn't think so, but I was certain Winn and Greer would accept it as the low-hanging fruit.

I was on my own.

I got up from my desk and walked into Phish's office. He usually worked long hours. "You still here?" he asked.

"Just working on a few things and getting prepared for the morning. I'm interested in whether Miller has a criminal record here in Seattle. Any thoughts?"

"Not really sure there's an easy way to go about it. Blunt could possibly help."

"Yeah," I said, not wanting to go to Blunt. "I tried him but he's too busy with the trial and all."

"Well, I suppose you could go through the back issues of the paper in the vault." Which is what Phish called the room where he kept the *Star*'s back issues. "Monday mornings we list the court cases for the week. You might find something in there."

Some weeks the court calendar was full. Others only one or two cases. The vault was located on the second story with the printing equipment—where the typesetters and press operator worked. I climbed the stairs. The second floor was hot even with the machines off and the hinged windows swung open. A couple of typesetters worked at long wooden tables but paid me no attention.

I went inside the vault and stared at the shelves of bound volumes—black books with red spines. A month's worth of newspapers in each volume, arranged by months of the year, with the most recent bound volume shelved near the front and older volumes shelved in the back. I pulled up my notes and confirmed when Miller had moved to Seattle. It had been three years ago, which narrowed the search to thirty-six volumes. Still a lot, but much less than I had anticipated.

I started with the most recent volumes and worked backward. I carried each volume to the typesetters' wooden bench and methodically went through the issues, running my finger down the page listing the legal cases before the court, though unsure what, exactly, I was looking for.

The task was painstakingly slow and the room uncomfortably hot. After a couple of hours, my handkerchief was wringing wet, and I'd been through just eighteen months of back issues. I decided to go back one more month in 1932 before I went downstairs to call my mother.

I pulled the volume for April 1932 from the shelf, opened the Monday, April 4, newspaper to the court cases section, and used my finger to scan the list. I didn't find George Miller's name but thought I recognized a name and read it twice. *The Musketeers.* McKinley had used that name in court to discredit Al Smith's testimony. He said it was a company owned by George Miller and Syd Brunn.

The Musketeers also owned the Lodge Café. I looked more closely and noticed the names of other establishments I thought I recognized. The Jungle Temple. The Olympic Tavern Roadhouse. In every instance, the Musketeers Company was identified as the owner and named as the defendant in an action brought by the state tax advisory commission. Case numbers were given for each separate action. I jotted down the information, then went back downstairs to my desk. The air on the first floor felt about twenty degrees cooler.

I opened my desk drawer where I kept my spent notebooks. I dated them and kept them in order so the information inside each was more readily accessible. I found the notebook I'd used when the Pom Pom case first broke and flipped through my notes to Detective Blunt telling me about his interview of George Miller with his attorney, John Sullivan, present. Blunt and McKinley had asked Miller about other establishments Miller owned. Miller had named ten, including the Lodge Café, the Jungle Temple, and the Olympic Tavern Roadhouse, as well as half a dozen disorderly houses he was rumored to own.

Interesting.

I'd get to the court clerk's office early and have the case files pulled to determine what the cases had been about, though I assumed it had to do with a failure to pay taxes.

Not very sexy, unless of course it meant the defendants had hidden a pile of money somewhere to avoid paying taxes. Enough money to change lives, which made me think of my mother and my family.

I was getting carried away, counting my chickens before they hatched, as my mother would say. I had no facts to support the accuracy of my speculation.

I picked up the phone, dialed the operator, and gave her the number of my home in Kansas City. She told me to hold. I'd have to tell Phish about the call. The office phones were for work only, and he'd question a call to Kansas City.

On the third ring my aunt Ida answered. It took me several questions before I learned my mother was home, and then another minute to get Aunt Ida to cede her the phone.

"Hi, William." My mother sounded tired.

"How is he, Mom?"

"He's resting."

"What does that mean? Is he going to be all right?"

"He's alert, talking, and he's moving all his extremities. At this point the doctors want him to rest."

"But he's going to be okay. Like he was before."

"The doctors said we have to be patient, give him some time, and let him recover. He's underweight and dehydrated."

"When will he be able to go home?"

"It will be a while, but not too long. When he's strong enough."

"I should come home, Mom. I can look for work in Kansas City."

"You have a job, William, and right now you can't do anything to jeopardize your income. We need your income, William. I'm sorry to lay that on your shoulders . . ."

"It's okay, Mom. I can spare a few more dollars each month. I just want to be sure you and Thomas and Ellie are all okay."

"We'll be fine. We'll get by."

"What about the house, Mom? The mortgage? And now the hospital bills?"

"They'll always be there, William."

"They'll take our house, Mom."

"I can't think of that now, William. The only thing I care about is your father getting better and coming home."

"Of course," I said, feeling guilty for adding to her worries. "How are Thomas and Ellie handling everything?"

"They've both been a big help. Thomas has stepped up around here, keeping things running, and Ellie has too. I'm going to take them to the hospital tomorrow. The nurse said your father could have visitors then."

"Tell him I wish I was there, and if he needs me, if he needs anything, I'll be on the first train to Kansas City."

"He knows, William. He's been reading your articles in the papers you've been sending home. He's so proud of you. He takes the paper and shows it to all the neighbors and now the nurses. He'd want you to stay in Seattle, at your job, covering this trial. I know he would."

"Okay," I said.

"Has Oma's ring shown up yet?"

"I don't know. I haven't been back to my boardinghouse today."

"I want every detail—how you propose to this young lady. And a photograph. Can you have someone take a photograph and send it to us? I'd like to see who's captured my son's heart."

"I will, Mom. And first chance we get, we'll come home to visit, so you can meet her in person. She's wonderful, Mom. You're going to love her . . . and her family. Two older brothers."

"I'll look forward to it. I need to go lie down. I'm very tired."

"I'll call again on Sunday."

"I love you, son."

The phone clicked just before I said, "I love you . . . Mom."

I went to bed that night missing Amara and my family, and troubled by Joan Daley's death and what I was learning about the trial. I locked my door, then shoved my chair under the doorknob, but I still couldn't fall asleep. My mind kept circling over the information I had learned and what it could all mean. To settle my thoughts, I read from *The Count of Monte Cristo*. I hoped it would lull me to sleep, but the plot was so engaging I didn't stop reading until a little after two a.m. I thought about Edmond Dantès and the treasure he'd found, how it could change lives. How it could change my family's lives.

Chapter 17

Friday morning, I slept an extra hour, physically and mentally exhausted. The jury would spend the first couple of hours at the Pom Pom Club with Judge Kincaid, who had forbidden anyone but the jurors, litigants, and attorneys from attending. That didn't deter Phish from sending Richard Kneip to photograph the jurors outside the nightclub.

I didn't stop at the bakery. I didn't want to intrude during the busiest time of the day and just have snippets of conversation with Amara. I'd wait until I had more time to tell her about my father. I walked downtown at a leisurely pace, intending to review the legal cases against the Musketeers for tax evasion in the clerk's office on the first floor of the courthouse. I picked up discarded copies of the *Seattle Daily Times* and the *Post-Intelligencer* from bus benches and arrived at the courthouse at nine thirty, giving me an hour and a half before the jurors and litigants returned. A line of six people waited inside the clerk's office. The matronly woman behind the counter moved at a snail's pace. I read the newspapers while waiting. When I finally reached the counter, forty-five minutes had passed. I smiled, but the woman was impassive. She listened to my request without comment then shoved forms at me.

"Fill out a separate form for each file you are seeking. Use pressure because there are carbon copies. When the form is filled out satisfactorily, tear off the pink copy. Put the remainder of the form in the basket. Someone will help you."

She looked over my shoulder to the next person waiting in line. I left the counter wondering why no one told me to fill out the forms when I first walked in, to save time.

Things went from bad to worse. I had to fill out the forms three times; my first two attempts were not to the clerk's approval because I'd smeared the carbons when I'd made a mistake and tried to scratch it out. When, at last, I'd satisfactorily completed the task, I didn't ask how long it would take for someone to pull the files, figuring my questions wouldn't expedite their retrieval and might prolong it.

I watched the minute hand tick on the clock above the clerk's counter. It was 10:37 a.m. when a man older than Moses, and a lot less lively, picked up my case slips from the in-box. He returned with the files at 10:46, just fourteen minutes before court would be in session.

I hurried to the counter and grabbed the files.

"Hold on," the clerk said. "I need to check each form with the case file to ensure you have the correct files."

"I'm sure it's fine," I said.

"It's procedure," she said.

"I'm in a hurry. I'm a reporter for the *Daily Star*, and I have to be in court for the Pom Pom trial by eleven sharp."

"Well, why didn't you say so?" She smiled but it quickly faded. Sarcasm. She held out her hand. "Forms. It's procedure."

She took her sweet time confirming the case numbers with the numbers on my forms before she released the files to me. "You can't remove them from the office . . ."

I wasn't listening. At 10:48 I hurried to a chair and quickly opened the first case file. As I had deduced from the litigants' names, the State Tax Commission had sued each establishment for tax evasion, specifically the failure to pay Business and Occupation Tax on pinball machine income, as well as the sale of cigarettes and alcohol. I scanned the pleading for the accused owners of the Musketeers and found George Miller and Syd Brunn listed as limited partners, whatever that meant.

My pulse quickened.

I put the first file aside, opened the second file, and gathered the same information. I glanced at the clock on the wall. I had about eight minutes to get to court. I scanned the other case files and found the same information. The State Tax Commission alleged the Musketeers to be a holding company for the individual bars and taverns, which I deduced meant technically the Musketeers Company owned the bars and taverns, not Miller or Brunn. In each instance, the commission estimated the amount of tax each establishment had either underpaid or failed to pay for each year. I wrote down the amounts but didn't have time to add them up, though it seemed a significant amount. I was about to close the last file when I had a thought. I searched for the state prosecuting attorney.

Laurence McKinley.

Again, I felt a quiver in my stomach. A coincidence?

I didn't have time to look at the other files, but I also didn't doubt I'd find McKinley's name. He clearly knew about the company, the Musketeers, because he'd brought the incorporation papers to court. The charges were the same in each file. There would have been no reason to assign a different prosecutor. I also didn't have time to assess what all this could possibly mean.

With just minutes to spare, I scanned the pleading for the State Tax Commission agent who had gone after the Jungle Temple. I wrote his name in my notebook, returned the files to the counter, slapped the bell, and took off running for the elevators in the lobby.

I made it to the courtroom doors just moments before the bailiff announced Judge Kincaid, and the jurist stormed up the steps to his desk. He looked even less happy than usual.

"Counsel." He addressed John Sullivan. "I have your pleading papers and understand you intend to bring a motion?"

Sullivan rose from his chair. The jury had not been recalled. "The defense requests this court grant a motion for directed verdict and dismiss all charges forthwith." The murmur in the gallery grew. I could hear reporters, caught off guard, hurriedly opening their satchels and pulling out notebooks and pencils, scratching furiously, myself included.

"And the basis for the defense's motion for directed verdict?" Judge Kincaid asked.

"The State has failed to meet its burden of proving that George Miller did not have a reasonable basis for fearing for his life when he shot Frankie Ray in self-defense. This was admitted by criminologist Luke May and the witnesses in the club the morning of the shooting. All testified Mr. Ray was quarrelsome and threatened Mr. Miller. They testified Mr. Ray had been in a violent mood and had shown a threatening attitude toward Miller."

It was apparent to me this was what Sullivan had been up to in court the prior few days. He hadn't asked a lot of questions on cross-examination because he didn't want to elicit testimony that could hurt the defense's motion. After several more minutes of argument by Sullivan, Kincaid turned to McKinley for rebuttal, and it dawned on me the judge would not have done so if he wasn't seriously considering throwing out the case.

McKinley stood. "Your Honor, the State concedes certain witnesses gave contradictory stories in court than they told detectives immediately after, or shortly after, the shooting. The jury can infer from these discrepancies that the witnesses did not tell the truth here in court. The veracity of each witness is for the jurors to decide, not defense counsel. Moreover, the burden is on the defense, not the State, to prove the killing of Frankie Ray was in self-defense. It's ludicrous for counsel to argue the State must prove the killing was *not* in self-defense."

Sullivan said, "The State's witnesses have not shaken the defense's plea of self-defense. The State has the burden to prove beyond a reasonable doubt Mr. Miller killed Mr. Ray without justification of any kind. The defense can and has certainly proven its case through cross-examination. Mr. Brunn, Mr. Smith, and Mr. Vahle all testified, under intense scrutiny, that Mr. Ray was quarrelsome, threatened Mr. Miller, and acted aggressively toward him, which would justify the killing. None testified, as postulated by State's counsel in his opening statement, that Mr. Ray came to collect a hospital debt incurred by Joan Daley. Miss Daley was not presented here in court to affirm the assertion. Nor has any other witness affirmed it. Moreover, criminologist Luke May admitted Mr. Miller could not have known whether Mr. Ray was or was not armed at the time Mr. Miller fired his weapon."

Not exactly, I thought, *but a good argument.*

"That was a ludicrous fabrication by the State, not the defense. That is the testimony before this jury," Sullivan said.

McKinley grew red in the face. "Mr. Smith changed his story. Mr. Brunn has changed his story, *twice*. It is for the good ladies and gentlemen of the jury to determine whether the witnesses lied on the witness stand and what is and is not ludicrous. Not defense counsel. Moreover, I resent being called a fabricator in a court of law."

Judge Kincaid rapped his gavel. "Gentlemen. You seem to have forgotten my admonition that each of you address this bench and not one another. I am issuing sanctions against both State and defense counsel in the amount of twenty-five dollars. Does anyone wish to try for fifty dollars? If you do, just open your mouth again."

Neither McKinley nor Sullivan responded.

Kincaid eyed them both. After a good while he said, "Now, as to the defense's motion for a directed verdict. The motion is denied. The State is correct in its assertion the witnesses presented seem to have changed their testimony between the time they were initially interviewed and the time they were called to this court to testify. Whether these witnesses are credible in their testimony will be for the jury to decide. Regardless, their failure to testify as anticipated does not equate to a finding that the defendant acted in self-defense. What it equates to is they either did not tell detectives the truth when questioned following the incident, or they did not tell the truth here in my courtroom, which has far graver consequences. Moreover, Luke May testified, given the victim's injuries, that Mr. Miller could not have shot in self-defense. Whether the defendant reasonably believed the victim was armed is up to the jury to decide.

"Unless there is anything else, I will instruct the bailiff to bring in the jury and we will proceed with the defense's opening statement."

Neither McKinley nor Sullivan dared raise another issue, and the judge instructed the bailiff to retrieve the jury. From the expressions on their faces, the jurors seemed curious about the delay. Once the jurors were seated, Judge Kincaid said, "Mr. Sullivan, does the defense wish to make an opening statement?"

Sullivan stood with a legal pad. "The defense does."

Sullivan approached the lectern looking like a Virginian cotton farmer in a tan seersucker suit and red bow tie.

"Ladies and gentlemen. In this instance, I'm afraid we must override the custom of not speaking ill of the dead. Frankie Ray was a professional boxer, with many bouts to his name. He was, at one time, considered a contender for the lightweight championship. But Frankie Ray didn't limit his fights to the boxing ring. Unfortunately, Mr. Ray also had a medical ailment. An ailment that made Ray a dangerous, violent man, a potential murderer, especially when drinking." Sullivan's voice rose like a Baptist minister preaching. "If ever a man courted death, on the morning of June 13, 1933, it was Frankie Ray."

Sullivan paced the jury box, running his hand along the railing and smiling as if he and the jurors were good friends. "Witnesses will testify to a long series of violent acts dating as far back as 1929—including spitting in a policeman's face, slashing a man's ear with a knife, badly wounding a girl by hurling a glass in her face, and frequent fights. Two physicians will testify Ray had a cerebral infection and suffered from delusions. My client, George Miller, is charged with killing a *man*. But he actually killed a brutal beast who was a menace to the community. Mr. Miller is not afraid to tell you this himself. He will, in fact, do so."

That answered the first question on my mind and, I suspected, everyone else's. George Miller would testify.

As Sullivan gave his opening, curiosity got the better of me, and I flipped back several pages to the notes I had taken on the tax cases. I added up the amounts the tax commissioner had deemed delinquent from each establishment. By the time I had finished, I'd calculated $54,000 owed in 1931 and another $52,000 in 1932.

"Whew," I said, louder than I expected. I looked up. Sullivan had turned his head to look at me, as had the jurors and others sitting in the gallery.

Kincaid rapped his gavel. "There will be no comments of any kind from the gallery," he said. "If there are, I will have that person escorted from the courtroom."

I put my head down, embarrassed, though I had no idea what I had even commented on in Sullivan's opening since I hadn't been listening to him.

I double-checked the amounts I had scribbled. The total number was staggering to a man who made $5.40 a week, and probably staggering to just about every other man fortunate to have a job in these hard times. The obvious question was what happened to all that money? Did Frankie Ray have it? That made sense if Miller and Brunn thought their residences and businesses might be searched by tax agents. In fact, Miller's disreputable houses had been raided. They could have given the loot to Ray and told him to safeguard it, maybe even paid him a bit to do so. Had Ray used some of the tax money to make payments on the Cadillac? Is that what made George Miller angry? Had he feared that the tax commissioner would become suspicious as to how Ray, a known friend of theirs, was making the payments and further investigate Miller and Brunn? It would explain why Frankie Ray was in the club, and maybe why he brought Al Smith, wrongly deducing Miller wouldn't harm him with a witness present. He might have misjudged Miller's temper. It also explained why Brunn and Miller had lied about what had happened. They couldn't testify they were having a meeting about money they had withheld from their taxes, not without implicating themselves. They had a vested interest to lie. And what of the other three men? Vahle, the waiter, and the caretaker? Maybe Miller made it worth each man's while to stick to the same story, thus corroborating his rushed explanation. Or maybe he threatened to fire them if they didn't go along. During a depression, the men couldn't take the chance they'd be out on the street, standing in a soup line and living beneath cardboard in Hooverville. It would explain why the three men, who hadn't witnessed the shooting, had stayed at the club. It could also be why Frankie Ray had Joan Daley making payments on the Cadillac, so he could tell Miller and Brunn, if they asked, that the money came from Daley. The lie would have worked, too, until Joan Daley got hurt jumping from a second-story window and no longer had a means to make an income, let alone pay fifty-five dollars a month on a Cadillac.

Miller and Brunn had likely questioned Ray, maybe even were friendly at first. It would explain why the witnesses said Ray and Brunn were smiling and getting along. Brunn was likely smart enough to know they couldn't kill Ray until they knew where he'd hidden their money. But then the quarrel escalated, and Miller had let his temper get the best of him. He shot Ray before he and Brunn had determined where Ray hid the money. That explained why someone went through Joan Daley's room. She was the logical starting point.

"The defense calls George Miller to the witness stand," Sullivan said.

I raised my gaze and watched George Miller rise, button his suit jacket, and stride toward the witness stand, ear trumpet in hand.

This is all one big con, I thought.

This trial was a sucker's game, as Ernie Blunt had called the craps played at the club with shaved dice. Miller and the others were lying to protect a fortune. And Blunt was lying about what Frankie had said to him while dying in the hospital, maybe intent on finding the missing fortune for himself.

Then I had another thought.

Maybe that's why Blunt called me with the scoop in the first place, and not a more experienced reporter like Winn or Greer. Maybe he knew from the moment he got the call of a murder at the Pom Pom Club that money was involved, a lot of money. Maybe he'd used me and the *Daily Star* to disseminate information to the public from which the jury would be chosen. Maybe he knew I'd be so happy to have the scoop that I wouldn't question the reason he'd called me. Maybe I was just a sucker in the game, and Early Winn had been correct.

I don't know what you're playing at, son, but you're playing with fire. You're the one who's going to get burned, he had said. *You don't have the experience for a story this big.*

Maybe not, but I was now in it up to my eyeballs. Like it or not.

And I didn't like being made to feel like a chump.

Chapter 18

Everyone in the gallery sat up, anticipating this, the main act. George Miller took the stand looking like a matinee idol. He used his ear trumpet when he took the oath to tell the truth, the whole truth, and nothing but the truth.

I doubted it.

Miller appeared composed, not the least bit like a man facing the death penalty or life behind bars. Maybe because he already knew the State would never convict him. Maybe Miller had already reached a juror, the way someone had reached the witnesses. Maybe he'd already made it worth a juror's while to hold out and find Miller not guilty.

Miller raised his ear trumpet and leaned forward as Sullivan ran him through preliminaries. Then Sullivan asked, "Did Ray come to the club alone?"

"No. He came in with another man and they went to a table. Ray said to me, 'George, have a drink,' and I did. I drank a little bourbon with water in it."

"Did Ray talk to you about a girl?"

"Ray said to me at one point, 'Why don't you ask me about my girl?' He sounded angry. So I said, 'Pardon me. How is your gal, Frankie?'"

"Did he tell you he needed money to pay Joan Daley's medical bills?"

"No. He did not."

Sullivan moved to different areas, questioning Miller about his dream to own a classy nightclub. He then asked about the fatal shooting, and for the first time Miller's voice broke. If it was an act, I couldn't tell. Miller was very convincing.

"Can you tell us why Mr. Ray was quarrelsome with you?" Sullivan asked.

"Ray wanted money to make a payment on an automobile, a Cadillac, and I told him I wouldn't lend him the money. I said he shouldn't have bought such an expensive car in these difficult times if he couldn't afford it."

It was a lie. I was certain. A lie to appeal to the jurors who couldn't afford such a car, but Miller said it with such conviction and ease it sounded natural, and some jurors looked like they believed him.

"What happened next?" Sullivan asked.

"He followed me into the washroom, yelling and screaming and gnashing his teeth."

That odd saying again. *Gnashing his teeth.* It was certainly scripted.

"What happened next?"

"I stepped from the washroom, and I heard a growl behind me. When I turned, Frankie was standing there, wild eyed." Miller was laying it on thick. "So I said, 'What's the matter, Frankie? Are you blowing your top off?'"

"What did you do?"

"I hurried to the ballroom, figuring it best to get away from him. But Frankie came after me. He was crouching, like a prizefighter. I said, 'Don't do that, Frankie.' But he kept coming toward me. He was grinding his teeth. It was making a peculiar sound. I backed away from him, but he followed. Then he hollered, 'I'll kill you. I'll rob you if you won't give me the money.'"

"Then what did you do?"

"What could I do? I pulled my gun."

Miller's voice became a whisper. This was an Academy Award–winning, rehearsed performance. "I didn't want to, but he kept coming, so I shot him. He lunged at me. So, I shot him again." His voice broke.

"Did you intend to kill Ray?"

"No. Absolutely not."

"Did you fear for your life?"

McKinley pushed back his chair to stand, but Miller answered the leading question quickly.

"Absolutely."

"What did you do after you fired the second shot?"

"I hesitated a moment. Then I went into the barroom and I told my partner, Syd Brunn, to call the police, and I put the gun on the safe and we waited."

"How long before the police arrived?"

"Just a few minutes."

"And did detectives arrive also?"

"After the ambulance took the victim away."

Sullivan stepped back and pointed to State's counsel table. "Did you speak to Detective Blunt?"

"Several times. He wouldn't let any of us leave the club, though I hadn't had any sleep and was dog tired and upset."

Sullivan paused here to give Miller a chance to drink from a glass of water and presumably to give the jurors a respite.

"Now, George, when Detective Blunt and the other officers arrived, you told them a false story; didn't you?" Sullivan made it sound like Miller was a child who'd taken a cookie without getting his mother's permission.

"I did," Miller replied. "I was frightened, and I wasn't thinking clearly."

"You, however, feared for your life?" Sullivan said, clearly prompting Miller.

McKinley didn't let it slip. "Objection, Your Honor. Counsel is testifying for the witness."

"Keep your shirt on," Sullivan retorted.

"The objection is sustained," Kincaid said. "Do not testify for the witness, Counsel. Moreover, your remark is improper and will be noted, as I previously warned both attorneys."

"I apologize, Your Honor." Sullivan addressed Miller. "Were there other incidents you experienced in which Mr. Ray made you believe he was a highly dangerous character?"

McKinley again objected. "Still testifying. No foundation."

Kincaid sighed. "Mr. Sullivan, set a foundation without testifying."

"Mr. Miller, did you believe Mr. Ray was a highly dangerous character?"

"From past incidents I did."

"Can you tell the jurors about those incidents?"

"There was a time . . . April eleventh, I believe it was, when Frankie came into the nightclub drunk, and he started in with a gal at the bar, and her date told Frankie to ease off. Frankie laid him out with one punch. So I had the bartender get Frankie out of the club."

"Any other incidents?"

"Another time, also in April, we were in a café and Frankie pulled a knife, but I talked him into putting it down."

"Did Mr. Ray tell you he suffered from a cerebral malady?"

McKinley rose. "Objection, Your Honor. There is no foundation this witness, who is not in the medical profession, has any basis to make such a determination. The defense should be admonished to first put on some scientific evidence to support such innuendo."

Sullivan turned on McKinley. "That is exactly our intention," he said. "I am simply asking Mr. Miller if Mr. Ray ever told him he was suffering from a cerebral malady."

"I will allow the question, but I will also caution the jury that it should not conclude from Mr. Miller's testimony that if Mr. Ray said he had a cerebral malady that Mr. Ray did indeed have one."

Sullivan asked the question again.

"He told me he had a cerebral malady, and was seeing a doctor, a urologist, for treatment," Miller said on cue. The insinuation was Ray had a venereal disease and it had impacted his brain, like Al Capone. Several jurors made a face or shook their heads.

After another hour of questioning, Sullivan concluded. "Your witness," he said to McKinley.

McKinley rose slowly and took his time approaching the witness stand. After a dramatic pause he said, "Mr. Miller, who is Catherine Miller?"

Sullivan had barely put his butt on his chair seat when he shot back up. "Objection. No foundation."

McKinley said, "Your Honor, the State endeavors to prove what the State believes to have been the motive for the killing, as has been discussed in court."

"The witness will answer the question," Kincaid said.

Miller held his trumpet to his ear and replied softly, "An acquaintance."

"Miss Miller is also known as Katheryn Conner; is she not?"

The woman at his home, I thought. The one sitting in the first row in the gallery dressed to the nines. "I don't know."

"You live with her, do you not?"

"I do."

"But you don't know her surname?"

"She never told me."

"And you say, although living with her, she is just an acquaintance?"

"She is."

"You and she owned and operated the establishment the Pink Fox; didn't you?"

"I didn't."

"Miss Conner did; didn't she?"

"I don't know."

"You also don't know how she makes a living?"

"I don't know."

"Joan Daley worked at the Pink Fox establishment; didn't she?"

"I don't know."

"But you do know Joan Daley; don't you?"

"I know her slightly."

"Another female acquaintance?"

"Ray introduced me to her sometime in the spring, I think. The spring of 1932."

"Where did this introduction take place?"

"It was a café in Seattle. In fact, I tried to patch up a quarrel between Frankie and Joan, but she said she was through with Ray because of his drinking and his fighting."

"Would this be at the Lodge Café?" McKinley asked.

"It would."

"You own that establishment; don't you?"

"Not me," Miller said.

"What other establishments do you have an interest in?"

"Just the Pom Pom Club."

"Don't you also have an interest in the Lodge Café, the Jungle Temple on the Everett Highway, and the Olympic Tavern Roadhouse?"

Miller shook his head, defiant. "Not me."

McKinley went back to his table and picked up sheets of paper. "I have here incorporation papers for those establishments, which are held under an umbrella company called the Musketeers. Those business papers were filed by your personal business attorney, Arnie A. Chevas."

"He's a very good lawyer."

"The incorporation papers indicate the company owners are you and Syd Brunn."

"I was told I didn't own those companies, that the umbrella company owns them. I don't really know how it all works. I leave that to you suits to handle."

"Mr. Ray asked you for money to pay Miss Daley's hospital expenses for injuries she suffered when she jumped from a second-story window of the Pink Fox during a federal raid on that establishment; didn't he?"

"No. He never did."

"You say Joan Daley confided in you she was done with Frankie Ray?"

"That's what she told me."

"She confided this very personal information about breaking up with Frankie Ray when, as you earlier testified, you hardly knew her?"

Miller didn't immediately answer. Then he said, "I guess she didn't have no one else to talk to."

"I guess not," McKinley said. "Mr. Miller, you testified you told falsehoods to the officers and detectives who arrived and questioned you. Let's be clear and call a spade a spade, shall we. By *falsehood* you mean you lied."

"My mind was in turmoil. I was excited and panicky, sir. I was frightened. And I was tired from no sleep. Why, eight or nine policemen shot questions at me. *You did this! You did that!* It was enough to get anybody rattled."

"You concocted a story that Frankie Ray had a gun and tried to engage in a holdup, and then you got the men remaining in the bar to back up your story. That's why not one of you called for an ambulance. You were too busy making up the story."

"I didn't concoct nothing."

"And yet Mr. Brunn, Mr. Vahle, Archie Brown, and Sandy Allen each told the exact same lie that you told Detective Blunt."

"Maybe they overheard what I was telling Ernie. I don't hear so good, so maybe I was talking louder than I should have been," Miller said. Then he rushed the next two sentences. "I wanted to protect the place. I was trying to protect the police too."

This last comment seemed to catch everyone by surprise, including McKinley. "Protect the police? How?"

"The police knew about the drinking and gambling in the club, but so long as there were no problems, they let us be. I thought the shooting would drag those officers into the mix and maybe get them in trouble for not coming down on us."

A murmur rippled over the gallery. I had my lede.

Police knew about Pom Pom nightclub drinking and gambling.

Pizzazz, Shoe! Pizzazz!

McKinley said, "And who were these policemen who permitted gambling and the drinking of liquor? Can you name them?" It sounded like a challenge.

Miller took it. "Officers Foster Heslop and Carl Norris."

It felt like two poker players calling each other's bluffs. "Did Officers Foster Heslop and Carl Norris go to the Pom Pom Club when they were on duty?"

"And off duty."

More ripples. This time loud enough to get the attention of Judge Kincaid, who scowled and moved to raise the gavel.

"Did other police officers go there while on or off duty?"

"Sure. And a lot of politicians too."

Larger ripples, waves. Miller's testimony had the hallmarks of a subtle threat that he would name names if pushed. It made me think of the black book Detective Blunt had found at the club that included the names of prominent Seattleites.

"You lied to protect the police and the politicians? Is that your testimony?" McKinley asked without asking the names of the politicians.

"Yes."

"You admitted to gambling taking place at your club. Did you admit that the craps tables were rigged?"

Sullivan rose quickly, red in the face. "Objection, Your Honor. The question is completely inappropriate and impugns my client's integrity. The defense requests an immediate mistrial."

"The objection is sustained—for lack of relevance to these proceedings, not because anyone was impugned. Mr. McKinley, you will refrain from any further line of questioning along that subject. The defense's request for a mistrial is, again, denied. I also want to caution the jury this case is not to be decided on the basis of 'pleasantries' between opposing counsel. Continue, Mr. McKinley."

"Isn't it true you shot Ray because of a quarrel regarding Joan Daley's hospital bill?" McKinley said.

"I told you I shot him because I was afraid he had a knife or a pistol and wanted to kill me."

"You didn't see a knife or a pistol though; did you?"

"He put his hand to his hip, and I was afraid he was reaching for a weapon, that he was going to kill me. I shot him to protect my life."

"I want to read to you statements you gave to Detective Blunt the morning of the murder."

"I don't remember talking to Detective Blunt. I was panicky and I hadn't had any sleep."

McKinley went through the statement anyway. He clearly intended to establish Miller would lie about anything. After each transcribed sentence, McKinley asked if the statement was a lie.

It was painstakingly slow.

When McKinley finished with the statement, he set it down on counsel's table, then approached the witness stand. "Why'd you shoot him twice?" McKinley asked.

"Frankie had this social disease and it got worse when he was intoxicated. He became violent. I'd heard about it, and I'd personally seen it. Anyone would have feared him."

"You testified you had a drink with Mr. Ray that morning and later saw him drinking at the bar?"

"I told you he had like twelve drinks. They were all buying rounds."

"You owned the club, but you did nothing to stop your bartender from serving alcohol to Mr. Ray, whom you now claim you knew was a vicious drunk whom you feared?"

Miller paused like a spider caught in his own web. Then he said, "Well, a man has the money . . . Who am I to decide how he spends it? Maybe I didn't want to make Ray angry, knowing how he could get."

"Or maybe you knew you had nothing to fear because you carried a loaded gun?"

"That's not true."

McKinley chuckled. "I think we've established you wouldn't know the truth, Mr. Miller, if it bit you in the nose."

"Objection," Sullivan said. "The defense moves for an immediate mistrial."

Kincaid leaned forward. "The objection is sustained. The motion is, again, denied."

Before he could be admonished, McKinley said, "The State has concluded its cross-examination, Your Honor."

Sullivan's brief redirect examination focused on the police officers who had regularly come into the club, trying to smear the bright line between law and order and underworld crime.

When we broke for our afternoon recess, I hurried from the courtroom to the phone booth. As I settled in and dialed my office, Early Winn slid into the booth beside me. I lowered my voice, sensing he was eavesdropping.

"Shoe? I can hardly hear you," Phish said.

"Have to keep my voice down. Winn is in the booth beside me."

"They let photographers into the club this morning. Kneip got in and got some great pictures and we put together the lede of a story. What else do you have?"

"Miller testified," I said. "About social diseases and about police coming into the Pom Pom Club and turning a blind eye to the gambling and liquor."

"Now you're getting it, Shoe! Let me get Kravitz and you can dictate what you have so far. I'll reach out to L. L. Norton, and the named officers, for comment. Shoot me their names."

When finished, I pushed from the phone booth. Winn stepped out of his phone booth at that same moment. I didn't for a minute believe it was a coincidence.

"Early," I said.

"Not lately. Seems you keep beating me to the punch, William."

"Well, the *Star is* an afternoon newspaper," I said.

"Yes. What did you think of Miller?"

"He sounded convincing." He didn't. Not to me.

"But you don't think he's telling the truth."

"Do you?"

"Tell me why you don't think he is."

I wasn't about to tell Winn anything. "The witnesses all changed their stories. Some multiple times. It was orchestrated, and Miller had incentive to be the orchestra leader."

"So why do you think Miller shot Ray?"

I stuck to the testimony. "The evidence indicates Ray wanted the money to pay Joan Daley's hospital bill, and when Miller wouldn't give it to him, an argument ensued and got out of hand."

"Seems flimsy; doesn't it?"

It did, certainly, and Winn's question made me wonder if Winn knew more than I was giving him credit for. "I don't know. Not if Ray became violent and Miller had such a bad temper."

"You buy the argument of self-defense?"

"Not for me to decide. That's for the jury."

"Shame about Joan Daley; don't you think?"

"Shame," I said.

"Heck of a coincidence. The timing, I mean."

"Yeah. Seems odd," I said.

"Heard you were at her boardinghouse," he said.

"Who told you that?" I asked, momentarily panicked.

"A police officer said he spoke to you the morning of Joan Daley's death at the boardinghouse."

"Oh. Yeah. Phish got a tip and sent me over."

"See or hear anything of interest?"

I shook my head. Winn gave me a curious look, like he didn't believe me. "I better get back to the courtroom," I said. Winn's meaty hand stopped me.

"The offer still stands. To share information."

I didn't reply and hurried to the courtroom.

I wondered if Winn was fishing, or if he knew I was onto something. I wondered if maybe he'd seen me in the court clerk's office. I didn't have time to ponder it for long. The afternoon was a series of defense witnesses called to corroborate Miller's testimony regarding the prior occasions in which Ray had become violent. The subject of the police at the club again came up.

On cross-examination of Lloyd Inglis, who ran the ballroom at the Pom Pom Club, McKinley asked if the front door was used to warn the operators of approaching police officers. Inglis chuckled. "That wasn't necessary."

"No? Why not?"

"Because the police were usually in the club. Politicians too. Like the night Ray was ejected for fighting. Ray kept yelling, 'I'm a friend of Johnnie Dore's and I'll have your job.'"

"Johnnie Dore, the mayor?" McKinley asked, which got the attention of everyone in the courtroom.

Inglis shrugged. "That's what Ray said."

Dolores Palmer, an acquaintance of Ray's, was the last witness of the week and testified Ray had hurled a heavy water tumbler into her friend's face after she refused to dance with him at the Hungerford Hotel.

Although it was only four o'clock, Judge Kincaid concluded early. "It's Friday afternoon, after all, and I'm sure you're eager to get home to your loved ones and enjoy a relaxing weekend." He cautioned the jurors not to read the newspapers or listen to the radio, and not to speak to anyone about the trial or what the witnesses said in court. Then he dismissed them.

Chapter 19

I rode the elevator to the first floor. Not wanting to leave the courthouse and have another encounter with Early Winn, I turned for the exit onto Fourth Avenue. It was a shorter walk up the hill to the *Daily Star* offices anyway, and since Amara was with her cousins this weekend, I had no reason to walk up First Avenue.

As I made my way along the hallways, I came upon the stenciled glass of a door identifying the office of the State Tax Commission. The lights behind the glass remained on.

I stopped to pull out my notepad from my satchel and flipped through the pages for the name of the tax commissioner who had pursued George Miller for withholding business taxes. Jacob Rosen.

I tried the door handle and found it unlocked. Before entering I checked the hallway to be sure no one had followed me or was watching me. No one was. Paranoid for certain, but with good reason. I stepped inside to a wooden counter and a young woman seated at her desk.

"Can I help you?" she asked, pleasant enough and about my age.

"I was hoping to speak with Commissioner Jacob Rosen."

"Do you have an appointment with Commissioner Rosen?"

"I don't." I smiled, recognizing she was perhaps the gatekeeper. "I don't make enough money to have tax issues."

She returned my smile and lowered her voice conspiratorially. "I'd say you're lucky. What do you do?"

"I'm a reporter for the *Daily Star*," I said. "I was in Judge Kincaid's courtroom on the eighth floor—"

"The Pom Pom Club trial," she interjected. "I've been reading about it every day. You make it sound so exciting. I mean, all the different kinds of people and what they're wearing, everything. It sounds glamorous. And horrific. The shooting part," she rushed to add. So maybe Phish was onto something.

"So a tax issue came up in court today, and I was hoping to talk to Commissioner Rosen about the matter. Is he still in?"

"Nobody here leaves before five o'clock sharp," she said. "It's a rule."

"Is he available, then?"

"I can check." She picked up the phone and a moment later she whispered, though I could tell from her facial expressions and pauses that Rosen was perplexed as to what I might have questions about. She covered the mouthpiece. "What's your name?"

"William Shumacher with the *Daily Star*."

She repeated the information into the phone. Then she added, "He's covering the Pom Pom nightclub shooting. He said a tax issue came up in court—" She made a face and slowly replaced the handset. "He hung up."

"He did?"

"Sorry. So do you work nights?" she asked.

"Not usually," I said.

"I don't either," she said. "I'm almost always free."

It dawned on me that she wanted me to ask her out, creating an awkward pause, but I was rescued when a young man quickly came around the corner.

"William Shumacher?" He put out his hand. "Jacob Rosen. You say a tax issue came up in court today?"

Rosen had clearly hung up his phone and hurried to the counter. He looked to be early thirties, with dark hair. I had expected an overweight, middle-aged man reluctant to talk. "I was hoping to ask you a few questions about some testimony in court. A case you worked on. The Lodge Café?"

He swung open a gate for me to step through. "We can talk in my office."

"I work until five, Mr. Shumacher," the woman at the counter said.

I followed Rosen along narrow hallways with small exterior offices. The interior was a bullpen of desks—men and women hard at work stabbing the keys of adding machines and typewriters. Rosen directed me into an office, then followed and closed the door. He squeezed behind a desk almost the width of the office. On the floor were file boxes filled with documents. Stacks on his desk teetered as if in danger of toppling.

"Sorry for the mess," he said. It was no doubt a programmed response since he had his back to me and couldn't have seen me eyeing the clutter.

"Looks like my office," I said. "Except I don't have an office. Just a desk."

He sat in what looked like an uncomfortable wooden chair that creaked in protest each time he moved. "What is it I can help you with?"

I had to be careful how I approached the subject, not certain of his thoughts and whether he might be guarded. I stuck to what we'd already discussed. "Like I said, the prosecutor, Laurence McKinley, was asking George Miller questions about the Lodge Café, and the subject of ownership came up."

"And Mr. Miller said the café was owned by a holding company."

"He actually denied owning the company."

Rosen shook his head and chuckled.

"But McKinley introduced evidence Miller and Syd Brunn owned the Musketeers holding company. I don't know what that means, exactly."

"We're starting to see more and more of this with the recent change to the tax laws designed to relieve the tax burden on farmers and make the tax laws more equitable by taxing business owners. Attorneys are creating these holding companies to shield their clients from personal tax liability when someone gets hurt in the establishment or we bring a delinquency action."

"It appears that the Musketeers owned other companies also," I said, going back over my notes. "I believe in addition to the Pom Pom Club and the Lodge Café, it also owned the Jungle Temple and the Olympic Tavern Roadhouse."

Rosen didn't immediately respond.

"Am I right?"

"Sorry. I thought you were going to continue."

"Are there more?" I asked.

Rosen laughed. "About a dozen if you count the disorderly houses Miller owns. It's a lawyer's ploy, and Miller has one of the best business lawyers in the state. They lobbied the legislature to pass the law to protect individual assets, but it's being abused to *hide* assets."

"Is that what happened in the actions against Mr. Miller's businesses?"

"I can't say specifically, but I can give you a scenario we frequently encounter. The businesses have a cash register, but the owner only rings up maybe one in five or one in ten sales. This lowers the business's taxable income. The money not rung up goes into the business owner's pockets."

"I pulled the litigation files in the clerk's office and added up the numbers for 1931 and 1932. It was over a hundred thousand dollars delinquent. Is that right?"

Rosen sat back with a creak from his chair and gave me a thin smile. "Off the record?"

I hadn't yet pulled out my notebook and pencil. "Absolutely," I said.

"That's the amount we could document. The actual amount is likely far higher, in my experience with these cases. Possibly double that. Maybe closer to two hundred and fifty thousand." My jaw must have hit the floor because Rosen said, "Jaw dropping; isn't it? You have to remember we're talking about cash spent on liquor, cigarettes, gaming machines, and gambling."

"So where is the money?"

Rosen shrugged. "Hidden somewhere. They can't put it in the bank because we can track the deposits and compare it with the documented sales on their tax forms. We had federal agents raid several of Mr. Miller's establishments, including his disorderly houses and his personal residence." Which is why Joan Daley had jumped out a second-story window. "We found some money, but nowhere near that amount. I suspect Miller has someone keeping a close watch on it for him."

The most likely person would have been Katheryn Conner, but if that was the case, it didn't explain how Frankie Ray got his hands on the money to pay for the Cadillac. So maybe Miller didn't trust Conner and chose Ray instead, a rube they thought they could manipulate.

"What's the investigation's status?" I asked.

"It remains open. We were negotiating with Miller's personal counsel on a payment plan to close the files when the Pom Pom shooting occurred. That put everything on hold."

"'A payment plan'?"

"Like paying off a car or a house bought on credit," Rosen said. "The deputy prosecutor will reach a deal with the business owner's counsel and agree to accept pennies on the dollar. Likely ten percent."

"Why would the deputy prosecutor agree to pennies on the dollar?"

"Again, we're off the record?"

"Still off."

"It happens in all our cases. It's next to impossible to conclusively prove how much alcohol or how many cigarettes a business sells, or how much money it makes on the pinball machines and the gambling. It would take a prolonged and expensive forensic examination, and the government doesn't have the money to hire more agents during a depression. The prosecutor's office encourages their prosecutors to reach a compromise based on a commissioner's estimates. We know it. And the attorneys for the business owners know it. Just like everyone knows the police and the politicians are paid to look the other way when it comes to vices like drinking alcohol, gambling, and prostitution. If the crime isn't hurting anyone, they're just not interested in devoting time and resources to pursuing it. Besides, most of them have a vested interest."

"They're paid off?"

"I didn't say that. It would cost me my job. You can infer what you want. But don't be naïve, and for God's sake don't quote me."

"No, I was just—this is just background."

"The businesses don't become a problem until something like the Pom Pom Club shooting happens and the club is in the spotlight. Then everyone gets worried about whose name is going to come out in the newspapers."

Which was exactly what Miller seemed to have done today by implicating the police officers and mentioning the mayor by name. Maybe it was an intended shot over the bow, a warning.

Rosen looked suddenly concerned. "I could lose my job," he said, "telling you some of this that isn't public record."

"You won't," I said. "It was off the record, and I'll honor that agreement."

Rosen considered the clock on his desk.

"I don't want to keep you," I said.

He walked me to his office door but didn't immediately open it. "If I might offer a piece of advice, Mr. Shumacher?"

"Sure."

"I get paid to look for hidden money. It's my job, and everyone—the business owners, the attorneys, and the politicians—accepts it, just like we accept that businesses are going to do everything possible to cheat on paying their taxes."

"Okay."

"Two hundred thousand dollars is a lot of money. In my line of work, I've seen people do some horrible things to protect far less."

Like shooting Frankie Ray, I thought. *And pushing Joan Daley out a window.*

"You're saying I need to be careful."

"I'm telling you not to dig too deep. You don't have the tax commissioner's office to protect you if you turn over stones someone doesn't want turned over."

Joan Daley had said much the same thing.

I paused in the hallway with another problem. The young woman at the counter.

"There's a back exit," Rosen said. "I've helped others to escape."

As I departed, I was more worried than I had ever been, and more certain than I had previously been that Joan Daley had not jumped out a window. Rosen was right. A quarter of a million dollars could change lives, and the fewer people who knew about it, or had access to it, the larger the share. And the people in line to get a share weren't exactly upstanding citizens. They were underworld members and, in George Miller's case, willing to kill.

I stepped outside, turned the corner at James Street, and nearly walked into Ernie Blunt, who stood with his back against the King County Correctional Facility, smoking a cigarette.

"Holy moly," I said, startled.

Blunt smiled. "You're awful jumpy, Shoe."

"What are you doing here?" I asked.

"I could ask you the same question. Court adjourned nearly an hour ago. Don't you have plans with that nice young lady from Giovacchini's Bakery on a Friday night?"

"No. She's . . ." I stopped. "How do you know about her? I've never mentioned her."

Another smile. "It's my business to know things. You should know that, Shoe."

"She's with her family this weekend."

"So you thought you'd hang around the State Tax Commission." Blunt flicked the cigarette into the gutter and poked at his teeth with a toothpick. "Seems a young man like you could find something more interesting to do with a free evening. *King Kong* is opening at the Green Parrot."

Before I could answer, the receptionist rounded the building corner and smiled at me. "Oh," she said. "Hi again."

"Hi," I said. "I was waiting for you. I was wondering if you wanted to have a drink?" She beamed. I felt awful leading her on, but asking her out had been the only excuse I could think of for why I had been in the tax commissioner's office.

"Sure. Give me a minute to fix my face." She removed a compact from her purse and stepped back around the building corner.

Blunt smiled but his eyebrows knitted together. "The cat's away, so young William will play? Good for you. You're young. You should play the field a bit."

"So, what then are you doing here?" I asked to change the subject.

"Me? I'm old and divorced," Blunt said. "Not in a rush to get anywhere."

The young woman came back wearing mascara, face powder, and red lipstick. "Ready," she said.

"Don't let me keep you." Blunt tipped his fedora. "You two have a nice evening."

I started up the street with the young woman at my side. "This is such a surprise," she said. "I mean, I'm hardly ever available at this late notice on a Friday night."

"Shoe?" I turned at the sound of Blunt's voice. "The woman who lives behind Joan Daley's boardinghouse couldn't help us out with a sketch of the mystery man she saw leaving the building the night Daley jumped out the window."

"No?" I said. "That's too bad, I guess."

"Only if it wasn't a suicide. Everything indicates it was. Unless you found out anything more?"

Was he giving me a chance to come clean? I couldn't tell. I shook my head. "I haven't."

"What did you think about Miller's testimony police officers frequented the club and saw people drink liquor and gamble?"

I recalled what Commissioner Rosen had said. "I guess it's okay, so long as nobody gets hurt."

Blunt flicked his toothpick onto the sidewalk. "Seems to be the separation line; doesn't it? Until somebody gets hurt."

Chapter 20

Out of the stream of words that flowed without commas or periods, I learned the woman's name was Helen Ruth. "Like the baseball player, though we aren't related."

I took her to the Central Cafe, in part because I didn't know any other bars. It was crowded, and I didn't think we'd be able to get a booth, which meant a quick beer and a quicker getaway.

"There's a booth opening." Helen grabbed my hand and yanked me to a booth near the back. The two men had barely stood when Helen slid onto the vinyl seat. "Take the other side," she said. "If you aren't assertive here you can end up standing all night."

My luck. She'd been here before.

The waitress was the same woman who had served me and Ernie Blunt our free lunches. "You're back," she said to me. "The reporter for the *Daily Star*."

"Yes," I said, wilting under her intense glare.

"What can I get you?" she asked Helen.

Helen looked about, then lowered her voice. "Any chance a girl could get a gin rickey?"

I'd never heard of it, but it sounded expensive.

"We'll put it in a beer glass," the waitress said.

"And how about you?" the waitress asked me.

"I'll have a beer," I said.

"Aren't you going to eat?" the waitress asked Helen.

"I'm famished," Helen said.

I mentally added up the money in my pocket and knew I didn't have enough for two meals. "I ate late," I said. "During a break in the trial."

"I'll have the macaroni and cheese," Helen said without contemplating the menu. She'd definitely been here before.

The waitress gave me a sardonic smile as if to say, *What goes around comes around,* and she was going to enjoy it.

"Wow. You're famous," Helen said, gushing. "Even the waitresses know who you are."

I smiled.

Helen kept up an animated, one-sided conversation about her job, her aunt who worked in the mayor's office and knew a lot of people, and her family. I nodded politely and smiled when appropriate in between sips of my beer. I kept thinking about what Commissioner Rosen had said, which Blunt had also seemed to confirm. A quarter of a million dollars was a lot of money, enough to change lives, especially with no end in sight to the Depression. Someone who dug too deeply for information that could put that much money in jeopardy could get hurt.

Helen's macaroni and cheese arrived. The waitress seemed to delight in putting the check on the tabletop. "I'll take care of that when you're ready," she said to me. "Unless the young lady will be wanting something more?"

"I'll let you know," Helen said.

Helen didn't offer me any macaroni and cheese and continued her soliloquy while eating.

"I've been blabbering on and on," she finally said. "I haven't asked you anything about yourself."

"Not much to tell." I explained I had moved from Kansas City to Seattle for a reporter's position at the *Star*.

"How exciting," she said. "I would never have the courage to move that far from home. I mean, I wouldn't know anybody. No family. No relatives. No friends. Gosh." She reached across the table and squeezed my hand. "You're so brave, William." She pushed aside half her macaroni. "I can't eat another bite. Should we share a dessert? They have apple pie à la mode."

"I have to get home," I said. "I have to be at the newspaper early in the morning."

"Tomorrow's Saturday." She sounded disappointed—though I couldn't be sure whether it was about me cutting short the date or not getting the apple pie à la mode.

"The paper never sleeps," I said, quoting Phish. "Seven days a week."

"I hadn't even thought about that," she said. "No days off. Not even the holidays. I once visited my aunt in the hospital on Thanksgiving. Can you imagine? Pretty much ruined my holiday."

I'm sure it didn't do much for her aunt either, but I didn't say that.

"So, you don't have much free time at all?"

"I really don't. Very little. Hardly any. The pay isn't very good either."

That was all Helen needed to hear to slide to the edge of her seat. "You'll at least walk me home; won't you? I mean, it wouldn't look proper for a young woman to be leaving a bar alone; would it?"

"Sure," I said, happy to be leaving. I slid from the booth and let others standing know it was free. I retrieved Helen's jacket from a hook on the outside of our booth and helped her slip it on, then slid on my own jacket and my cap.

I left money on the table for the check, and as Helen and I started for the door, she slid her arm beneath mine. "I hope you don't mind. I'm afraid I may be a little tipsy."

"Where do you live?" I asked.

"Just up the hill. On Ninth and University."

At least it wasn't far. We left the bar and walked to the intersection of First Avenue and Yesler Way when Helen turned and said, "We don't have to go home so early." Then she rose on her toes and kissed me hard on the lips. I pulled back, surprised. When I did, I spotted her.

Amara stood at the corner across the street with her father, mother, two brothers, and a host of others, presumably her cousins. They all stared at me, their faces uniformly shocked. Amara burst into tears, covered her face, then turned and ran. Her mother hurried after her.

After a moment of stunned paralysis, I shouted, "Amara, wait! I can explain." I took off running across the street, avoiding two cars that blew their bugles and nearly hit me. Amara's brothers stepped in front of me. "I can explain," I said to them.

"We think a picture is worth a thousand words of explaining, Bub," Ernesto said.

"But it's not what it seems," I said, nearly pleading with them.

"It certainly isn't," Arthur said, sticking a finger in my chest. "You've hurt our sister enough. If you don't get out of here, we'll return the favor."

He shoved me backward from the curb and I stumbled into the street. Mr. Giovacchini stepped past me and, as my mother liked to say: *If looks could kill, I'd be six feet underground.*

"It's not how it looks," I said. "Mr. Giovacchini, please."

But he didn't respond. The entire group turned their backs and walked in the direction Amara and her mother had run.

For a brief moment I considered running after Amara, but I would never get past her brothers and her father, and they might do more than just shove me away. I'd have to try to find another time to explain. I stood there, feeling horrible about the misunderstanding, then realized I'd left Helen Ruth standing on the sidewalk across the street. I turned and spotted her chatting with two sailors in their white uniforms and Dixie Cup caps. Then she linked arms with each sailor, and the three of them headed back inside the Central Cafe. I guess Ernesto was right. A picture was worth a thousand words.

Now I knew why the waitress had been so glib. Helen was definitely a regular.

Feeling as alone and uncertain as I'd felt that first day I stepped from Union Station, I made my way slowly up First Avenue, wondering what more could go wrong. My father's heart attack, Joan Daley's death, and now I'd hurt Amara. I'd have to think of a way to talk to her when her brothers and father weren't around, and explain to Amara why they all had witnessed me kissing a woman on the sidewalk. Both felt like tall tasks at the moment.

I walked past the Green Parrot Theatre where Amara and I had our first date. The marquee advertised *King Kong* in big red letters, and movie posters adorned the windows and the ticket box. I walked past Giovacchini's Bakery, a "Closed" sign on the door, the windows cleared of pastries. For the first time since I'd arrived in Seattle, I missed home. I missed my mother and father and my siblings. I missed my friends. I missed the familiarity of things. I seriously thought the best thing I could do was take the train back to Kansas City.

But that would put my family in further jeopardy, and it would mean walking away from Amara without even trying to explain what she had just witnessed.

I made my way to Pike Street and trudged up the steps of my boardinghouse. I wasn't three steps into the entry when Mrs. Alderbrook called out. "William. You have a package."

"A package?" I said, uncertain.

"It came by post today. From Kansas City."

My Oma's wedding ring, so I could propose to Amara. I groaned. It felt like someone had twisted a knife in my back. Unless I could clear things up with Amara, I'd have to explain to my mother that the proposal wasn't going to happen. She'd be more heartbroken than I already felt. She'd wonder what I was doing out here in Seattle, proposing to every woman I met?

I took the brown paper package. "Thank you," I said.

"What is it? Aren't you going to open it?" Mrs. Alderbrook asked.

"Just socks," I said.

"Socks?" She sounded disappointed.

"My mother knits them for the winter."

"Well, I guess that's useful." She eyed me, distrusting. "Is everything all right with your father? Have you heard more?"

"My mother says he'll be in the hospital awhile but he's going to pull through."

"That's something positive to hold on to," she said.

"Yes," I said. "It is. I'm tired. It's been a long week. Good night."

I left her standing behind her counter. "William?"

"Huh?" I said, turning back.

"Your key."

I retrieved my key and made my way up the staircase and down the hall to my room, thinking about how happy Amara had been the night I almost proposed to her. How happy I had been. When I reached to insert my key in the door lock, the door swung inward a few inches. It had been ajar. I was certain I had locked it that morning. I locked it every morning. I felt the rush of adrenaline and reached out my hand, though my inner voice told me to stop.

The door made a creaking sound when I pushed it in. My lamp had been switched on, casting a glow across my room and my belongings, which were strewn across the floor. The armoire had been emptied—my lone suitcase lay open like a book. My bedding had been pulled off the mattress. Notebooks had been scattered, the pages fanned open.

Just like Joan Daley's room.

Someone searching—for something.

The floor creaked beneath someone's weight. Before I could turn, I felt a sharp blow to the back of my head and I pitched forward, the floor and my bedding getting closer, along with a pair of black wing-tip shoes.

I awoke to someone calling my name and shaking my shoulder. "William? William?"

Mrs. Alderbrook hovered over me, a concerned look on her face. I tried to sit up, but she pushed me back down. "Don't get up," she said.

My surroundings, initially blurred, came into focus. White walls, white linoleum flooring, white bedding. "Where am I?"

"Harborview," she said.

"The hospital?"

"An ambulance transported you. Mrs. Schroeder passed your room. The door was open. You were on the floor, bleeding from a cut on your head."

I remembered the blow to the back of my head and reached up, touching a bandage.

"The doctor said you were lucky."

"I don't feel so lucky."

"The cut didn't require any stitches."

Some luck.

"William . . . Your room? What happened? Why did you tear your room apart?"

"What?"

"Your clothes and bedding. They were all over the floor. Did you go berserk? You seemed off when you came in, upset about something."

"I didn't go berserk," I said. "Someone went through my things."

"What?" She stepped back. "That's not possible. I had the key to your room. I gave it to you."

But I knew how easy it would be to grab the key when Mrs. Alderbrook wasn't at the desk, or to use the back stairs and pick my simple door lock.

"I gave you the key with your package from home."

The package.

I reached for my pockets but realized I was in a white gown. "Where are my clothes?"

"They're hanging on the wall behind you."

I moved to retrieve them, the room spun, and I fell back onto the pillow.

"The doctor said you could be dizzy."

"The package. I put the package in my pants pocket."

Mrs. Alderbrook moved to my clothes and felt inside my pockets. She pulled out the package. "Here it is."

I felt a sense of relief and sighed.

"You said it was just socks."

"It's a ring my mother sent, my Oma's ring, so I could propose to Amara. That won't happen now."

A middle-aged man wearing a white smock walked in carrying a clipboard. "Mr. Shumacher. Good to see you're awake. How are you feeling?"

"Okay," I said.

"You have a nasty bump on your head, but the orderly who accompanied the ambulance said your bedding on the floor softened the blow to your head."

I almost told them the blow had been administered before I hit the floor, but I didn't see the point. It would only lead to more questions to which I didn't have answers. "I was lucky," I said.

"Have you had fainting spells like this before?"

Fainting? "No. Never. I guess I forgot to eat lunch and dinner. I was working."

"He's the reporter for the *Daily Star* covering the Pom Pom trial," Mrs. Alderbrook offered.

"Your landlady said something about your room being torn apart . . . ," he said to me.

"I was just upset," I said. "I'll clean it when I get back. How much is this going to cost?" I asked, mindful of my limited funds.

"This is the charitable hospital, Mr. Shumacher. The county covers your expenses."

"When can I leave?"

"How do you feel?"

"I'm okay," I said.

"You don't appear to have any other injuries. I'd say you're free to go whenever you feel up to it. You may be dizzy, however. I'd suggest taking it easy for a day or two. And remember to eat."

The doctor left the room.

Mrs. Alderbrook said, "Maybe you should spend the night. You seem a bit wobbly." She sounded concerned, but I could also tell she thought I had gone berserk. She hadn't yet said anything about the door lock or jamb having been broken or asked how I was going to pay for any damage, which meant whoever broke into my room had likely picked the door lock. Someone who knew I wouldn't be home and believed they had time to go through my things.

I thought of Detective Blunt detaining me outside the courthouse. He knew I had gone to the county tax office, and that I'd gone to get a drink with Helen Ruth and wasn't going back to my boardinghouse right away.

I didn't want to go back to my room. Not tonight.

"I think maybe you're right," I said. "Why don't you go back, and I'll spend the night. I'll come by in the morning and get everything straightened up. Thank you for taking care of me. I hope it wasn't too much of an inconvenience."

She smiled. "You're sure you're all right?"

Which was her way of asking whether I was going to have any more crazed episodes. "I'm fine," I said.

"Do you want me to call your mother?"

"No," I said. "She has enough to worry about."

"I suppose she does."

After Mrs. Alderbrook departed, I swung my feet to the floor but remained seated on the bed's edge until the room stopped spinning. I got up gingerly and slowly dressed. It took almost twenty minutes for the nausea to pass before I could think clearly. I now knew for certain someone was searching for something, and they thought either I had it or I knew where to find it. I had no other explanation for someone going through my things. Miller's treasure, hidden somewhere. Enough money to change lives. My parents'. My siblings'. Maybe mine and Amara's. I decided then and there if the treasure existed, I would find it. For my family's sake. For Joan Daley's sake, and for Amara's sake.

But I had another problem.

Where would I go tonight? I didn't know anyone in town besides Amara, who at the moment didn't want anything to do with me, and I didn't have money to get a hotel room for the night. After buying drinks and Helen's half-eaten dinner at the Central Cafe, I was down to the few nickels Phish gave me each day to call in my stories.

Phish.

I made my way to the hallway and found a pay phone. I inserted a nickel and asked to be connected to Phish's home number. He'd given his reporters the number in the event of a breaking news story. He wanted us to be able to communicate with him quickly.

Twenty minutes later, now close to midnight, I stepped off the trolley car onto Capitol Hill near Lake Union and made my way up Roy Street. Phish rarely talked about his personal life, but from the snippets, I'd gleaned he was married and lived with his wife. They had two grown boys, both gainfully employed. I assumed the latter because Phish was fond of saying of his sons, "They're off my payroll."

The house was two stories, forest-green stucco with brown wood trim, a wraparound porch with potted plants, and a hanging porch swing where I could imagine Phish and his wife sat on warm summer nights. It made me think of Amara, of the porch swing at her parents' home, and what I had lost, and how I could get her back.

I knocked gently. A porch light flickered on overhead before Phish pulled open the door. He wore a red-and-white checked robe over striped pajamas and slippers. "Shoe. Are you all right?" he said, his gaze going to the bandage on my head.

"Yes," I said. "Though I'm a little dizzy. I'm sorry to call so late. I hope I didn't wake anyone."

"Nonsense. Come in."

Phish led me to a sitting room just off the entry. He closed the door behind us and turned on several lamps. I sat on the plush purple sofa. Phish went to a bookshelf, moved aside several books, and pulled out a bottle. "Cognac," he said. "Mrs. Phishbaum doesn't allow drinking in the house but for her glass of sherry at night." He poured two glasses and handed me one. Then he hid the Cognac again. "My mother swore by it to help her sleep. Given the amount she drank, that wasn't a problem."

I took the glass and sipped the liquor, which made my taste buds tingle. Phish moved to a maroon winged armchair by the fireplace. "Now, tell me what's going on."

For the next forty-five minutes I told Phish about my father's heart attack, my conversation with my mother, and my conversation with Joan Daley the night she had supposedly jumped from her boarding-house window. I told him about the black Ford that had followed me down the alley, what I had learned at the city clerk's office about the delinquent tax cases, what Commissioner Rosen had clarified, Detective Blunt's peculiar conversation with Frankie Ray on his deathbed, and Blunt's conversation with me late that afternoon. I told him how Miller and Brunn had been partners in a company that owned the establishments under indictment for skimming taxes.

"The tax commissioner estimates as much as $250,000 could be floating around out there."

Phish's eyes widened, and he whistled. He set down his Cognac. Though he didn't say it, I knew his first thought. *Pizzazz!*

"I don't think Frankie Ray was killed because he pushed George Miller to pay for Joan Daley's hospital bill. I think Miller called Ray into the club that morning because he found out about Ray's new Cadillac and he wanted to know how Ray was paying for it. That's why Ray put the lease in Joan Daley's name in the first place, but then Joan got hurt and couldn't pay. I think Miller figured Ray used some of the tax money to pay for the Cadillac, and Miller was angry Ray was cheating them, and putting the rest of the money at risk. It also explains why Ray, a regular at the club who'd known Miller a long time, decided to bring Al Smith that morning. Ray anticipated a confrontation with Miller and thought, wrongly, that Miller wouldn't kill him with a stranger present. He underestimated Miller's temper."

"Miller's motivation for killing Ray is as old as time itself, then. Greed. And you think Blunt knows about this pot of gold?"

"I do, based on his conversation with Frankie Ray in the emergency room, and because of all the questions Blunt's been asking me. He hinted at knowing I spoke to Joan Daley just before she died. And he was waiting for me outside the courthouse this afternoon and knew I'd been to the tax commissioner's office."

"When did you speak to Joan Daley?"

"Just before someone killed her."

"What did she have to say?"

"Basically what I told you, that the dispute between Miller and Ray wasn't about a hospital bill. It was about Miller's money that Ray was using to pay off his Cadillac."

"You said Blunt hinted at knowing you spoke to Daley—how?"

"He said a woman who lived behind the boardinghouse was feeding her chickens and saw a man leaving the building by the back door leading into the alley. But I checked the backyards along the alley, and I didn't see any chickens or a chicken coop."

"Why do you think that means he knows you were there?"

"The black car outside the boardinghouse followed me down the alley before I hopped a trolley car and made my way back to the boardinghouse and saw it again, this time close enough to determine the make and model. I can't be certain it was Blunt, but Blunt drives a black Ford sedan."

"A lot of those cars in town, Shoe. Especially black."

"I know."

"But if it was Blunt, then he had to have been tailing Daley, thinking she knew where the money was, and spotted you," Phish said. "And the fact that her room and your room were both ransacked in the same manner certainly indicates someone *is* looking for something."

"Thank God you believe me."

"Of course I do."

"The way they went through my notebooks indicates they think I have notes, maybe from my conversation with Joan Daley."

Phish stood, his eyes wide. "The newspaper."

"What?"

"It stands to reason they'll search for notes in the notebooks you keep in your desk." He moved to the closet in the room, opened it, and pulled out a cardboard box. He opened the box and removed a handgun and a holster.

"What are you going to do?" I asked.

"Defend the First Amendment's guarantee to a free press," he said and hurried from the room like Paul Revere readying for his nighttime ride, though hopefully to first change from his pajamas.

Fifteen minutes later, Phish and I were on Seventh Avenue unlocking the *Daily Star*'s front door. Phish had his gun out when he pushed in the door, bells jingling, and flicked on the lights, but it was unnecessary. The pressroom looked as it always did, the desks in a bit of disarray and cluttered beneath notes and documents, newspapers strewn about. I moved to my desk and pulled open my drawer. My used notebooks remained where I always kept them.

"Do you have any notes of your conversation with Joan Daley?"

"No. Nothing. She wasn't in a condition to say much of anything."

"Hand me your notebooks. We'll put them in the safe in my office and sleep here tonight."

"Do you really think someone would break into the newspaper office?"

"For a quarter of a million dollars I don't put anything past anybody. You take the small couch in my office."

"I don't want to take your couch, Phish. Besides, I don't think I'll sleep much."

"Listen, what we do, we do every day. Newspaper reporting is in our blood. It's what keeps us alive. I told you I bleed ink, and I think you do too. You got a nose for a story, but you have to learn to shut it off and not let it consume you. If you don't, you'll be an old man without much of a relationship to the children you and that young lady are going to have."

It was a rare glimpse into Phish's personal life. And it was painful to hear.

"I don't think I have to worry about that."

"What do you mean?"

I told him what had happened, about seeing Amara and her family while Helen Ruth clutched my arm, then rose unexpectedly and kissed me.

"I wondered why you called me and not her."

I told Phish about Helen coming around the corner of the building as I spoke with Blunt, and how I'd seized the opportunity to make it look like I'd gone to the tax commission office to ask her out.

"Quick thinking, but an unfortunate turn of events with Amara. There's nothing you can do about it tonight. Get some sleep. A new day brings new stories and sometimes solutions to our problems. Go on. Take the couch in my office. We'll see what the morning brings. Until we get to the bottom of this, you'll stay at my house. How much was the dinner and drinks tonight?"

"It came to $1.85."

"Did you get a receipt?" I told him I had. "Submit it as a business expense and I'll reimburse you."

"You don't have to do that, Phish."

"You keep telling me what I don't have to do, and I'll think I work for you. Expense it. Now get some shut-eye."

I thanked him, went into his office, and closed the door. As I predicted, I lay down on the sofa, but I didn't fall asleep. I imagined Phish had spent many nights on this couch when covering a breaking news story. The thought was both exhilarating and daunting. I could imagine how the hours had taken a toll on his family. I didn't want that for my own family—if I ever had one.

The thought of Amara propelled me upright. The light in the newsroom penetrated Phish's glass wall. I picked up the afternoon paper from his desk. I hadn't had time to read it. The front page was split. The lead story was my late-afternoon piece on Miller's theatrics in the courtroom, and his seeming implication of the police. Below the headline and article, Phish ran Kneip's photograph of the jurors inside the Pom Pom Club looking like schoolchildren on a field trip, their faces showing both awe and amazement.

I went back and read the story under the banner. Phish had supplemented my facts after he'd spoken to the two officers and the chief of police.

Miller Implicates Police

Officers in Pom Pom Club

Says Patrolmen Frequented Club,

Knew about Liquor, Gaming

The door to the Pom Pom Club was sometimes wide open, even while craps games were going on and liquor was being dispensed openly over the bar. The shades were not always drawn at the windows, and the night revelers, particularly in the private dining rooms, could be seen by passersby. George Miller, club proprietor and murder trial defendant, testified under a blistering cross-examination by Deputy Prosecutor Laurence McKinley and dropped a bomb on the proceedings—that he concocted a story to protect two patrolmen who frequented the club and knew of its illegal activities, Foster Heslop and Carl Norris.

Questioned at his home about Miller's testimony, Patrolman Heslop said, "I guess I haven't anything to say about that."

Patrolman Norris could not be reached for comment at the time the *Star* went to press.

Heslop and Norris will have something to say. Defense counsel John Sullivan has listed both as witnesses in the murder trial, which is to resume Monday in Judge Peter Kincaid's King County courtroom.

Police Chief L. L. Norton, questioned regarding Miller's statement the club operated openly and under the noses of his officers, said an investigation of Miller's allegations was underway.

"We have to get someone to corroborate Miller's story. Most of those who would know have been subpoenaed in the Miller case, and we cannot take them from so important a trial.

"As soon as they are free, they will be questioned, and if Miller's statement that police officers were in the club and knew of its illegal practices is accurate, those officers will be immediately dismissed."

Norton said Seattle Police had very few complaints about the Pom Pom Club and nothing alarming, and therefore the club had never been investigated. "It is

> like a lot of these nightclubs that are patronized by your very best people. Unless we have a complaint, we don't get into it much."

And since the club paid the police—of this I was now quite sure—there would have been no complaints, and no reason for the police to look into "illegal activities" participated in by Seattle's very best people. This, too, sounded like a shot over the bow, Norton intimating if the courtroom allegations implicated the police department, he would have no choice but to name others. It seemed a startling admission by Norton—the police and the politicians turning a blind eye to illegal activities conducted within these establishments—and it made me realize a lot of important people could be involved.

And Blunt held the black book with the names of all the club's patrons.

Was he protecting them? Or perhaps protecting himself? Maybe he believed the book and the names would come in handy down the road for some future use. Or maybe his name was also in that book.

Seattle, I was learning, was a lot more interesting, though also more dangerous, than at first blush. Yes, the waters were a crystal-clear blue, and the majestic mountains were covered in virgin white snow, but the city's underbelly was as dark and dirty as the waterfront at night. And, as Joan Daley had said, maybe it wasn't the underworld who needed to be feared. With the underworld, you knew the players and what to expect from each. It was the people you didn't know, the upstanding citizens of Seattle, some sworn to protect and to serve, who needed to be feared.

Chapter 21

Phish insisted I take the weekend off. Saturday morning, with a lot of trepidation, I bought flowers, took a deep breath, and walked to Giovacchini's Bakery. I wanted to talk to Amara and explain what happened. If she wanted nothing more to do with me, then I could at least say I had tried. I didn't want to walk away from the best thing in my life without trying.

When I stepped inside the bakery, Mr. Giovacchini approached from around the corner, and before I uttered a word, he pointed to the door and said, "Out!"

"Mr. Giovacchini, if you'll just let me talk to Amara, I can explain—"

"Amara is not here," he said. "She is at home with her cousins. And no explaining. We saw what we saw."

"But—"

"No buts. You have hurt my daughter and embarrassed my family. I think perhaps Mr. Big-Shot Reporter has grown too big for his britches."

"I haven't—"

"Leave now. Or I'll call Arthur and Ernesto to throw you out."

"Mr. Giovacchini—"

"Out!"

He was not going to let me explain, and with Amara not present, persisting would be a waste of time. I left the bakery, but I had not given up. I'd come back when Amara was there, or try to talk to her after work, when her father went to buy more supplies.

I killed time at the Green Parrot watching *King Kong*. The sold-out theater crowd was animated, and *King Kong* didn't disappoint, which only made me more depressed I didn't have Amara at my side to share the experience. As promised, I went back to my room to clean up the disarray and pack clothing for my stay with Phish, but when I arrived, I found Mrs. Alderbrook had straightened up for me.

When I came downstairs, suitcase in hand, her eyes widened like someone who'd just come from a horror show. "You're not leaving; are you?"

"What?"

"Your suitcase. You're not leaving?"

"No. Just going to visit a friend for a few days." She sighed in relief. "Thanks for cleaning up my room. You didn't have to do that."

"You seemed upset after the hospital visit. What happened? No. Let me guess. You proposed and she turned you down."

She wasn't far off, so I nodded.

"I knew it. If there's one thing that can make a young man go berserk, it's a young lady. Give her some time, William. Women don't like to be rushed into these things. She'll come around."

"I'm not so sure about that."

"Of course she will. You're a catch. You have a good job and you work hard. You're industrious. A young woman would be crazy to pass up an opportunity to marry you. Especially during a depression."

I smiled. I guess anyone with a job was a good catch during a depression. But I certainly didn't feel like one.

I was glad when Monday came. The routine of covering the trial gave me something besides my father's health and Amara's absence on which to focus my attention.

When I stepped into the courtroom, early for a change, Detective Blunt gave me a curious look from counsel's table, almost as if he hadn't expected me. I took my regular seat, Judge Kincaid called his courtroom to order, and we were underway.

Sullivan rose and called Officer Carl L. Norris, one of the two police officers Miller had implicated Friday in knowing about and permitting gambling and liquor sales in the Pom Pom Club.

The patrolman was a big man with a gut and a shock of thick white hair and equally thick tufts for eyebrows.

After preliminaries, Sullivan asked, "How often would you go into the Pom Pom Club?"

"It was on my patrol, so I'd stop by there every evening on my regular beat, just to have a presence. Let them know I was around. It tended to keep away the riffraff."

"Did you see any liquor being served or gambling on those occasions?"

"No need to go inside. The neighbors didn't complain, and everything seemed in order."

"What about the occasions you did go in? Did you see liquor being served, or gambling?"

"When I did go in, which was rare, I'd see glasses of liquor on some tables but no gambling. I'm not a rube. I knew they flipped the tables when I showed up to make them look like ordinary tables. So long as there wasn't any trouble, I didn't pay it no mind."

"But you knew they were gaming tables?"

"I suspected as much. Look, a lot of good people are suffering during this depression. They go to the clubs to blow off a little steam. If the clubs and speakeasies . . . the roadhouse taverns weren't around, who's to say what would happen? I wasn't about to come down hard on people, or on an establishment, for providing people with an outlet. So long as the place was orderly and kept everything within the four walls, I cut them a break."

"Was there ever an occasion at the Pom Pom Club in which things were not orderly?"

Norris made a face like he had indigestion. "I was called to a disturbance there on April eleventh."

"Tell us what happened."

"I met George Miller outside the club. He said a fellow was raising Cain inside and asked me to take care of it. I said I didn't want anything to do with it, that Miller was barking up a tree I didn't want to climb. I said he ought to hire his own bouncer, but he said Frankie Ray was driving his trade away. The next thing I heard were glasses breaking and shouting. Miller said, 'He's breaking up my joint. You'll have to arrest him.'"

"And did you arrest him?"

"I tried but it wasn't easy."

"Why not?"

"I'm about twice Ray's size, but I had considerable difficulty subduing him. He was that strong."

"Did Mr. Ray say anything?"

"He said, 'I'm a friend of Johnnie Dore's and I'll have your job.'"

"Johnnie Dore, the mayor of Seattle?" Sullivan asked, voice rising as if surprised. I was sure he wasn't. The gallery gave a collective gasp.

"That's what he said. I had my doubts."

"Why is that?"

"In situations like that, guys will just throw out names."

"Did you learn what had set Mr. Ray off?"

"Ray tried to dance with another patron's date, but she refused. When Ray persisted, the patron stepped in, and Ray attacked him."

"Were you able to eventually subdue Mr. Ray?"

"You bet. He called me a vile name I won't repeat in mixed company and spat at me. So I socked him in the nose and put an end to his nonsense."

"Were you aware Mr. Ray was once a lightweight boxing contender?"

"I knew, but I did a fair bit of boxing in my day as well," Norris said, puffing out his chest. "And I could give as good as I could take."

"Did you form an opinion whether Mr. Ray was a violent person?"

McKinley objected but Kincaid overruled him.

"In my opinion, Ray was a violent, dangerous person, drunk or sober."

On that note, Sullivan sat.

McKinley rose. "Officer Norris, was it up to you to decide whether or not to enforce the law?"

"Well, I'm the one out there on the beat, so I guess you could say it was every beat cop's prerogative."

"Did your captain or the chief of police know you were arbitrarily deciding when and when not to enforce the law?"

Norris gave McKinley a tight smile. "It's how things are done, son. Like I said. It's the Depression. A lot of people are hurting and living in Hoovervilles. The jails are overflowing. So yeah, I decide whether or not I'm going to crowd those already overflowing jails with more people for misdemeanor offenses."

"I didn't find any arrests of Mr. Ray recorded in the police log. Why not?"

"Mr. Ray got what was coming to him. The club called him a cab and the cabbie took him home."

"You cut Mr. Ray a break, then."

"I did."

"I guess, then, you didn't consider him too dangerous." It was a good point by McKinley. Before Norris might explain, McKinley asked, "During your altercation with Mr. Ray, did he pull a gun or a knife?"

"Not on his life."

"You never told Mr. Miller that Mr. Ray had a gun or a knife?"

"He didn't. So I didn't."

"The occasion you socked Frankie Ray he was intoxicated, wasn't he?"

"He was three sheets to the wind."

"Did you ever see him violent when not intoxicated?"

"Can't say that I did."

"So you have no personal knowledge Frankie Ray was 'dangerous'—your word—when sober."

"I don't."

"Did you ever visit the Pom Pom Club off duty?"

Norris paused like a thief caught red-handed.

"Officer, you're under oath," McKinley said.

"Objection," Sullivan said. "The question is irrelevant."

"It goes to credibility," McKinley said.

"The officer will answer the question," Kincaid said.

Norris said, "Mr. Miller and Mr. Brunn, in gratitude for my handling Mr. Ray, invited me and the missus to return to the club, on the house."

"And did you take them up on their offer?"

"The wife doesn't have much opportunity to go to a club like that, me being a public servant, and I felt she deserved a night out. So yeah, I took them up on it, for her sake."

"Did you and your wife dine there?"

"Yes."

"Did you imbibe alcoholic drinks?"

"My wife had a cocktail. I drank beer, which is legal."

"And did you or your wife gamble?"

"My wife got a thrill rolling the dice. I did not."

"And did she win?"

"Fifty dollars."

"That's a good night," McKinley said, "especially since the games were rigged against you."

"Objection," Sullivan said.

"Sustained."

After Norris, Sullivan called Patrolman Foster Heslop, and Heslop testified similarly about walking the beat and knowing about the gambling and drinking but letting the matter slide if there were no disturbances. He also described a violent incident involving Ray, but this one at the Lodge Café.

McKinley approached on cross-examination and asked, "The incident involving the Lodge Café—that's not your regular beat; is it?"

"No, it is not."

"What were you doing at the Lodge Café on your night off from work?"

"Moonlighting."

"And what is moonlighting?"

"It was my off-duty job. I worked security."

"You were employed by Mr. Miller?"

"That's right," Heslop said, and it sounded like *What of it?*

"Mr. Miller paid you?"

"I don't work for free, Counselor; do you?"

"Just answer the questions, Officer," Judge Kincaid said.

Heslop made a disgruntled face but nodded.

"What is your salary as a patrolman?"

"One thousand, eight hundred, and thirty-two dollars a year."

"So roughly one hundred and fifty dollars a month."

"If you say so. I've never done the math."

"How much was your salary at the Lodge Café?"

"Twenty dollars a night. Fifty dollars on a weekend."

"So how much money did you earn in a month from the club?"

"Two to three hundred dollars."

McKinley made a surprised expression, though I'm certain he wasn't. "Moonlighting was lucrative."

"It paid the bills."

"I'm sure it did. But tell the ladies and gentlemen of the jury, why would a café need a policeman for security?"

Heslop turned to Kincaid. "I'd like to not answer that question on the grounds it could cost me my job."

"I'm afraid you don't have that luxury, Officer. This is a court of law, and you are sworn to tell the truth," Kincaid said.

Heslop's jaw undulated like he was chewing on his words. "The café needed security because they had some games going on there, and a person on the losing end could become disgruntled."

"And by 'games' you mean gambling?"

"I'm not talking about hopscotch and kick the can, Counselor."

"Answer the question, Officer, without the sarcasm," Kincaid said.

"Yes. Gambling."

"Poker and craps?"

"Among others."

"Did you ever moonlight on a night when Mr. Ray came into the Lodge?"

"Sure, many times."

"And what was his demeanor on those occasions?"

"Frankie was all right. Not a bad guy."

"Did you ever see him wield a knife at the café?"

"Not with me working there. He knew better. I'd toss him out on his can."

"A gun?"

"Never."

"Did any other officers who moonlighted ever tell you Mr. Ray pulled a knife or a gun?"

Heslop shook his head. "Never heard such a thing."

"Did you know Mr. Miller to carry a gun?"

Heslop gave it some thought before he said, "Knew of it. Heard of it, I should say, but never saw him with a gun."

Following Heslop, Sullivan proceeded to call what Phish had deemed "the parade of pals"—people who had, at one time, been Frankie Ray's pals but now turned on him. The first was Jake Woitt, serving a term at a federal road camp for illegal distribution of liquor during Prohibition.

Sullivan asked, "Mr. Woitt, how did you and Mr. Ray know each other?"

"Frankie used to work for me distributing liquor to some establishments I had a contract with, but I fired him after he attempted to knife me during the Christmas holidays at the Bucket of Blood Nightclub on King Street in Pioneer Square."

McKinley rose. "Objection, Your Honor, these previous fights, even if believed, are too far afield to be relevant to these proceedings."

"Your Honor, I can make them relevant with one question," Sullivan said.

"Please do."

"Mr. Woitt, did you tell Mr. Miller about this incident in which Mr. Ray pulled a knife on you?"

"I sure did," Woitt said.

Sullivan sat with a satisfied smile.

McKinley rose. "Mr. Woitt, you're a convicted liquor runner; is that right?"

"Well, I distributed liquor, so if that's a runner, then, yes."

"Did you distribute your liquor to the Pom Pom Club?"

"Sure. They were one of my best customers. A lot of booze went through that joint."

"And the Lodge Café?"

"Yep."

"The Jungle Temple?"

"Yep. And I know what you're going to ask, and I can make it easy on you. I distributed liquor to all of Mr. Miller's businesses. He was my best customer."

McKinley smiled like it was too easy. Then he sat.

Kincaid ended the day early. He had a sentencing in another case. Without need to rush to the phones in the hallway, I went back to the office, filled in Phish, then typed up my story for the afternoon edition. Phish didn't pull any punches with his headline, which was sure to get attention, especially from the boys in blue.

Seattle Police Knew of Drinking and Gaming Violations

Frankie Ray Ran Amok

in Pom Pom Club

I hoped they didn't pull my press pass and expressed this concern to Phish.

"Are you kidding? You made them sound like good shepherds, allowing people to blow off steam in difficult financial times. Besides, we have to call them as we see them. A strike's a strike and a ball's a ball. The strike zone shouldn't change depending on who's at bat, and neither should the article."

I used my unexpected time in the office to put together a timeline. I wanted to see things in chronological order, hoping something jumped out at me that I hadn't yet considered. I was more convinced than ever the dispute in the club had been about hidden tax money, and Joan Daley was killed because she knew too much.

I checked off Miller's home as an unlikely location for the cash. It was too obvious, and Commissioner Rosen said it had already been searched. Someone had also searched Joan Daley's room, so I checked that off as well. Then I had a thought. An epiphany really.

What about Frankie Ray's room or house?

Had anyone gone through his belongings? I didn't see anything in my notes, and I never heard Blunt tell any of his detectives to find out where Ray had lived.

That seemed a logical starting place; didn't it?

I went to Kravitz and asked him to find the last known address for Frankie Ray. Within minutes he'd come back to my desk.

"That was fast," I said.

"I called the Cadillac company. Ray needed to show his driver's license to take out the loan for the car. The salesman had written the address down in the file."

"Good thinking," I said.

The address was for a brick apartment house on Jackson Street a block up from the waterfront, a rough neighborhood. I put my police press pass on my jacket, hoping those at the waterfront wouldn't give it too close a look, think I was a detective, and leave me be.

At the waterfront, vagrants rummaged through garbage cans and walked alongside sailors who'd just deboarded a ship at the pier and were headed up to First Avenue, likely to talk to the shoeshine boys about dates for the evening. The shoeshine boys would do well this night collecting their quarters.

When I reached Frankie Ray's building, I removed the badge, now more concerned people wouldn't want a reporter sticking his nose in their business. I stepped inside a shabby lobby to a woman behind a desk with ratted hair pinned atop her head. Smoke filtered from a cigarette in her hands, and from her mouth and nostrils. She squinted through the haze at me.

"Help you?"

"I'm looking for a room rented in this building by a man named Frankie Ray."

"You his son?" she barked, then started a coughing fit that ended in her taking another drag.

I figured maybe being family might gain me some sympathy. "Yes."

"Where the hell have you been?"

"Mourning," I said.

"I have a thirty-day policy. If the person doesn't pay rent, I put his belongings in storage. After thirty days I throw them out. He paid rent for June, but nothing since then."

"So you threw out his belongings?"

"I said I have a policy. I didn't say I did it."

"He still has the apartment?"

"Who do I look like? Daddy Warbucks?"

She didn't. She looked more like the mean Miss Hannigan who ran the orphanage.

"I can't afford to have a room unrented. But I figured with the trial going on and all, maybe I'd better hang on to his stuff. I've had enough of these where eventually the police get around to calling."

"But they haven't yet in this case?"

"You're the first."

"Can I see his things?"

"I charge fifty cents a month for storage. He owes me a dollar fifty."

"But he's dead."

"That isn't my fault or my concern. Dead or alive, he owes me a dollar fifty. You want his things, that will cost you. Otherwise, I'll dump them."

I recalled Phish telling me to expense the dinner, and I was confident he'd allow me to expense the cost of looking through Frankie Ray's belongings. I reached into my pocket and pulled out three quarters, two nickels, and six pennies. "All I have is ninety-one cents. Can I bring you the fifty-nine cents tomorrow?"

"Sort of like Wimpy on the *Popeye* cartoons, huh? You'll pay me Tuesday for a hamburger today?"

"That's right."

"No."

"What if I call my boss, and he vouches for me?"

"Your boss, huh? Who is he?"

"He . . . He runs a bakery in . . . Rainier Valley," I said, worried if I mentioned the newspaper, she'd figure out I wasn't Ray's son.

"Okay, kid, get him on the phone." She pulled the candlestick telephone out from under the desk and handed it to me.

Phish was more than a little confused when I called.

"So I can't look at my father Frankie Ray's belongings unless I pay the storage fee of a dollar fifty," I said. "I told the manager here that you would cover the cost and take it out of my paycheck at the bakery."

After a moment the light must have gone on for Phish. "I got you, kid. Put her on."

Minutes later she replaced the speaker in the cradle and told me to follow her down a flight of stairs to the basement. "That's a hell of a boss you got, son. He offered to pay the full dollar fifty on your behalf."

"He'll take it out of my paycheck this week," I said.

"Too bad, but at least you'll get back your father's things. It isn't much. Just a couple of boxes."

At the bottom of a staircase, we came to a pitch-black room. The landlady waved her hand in front of her face, then pulled a string. A weak, pale light lit up a portion of the basement. Dark shadows danced along the walls. I could hear the plink, plink, plink of water dripping in a corner, and each time someone in the building flushed a toilet, the sewage flowed through the pipes. Something scurried about in the dark.

"Do you have a cat?" I asked.

"No. Why?" She pointed. "Those are his boxes there." I lifted the two boxes, which weren't heavy. I almost asked how putting them in the basement could cost a dollar fifty but let it alone.

I carried the two boxes to the building stoop. They weren't heavy, but they were awkward. I set them on the stoop and looked about for anyone loitering, which was just about everyone on the street, men and women suffering through hard times. I looked for a black car, but again there were many. I carried the boxes over to Yesler and maneuvered my way onto a trolley car, taking it to Seventh Avenue. I stepped off and carried Ray's belongings to the *Daily Star*'s offices.

Phish had left for the evening, but the typesetter remained upstairs putting together printing plates for the boilerplate articles and advertisements for tomorrow's edition.

I used my key to enter. The typesetter heard the bells over the door jingle and came down the steps to determine who had come into the office so late. I locked the door behind me and carried the boxes into Phish's office, not wanting to sit at my desk where I could be seen through the window facing the street.

I pulled off the tape holding down the lid on the first box. It looked like someone had just dumped belongings into it. I pulled out wrinkled dress shirts and ties, socks, a pair of slacks, and two pairs of shoes. Underwear. The clothes were of good quality and about my size, but something about wearing a dead man's garments gave me the heebie-jeebies. I'd donate them to Goodwill. I set the clothes aside. Beneath the clothes I found some jewelry, nothing expensive; half a pack of cigarettes; and some dice that had been altered, the edges shaved.

In the second box I found more clothes and what looked to be the contents to a desk drawer or a side table—paper, a couple of pencils, and a Bible. The papers had some scribblings on them, but I couldn't decipher much of it. I set them aside and pondered. My big idea had produced less than nothing.

The typesetter called out to let me know he was heading home and to lock the door behind him. I heard the chimes ring and the door click shut. I went through the pockets of Ray's clothes. Again, going through a dead man's trousers gave me more heebie-jeebies and caused the hairs on my arms to tingle. Being alone in the newspaper office didn't help. In a pocket of the lone pair of khakis I pulled out paper balled into a wad. I carefully unwrapped it, smoothed it, and put it under the desk lamp.

It was a receipt from the Universal Concrete Company in Seattle.

3 sacks of Universal Concrete 3 x 95¢ = $2.85

1 sledgehammer $1.10

1 trowel 85¢

Total: $4.80

Payment: Total $4.80

The receipt seemed at odds with the Frankie Ray described every day in court—a pugilist who worked in the nightclubs owned by Miller and Brunn. I didn't see Ray mixing and spreading concrete . . . And then it hit me. *Unless he was burying something.* Like a suitcase or two full of money. I got excited at the prospect, then realized he could have buried the loot almost anywhere in Seattle.

So what really had I gained? It would take an act of God for me to figure out the location, if I was even correct that Ray had buried the money someplace.

I considered the Bible I'd set on Phish's desk.

An act of God.

Like the concrete receipt, the Bible didn't fit the man described in court as a violent drunk and underworld hanger-on. I opened the cover. Nothing written on the first page. I flipped through the pages, uncertain what I was searching for, but did not find writing. I looked at the back cover. Nothing. The final two pages were also blank.

I fanned the book again, holding it upside down. No papers fell out. I fanned the pages more slowly, and this time, I saw a couple of pencil marks. I stopped, licked my finger, and thumbed the pages until I'd found what I had seen. The number 13 in the corner of the page had been circled. Why? I scanned the text of chapter 10 and the first paragraph of chapter 11 of the book of Genesis to see if maybe it was a favorite passage or something but found no other marks. I flipped through the pages again, this time focusing on the page numbers in the corner. I didn't have to go far before I found the number 45 had also been circled. The page corresponded to chapter 39 in the book of Genesis. Joseph's temptation. Again, no other pencil markings. I read the chapter. It was about a man seduced by his boss's wife. I paused, but nothing more came to me as to why Frankie Ray, if it had been Frankie Ray, circled the numbers.

I flipped through the remaining pages more carefully but didn't see any other page numbers circled.

I went back to the beginning and fanned the pages again, this time more slowly, but again I noted nothing of interest. I did it once more and saw a pencil mark. I went back page by page and found the mark. The word "East" had been circled, but no other word on the page was circled or underlined. I continued flipping the pages, scanning the text, looking for pencil marks. It was tedious and my eyes strained in the poor desk light, but I found a second mark. The word "John" had been circled atop a page in the right-hand corner.

On a scrap of paper I wrote down the markings in order: 13 45 East John.

I didn't know Seattle well, but that sounded like an address. I went to the large map Phish kept pinned to the wall in his office and traced my finger along the index of streets at the bottom left corner and found East John Street on Capitol Hill.

Could it be possible?

Was this where Frankie Ray had hidden the money, somewhere beneath concrete? It made me think of Ernie Blunt at George Miller's house. He'd gone into the basement and walked around. Could he have been interested in the concrete floor?

In the morning, I'd ask Kravitz to determine if the address existed and, if so, whether a house or a building was there and who owned it. The bigger question was what to do with the receipt and the Bible for the night. I didn't dare take them with me in case whoever hit me in the head had followed me.

The logical solution was to lock both in the *Daily Star*'s safe, but I didn't know the combination. I picked up the phone to call Phish at home. I wasn't certain he'd provide me with the combination, but maybe if I explained the circumstances to him, he would.

A scratching noise came from the newsroom. I hung up the phone and shut off Phish's desk lamp, then duckwalked to the door of his office. Outside the plate-glass window, hunched over at the outer door, was a man in a coat and fedora. His face was obscured in the shadows.

At that same moment, I realized I hadn't locked the door after the typesetter left for the night.

The door handle turned, and the door slowly creaked open. The bells barely made a sound.

I crawled back to the desk, heart pounding, and slipped the receipt inside the Bible, then put the Bible in Phish's top desk drawer, as if he owned it. I shut the drawer slowly. In the newsroom a beam from a flashlight swept left and right over the news desks. Quietly, I replaced the few remaining belongings in the two boxes. The newsroom floor creaked—someone walking across it. I heard the man open and close desk drawers.

I stacked the two boxes and slid them against the wall, positioning them like they belonged. Hiding myself would not be so easy. The wooden floor continued to creak under the man's weight. I crawled on my hands and knees to the desk. Phish's autographed baseball bat hung on the wall, but I didn't have time to grab it. And if the man had a gun . . .

I carefully rolled back Phish's chair and climbed under his desk, then pulled the chair back toward me, curling into a tight ball.

Footsteps. Closer. I hoped the person would survey the room and leave, but I heard him enter and move to the far side of Phish's desk. He rummaged through papers, then stepped around the desk and slid open drawers—first the top drawer, then the middle, and finally the bottom drawer. More rummaging.

From beneath the desk, I saw pants and dark wing-tip shoes.

My legs cramped. I felt the start of a charley horse in my right hamstring. I had no way to straighten my leg to relieve the pain, not without pushing back the chair and giving away my location. I was perspiring profusely and trying my best to control my breathing and not cry out. I bit my lower lip, swallowing the pain. I reached down with my right hand. My hamstring felt like piano strings pulled taut. I tried to gently massage it.

The floor creaked, followed by what sounded like someone removing the lid on the top box. Seconds passed. The pain in my hamstring worsened. The footsteps started again, this time more deliberately. The steps grew faint. I heard the bells over the door and the door shut. I waited, in case it was a trick.

When I didn't hear another sound, I kicked out the chair and struggled to straighten my leg. In the process I banged my head where I'd previously been struck. The pain radiated from the top of my scalp down every inch of my body. Stars flashed. I straightened my leg and jiggled it, as I had done in bed after high school cross-country practice when I would regularly get these cramps. Eventually the cramp faded and I was able to slide out from under the desk and stand. Walking gingerly, I limped around the office to relieve the pain in my hamstring and looked to where I had placed the two boxes.

They were gone.

Chapter 22

I startled awake. Someone hovered over me. I sat up quickly and raised the baseball bat to defend myself.

"Easy," Phish said, taking a step back, his hands raised.

I took a moment to catch my breath. "Crap," I said.

"Is that my Tioga George autographed baseball bat?" He looked and sounded astonished. I handed him the bat I'd taken from his wall before locking the front door and lying down on his couch. "What the hell is going on? What did you find at Frankie Ray's boardinghouse?"

I looked to the empty space on the floor where the two boxes had been, then to the clock on the wall. Seven a.m.

"Someone came into the newspaper office last night and took the two boxes I retrieved from Frankie Ray's landlady."

"What do you mean, someone came in? Here? They came into my newspaper office?"

I nodded.

"Who was it?"

"I don't know. A man. At least I'm fairly certain it was a man from the shadow in the front window and the pants and shoes I saw from under your desk."

"Under my desk?"

"I was hiding."

Phish frowned. Then he asked, "How did he get in with the door locked?"

I didn't want to tell Phish I had neglected to lock the door after the typesetter left for the evening. "He must have picked the lock," I said.

"Start from the beginning," Phish said, leaning the baseball bat against the side of his desk and sitting on the edge. "And don't leave out anything."

I told Phish what had happened. As I did, he moved to his upper drawer on the left side of his desk and removed Ray's Bible. I first showed him the receipt for the concrete, sledgehammer, and trowel, then showed him the circles I'd found around certain numbers and words on the otherwise clean pages.

"Thirteen forty-five East John," Phish said.

"I looked it up on the map. If I'm right about the bags of concrete and the tools, and about the numbers and words Ray circled, I suspect that might be the address where Ray hid the money, buried under a layer of concrete."

"Seems a leap. And convoluted. Why would Ray go to so much . . . mystery?"

"Don't know, but it seems unusual Ray would buy concrete and also keep a Bible; doesn't it?"

"I'll give you that. What else was in his personal effects?"

"Nothing of interest. Clothes mostly, a few pieces of jewelry, some paper. Pencils. Sad, really, a man could die and leave behind so little."

"Our physical possessions don't define us, Shoe. What will be remembered is how we lived our lives." Phish gave me a concerned expression and sighed. "How did this person find you here?"

"I don't know, but I assume he followed me from Ray's boardinghouse."

"Which means he knew you went to Frankie Ray's last known address."

"He must have waited outside the building and thought I was the typesetter when he went home for the evening. I heard him go through desk drawers before he came into your office and found Frankie Ray's boxes."

"You should not have stayed here alone. That was stupid."

"Maybe," I said, glad I didn't tell Phish I had neglected to lock the front door after the typesetter had left.

"No maybes about it. From now on promise me you won't do anything stupid."

I wasn't exactly sure how to do that, but I got his point, and I agreed to be more careful, or at least more discerning. "What do we do now?" I asked.

"That's what I was just considering. We can't call the police, not if Detective Blunt is the person who broke in. For now, we'll keep this between us. I'll send Kravitz to determine if the address even exists and, if it does, what kind of establishment is there and who owns it." He pulled a pocket watch from his vest and clicked it open. "You need to get to court. Trial will be starting soon. We don't want it to look like anything is up. Not until we get to the bottom of this."

The courtroom gallery was again packed. New faces mixed with the regular attendees: Katheryn Conner, Early Winn, Archibald Greer, and George Miller's friends and supporters. I wondered just how much money the guard at the door was making each day and whether he was spreading the wealth to his fellow guards. No doubt the take was a heck of a lot more than $5.40 a week, which got me to thinking about the nightclubs George Miller owned and the amounts of money each of those clubs brought in. Miller made a lot of cash, but he also spread that money far and wide, to the clothiers and tailors who made his expensive suits, the haberdasher who made his hats, the cobbler who made his leather shoes, and the stores where he purchased Katheryn Conner's fancy dresses, jewelry, and furs. He paid the cooks and the waiters he employed at his clubs, the orchestra musicians and the singers and entertainers, the bootleggers from whom he bought illegal liquor, and the box person in charge of the craps tables and the dealers who ran the card games. The money also lined the pockets of police officers and politicians Miller paid to look the other way.

And why wouldn't they look away? As Officer Norris had said, people were hurting, starving, some with no roof over their heads.

Whoever said "crime doesn't pay" had never sat through a trial like this one. It paid handsomely.

The thought of George Miller's cobbler caused me to consider the shoes worn by Ernie Blunt. I had to lean forward to look over the railing and under counsel table. Blunt wore brown wing tips. McKinley wore black wing tips; the defense attorneys, bailiff, and the other courtroom officers also wore dark-colored wing tips.

The color and style of the shoes wouldn't be much help, as Phish had suggested.

Upon the bailiff's announcement, Judge Kincaid climbed to his seat behind his elevated bench and spoke to Sullivan and McKinley, telling each he expected to end the trial no later than Friday. He wasn't seeking their opinion on the matter; he was dictating it to them. With that understanding, he directed the bailiff to bring in the jury, and upon the jurors retaking their seats, Sullivan rose and called several club performers, the most interesting of whom was singer Arthur Trent. Trent's shaved head reflected the overhead courtroom lights as he crossed to the witness stand in a sparkling blue suit with a light-blue shirt and matching tie.

"Good morning, Judge," Trent said to Kincaid. "Beautiful morning out there. Beautiful." He turned to the jury. "Ladies and gentlemen."

The bailiff administered the oath and asked if Trent swore to tell the truth, the whole truth, and nothing but the truth. "I won't swear," Trent said. "Not in front of the womenfolk. But I will tell you the truth."

The bailiff looked to Judge Kincaid, and Kincaid gave him a subtle nod. As the bailiff left, Sullivan approached. "Good morning, Mr. Trent."

"Good morning, Mr. Sullivan. And you can call me Happy. Everyone does. Since I was a little one."

"Okay," Sullivan said with a smile. "You're an entertainer?"

"My entire adult life." Trent's smile and animation were contagious, and the jurors smiled along with him.

"Where have you entertained audiences?"

"I appeared for four years at Doc Hamilton's speakeasy in the Central District before a Prohibition raid shut it down."

"That was a Negro speakeasy, was it not?"

"Well, I'd say predominantly Negro, but certainly not exclusive. We had a lot of white folk come to the club. Best jazz in the city before we got shut down."

"What did you do after the club was shut down?"

Happy smiled brightly. "You can't keep a good man like Doc Hamilton down long. As soon as they shut down his club, he opened up Doc Hamilton's Barbecue Ranch, a roadhouse out in Snohomish County, far enough from the city where the police wouldn't bother him none. Classy joint with an elegant interior that attracted folks far and wide. Some people said it was like the Cotton Club in New York's Harlem."

"Did the police eventually shut down Doc Hamilton's Barbecue Ranch also?" Sullivan asked.

"No, sir. That wasn't about to happen."

"And why not?"

"Well, I suppose the police didn't want to get fired," Trent said, his voice rising and a smile lighting his face.

"Can you explain?" Sullivan said.

"Seattle's most important businessmen and political folk frequented Doc's places. Why, even a few judges and the mayor." Trent smiled at Kincaid. "Not you though, Judge. Never did see you there."

Ripples of laughter rolled over the courtroom. Even Judge Kincaid gave a rare smile.

McKinley objected that the questioning was irrelevant.

"Granted," Kincaid said. "But certainly not dull."

Sullivan asked questions about how George Miller recruited Trent to work three nights a week at the Pom Pom Club.

"Was the pay good at the Pom Pom Club?"

"It was the best."

Trent then testified about the incident on April 11.

"I saw Mr. Frankie Ray insulting a young lady in the ballroom and the man she had come with. Mr. Miller stepped in, and Mr. Ray called Mr. Miller every name in the book on his way to being tossed out the door by the police."

Sullivan asked a few more questions about the incident, then sat.

McKinley approached the witness chair.

"Did you help remove Ray from the club?" McKinley asked.

"No, sir. I'm built for peace," Happy said, drawing more smiles.

"Do you know why Mr. Ray called Mr. Miller 'every name in the book'?"

"No, sir. Just heard it. Didn't decipher it."

"During the many hours you were at the club did you see Frankie Ray on other occasions?"

"Oh yes, sir. Mr. Ray was at the club frequently. I'd say a couple times a week, at least."

"Did Mr. Ray and Mr. Miller engage one another at the club?"

"Not all the time. Sometimes Mr. Ray or Mr. Miller had young ladies on their arms to attend to." Another smile.

"Did Mr. Miller look to be afraid of Mr. Ray?"

"Afraid?" he asked, voice rising. "No, sir. I saw the two of them at times laughing and smiling."

"No cussing at one another or yelling and screaming."

"I didn't see none of that, except that one time I told you about."

After Trent's testimony, Kincaid broke for lunch, and I hurried to the office rather than use a pay phone. I told Phish the testimony provided some pizzazz, but no fireworks. "The defense appears to be hanging their hats on one or two incidences, but McKinley is making inroads by getting the witnesses to say Mr. Ray and Mr. Miller were together often, and Miller wasn't afraid of him."

"Hmm," Phish said, and I could see his mind spinning over a potential headline.

"What did Kravitz find out about 1345 East John Street?" I asked.

"There's a building but it's vacant, like many on that block. I had him do a little digging into its past. The building had at one time been a supper club with a speakeasy in the basement called the Topsy Turvy."

"Did George Miller own it?"

"No. And it got shut down almost as quickly as it opened."

"Which means someone wasn't paying the right people."

"Likely a correct deduction," Phish said.

"What's there now?" I asked.

"Just an empty building. It's going to the wrecking ball to make way for government-built housing, another of Roosevelt's New Deal programs."

"When?" I asked, alarmed.

"Relax. Nothing is being demolished for some time," Phish assured me. "The government is just getting things established. These programs take time."

At my desk I typed up my notes from the morning testimony, provided the article to Kravitz, and hustled back to court. As I stepped off the elevator onto the eighth floor, I had my head down, thinking about the deserted building. I had a plan formulating. Phish had made me promise not to do something stupid, which was a pretty broad spectrum. What I intended wasn't stupid. It was well thought out.

I was so absorbed in my thoughts I didn't see Detective Ernie Blunt until I nearly walked into him in the marble foyer.

"Whoa." Blunt touched my shoulders to stop me. "What are you thinking about so deeply?"

"Oh, uh . . . nothing really. My mind is just wandering."

"So are your legs and your feet," he said.

It occurred to me court was about to start. "What are you doing out here? Shouldn't you be inside at counsel table?"

"I'm on my way. Just wanted to ask how your date was the other night with that woman from the county tax assessor's office?"

"Oh. That. It wasn't great," I said.

"No? That's too bad. What did you end up doing?"

"Just got a drink and some dinner and walked her home," I said, then added, "and I caught *King Kong* at the Green Parrot." I hadn't, not that night, but I wanted to see Blunt's response.

"Did you? How was it?"

"Great."

"Expensive evening. Drinks. Dinner. A show."

"I didn't take her to the show. We better get in the courtroom. The guard at the door doesn't like me much."

"He won't lock me out. You want me to have a word with him on your behalf?"

"No, that's all right."

"You sure? I wouldn't mind helping you out. I'd like to believe you'd do the same. Help me out."

I smiled. "Of course."

"You haven't learned anything more of interest, then . . . about the case, I mean? Anything you think I should know?"

"No. Nothing. The entertainers on the witness stand this morning were . . . entertaining though; huh?" I said.

"Very," Blunt said.

"I better get inside," I said.

"Don't let me stop you." Blunt stepped aside.

I hurried inside the courtroom with the feeling Blunt's gaze was burning holes in the back of my head.

Sullivan continued with his "parade of pals," one witness after the other, each of whom at one time had been Frankie Ray's friend, but that friendship didn't stop the witness from stomping on Ray's grave and testifying he was a violent man. Each witness was on and off the stand quickly, and McKinley was like a knight with a sword and shield, fending off one after the next, showing a bias.

Sullivan called Joe Gideon to the stand. Gideon was a small man with a nervous look who worked as a molder, a man who made molds for the decorative cornices of buildings.

"Did you know Mr. Frankie Ray?"

"Sure, I knew Frankie."

"And Mr. George Miller, the defendant. Do you know him?"

"I know George also." Gideon nodded to Miller, who returned the gesture.

"Were you ever present when Mr. Miller and Mr. Ray quarreled?"

"Yes, sir. I was present one time when Mr. Ray pulled a knife on Mr. Miller."

McKinley looked up from his notes, then to Blunt. He had not expected this testimony. This was exactly what Miller needed. It lent credibility to his assertion that he believed Ray had been reaching behind his back for a knife or a gun. It could establish self-defense. You could have heard a pin drop inside the courtroom.

"Where did this take place?" Sullivan asked in a soft voice.

Gideon had a habit of leaning forward when speaking, and he looked like he might topple off the front of the witness chair. "The Lodge Café."

"Can you tell the jurors about the quarrel leading to Mr. Ray pulling a knife on Mr. Miller?"

McKinley looked like he wanted to stand but couldn't think of the proper objection.

"They were arguing about a dame. I don't recall the dame's name, but Mr. Ray seemed to get more and more upset as the conversation went on. The next thing I know, he's practically foaming at the mouth."

I looked quickly to the jury and saw several frown.

"And he had a knife in his hand. And Mr. Miller, he backed from the booth and said, 'Take it easy, Frankie. Are you blowing your top off?'"

Foaming at the mouth. Blowing your top off. Close to Miller's testimony—words he'd supposedly said to Ray at the Pom Pom Club. Several jurors looked as if they weren't buying Gideon's testimony.

"And then what happened?" Sullivan asked.

"Well . . ." Gideon paused, like an actor in a play who had forgotten his lines. After a bit, he said, "Frankie just sort of stood there, like he was frozen or something, or maybe unsure as to what he was doing, and Mr. Miller, he just backed away, like I said, and left."

Blunt had leaned over to whisper in McKinley's ear while the prosecutor scribbled on his notepad.

"Did Mr. Miller look afraid to you?" Sullivan asked.

"Well, sure he did," Gideon said. "Anyone would have been, a guy pointing a knife at you. Scared for sure."

Sullivan turned from the witness stand with a smug expression. "Your witness."

McKinley finished listening to Blunt, then slid back his chair and approached the witness stand. "Are you working as a molder now, Mr. Gideon?"

Gideon slid back in his seat. "No. Not for about four years."

"I take it times are hard, then, after four years of unemployment?"

"I'm not unemployed."

"No?" McKinley's voice rose, and he looked toward the jury. "What do you do now?"

"I deal cards now."

"Gambling?"

"I guess so."

"Which is illegal."

"Well . . ."

"Where do you deal cards?"

"The Game Room."

"George Miller owns that establishment; doesn't he?"

"Well, I don't know for certain."

"Who pays your salary?"

"A company."

"The Musketeers?"

"That's right."

"George Miller's company."

"Is it?" Gideon said, trying to sound surprised but failing.

"You feel like maybe you owe Mr. Miller for giving you a job?"

"Well . . . I'll say this. Times are tough now. And jobs are hard to come by. You could say I owe him one."

"Did you owe one to Albert Dickey?"

Gideon had leaned forward to answer, but his lips didn't move.

"You were an alibi witness for the defense in the recent conviction of Albert Dickey for bank robbery; weren't you?"

"Well, yeah, I testified for Albert."

"Gave him an alibi that supposedly placed him at your card table in the Game Room at the time of the robbery in question."

"That's right."

"And you testified as an alibi witness in the trial of Frank Geysl, a card dealer in a downtown speakeasy who stabbed a man."

"The guy was stealing chips."

"Mr. Geysl and Mr. Dickey were both convicted despite your testimony; weren't they?"

"Yeah, they were."

"The juries didn't believe your testimony, did they?"

"Objection," Sullivan said.

"Sustained."

"I thought maybe you might have found yourself a new career," McKinley said.

"Objection," Sullivan said, more forceful.

"Sustained."

"The State has no further use of this witness, Your Honor."

It being close to the afternoon break, Sullivan needed to finish the day with a bang. He called Emmaline Cartman, a French hatcheck girl who worked the Pom Pom Club coatroom.

Cartman sauntered into the room in a tight green dress, hips swaying like the pendulum on a grandfather clock. A striking brunette, she was petite but entered with the aplomb of a grand duchess, which I wrote down for my article. She pulled white gloves from her fingers as she sashayed to the stand and laid them over the oak railing. I caught a glimpse of Katheryn Conner's facial expression, as pale and rigid as a marble statue. Conner's withering gaze shifted from Cartman to George Miller, who had subtly glanced over his shoulder at his sweetheart.

After preliminaries, Sullivan asked Cartman, "Where were you stationed inside the Pom Pom Club?"

"The coatroom was in the hall near the front door, but I could see into the bar and the dance hall," she said. Her French accent caused several male jurors to smile.

Conner, now red in the face, occasionally closed her eyes, the muscles of her jaw so tight they looked like they might snap.

Cartman testified about the April 11 incident and said Ray told Miller, "I'll get you."

Sullivan sat.

McKinley walked slowly to the center of the room. "Are you married?" he asked.

"I don't believe that is any business of yours."

"Answer the question, Miss Cartman," Kincaid said, not sounding at all bewitched.

"No. I am not married."

It was an interesting question. It seemed irrelevant, but I deduced the relevance when McKinley asked his next question. "Who hired you to work at the Pom Pom Club?"

"MisterGeorgeMiller." She said Miller's full name like it was one word, smiled, and gave Miller a small wink. Conner shifted in her seat with clenched hands in her lap.

"A lot of people were at the Pom Pom Club the night of April eleventh?" McKinley asked.

"A lot of people are at the club every night. It is a popular club."

"And you're busy checking hats and coats?"

"'Tis my job."

"Let me direct you to this chart." McKinley pointed to a chart of the nightclub's interior he had placed on an easel facing the jury. It clearly showed Cartman could not have seen the incident in the ballroom from her position checking coats and hats.

"You won't 'get' me on that chart," Cartman said.

"'Get' you?" McKinley asked, sounding innocent.

"I won't get mixed up."

"I'm just wondering how you saw and heard so much from way over here at the coat check on a busy night?"

"It was no problem," she said.

"You can't see or hear through walls; can you?" McKinley said.

"Objection," Sullivan said.

"Sustained."

"No further questions," McKinley said.

Cartman picked up her gloves, tossed them over her arm, and stalked haughtily off the stand, hips in full swing again.

Miller again turned in his seat, but Conner kept her head down and did not meet his gaze.

Chapter 23

I had my story. Phish would be enamored with Cartman. Talk about pizzazz. I hurried to the pay phone, called Kravitz, and dictated my story, then asked to speak to Phish and told him about Cartman. He told me he'd rush the article up to the typesetter.

When the day ended, I hurried from the courtroom back to the *Daily Star*.

Phish handed me the paper.

Hatcheck Girl

Steals the Show

Other Witnesses Claim

Ray Brawled at Club.

Once Pulled a Knife.

Negro performer Arthur "Happy" Trent and a parade of Frankie Ray's pals-turned-his-enemies testified in the murder trial of George Miller, but it was diminutive hatcheck girl Emmaline Cartman who stole the show this day.

"Nice article." Phish spoke from over my shoulder as I read at my desk.

"Thanks, but the most interesting thing about today isn't in the article," I said.

Phish looked wounded. "Why not?"

"Because I don't have any facts to support my intuition."

"I'll be the judge of that." He grabbed Nathan Kawolski's chair from his desk, turned it backward, and faced me, forearms on the chair back. "Spill."

"I think George Miller had a thing with Emmaline Cartman, and Katheryn Conner knows it."

"Okay. What evidence do you have? Attractive?"

I thought about that word. "Different."

"Sensual?"

"That would be the better word." I explained how Cartman dressed and entered the courtroom.

Phish smiled. "My own mother, God rest her soul, said a woman like that 'has more coal burning in her skirt than the boilers of the *Titanic*.'"

I laughed. "From the moment Cartman entered the courtroom, Conner went rigid as a statue, but her eyes shot hot daggers at both Cartman and, when he turned to look at her, George Miller."

"Really? Now *that* is an opening sentence, Shoe."

"When Miller turned around, he looked more afraid of Conner than the witnesses said he was of Ray."

"Even better," Phish said. "Now you're getting it." He gave this some quick thought. "Yet Conner's been in court."

"Every day. Front row," I said. "Dressed to the nines."

"But you don't think her presence is genuine?"

"I don't know."

"She doesn't love him?"

"No," I said, emphatic. "I think she does."

"Ah. I see."

"She wouldn't have had the reaction she had in court today if she didn't legitimately love Miller, or at least have strong feelings for him; would she?"

"Likely not."

"I think Cartman opened up some deep wounds."

"Speaking of which . . . Any luck with that bakery gal, Amara?"

"I went to the bakery, but she wasn't there, and her father made it very clear if I tried to speak to her, his two sons would pay me a visit. If I could just talk to her alone . . . without her father or her two brothers around. But I don't see that happening at the moment."

"Don't give up just yet, Shoe. 'It's hard to fail, but it is worse to have never tried to succeed.' Teddy Roosevelt."

"Did he say anything about confronting an angry Italian father?"

"Time heals wounds. Give her time, Shoe." He stood from his chair and spun it like twirling a woman on the dance floor back to Kawolski's desk. "I have an engagement this evening. I want you to go back to the house. Don't go looking for that speakeasy on East John Street. It isn't going anywhere, and it's clear someone is watching you."

"I know, 'Don't do anything stupid.'"

I thought back to Ernie Blunt confronting me in the foyer outside Judge Kincaid's courtroom. He clearly knew I wasn't telling him everything. I also thought of Teddy Roosevelt and his Rough Riders. They would have ridden horses down the hill to First Avenue and charged in the bakery's front door, but I was a long way from Teddy Roosevelt and his men. For one, I couldn't ride a horse.

I had something else in mind.

After Phish departed, I went into his office and removed the flashlight I had seen in his desk drawer when I had slipped in the Bible. He kept the light in case the power went out at the paper. I put it in my reporter's satchel and departed. On the street, I checked my surroundings. Plenty of black cars passed, but no driver seemed interested in me, nor did I notice anyone loitering or watching me. I walked north, then turned right on East Madison Street. My intent was to catch a trolley car, but it seemed I reached each stop just in time to miss one. I didn't mind. Walking would give me more time to not be stupid, which was really all I had promised Phish.

I stepped into an entry for a closed business but didn't detect a familiar car, nor a person watching me. I made a right turn at the end of the block, another right at the next corner, then a third right, and returned to where I had started. Again, I didn't notice anything peculiar. I continued north and came to Seattle College. I decided to get off the main road and cross the campus on foot.

I exited on East Madison Street, took a left on Twelfth Avenue, and walked six blocks to East John Street. I took a right and checked the addresses on the buildings, then turned and walked the opposite direction, which I figured wasn't a bad thing if I was trying to detect a tail. I didn't.

I walked on the north side of the street. When I got to the 1300 block, I looked across the street at an empty lot, and beside the lot a one-story structure with a skeletal metal awning that had likely once been covered with cloth to protect customers entering the building from the rain. I slid back into a doorway of a closed storefront with newspapers taped on the inside of the windows. From there I watched for anything out of the ordinary.

After a few minutes, when nothing alarming caught my attention, I hurried across the street and stepped into the building's shadow. I tried sliding windows open. None budged. At the back I located a door at the bottom of two steps and tried the doorknob. Locked. I went to the other side of the building. A windowpane had been broken. It looked as if a rock had been thrown through it. I reached my arm inside the broken glass, careful not to catch my coat on a jagged edge, and stretched for the window lock. I was just able to grab it, but I had trouble pulling the lever. I was about to give up when I felt the lever give. I stretched a bit farther to get a better grip. The lever pulled to the right. I removed my arm and raised the window sash.

I found a box in the vacant lot, set it under the window, and climbed through.

I was inside.

Phish said the Topsy Turvy was a speakeasy, which were usually in building basements and entered by either showing a club card or speaking a password through a slot in the back door. The two stairs leading to a door at the back of the building indicated a basement, but where was the interior stairwell?

I removed the flashlight from my satchel and turned it on. The light cast a tunnel through the murky interior. The room was empty but for strewn garbage and structural pillars. I scanned the room for stairs but didn't readily see any. I did see a few doors. One led to the bathroom. A second to a large closet. I walked to another door and opened it.

Jackpot.

Stairs descended into darkness. I shone the torch beam down to the bottom, then along the wall. I found a switch. I flicked it, but no light illuminated the staircase. With one hand on the stair railing, I descended. My heart pounded. The wooden stairs creaked and groaned. When I reached the floor, I stepped forward into cobwebs, managed not to panic, and wiped them away. The walls were painted with murals of Seattle—Elliott Bay and Mount Rainier among other iconic images.

I shone the light on a waist-high counter, likely the makeshift bar, and on a small wooden platform—a place for musicians and singers perhaps. The floor was black-and-white linoleum squares.

A speakeasy for certain.

I crept forward, following the light, uncertain what I was looking for. After five minutes I noted nothing unusual. Maybe I'd been wrong. Maybe the markings in the Bible weren't some clues to a treasure.

I noted a rectangular rug at the foot of the stairs I had descended. I hadn't given it much thought before, thinking it was for those arriving to wipe their feet. But revelers wouldn't have likely come through the front door. They would have entered the back door off the alley. The carpet location seemed out of place. I walked over and lifted it. I pushed on the linoleum squares. They moved. I grabbed a corner and the square lifted. I removed another tile, then another, in a pattern roughly the size of the carpet.

The cement beneath the tiles was lighter in color and not as smoothly finished as the cement along the edges. I also didn't see any glue marks normally used to hold the linoleum squares to the concrete. The rectangle had been poured after the floor was tiled. I was sure of it.

With my heart pounding, I thought again of the Count of Monte Cristo, Edmond Dantès, and the riches he had found.

And the misery those riches had brought him.

Chapter 24

The following morning, Wednesday, I awoke before Phish and his wife and left the house for the office. I had not told Phish what I had uncovered at the Topsy Turvy. I had every intention of telling him, but when I walked in the door and he asked where I had been, I said I went by the bakery, but it was closed by the time I had arrived. Phish didn't push me on this lie, which made me feel worse for not telling him the truth. Maybe I didn't want another lecture on doing something stupid.

But that wasn't the reason.

I kept thinking of all that money. If he was convicted, George Miller wouldn't be able to use the money. Frankie Ray was dead, and Miller's remaining partner, Syd Brunn, wouldn't suspect a reporter of having solved the clues Frankie Ray had left. I kept thinking I could pay off the mortgage on my parents' home and pay my father's hospital bills. But my mother would never let me. I could do it all anonymously. They'd certainly never suspect me, making $5.40 a week. Maybe I could also buy a headstone for Joan Daley's grave, though I'd have to be careful how I spent the money. Anything too extravagant, like buying a Cadillac, would make Blunt suspicious, and I'd end up like Frankie Ray.

I stopped my thoughts.

I knew I would never do it, even if I found the money.

My mother would say no good comes from dirty money. The money, if I ever found any, should go to those who really needed it, and God knew that was a lot of people.

◆ ◆ ◆

I arrived in court, and once Judge Kincaid got the trial back underway, I focused. Sullivan called Dr. John L. Thomas, Frankie Ray's urologist. Those of us in the press knew Sullivan had subpoenaed the doctor to get him to admit Ray suffered from syphilis or gonorrhea.

"Was Frankie Ray a patient of yours?" Sullivan asked Dr. Thomas.

"He was."

"What was he suffering from?"

McKinley stood. "Objection, Your Honor, statutory privilege."

Kincaid asked, "Is it your intent, Dr. Thomas, to claim statutory privilege and refuse to reveal anything you learned from Mr. Ray while he was your patient?"

"It is," Dr. Thomas said.

"I will ask the bailiff to remove the jury from the courtroom," Kincaid said. Before the bailiff did so, Judge Kincaid explained. "Ladies and gentlemen of the jury, counsel and I have a legal matter to discuss. When we conclude, the bailiff will bring you back into court."

When the bailiff had cleared the courtroom, Kincaid told Sullivan to proceed.

"Your Honor, this information is highly relevant to the defense's theory of this case. The State contends Mr. Ray was a peaceful man on a mission of charity the night in question. We contend Mr. Ray sought the money to make payments on a Cadillac he was in danger of forfeiting, and when he didn't get the money from Mr. Miller, he went berserk. We wish to prove Mr. Ray was prone to fits of violence caused by the medical condition for which Dr. Thomas was treating him."

McKinley said, "That's all well and good, Your Honor, but Dr. Thomas has claimed his statutory privilege to refuse to reveal anything he learned from a patient, and the privilege is statutorily protected."

"No doubt at your advice," Sullivan shot back. When McKinley didn't respond, Sullivan turned back to the bench. "Your Honor, the defense requests this court order Dr. Thomas to answer questions. It is prejudicial that, had the State called the physician as a witness, the physician could not have invoked the privilege, but he can in this instance when called by the defense."

McKinley said, "Your Honor, that is for the legislature, not this court, to decide."

"Your Honor," Sullivan said, "the State is quick to argue it is the defendant's burden to prove he acted in self-defense—that Mr. Miller must prove he knew of and was afraid of Mr. Ray's propensity for violence. The doctor's testimony will go directly toward that proof."

Kincaid listened to the debate with little interruption or admonishment of either counsel, which was against what had been, to this point, his common practice. It was like a schoolmaster handing out boxing gloves to two boys constantly arguing and letting them slug it out once and for all. When the attorneys had finished throwing punches, Kincaid leaned forward.

"I confess this question is most troublesome," Kincaid said. "The statute provides a physician shall not be compelled to reveal information obtained from a patient in his professional relations. There can be no doubt the purpose of the statute is to permit a patient to freely disclose matters to his physician without the danger of being embarrassed while living, or having his memory disgraced after he is dead, as the State so argues.

"Keeping in mind this purpose, and there is no one in court to give his consent to the doctor's testimony on the deceased's behalf, I feel the physician's lips are sealed, and the court is powerless to pry those lips open absent a decision by the legislature."

I could see Phish's potential headline now.

Judge Refuses to Pry Open

Doctor's Lips

Sullivan stood. "Your Honor, the defense does not agree but will respect your decision and not ask Dr. Thomas to reveal any confidential communications with Mr. Ray."

Kincaid summoned the jury, and Sullivan recalled Dr. Thomas.

"Dr. Thomas, without revealing anything discussed between you and Mr. Ray, I would like to know whether the unstated malady from which Mr. Ray sought your treatment is recognized as creating homicidal tendencies?"

McKinley objected strenuously, but Judge Kincaid overruled the objection. Early Winn whispered to the person seated beside him, "The judge doesn't want to give the defense an appealable issue to take to the appellate court."

Dr. Thomas said, "Without specifics, I can say that in latent types of *some* diseases, a disturbance of the central nervous system can materially affect the patient's mental condition."

"Is that a yes?"

"Yes. It has been," Thomas said.

"And to your expert knowledge, does the use of intoxicating liquor intensify the disease's effects?"

"Yes, it can, in *some* cases . . . that is, with *some* diseases."

Though I was no expert, the testimony seemed to be a decisive victory for the defense, which had now corroborated the statements of laymen with Dr. Thomas's expert testimony.

McKinley stood and approached the doctor. "Dr. Thomas, let us focus only on the victim, Mr. Ray. Can you say the violent acts, which the defense attorneys have put before you, are symptomatic of any such malady with which he was afflicted?"

"No. Not symptomatic. The violent acts can be caused by any number of things not related to any malady."

"Does spitting in a policeman's face indicate the person has this malady?"

"No. The person might simply dislike police officers or authority figures."

"And if the victim was upset with the defendant for reneging on an agreement to pay someone's hospital bill, and an argument ensued, that argument would not necessarily be due to the victim's alleged malady; would it?"

"No. He could simply have become upset."

"So, while the victim may have suffered from a malady, you have no expert knowledge the malady had any causal connection to creating anger or violence in this particular instance; do you?"

"I do not. As I said, it is not symptomatic."

I thought it a good cross-examination, under the circumstances.

Following Thomas's dismissal, Kincaid turned to the clock, then said, "Call your next witness."

Sullivan walked to counsel table and he, attorney Chevas, and Miller huddled closely for less than a minute. Then Sullivan turned and faced the bench. "The defense rests, Your Honor."

A murmur rippled through the courtroom. This was unexpected, and I, along with the others in the gallery, wondered what it could mean.

"Very well. Then we will break for the day and begin tomorrow with any rebuttal witnesses for the State." Kincaid rapped his gavel and dismissed the jury.

Given the buildup of the case as the Trial of the Century, the ending, if it was the ending, felt anticlimactic.

I hurried back to the *Daily Star* and went to Phish's office to tell him the defense had rested unexpectedly but found his office empty. His coat was not on the stand.

"He has another engagement," Kravitz said, entering to put copy on Phish's desk.

I left the office, and when I arrived at Phish's home, his wife said her husband had a charitable function to attend and told her not to wait up for him. We had dinner together and after dinner we played canasta until I tired and turned in. When I awoke, Phish had already departed for the office.

Chapter 25

Thursday morning, the line snaking its way from the courtroom doors down the marbled hallways had returned. Word had no doubt spread from the short statement I'd managed to get into my afternoon article, and the headlines in the *Daily Times* and *Post-Intelligencer* that morning, that the defense had rested and the two sides might give closing arguments. The gallery in the courtroom was once again standing room only. We sat in the pews shoulder to shoulder.

When Kincaid took the bench, he wanted to be sure order was maintained and admonished us, though most of us were familiar with his lecture and his threats to close the trial to the public if he deemed it necessary.

Perhaps sensing the anticipation in the crowd, or confident in his case, McKinley declined to call any rebuttal witnesses and told Kincaid he wished to move directly to closing argument. This tactic seemed to catch the defense off guard. Sullivan huddled quickly with Miller and Chevas, then proclaimed the defense ready. He stood and moved for a directed verdict, asking Kincaid to find for the defendant.

"The State has failed to put on sufficient evidence to rebut defendant's plea of self-defense, the evidence for which is overwhelming, and from which the jury could only reach one conclusion. George Miller acted in self-defense when he shot Frankie Ray."

McKinley's response was brief, going over all the evidence the State had presented and the contradictory evidence the defense had presented. To no one's surprise, Kincaid denied the motion.

With that, the jury was brought in. Kincaid briefly told the jurors closing arguments were not evidence but simply the attorneys' opinions regarding the testimony and the evidence. Following these instructions Kincaid took a moment to arrange materials on his desk, but one got the impression he was giving counsel time to prepare. The silence in the courtroom was deafening and the anticipation electric.

"Deputy Prosecutor McKinley, you may proceed."

McKinley slid back his chair, buttoned his gray suit jacket, and approached the jury. He thanked them, then said, "At the beginning of the trial I told you the State might or might not seek the death penalty for Mr. Miller's first-degree killing of Frankie Ray. This morning I am here to tell you the State will not seek the death penalty."

Murmurs in the gallery drew the glare of Judge Kincaid, and the attorneys at the defense table glanced at one another as if taken off guard by this concession.

"Brilliant," Early Winn whispered to the person beside him. "He doesn't want the death penalty to hang up this jury and possibly have to retry the case."

"Instead," McKinley said. "The State asks you to find the defendant guilty of first-degree murder with a penalty of life in prison."

McKinley then ripped into Miller's self-defense argument, calling it a fabrication. "Counsel has attempted to paint Mr. Miller as the victim and Mr. Ray as the killer. He has called Mr. Ray a beast, something below human. But no matter how low on the human scale Mr. Ray might have fallen, one man stood beside him. George Miller.

"Mr. Miller and the men in the bar that morning changed their stories 180 degrees from the statements they gave to police immediately following the shooting. The story they each told the police was a complete fabrication—one Mr. Miller concocted while Frankie Ray bled to death on the Pom Pom Club's floor, within feet of where he stood.

They didn't call an ambulance. Mr. Miller was content to let Mr. Ray die, because a dead man couldn't tell what really happened."

No, he couldn't, I thought. Though I doubted McKinley and I agreed on what had really happened that morning.

"Then," McKinley continued, "after consulting with counsel, and no doubt being told his story had more holes than Swiss cheese, the defense fabricated and concocted here, in this very courtroom, another fable, that Frankie Ray was this wild and violent creature of whom Mr. Miller was afraid. In short, Mr. Miller lied to the police, and he is lying to you. You can decide for yourself why he has repeatedly lied."

Indeed, that seemed to be the pertinent question. But while McKinley said the motive was a debt, be it to pay Joan Daley's hospital bill or to make payments on the Cadillac, I was confident what had led to the shooting was, as Phish had said, as old as time itself. Greed.

"When the Pom Pom Club closed, those who had worked there joined the unemployed—witnesses in need of money and who, the State has proven, were willing to say just about anything for the right price."

McKinley went through each of the defense's witnesses and pointed out why each had a reason to lie and could not be trusted. McKinley then created a stir when he donned Ray's bullet-riddled and blood-stained coat and reenacted the killing to show it could not have happened as Miller testified.

"Mr. Miller shot Frankie Ray, the victim, in cold blood, and Mr. Miller should be put away for life." McKinley raised his voice, his inflections and his gestures reminding me so much of the sermons in church in Kansas City.

"I say now to you. To each of you. There is but one verdict you can reasonably find from all the evidence put forward these past weeks. There is but one conclusion. George Miller is guilty of first-degree murder and should be imprisoned for the remainder of his life."

McKinley left the jury railing and pointed his finger at George Miller, the trumpet projecting from Miller's ear. "This man has respected neither the laws of God nor the laws of man. If you don't hang him, you should at least put him where he'll be kept away from society for the rest of his life. Send him to jail, ladies and gentlemen. Send him to jail so no law-abiding citizen will be susceptible to his violence and depravity. The defense called Frankie Ray a beast. I say to each of you, the beast remains alive, and he sits here in this courtroom at defense counsel's table."

Sullivan objected. "State's deputy prosecutor is testifying about matters never introduced. We demand a mistrial."

"Your objection is sustained. Your demand is denied. The jury is to disregard counsel's opinion about the defendant being a beast."

McKinley didn't care. He'd let loose a fury, relating Miller to the beast in the Bible, to Lucifer, the devil himself. "Manslaughter is entirely out of the question," he thundered. "If you return a verdict of manslaughter, there would be a celebration in the underworld tonight."

Again, Sullivan rose and loudly objected. Again, it was sustained. Again, it didn't matter.

"This is not just a conflict between Miller and Ray. It is a conflict between organized society—people who believe in enforcing the law—and the underworld."

Another objection. Same result.

"The defense attempts to cloud the issue by putting Mr. Ray on trial," McKinley said. "Don't let them get away with it. Don't you forget the man lying in a casket six feet under the ground is Frankie Ray, the victim, and he was put there by the defendant, George Miller. Do not be misled by the fancy clothes and the movie-star good looks. The defendant is not a movie star. He is not a good person. He is the beast. Find the beast, George Miller, guilty of first-degree murder."

Sullivan didn't bother to object.

When McKinley sat, Judge Kincaid broke for a short recess to allow everyone to "catch his or her breath" before the defense's closing argument. Outside the courtroom, the gallery mingled in the hallway, talking.

"Brilliant," Early Winn said again. "Likening Miller to the beast was brilliant. The Bible is filled with references of Lucifer changing his appearance to something aesthetically pleasing to lure others to do his will."

I thought so as well, and I thought Phish would too. I used the short break to phone into the office. Kravitz answered and I dictated my story, using McKinley's references to the beast to give it some pizzazz. I told him I'd call again after Sullivan closed.

I hung up the phone and looked down the hall. The crowd had gone back inside the courtroom. I slid back the phone booth accordion door, noticed Blunt coming from the men's room, and decided to wait, not wanting to give him another chance to ask me questions. As he crossed the rotunda, a woman stepped out from behind a pillar—she'd apparently been waiting for him. Blunt stopped dead in his tracks.

Katheryn Conner.

Blunt looked over both shoulders but thankfully didn't turn around. The two spoke for only seconds, and I couldn't hear them or read their lips. I also couldn't tell from Conner's facial expressions what the two talked about. Blunt stepped past her to the courtroom. Conner lingered a second longer, as if to allow Blunt a sufficient head start and avoid any appearance of impropriety. Then she walked past the guard at the door.

I walked to the courtroom door. "Well, at least you're consistent," the guard said. "Always late to the party, aren't you?"

I'd had enough of him. "Looks like you got a haircut," I said. "Shoes are shined. Uniform looks freshly pressed. It's almost as if you suddenly have money to burn. I wonder what the judge would think if he knew you were selling seats in his gallery?"

I expected the guard to sputter and cough. I expected him to be concerned. Instead, he smiled. "I don't think the judge would mind, but you're free to ask him," he said. Then he lost the smile. "There's a depression going on, son, and everyone is doing all he can to avoid renting a room in Hooverville. The quicker you accept that, the quicker you'll have a nickel or two in your pocket at the end of each day."

I walked forward but my thoughts stayed behind, deciphering what I'd just been told. I thought it more fabrication. I'd certainly witnessed my fill inside the courtroom, but the guard's demeanor and the conviction with which he'd spoken, the confidence with which he'd dared me, without revealing any concern, to speak to the judge, indicated what he'd said was not a fabrication.

Judge Kincaid was getting a cut from the courtroom attendance.

My God. Everyone *was* in on the take. Phish had said as much, but it hadn't really set in. Not until that moment.

I retook my designated seat in the crowded gallery and thought again of my buried treasure, and of Edmond Dantès. I thought of leaving the courtroom, finding the treasure, and leaving Seattle. I'd reappear in Kansas City as a different man, one who would save my family home and pay off my family's debts.

Judge Kincaid retook the bench, but I no longer viewed him as Wyatt Earp at the O.K. Corral. Maybe the guard at the courtroom door was right. Maybe it was time to open my eyes and get what I could, like everyone else.

Judge Kincaid had the jury brought in and invited Sullivan to give his closing. This morning Sullivan wore an off-white suit, and I wondered if it was symbolic. I'd seen similar suits worn in church, usually on Easter Sunday. Was his choice intended to foretell George Miller's resurrection?

But Sullivan did not approach the jury or begin his closing like a dime-store preacher curing the sick and selling potions. He spoke to the jury in a quiet, almost intimate voice.

"The State brought this case. The State accused George Miller of murder. The State initially sought to put my client to death, to have you impose the death sentence. In the face of this possibility, my client was understandably terrified and said things he shouldn't have said. Things that were not the truth. Why did he do it?

"Fear.

"He knew if a jury such as yourself found him guilty of murder, it was possible the State would seek to put him to death.

"He has been called an underworld member. He has been accused of illegal acts in his club. Selling liquor and promoting gambling. But he isn't the person drinking the liquor or rolling the dice. That was the good citizens of Seattle. All he did was provide a little entertainment, an oasis in the midst of a great depression that has sucked the life out of so many.

"You heard his testimony. He panicked and made up a story. Who amongst you would not have made up a story to save your life?" Sullivan pointed to the witness chair. "But he didn't lie in court. He didn't lie under oath on that witness stand. No, he did not. He sat in that chair, and he told you the truth—truth corroborated by the witnesses." Sullivan took in a deep breath and pushed away from the railing. "In that chair, sworn to tell the truth, the whole truth, and nothing but the truth, witness after witness told you Frankie Ray was a violent and disturbed man when drinking. They told you of incidents in which he had pulled a knife on the defendant. They told you he spat in the face of a patrolman, threw a glass in a young woman's face, and had to be physically removed from the Pom Pom Club. The State can paint Mr. Miller as a liar. It can paint his friends as liars. But for you to find in the State's favor, you will also have to believe the patrolmen who testified in this trial also lied to you. Do you believe that to be so?"

The guard stood at the door with his hair freshly cut, his shoe tops reflecting the courtroom lights, his freshly pressed suit starched so heavy you could bounce a quarter off it. "Yes," I said softly. I didn't believe it when I'd first come through those courtroom doors. But I believed it now. They could all be bought. Including Judge Kincaid.

"The State accuses the defense of impugning the victim's integrity. Hypocrisy! Hypocrisy!" Sullivan said, the fire building, and the brimstone sure to follow. "The State would have you believe the defendant is part of the underworld, that he is evil, and Mr. Ray was just a poor helpless victim.

"I told you at the beginning of this trial the defense would have to break the time-entrusted rule of speaking ill of the dead. Mr. Ray was violent. He was violent inside the boxing ring, and he was violent outside the ring when he drank. The defendant knew this. Did he turn his back on Mr. Ray? Did he prevent Mr. Ray from entering his club? No. He did not. He gave Mr. Ray the benefit of the doubt, but with the lingering knowledge Mr. Ray was a ticking time bomb who could go off at any moment.

"He went off the morning of June thirteenth. What the argument was about doesn't matter, does it? What matters was Mr. Ray's reaction when Mr. Miller refused to give him the money. And the result is something everyone who testified agreed on. Mr. Ray came at Mr. Miller. He came at him like a fighter in the ring coming at his opponent." Sullivan crouched, hands in front of him like a wrestler. "Mr. Miller backed away, tried to reason with Mr. Ray. Tried to calm him. But Mr. Ray kept coming. Then he reached behind his back, and Mr. Miller, having once confronted Mr. Ray holding a knife, pulled his gun and shot him. And when Mr. Ray did not go down, when he kept moving forward, Mr. Miller shot him a second time."

It was a convincing closing. I could tell from the jurors' expressions they were listening intently, perhaps even considering leniency. At the defense table Miller lowered his head; tears rolled down his cheeks. Again, if it was a performance, it was as good as any Broadway-trained actor's. I turned my attention to Katheryn Conner. She, too, had lowered her head to her chest, but from my angle I could see the side of her face. No tears left trails in her pancake makeup.

Sullivan went on to attack the State's case, and when he had finished, he took a step back and caught his breath. He gently touched the jury railing, once more lowering his voice, making the moment more intimate.

"It is a terrible thing when a man loses his life. But in this instance and under these circumstances, if ever a man courted death, if ever a man asked to be shot, that man was Frankie Ray. Mr. George Miller shot Mr. Ray in self-defense. I trust you will agree."

The State having the last word, McKinley rose as Sullivan sat, and I could tell from his intense look that he would not hold back. He built his argument slowly, first rebutting Sullivan's theatrics with "facts." After he had done so, he unleashed fury.

"This is a conflict between good and evil, between justice and injustice, between truth and deceit. The defense has put on witness after witness who thought nothing of lying, first to the police and then to you, ladies and gentlemen. Why? Because they do not respect this process and they do not respect your intelligence. They needed a story to pull the wool over your eyes." McKinley went through the various stories, calling each "Preposterous." "How many witnesses told you Frankie Ray was 'gnashing his teeth'? Preposterous. How many told you George Miller feared Frankie Ray? Preposterous. Mr. Miller claims he feared Ray when he drank, and yet Mr. Miller let Ray into the Pom Pom Club frequently and let him drink shot after shot of alcohol at the bar? Preposterous. Mr. Miller claims he didn't want to throw Ray out, and yet he'd previously had him thrown out, twice. The entire defense is preposterous. The entire defense is an affront to your intelligence. Do not let the defense insult your intelligence. Do not fall for all the lies and fabrications. Do not fall for the wolf in sheep's clothing. Do not let George Miller get away with murder."

When McKinley finished, Judge Kincaid instructed the jury on the elements of first-degree murder, second-degree murder, and manslaughter. Or, he said, they could acquit Miller entirely. The law, he said, presumes every killing to be murder in the second degree, the burden resting with the State to raise the degree, and upon the defense to reduce it or to prove the killing justifiable.

With those final words, Kincaid instructed the bailiff to take the five women and eight men to the jury room. It was 4:20 in the afternoon. Kincaid asked the jury to deliberate as far into the evening as they deemed prudent. He didn't say, though it was clear, that he wanted a verdict by Friday.

I gave the court clerk my name and the *Daily Star*'s number and asked for a phone call in the event the jurors reached a verdict, then exited the courthouse and made my way back to the newsroom to talk with Phish. He was in his office. He had his sleeves rolled up and ink on his hands along with a few cuts and scrapes.

"What's going on?" I asked.

"Trouble with a printer."

"Is it working?"

"It is now. Why? Do you have a verdict?"

I told him what had transpired. "Let's hope we don't get a verdict tonight and miss out on the opportunity to sell a lot of papers," he said. "What's your gut telling you?"

"I don't think we'll get a verdict tonight, though Kincaid wants one by tomorrow. What the jury will ultimately decide? I just don't know. It won't be first-degree murder. I think the defense did their best to muddy those waters."

"I'll have Kravitz grab some dinner and bring it back to the newsroom. Then I want you to go back to the courtroom. One never knows what might transpire."

Chapter 26

I ate dinner, then hurried back down the hill to the courthouse. Unlike the past two weeks, only the journalists and the hangers-on remained in the gallery. Everyone looked tired and worn out. I watched the interaction between Miller and Katheryn Conner. They spoke to one another but showed no affection. No hand-holding. No kisses. Just sullen expressions and voices.

"What do you think?" Detective Blunt hovered over me.

"About what?" I asked.

He chuckled. "About what's on everyone's mind right now. The verdict."

"I don't know," I said.

"You were here every day. You heard all the testimony. You have to have some opinion."

"I was surprised the State took the death penalty off the table, but I suppose it was strategic," I said. "It eliminated the possibility of a holdout juror opposed to imposing death."

"That's exactly why we did it. Do you think the State still has a chance at first-degree murder?" Blunt asked.

"I don't know," I said and just then heard squeals of laughter that were so incongruous with the setting it sent a chill down my spine. The squeals came from behind the wall to the jury room.

The defense attorneys looked at one another, first surprised, then confident. They nodded to George Miller as if to say, *We got this.*

Maybe, but as the hours passed, rumors circulated among the court staff that the verdict would not be this night. Confident in the staff's assessment, I made a call to let Phish know, then I double-checked that the court clerk still had the *Star*'s number and would call me with any news, then went back to the office. The typesetter told me Phish had taken off shortly after my phone call advising that the jury was unlikely to reach a verdict. I stayed at the office until the court clerk called to say there would be no verdict this night, but that the jury had not sought any further evidence or instruction.

I spoke to Phish at his home late at night.

"Nothing from the court?" he asked.

"It won't be tonight," I said. "But I think soon."

"Why is that?"

"When the clerk called, he said that before the jury stopped for the night it did not indicate they would *not* be able to reach a verdict, and they didn't ask for further instructions."

"We'll get a verdict, then."

"Looks that way."

"Let's hope it's in the morning. We'll sell a lot of newspapers, whatever the jurors decide."

Of that, I had no doubt. It was about the only thing I didn't doubt.

Chapter 27

Friday morning, I was exhausted from the marathon Thursday night and had no sooner sat at my desk when Phish stormed out of his office like Teddy Roosevelt charging a mountain. "Jury is coming back this morning," he said sliding on his suit coat. "Monte, keep the phone lines cleared. Richard, get your camera. We'll run the photo just beneath the banner. Let's go, Shoe. Chop chop. Time waits for no man."

"You're coming to court?"

"I created this Trial of the Century. And I damn well am going to see its conclusion in person."

I threw my satchel strap over my shoulder and hurried out the door, practically running to keep up with Phish's long strides down the block.

"I didn't get a call," I said, catching up to him.

"You will, at nine this morning." He pulled his watch from his vest pocket and snapped it open. "In about twenty minutes."

"How did you hear?"

He gave me a glance out of his peripheral vision. "I didn't always sit behind a desk in my glass office, Shoe. I used to pound the pavement just like you, make contacts. Some of those contacts and I go back a long way."

We arrived before counsel. Marshals brought Miller down from the county jail. Word of a possible verdict had spread quickly and the gallery was already filling and would no doubt be packed. Eventually, Miller was brought in wearing handcuffs. He smiled, but it was nerves. He wore the neat brown suit he'd worn many times. When the handcuffs were removed, he turned to his personal counsel, the only attorney yet in the courtroom. "This looks bad," he said. "It's Friday the thirteenth."

A friend stepped forward from the gallery and handed Miller two tickets. "It's for a performance tonight," the friend said. "For you and Katheryn to attend after you're acquitted."

Miller thanked him and slid the tickets into his coat.

As the gallery filled, I made a note of what Miller had said about it being Friday the thirteenth and about the tickets he received. I also noted the verdict, whatever it was, would come exactly four months to the day Miller shot Frankie Ray. It would make a good lede.

Twenty minutes later, with McKinley and Sullivan in court, Katheryn Conner seated in her usual spot, and the courtroom gallery bursting at the seams, what looked to be an entire shift of police officers entered and spread along the courtroom's walls.

Kincaid took the bench. "Before I bring in the jury, I want to admonish the gallery that there will be decorum in my courtroom. I have requested extra police officers to ensure law and order will prevail. And I will have no trouble having those police officers arrest anyone who does not heed my warning. That being said, the bailiff will bring in the jurors."

The jurors walked in grim faced, their heads and gazes lowered. When they sat, they directed their eyes at Judge Kincaid.

"Never a good sign when the jury doesn't look at the defendant or his attorneys," Phish whispered. "Do you have a read?"

I shook my head. We'd know soon enough.

"Ladies and gentlemen of the jury. Am I correct that you have reached a verdict?" Judge Kincaid asked.

Surprisingly, one of the five women responded. "We have, Your Honor."

Kincaid scanned his jurors' chart. "Juror number six, am I correct you have been selected by your fellow jurors to deliver their verdict?"

"You are," the woman said.

"So says one, so says all of you? Juror number one?"

"Yes."

Kincaid confirmed the verdict had been agreed to by all twelve jurors. Then he asked, "Juror six, please hand your verdict to the bailiff."

Juror six did so, and the bailiff handed the verdict to Kincaid, who reviewed it and handed it back. Judge Kincaid directed his gaze to the defense table. "The defendant will rise."

George Miller put both his hands on the table and rose from his chair. His knuckles turned white.

"Juror six, you may read the verdict."

"In the matter of the State of Washington versus George Andrew Mil—" Her voice cracked.

"Bailiff," Kincaid said, but his bailiff was already pouring a glass of water and delivering it to the woman. She thanked him and took a sip, then set the glass aside.

"In the matter of the State of Washington versus George Andrew Miller," she repeated. "On the count of murder in the first degree, we the jury find the defendant not guilty."

Miller gave a sigh of relief and his shoulders lowered. His attorney reached out and grabbed his hand. Sullivan clenched a fist. McKinley never blinked. He and Blunt remained stoic.

"On the count of murder in the second degree," juror number six read. "We the jury find the defendant guilty."

The gallery erupted with shouts and murmurs. Miller's friends voiced dissatisfaction. Others shouted approval. Judge Kincaid banged his gavel several times, and the police officers moved forward several steps. Miller bowed his head, eyes closed. His personal counsel had stood and placed a hand on his client's back. Sullivan sat, looking stunned. At State's table, McKinley turned and gave Blunt a knowing nod. The detective shifted his gaze, subtly, and not likely detected by anyone else in the courtroom, to the first pew in the gallery. To the center seat. Katheryn Conner had her head down, but I saw no tears. The corners of her mouth moved upward.

"Members of the jury. Having reached a verdict on murder in the second degree, the court will not question you on the State's third charge of manslaughter," Kincaid said. "I will ask each of you to confirm your verdict. Please answer 'aye' or 'nay.' Juror number one?"

"Aye."

"Juror number two?"

"Aye."

As Kincaid polled the jury, I reconsidered Conner. She had lifted her head, her expression stoic. Miller and his attorneys appeared to be stunned, as if they had expected an acquittal. I, too, was surprised—if I was being honest. I kept thinking Miller was guilty but the State would never get him. I thought the underworld would find a way to pay for a juror's vote, as they had paid the witnesses. Money could do that. Money could corrupt. And the underworld had a lot of it.

Then I thought of Judge Kincaid taking a cut of the money paid by those in the gallery. If that was in fact true. Could Miller have reached the judge?

When the final juror responded "aye," Kincaid took a moment. Then he said, "Members of the jury, having served your civic duty, you are free to leave. You may be contacted by counsel for the State or for the defense to discuss your verdict. You may speak to them or not. The decision is yours. On behalf of the State of Washington, County of King, I thank you for your service. You are excused."

As the jury exited, I turned to Phish. I could see the wheels already spinning over the front-page headline and the photograph. *Guilty!* We would sell a lot of newspapers this afternoon.

When the jury had cleared and everyone had taken their seats, Kincaid said, "Counsel, I will hear arguments for sentencing."

For more than thirty minutes, Sullivan asked Kincaid to render a verdict of not guilty, notwithstanding the jury verdict.

Kincaid declined.

Sullivan requested a new trial.

Kincaid declined.

Sullivan asked Kincaid to "take into consideration the deceased's character and impose the minimum sentence."

McKinley stood. "It is far more important," he said, "to take into consideration the defendant's character. And it is high time we do so." He mentioned Miller's criminal record.

"This is a moral leper, and he has lived off the moral weaknesses of others for years. It is time to put him where he belongs, in a jail cell where he can no longer take advantage of his prey and, in the process, corrupt the moral integrity of the good citizens of Seattle."

Judge Kincaid listened patiently to both sides. When they had finished, he formed a steeple with his hands beneath his chin and remained silent for what seemed a long time. No one in his courtroom moved. You could hear every cough, every sniffle, every creak of a chair.

Was this more theater? Did Kincaid want everyone to believe he was giving this matter due consideration? Or had the underworld not gotten to the jurors because there was no need? Had they gotten to Kincaid? Was he preparing to let George Miller go free?

Kincaid lifted his eyes. Quietly, he said, "The defendant shall rise."

Miller did so.

"Can you hear me, Mr. Miller?" Kincaid asked.

Miller picked up his ear trumpet and placed it beside his ear.

"Having been found guilty by a jury of your peers . . . this court sentences you to the maximum punishment of thirty-one years in the Walla Walla state penitentiary."

Some in the gallery gave a collective sigh of relief; others inhaled in disbelief. I didn't know what to think.

"The evidence put forward in this court clearly established you have no respect for the laws of this great state, including the law administered to you in my courtroom to tell the truth, the whole truth, and nothing but the truth. You and your band of witnesses flouted the truth, and that is a crime I cannot stomach. *You* will pay for your actions in a jail cell. As for your equally mendacious friends and business partner, time will tell if they will join you for their crimes of perjury." Kincaid looked over the gallery with a final, hard stare. "This court is adjourned. God bless the people of the great state of Washington."

He rapped his gavel and left the bench.

For a moment, I didn't think anyone else was going to stand, or maybe they couldn't stand. Like when a powerful movie finishes and the audience is struck dumb and still. But one person had no time for such foolishness. He had a job to do.

Phish bolted upright. "I'll get back to the office and get started on the verdict and the headlines. You find out if anyone has anything more to say. I'll see you back there and we'll craft your story. This is going to be big, Shoe. Maybe the paper's biggest bestseller ever." With that, he strode from the courtroom.

Those who had been seated in the gallery slowly departed, speaking quietly, expressing their dismay or their approval. Winn and Greer had cornered Katheryn Conner. I moved to the railing and called out to George Miller. To my surprise, he and his attorneys acknowledged me.

"Were you surprised by the verdict?" I asked.

"Mr. Miller—" Sullivan started but George Miller raised a hand.

"Yes," Miller said.

"You expected an acquittal?"

"I did," he said. "I guess you can't expect good news on Friday the thirteenth."

"The defense will appeal the jury's verdict and Judge Kincaid's sentencing, which was egregious," Sullivan said.

Then the guards turned Miller around and replaced the handcuffs on his wrists before leading him away.

I hurried out the courtroom doors and moved to where McKinley and Blunt held court.

"We are pleased with the jury's decision," McKinley was saying. "We believe justice has been served."

"The defense said it will appeal both the jury's decision and the sentencing," I said. "Any comment?"

"The State is not concerned with the defense's bluster," McKinley said. "The defense moved for a mistrial repeatedly throughout these proceedings, and Judge Kincaid rightfully denied those requests. We believe there are no grounds warranting a new trial, or a new verdict."

"How will you celebrate?" another reporter asked.

"Trials tend to take on a life of their own," McKinley said. "For the past few weeks, I have neglected my other cases and obligations. I intend to take a long weekend outdoors before getting back to work."

I found it interesting McKinley didn't mention having a family, and I realized I didn't know if he had one. He'd never mentioned a spouse or children.

"What about you, Detective?" someone asked Blunt.

"Me? I believe I'll have a scotch, a cigar, and a relaxing evening beside the radio."

"There are rumors you intend to retire," someone else said to Blunt.

I had not heard this before.

"And they shall remain rumors, gentlemen," Blunt said. "Until the day I decide I've had enough."

"Is that day today, with a guilty verdict in the Trial of the Century?" the person asked. "The pinnacle of a career serving the public?"

Blunt's eyes found mine. "One needs more than accolades to retire, I'm afraid. And pinnacle or not, I remain a public servant, living, like all of you, in unpredictable and uncertain times."

I hurried back to the *Star*, and Phish and I banged out my article to go immediately beneath the "guilty" headline and alongside Kneip's picture of Miller standing at the defense table. When we had finished printing ten thousand more copies than usual, and the papers were being shipped out the back of the building to the newspaper vans for delivery to the newsstands, Phish invited me into his office.

"Shut the door," he said. I did. "Take a seat."

I sat across from him. "That was good work, William. You handled yourself well."

"Thank you," I said.

He slid open his bottom desk drawer and pulled out a bottle of whiskey and two glasses along with two cigars. He poured the whiskey and handed me a glass, holding up his own. "To William Shumacher. I've often said one can only become a newspaper reporter through a baptism of fire, and you have certainly passed through the flames. Singed perhaps, but not too badly."

I thanked Phish and sipped my whiskey, nearly coughing but somehow managing to suppress the fire burning a trail down the back of my throat. Phish clipped the end of his cigar, then struck a match and lit the other end. He handed me the clipper and his matches. I'd never smoked a cigar. Never had the money for such a luxury. I followed his lead and managed not to cough up a lung with my first inhale.

As we celebrated, the whiskey gradually became smoother and the cigar less toxic. I don't know how much time passed, only that we consumed a good portion of the bottle and smoked our cigars to nubs. Outside the building windows, dusk had settled in.

"What will you do now?" Phish asked.

"I suppose you will have some hand in that," I said.

"I meant about your lost love?"

Fueled by the whiskey, I said, "I believe I will make like one of Teddy Roosevelt's Rough Riders and ride into the bakery again. I shouldn't just give up, not without talking to Amara directly."

Phish nodded. "And what of your buried treasure?"

I blew out a breath. I'd never told Phish about my excursion to what was once the Topsy Turvy. "It's likely a fantasy," I said, thinking of Edmond Dantès in *The Count of Monte Cristo*. "The musings of a poor reporter who too early in life read of great treasures and imagined himself a famous explorer."

Phish gave me a wry grin. "About that poor reporter jab. I will not be your Ebenezer Scrooge, Bob Cratchit. I intend to raise your salary to ten dollars a week."

My eyes widened and the nub of cigar fell out of my mouth and into my lap. I shot out of my chair, brushing away the ash, and retrieved the cigar from the floor while Phish laughed. My chest felt like it had burst into flames, though that could have been from the whiskey. "I don't know what to say!"

"'Thank you' is usually appropriate."

"Thank you," I said quickly. I reached a hand across his desk and Phish shook it. I could increase the amount I was sending home to my family. It might even save the house. Regardless, it would help.

"You are now a full-fledged reporter for the *Daily Star*, and this will make it official." He reached into his pocket and handed me a ten-dollar bill. "Consider it an advance on your first week's salary. My hope is sometime over the weekend you will find the courage to speak to your sweetheart and if so, that you will have sufficient funds to buy her flowers and make amends."

"I won't let you down, Phish. I mean the reporting."

"I know you won't. I see this as a good investment in the *Daily Star*'s future. Now, I better get home to *my* wife. Will you be coming?"

"I appreciate the offer, Phish. And I appreciate you taking me in this past week, but I think it's time to get on with my life, such as it may be." I thought of Amara and of going to her home to try to talk with her.

"You're always welcome."

"Thanks," I said, and departed his office. I cleaned up my desk, grabbed my coat, hat, and satchel, and walked outside. The cooling night air gave me a chill. The whiskey, on an empty stomach, made my head swirl, or maybe it was the cigar. I didn't know which, only that the combination was joyous.

I walked up First Avenue and secretly hoped the bakery remained open, but I knew at this late hour it had closed, and Amara had long since gone home. I wondered if she had plans for the weekend, if she had met someone new, someone who would be taking her to the picture show or on a ferry ride to the islands. I wasn't sure I could bear seeing something so painful. I thought also of the guard at Judge Kincaid's courtroom, about what he had said, and what I had learned during the past weeks—everyone in Seattle, from the shoeshine boys to the elite, even Judge Peter Kincaid, was susceptible to the allure of money during a depression.

I thought about 1345 East John Street.

I owed it to myself to at least find out if I was right about my buried treasure; didn't I? There was no harm in being certain; was there? And if I was wrong, at least I'd be satisfied that I'd looked. At least I would have no regrets.

The credit belongs to those who actually are in the arena . . . or whatever Teddy Roosevelt had once proclaimed.

A man stepped from the hardware store, about to lock up. I hurried across the street, calling out to him.

"Can I help you?" the man said.

"I need to buy a couple of things. Would it be possible?"

He made a face. "You're drunk."

"I am," I said. "But I have money."

In a depression, nothing more needed to be said. He turned and unlocked the door.

Chapter 28

I stopped at my boardinghouse to change my clothes, leaving what I had purchased hidden outside. Mrs. Alderbrook was behind her desk. Her eyes widened as I approached.

"William," she said, smiling. "You're back."

"I am," I said, keeping my distance and hoping she couldn't detect my intoxication.

"For good, I hope."

"Certainly for a while," I said.

"They convicted him. Guilty."

"Yes, I know," I said, struggling not to sway.

"Of course you do. Silly of me. You wrote the article."

"Can I get the key to my room?"

"Oh yes, sorry."

She held out my key, but when I reached for it, I stumbled off-balance, and the key fell to the floor. The wooden knob to which it was attached clattered and rolled along the wood. "Sorry," I said. "Clumsy of me."

"Are you all right?" she asked.

I decided that in this instance honesty, or partial honesty, was the best policy. "No, I'm not," I said. "There was a celebration following the jury verdict at the newspaper, and I believe I had one too many."

"William," she said.

"I know," I said. "But I couldn't turn down my boss. It would have been rude."

"I suppose you could not have," she said. "You smell of cigar smoke as well."

"Guilty," I said.

She frowned. "I have a strict no-smoking policy," she said. "If you're going to smoke, you must do it outside."

"And I shall not smoke a single puff while I reside here," I said. "Now, I think I better shuffle upstairs and get to bed."

"Do you want me to make you some coffee?" she asked.

"I will be sound asleep well before you have it made." With some difficulty, I picked the key up from the floor and wove my way up the staircase, only missing a single stair once.

I went down the hall to the bathroom, stood at the sink, and splashed cold water on my face, which only partially revived me. Inside my room I took off the clothes Amara had picked out for me, thought of her, and felt an overwhelming sadness. Not wanting to dwell on the subject, I quickly changed into my old clothes, ones I could now afford to get dirty, slipped on my cap, and made my way down the back staircase to the alley. There, I retrieved what I had purchased from the hardware store and made my way to Capitol Hill.

The long walk and the cold air further revived me. I remembered the possibility of my being followed and stopped occasionally to look around at my surroundings but saw nothing suspicious.

Once I reached 1345 East John Street, I moved to the window I'd previously managed to open, slid it up, then found the box to stand on. Doing so the other night was far easier than this night. I stumbled several times and, try as I might, couldn't find the delicate balance between lifting my left leg high enough to get it over the windowsill and not falling over backward. After my third failed attempt, I tossed my purchased possessions through the window, leaned over the windowsill until my weight was more forward than aft, and fell onto the floor. I landed with a loud thud. So much for keeping quiet.

I turned on my flashlight, my first purchase, and made my way to the hidden staircase. The stairs seemed steeper than they had the other night, particularly carrying an eight-pound pickax, a spade shovel, and the flashlight. I thought again of Teddy Roosevelt and his statement about the man who ventures into the arena knowing both victory and defeat, though I was hoping for victory.

I stepped down carefully, using the pickax and shovel to balance. It felt like an hour before I reached the bottom, but I'm sure it had only been minutes. I moved the rug aside, then the linoleum squares, revealing the fresh concrete. I set the flashlight down at an angle that provided light, raised the pickax over my head, stumbled, and nearly fell over backward. I tried again, this time bracing my legs to give me better purchase, raised the pickax, and used its weight to smash the concrete. It cracked, a spider's web.

After several more swings I was perspiring, but the exertion helped to further sober me. I dropped to a knee and removed several concrete pieces. The concrete was just two or three inches thick. Thinner than the concrete around it.

When I had removed the rectangle of concrete, I stepped back, breathing heavily. I wished I had brought water and wondered if I might find a working faucet in the abandoned and condemned building. I set down the pickax and turned.

I saw the silhouette of a man in a fedora and long coat standing beside a woman in the doorway.

"Hello, William," the man said. "Kind of you to do the heavy lifting for us."

Chapter 29

I raised a hand to cut the glare of a flashlight shining in my eyes, but still couldn't make out their faces, though I recognized the man's voice. I'd heard it every day in court for weeks.

"What are you doing here?" I asked.

"The same as you," Laurence McKinley said, lowering the beam of light and stepping farther inside. "Looking for Miller's unpaid tax money."

I could now see his and the woman's faces. Katheryn Conner. McKinley walked over to a light switch, flicked it, and an overhead bulb lit up a small section of the room. The rest remained in shadows.

I hadn't suspected McKinley. I thought it was Blunt who'd figured out a suitcase of cash existed somewhere, but now, faced with reality, McKinley made perfect sense.

"You knew about the money from the tax cases," I said.

"Yes and no. I knew Miller and Brunn had stashed away a large sum of money to keep Uncle Sam from getting his hands on it, but I didn't know where it was hidden."

"But you suspected Frankie Ray did know?"

"One doesn't show up with a new Cadillac without disposable income in these times, and Frankie Ray was not known to have disposable income," McKinley said.

Which had been my deduction as well. "You knew he and Miller didn't quarrel over Miller's refusal to pay Joan Daley's hospital bill."

"It was another lie in a string of lies. I knew Miller had to have learned of the Cadillac and likely called Frankie Ray to the club to find out if Ray had been skimming money. Miller likely questioned Ray, got angry when he learned Ray double-crossed him, and let his temper get the better of him—shooting Ray before learning where he had hidden the money. Or maybe he thought Joan Daley knew the location. From there it was easy to deduce from the fact that all the witnesses told the same story that Miller had coached them on what to say, likely for some substantial cash."

"Frankie Ray didn't tell Detective Blunt he wasn't a squealer," I said.

"No?" McKinley asked in a tone indicating he really hadn't known.

"Ray told him he'd hidden the money and to tell George Miller he'd never find it."

"I don't know for certain, but I suspect you are correct. I suspect Miller initially gave Ray the money and told him to hide it somewhere because he needed some distance between it and him and Syd Brunn. Maybe Ray really did want Miller to pay Joan Daley's medical expenses, and when Miller refused, Ray said he wouldn't tell Miller where he'd hid the money. Maybe Miller only took out the gun to scare Ray. It's unlikely we'll know for certain. The question thus became, where did Frankie Ray hide the money? Tell me, William, how did you figure it out?"

I wondered if I could somehow use the shovel as a weapon, make my way to the door, and run. "Joan Daley mentioned something to me when I spoke to her in her room. She mentioned it wasn't always easy to tell the difference between the good guys and the bad guys. From there I pieced things together. I found the tax cases brought against the Musketeers, and Joan had indicated the argument at the Pom Pom Club was about more than an eighty-dollar hospital bill. It made me believe Ray's presence in the club, his having brought Al Smith with him, was purposeful."

"You're sharp," McKinley said. "And dogged. I'll give you that."

"What happened to Joan Daley?"

Katheryn Conner smiled. "Joan had a little too much to drink and fell out the window of her boardinghouse."

"Only she didn't fall. When I left her, she was passed out in a chair."

"Where she had lured my George into her bed on more than one occasion," Conner said with bitterness. "Once I realized she wasn't about to tell me where Frankie hid the money, or that she didn't know, I got rid of her."

"We figured maybe she told you where it might be, offered you a reward or something to get it for her," McKinley said.

"You were the person in the car following me that night."

"And look where it has led us."

"You were supposed to be George Miller's sweetheart," I said to Conner.

"I *was* his sweetheart. It was George who kept forgetting that fact."

"I could tell by the look on your face when Emmaline Cartman testified that he'd had an affair."

"That little French bitch came into the club swinging her hips and making eyes at George from day one. George was weak. He'd have sex with anything on two legs. I wouldn't have cared if he hadn't hired her to work in the club, which meant I had to look at her cute little face every night I went there, knowing what the two of them were doing together when I wasn't around. After George shot Frankie, I saw an opportunity."

"With Frankie Ray dead, and with George Miller in prison, the money would be there for the taking," I said. "If you could find it."

"If I could find it," she agreed.

I felt proud that I had indeed figured out the mystery, but then concerned my intuition had been correct. I was in a pickle for certain, knowing so much, too much maybe for them to let me just walk away. "What about Syd Brunn?" I said, reaching for others who might know of the money.

"Scattered to the winds, as I predicted. With George gone, Brunn cut his losses. He makes enough as a bail bondsman and doesn't need the headache."

"So, you cut a deal with Mr. McKinley?"

"I actually cut the deal," McKinley said. "I figured one of two people knew where the money was hidden, Joan Daley or Miss Conner. Turns out I was wrong on both accounts."

"But a deal is a deal," Conner said.

"And I am a man of my word," McKinley said. "We agreed to split the money. If we found it."

I tried a different tack, appealing to McKinley's duty. "You're supposed to uphold the law," I said. It was a long shot, I knew. Duty meant little when you were looking at the type of money that would change your life forever.

"Miller is going to jail for the rest of his life; isn't he?"

"And Ernie Blunt? Is he also part of this?"

"Good old Ernie. Straight as an arrow and flies that way too. He never would have gone for something like this. Telling him would only have screwed the deal," McKinley said.

But I wasn't so sure Blunt was so straight. He'd clearly followed me that day at the courthouse, and I was certain he suspected something. And, we were talking about a fortune, which had to be hard for a man on the cusp of stepping away from his job to pass up, especially in these times.

"Now, we interrupted you just when it looks like you were about to pick up that shovel."

"And if I refuse?" I said, about to put my plan into action.

McKinley pulled out a gun from behind his back and pointed it at me. The barrel loomed as big as a cannon. My plan went out the window. "Then George Miller's gun will kill one more person before I put it back into evidence and it is destroyed."

I felt nauseated, realizing what McKinley and Conner were planning. "What happens after I dig up the money?"

"Let's cross that bridge when we get to it; shall we?" McKinley said. "Dig."

I picked up the shovel and started digging. With each shovel of dirt, I felt one step closer to my grave. It wasn't particularly hot, but by the time I had dug the hole as deep as my thighs, sweat was rolling down my face into my eyes and had caused my shirt to stick to my back. I kept thinking of ways to get out of the hole, maybe use the shovel as a weapon, but McKinley holding a gun on me made that unlikely. Unless I had a reason.

I took a momentary break, punctuated with a deep, exaggerated breath, and turned. "Can I get a drink of water?" I put down the shovel, about to get out of the hole, but McKinley stopped me.

"Keep digging," he said. "I'll try to find you some water."

He turned his back, presumably in search of a faucet. I picked up the shovel, as if to resume digging, and decided this would be my only chance. I was about to jump from the hole and rush forward when Katheryn Conner removed a gun from her handbag and shot McKinley in the back.

The prosecutor took two steps forward, like a man whose back had just seized, stumbled, and fell forward, hitting the bar counter before sliding to the floor.

I stood in stunned silence, disbelieving what I had just seen. I'd spent weeks with McKinley, nearly every day over the past two weeks.

Conner turned to me and smiled. "Men are so violent; aren't they?"

McKinley was not moving. Blood stained the back of his shirt. I dropped the shovel to move to him, but Conner stopped me, or I should say, her gun stopped me. "No. No. No. Don't do anything stupid. I need you to dig. I don't want to get my hands dirty."

I looked at her and another realization came. "You're going to shoot me when I find the money; aren't you?"

"As Mr. McKinley said, let's cross that bridge when we get to it."

"Let's cross it now, Katheryn." The voice came from a dark corner of the room. Conner turned toward the voice and fired her weapon. A second shot followed, a flash of light in the darkened corner, and Conner dropped to the ground. Blood flowed from a bullet wound in her forehead.

Fear gripped me. I'd never seen a murder, only the aftermath. I'd just watched two people die. I turned, gagging. Feeling like I might throw up.

Detective Ernie Blunt stepped from the shadows, gun in hand. "You okay, kid?"

I didn't move. Didn't say a word. My eyes focused on the gun in his hand.

"You did a good job. You kept them talking long enough for me to hear everything."

"How . . . how long have you been following me?"

"Not you, kid. The two of them."

I looked at Conner and McKinley. "How did you know?"

He smiled. "You cut me to the quick, kid. I am, after all, Seattle's most famous detective."

"You suspected them."

"I was keenly aware of the tax cases and the pot of gold that had disappeared. And, of course, Frankie Ray made it clear to me he had hidden the money. He just wouldn't tell me where."

My mind shifted back to my job. "That was in the hospital, when he was dying," I said.

"That's right."

"Why didn't you say anything?"

"To whom, kid? Haven't you figured it out yet? Nobody around here is innocent. Everyone is on the take. I figured it was better to let it play out, find out if McKinley was a snake or a guy trying to do the right thing. Turns out he was a snake. Let's just say I suspected he was on the same treasure hunt you're on."

So Blunt had known, and he believed I was going to take the money also.

"How did you find it? I didn't find anything in the two boxes you took from Frankie Ray's boardinghouse."

"That was you that night in the *Daily Star*'s offices?"

"That was me, kid. I waited until the place closed for the night and watched you leave."

"That wasn't me. It was the typesetter. I was there. I hid under the desk."

"I'll be. You keep surprising me. So how'd you figure this was where Frankie Ray buried his treasure?"

I told Blunt about the receipt for cement and about the Bible. He shook his head and laughed. "Again. I got to hand it to you."

"Why did Ray have the money?" I asked. "Why didn't Miller or Brunn hide it?"

"Don't know for certain, and I doubt any of us ever will. But if I were a betting man, I'd say Miller and Brunn were playing Frankie, using him to empty the gaming machines in their various bars and giving him the money they underreported from the sales on cigarettes and liquor, telling him to stash it so the feds wouldn't find it. He was their rube. If the government prosecuted, they'd each say Ray was stealing from them, and Ray would take the fall. I doubt either suspected Ray was savvy enough to hide the money as insurance they wouldn't sell him down the river while those tax cases were pending."

It made sense, but as Blunt said, we'd likely never know for certain.

"What do you say, kid? You want to find out if you were right?"

I no longer knew what I wanted. I just knew the money wasn't worth dying over. Would Blunt shoot me the way I believed Conner and McKinley would have? McKinley had said Blunt was straight as an arrow, but I suspected that wasn't true. "Are you going to make me dig up the money, then kill me?"

Blunt smiled. "Only one way to find out, kid. Dig."

I picked up the shovel and dug. The dirt was loose, not as compacted as I expected it to be beneath a slab of concrete. I removed shovelful after shovelful, until I was nearly waist deep in the hole and the ground was hard again.

"It isn't here," I said.

Blunt walked over, squatted at the hole's edge, and said, "Huh." I couldn't tell if he was disappointed or not. "I would have bet my year's salary you had it figured correctly."

"I guess I got something wrong."

"I guess you did, kid."

The rectangle I had dug was deep enough to be a grave. "What now?" I asked.

"First, I better find a pay phone and call this in."

"What about me?"

"I think you need to go home. I can't think of a legitimate reason why you would be here."

"You're not going to put me in the grave?"

Blunt looked startled. "Burying you would complicate my story about what happened here."

"What did happen, Detective?"

"I think you know. Some of it anyway. Frankie Ray told me he buried a fortune that rightfully belonged to the government. I told the deputy prosecutor, and he told me about the tax cases he prosecuted and confirmed money had been skimmed and was likely hidden. The question was where? Unbeknownst to me, McKinley made a deal with Katheryn Conner, which made sense because she was George Miller's sweetheart. Conner didn't know where the money was but said if anyone did, it would be Frankie Ray's girl, Joan Daley. She sent McKinley to Daley's boardinghouse to find out. Remember that witness I told you about? The one supposedly feeding her chickens who saw a man leaving the boardinghouse not long before Daley jumped out the window? I filed a report noting that piece of information."

"But there was no witness. Or chickens or pens."

"The police report says there was a man. It says the witness identified that man as being just about the same height and build as Laurence McKinley. And Luke May found McKinley's fingerprints all over Daley's room, which will be more than sufficient to establish he forced the information out of Daley, then killed her."

"But that didn't happen. You made up the police report."

Blunt shrugged. "If Seattle's most famed detective says it happened, then it happened, kid. McKinley and Conner then waited until George Miller was convicted to come and get the money. Only McKinley didn't realize Conner had set him up also, used him to find the loot's location. When she thought they had found it, she shot him. A classic double-cross. Which actually did happen."

"So then who shot her?"

"I did. I followed the two of them, suspecting they'd bring me to the pot of gold, which they did, except there wasn't any gold to be found. Conner shot McKinley, and when I told Conner to put the gun down, she turned on me and I had no choice but to shoot her in self-defense. Ironic; isn't it?"

"And me?"

"Like I said, kid, I don't have a good story why you'd be here. So, you need to leave."

"You're letting me go?"

"No reason to hold you. If you'd like, I can call your boardinghouse, tell you we have another crime, and you can show up here right along with the patrolmen and the others. Just like the Pom Pom Club. What do you say?"

"I think one Pom Pom Club murder is enough."

"There's always another case, kid, just like there's always another story. You'll learn soon enough. It's like my father used to say. 'The only things certain in life—'"

"'Are death and taxes,'" I said. "My father is . . . was an accountant. He said the same thing."

"Yes, but he wasn't a detective like my old man. Your father missed one certainty. The only things certain in life are death, taxes, and crime."

I couldn't argue with that.

"Go on. Get out of here. I'll wipe your fingerprints off the tools and make sure McKinley's are on them."

I climbed from the hole, no longer the least bit drunk. I had been scared sober. I walked toward the open back door half expecting to take a bullet, not fully believing Blunt was going to let me go.

"Hey, kid?"

I turned.

"Hypothetically, what would you have done? If you had found the money?"

I thought about it for what felt like a long moment, about my family in Kansas City, Joan Daley, Amara. But it was dirty money, more now than before. Three other people had already died because of it. I knew only that I didn't want it.

"I don't know," I said.

"Me neither," Blunt said. "I guess now we'll never know."

"Know what?"

"If we're as good and moral as we think we are."

Chapter 30

Police cars and an ambulance sped past me as I walked the streets. Dirty and disheveled, my clothes a mess, I looked like just another of Seattle's Hooverville residents, walking the streets in search of a scrap of food.

When I got back to my boardinghouse, I let myself into my room and sat on the bed. I thought about what Blunt had said, about neither of us knowing what we would have done, had I in fact found the money. I thought that was an honest answer. I didn't know, not for sure. Was I any better than George Miller? Who was to say?

I figured guys like me weren't built to be rich. My parents worked for everything they had, as their parents did before them, and their parents before them. I'd do the same because that's what guys like me did. We worked for the things in life. Having disposable income was simply not a part of my fiber. It was not part of the lexicon I had learned growing up. Wasn't that the lesson I had learned from reading F. Scott Fitzgerald's book *The Great Gatsby*? Jay Gatsby could have all the money in the world, but he could never be rich. He didn't understand the lifestyle. It wasn't in his blood. He faked it as best he could, put on extravagant parties, bought expensive champagne, and wore expensive clothes, but he was a fraud, and in the end, he was exposed.

One could find money.

Like Edmond Dantès.

But finding money and being accepted into the "rich" of society was not the same thing. That was something you were born into.

Edmond Dantès did not find happiness.

Neither did Jay Gatsby.

I wouldn't have either. The money was as dirty as the clothes I wore.

I lay awake much of the night. Not out of fear of Ernie Blunt or anyone else. I feared what awaited me in Seattle, my future, and decided I could not stay. I'd go home to Kansas City, get a job as a reporter, and be close to and help my family. Phish would write me a glowing recommendation, and I had the clippings covering the Trial of the Century. Phish certainly respected me, and that meant more to me than anything.

And I could not bear the thought of walking past the bakery each morning knowing Amara was inside. I could not bear the thought of running into her, of seeing her on someone else's arm. I'd done what I had set out to accomplish. I'd moved to a foreign city on my own, and I'd stood on my own two feet. I had even proven to be a pretty darn good reporter.

No, a voice inside my head said.

No. I was not leaving without first talking to Amara. After what I had just been through, I was no longer afraid of Mr. Giovacchini or Amara's two brothers. I'd go to the bakery, and I wouldn't leave until I had the chance to talk to her. Mr. Giovacchini could call his two sons and have me thrown out. But at least I'd be thrown out having tried. Like Phish had said about Teddy Roosevelt. At least I would have stepped into the arena and tried.

At some point, fatigue overtook my wandering thoughts and I fell into a deep sleep.

When I awoke the next morning, my head felt like it was about to split in two and my tongue like it had been glued to the roof of my mouth. To make matters worse, Mrs. Alderbrook was banging on my door, yet again. "William? William, are you awake?"

I put my feet on the floor, then had to wait until the room stopped spinning. Mrs. Alderbrook kept knocking. I'd passed out with all my dirty clothes on. I made my way to the door and opened it.

"William," she said, eyeing my disheveled appearance. "Are you all right?"

"I'm fine. What is it?" But as I asked the question, I already knew the answer. Phish was on the phone. There'd been two homicides. One was the deputy prosecutor Larry McKinley, the other Katheryn Conner.

Pizzazz on top of pizzazz.

We were going to sell a lot more newspapers.

"Someone here to see you."

"I'll be down in a moment. I have to use the bathroom," I managed.

I left Mrs. Alderbrook. In the bathroom I relieved myself, then made my way to the sink. The whites of my eyes were as lined with red as a city map, and I had dark circles beneath my lower lids. My skin was sallow. I splashed cold water on my face several times, and it both jarred me alert and made me want to throw up. I managed to hold everything down and washed the dirt from my hands then went back into the hall. Mrs. Alderbrook was not there.

I navigated the staircase, but I didn't see the phone on Mrs. Alderbrook's desk, nor was she behind it. She called to me. "William. Over here."

She stood with Mr. Giovacchini. He was dressed in a suit, his hat in his two hands, twisting the brim. I felt paralyzed but somehow managed to slowly walk over.

"You know Mr. Giovacchini from the bakery on First Avenue," Mrs. Alderbrook said. She sounded nervous.

"I wonder if I can have a moment of your time, William," Mr. Giovacchini said.

I nodded.

Mr. Giovacchini looked at Mrs. Alderbrook, and my gaze followed his.

"I'll go see about getting breakfast started." She left us standing in the lobby.

"Mr. Giovacchini," I said, but he shook his head and closed his eyes and I thought he wasn't interested in what I had to say.

"William, let me talk. I want to apologize."

"What?" Of all the things he could have said, that might have been the one I never thought I'd hear.

"I want to apologize. A big man accepts his mistakes. A bigger man apologizes for them. I was wrong."

"Mr. Giovacchini, I'm not—"

"Your editor, Mr. Phishbaum, came to talk to me at the bakery. He explained you were following a news story and the woman we saw you with that evening worked for the county tax assessor. He told me the woman asked you to walk her home since it was night and that you agreed, as any gentleman would have done, and she mistook your generosity for affection. I hope you can accept my apology, William."

Good old Phish. He was always there for me. He'd been a role model for me and a father figure, always looking out for me. I owed him.

"I'm sorry also, for the misunderstanding, and any embarrassment it caused your family."

We stood in an uncomfortable silence. Then I asked, "How is Amara?"

He shook his head. "Not good."

"Is something wrong?" I asked, alarmed.

He smiled. "She is a woman in love, William. She misses the man she loves. She hasn't been the same since that day. She is depressed. She is making mistakes at work. The other day she served the customers cold coffee."

I chuckled.

"I came to ask you, William. I know you love my daughter. She told me about the night you wanted to propose but you told her you would not do it without my permission."

Amara, also protecting me.

"That is also the sign of a good man. A good man for my Amara. I'm here now, William. If you still wish to marry my daughter. You may ask me."

"Mr. Giovacchini, I do want to marry your daughter, but Amara . . . I mean, will she be as understanding. I mean, she saw Helen Ruth—"

"Bosh," he said. "She is like her mother. She will play hard to get. She won't make it easy. But she loves you, William. And in the end, she is one hundred percent Italian. We were made to love. It is our heritage."

I felt suddenly lighter. A warmth spread through my body. I was also nervous to be asking for a woman's hand in marriage, but when I thought of Amara, saw her face in my mind, those nerves vanished.

"Then, I would like your permission, Mr. Giovacchini. I love your daughter and I will do everything in my power to make her happy. I'm not a rich man, Mr. Giovacchini, but I'm a hard worker, and I will work hard to give Amara everything she wants in life and to give you and Mrs. Giovacchini grandchildren."

Mr. Giovacchini had tears in his eyes. "And I would love to have you be a part of our family, William. I would love to call you my son."

He reached out and gripped me in a bear hug so tight I thought I might throw up. I wondered if he smelled the booze emanating from the pores of my skin, but if he did, he didn't say so.

"About your two sons," I said, smiling.

Chapter 31

I rode the 10 Mount Baker bus twenty minutes south to Rainier Valley wearing the clothes Amara had helped me pick out. I'd bought flowers. I didn't buy chocolates on this occasion, wanting to be careful with the money Phish had given to me and not spend any more of it unnecessarily.

I was nervous when I stepped off the bus. I had gone over the various scenarios in my head about what might happen this evening. In some, Amara flung herself into my arms. In others, she slammed the door in my face. Despite Mr. Giovacchini telling me Amara was depressed and still loved me, I knew nothing was certain. Still, I'd placed my Oma's ring in my pants pocket, and before leaving the boardinghouse, I'd told Mrs. Alderbrook about my intentions. She was aghast when I showed her the ring.

"You can't give a young lady a ring without a box," she said.

"I can't?"

"No. You need to get down on one knee and hold your hand out like this, then open the box when you ask her. Hold on a second. I think I have a jewelry box you can use." She went back into her private quarters and emerged with a small black box.

I knew Mrs. Alderbrook was a widow. She'd inherited the boardinghouse from her husband, who had passed away from consumption before I moved in. "I don't want to take something if it has personal meaning to you, Mrs. Alderbrook."

"Nonsense," she said. "This box isn't doing an old woman like me any good. Mr. Alderbrook and I would be proud if you would use it. Give me your ring."

I handed her Oma's ring.

She held it up to the light. It didn't look like much. Just a tiny diamond surrounded by even tinier rubies. Oma had apparently loved red flowers. "This is lovely, William. Any young woman would be lucky. Let's see how it fits." She pressed it into the seam. "Oh, it's even lovelier; isn't it? The black really makes the red stand out." She snapped the lid closed and handed me the box. "Do you want to practice?"

"I don't . . ."

"Go on, now. Show me how you're going to do it."

"I hadn't thought about it."

"William, you can't just hand a young woman a box and say, 'Here you go.' It has to be romantic. You have to tell her you love her and want to spend the rest of your life with her. Now, give it a go."

The lobby was deserted but I was still embarrassed. I dropped to a knee. "Amara, I love you, and I want to spend the rest of my life with you."

When I didn't continue, Mrs. Alderbrook said, "What else, William?"

"Oh yeah. Will you marry me?"

"Snap open the box and show her the ring when you say it." I did so just as two residents walked in the front door. Both gave me and Mrs. Alderbrook stunned expressions.

"Close your mouths," Mrs. Alderbrook said. "Haven't you ever seen a young man propose?"

That got them moving quickly up the staircase and got me off my knee. "I better get going," I said. "I don't want to miss my bus."

"Don't forget to get on a knee and to snap the box open when you ask."

"I won't," I said.

"And pick up flowers."

I walked up the long road to the Giovacchini farm. It was still light out and I didn't see the farm truck, nor did I see Ernesto or Arthur. When I knocked on the door, Mr. Giovacchini pulled it open. He was dressed in a black suit with a white shirt and a thin tie.

He smiled. "Welcome to my home, William," he said. "Please come in."

I stepped in more nervous than ever. Music played on the stand-up radio in the living room. An Italian aria, I think. Mrs. Giovacchini came out from the kitchen. She wore an apron over a floral dress with a strand of pearls draping her neck.

"Good evening, William," she said with a wry smile but also with watery eyes.

"Good evening, Mrs. Giovacchini."

"I'll get Amara for you," Mr. Giovacchini said and left the room.

After an awkward pause, Mrs. Giovacchini said, "You look very nice, William."

"Thank you. So do you."

"And don't worry. We sent Ernesto and Arthur out for the evening."

I smiled. "Thank you."

Mr. Giovacchini returned with Amara. He looked tentative, like he was leading an unbroken horse and unsure what she might do. Amara wore her red dress, complemented by a red rose pinned in her hair. Earrings dangled from her ears, and her gold necklace with a crucifix hung around her neck.

"Close your mouth," she said. "You'll catch a fly."

"Amara," her mother said.

"You look lovely," I said.

"Thank you," she said, curt. "Are those the clothes I helped pick out?"

"Yes."

"They look good on you."

"Thank you." I held out the roses. "These are for you."

She stepped forward to accept them and held the petals beneath her nose. "They're lovely. Thank you."

Another awkward pause followed. "Why don't you go sit on the porch swing and I'll get dinner ready," Mrs. Giovacchini said.

I walked back to the front door and pulled it open, then stepped aside for Amara to pass. Mr. Giovacchini gave me a nod for luck.

I closed the door and followed Amara to the swing on the wrap-around porch. She smoothed the back of her dress and sat, continuing to smell the roses. I sat beside her. We looked out over the pasture, where a lone black horse grazed in front of a barn, and the fields her two brothers farmed.

"This is beautiful," I said.

"It's one of my favorite places. I love to sit out here at night and read."

The chains of the porch swing creaked. "Do you think it will hold both of us?"

She frowned. "I think so, William."

"Amara, about the other night."

"My father told me Mr. Phishbaum came to the bakery and explained what happened, that you were working on a story and offered to walk the woman home because it was night."

"Yes," I said. "Her kissing me was totally unexpected, Amara."

"I just have one question, William. What took you so long?"

"I'm sorry," I said, confused.

"Why didn't you come and explain it to me right away?"

"You ran off crying, and your two brothers would have pummeled me."

"I don't mean that night. Why didn't you come to the house and explain? Why did Mr. Phishbaum have to do it?"

"I did come, to the bakery, but your father . . ." I caught myself, not wanting to blame her father.

"My father and my brothers weren't in love with you. I was. You hurt me, William. And you let me hurt for days."

"I'm sorry," I said. I'd been thinking of myself, my pain. I should have been thinking of Amara and her pain. She'd been the one who had witnessed Helen Ruth kissing me. She'd been the one who thought I was out carousing. I felt small and embarrassed. "I should have come to you. I didn't know Phish . . . You're right. I should have explained. I should have known you would understand."

"We're going to have difficult times, William. But we need to be able to talk through those difficult times so we can move forward."

"You're right," I said again and thought she sounded much more mature than I had acted.

I paused for a few seconds. The box with the ring was burning a hole in the front pocket of my khakis. "If there is a next time, I'll come and talk to you right away."

"I read your stories in the newspaper. They were very good. A lot of pizzazz! Phish must have been happy."

"He was," I said. "He gave me a raise."

"I know, you told me."

"No. He gave me another raise."

"So soon?"

"Ten dollars a week."

Her eyes widened. "William, that's wonderful. You'll be able to help your family."

I would, though I knew it wouldn't be enough to keep the bank from foreclosing when my parents couldn't pay the mortgage—or the hospital bills. But I didn't want to discuss that, not now.

"Phish said I couldn't support a wife and kids on $5.40 a week."

"No. I'm sure—What?"

I slid off the swing, reached into my pocket, and removed the ring box, then got down on my knee. I opened the box as I'd practiced. Amara dropped the flowers in her lap and put her hands to her face, covering her mouth.

"Amara Giovacchini, I love you. And I want to spend the rest of my life with you. Will you marry me?"

Amara's eyes widened. Tears rolled down her cheeks. She removed her hands. "William Shumacher, it would be my honor. Yes."

I slid the ring onto her finger. It would need to be sized, but it fit well enough. I felt tears well in my eyes, and I don't think my chest had ever puffed out so far. Amara Giovacchini would be my wife. I was nearly speechless.

I got up. "I'm—" I started, but Amara leapt forward, the porch swing swaying, chains rattling. She kissed me. Behind us, inside the curtained window, a cork popped. Mrs. Giovacchini rushed out the front door with champagne glasses, followed by Mr. Giovacchini. Amara's two brothers also came onto the porch from the far side of the house.

"I sent you two away," Mrs. Giovacchini said.

"Nonsense," Arthur said. "Did you think we were going to miss watching our baby sister get engaged or congratulating our new brother?"

I stuck out my hand, which they stepped around to grip me by the arms and lift me off the ground, dancing and singing.

This time, I didn't mind. I could have levitated on my own.

Chapter 32

Monday morning, I stopped off at the bakery for my cinnamon-raisin pastry and cup of coffee. Mr. Giovacchini was in work mode, filling customer orders and barking out his usual refrain. "Move down the line, please. Move down the line."

He acknowledged me, and Amara came out from the kitchen to work the counter. "How is your father doing?" she asked, which was so like her, to put others first. She knew I had called home to tell my mother the good news, that I was engaged. I thought my mother could use some good news.

"He's getting stronger," I said. "He can come home from the hospital this week, and I had the chance to talk to him. He sounded normal, like my dad."

"I'm happy for you, William. Did you tell him we're engaged?"

"Both my parents were so happy, Amara. My mother asked me when she gets to meet the woman who stole her son's heart."

"I told my friends," Amara said. "They want to throw us an engagement party. Won't that be fun? Maybe you can have your parents come out."

Maybe, I thought, but I wasn't sure how I could afford it.

"Will I see you tonight?" I asked.

"I don't know. What did you have in mind?" She smiled and winked at me.

"I thought we could get some clam chowder down at the pier and watch the sun set."

"Sounds romantic," she said.

"Amara, the customers," Mr. Giovacchini said but with a kinder voice than in the past.

"I'll pick you up after work," I said. "I better get out of here before your father calls off the wedding."

I slipped a nickel onto the counter and Amara picked it up.

"Amara." Mr. Giovacchini approached the cash register. He took the nickel from her hand and reached across the counter, handing it back to me. "You're family now. We don't charge family."

Amara smiled and I did too.

"Now move down the line," Mr. Giovacchini said to me, this time with a smile. Minutes later, I had barely stepped into the *Daily Star* offices when Phish called out from his office. "Shoe. Get in here."

I set my satchel over the back of my desk chair, put my coffee and pastry on my desk, and hurried into his office.

"What's going on?" I asked.

"What's going on?" he said. "What's going on is the shooting of Laurence McKinley and Katheryn Conner in what was once the Topsy Turvy on East John Street."

"I read the article. Nathan did a great job," I said. Kawolski had covered the story. The *Daily Times* and the *Post-Intelligencer* both had beat us to the punch, running morning editions with headlines that screamed "Pom Pom Prosecutor Gunned Down" and "Top Lawyer Slain."

Phish had called and told me he thought I might be too close to the story. He'd also sent Kawolski to cover a news conference held by Ernie Blunt.

"Kawolski just called in. Blunt is saying McKinley and Conner were on the hunt for the tax money, and Conner shot McKinley. Blunt, who had suspected something was up, had followed them, and when he told Conner to put the gun down, she turned the gun on him, and he shot her."

I felt like a young student in the principal's office, and the principal knew more than he was letting on and was waiting for me to confess.

"Will it impact the Pom Pom verdict?" I asked.

"I don't see how, but I'm sure Miller's attorneys will find some argument to appeal. Here's the interesting part. They said the concrete floor had been broken up and a hole dug, but the hole was empty."

"I guess I was wrong about the location of the money," I said. "Or someone beat them to it."

"Was it you?" Phish asked pointedly.

I was surprised by the question and didn't immediately answer. "No," I said. "I mean about the money. But I was there, Phish. I don't want to lie to you. You've been good to me. Treated me fairly. After I left the office Friday, I was drunk, and my head was spinning. I bought a pickax and a shovel, and I went to see if I was right. If the treasure was there."

Phish took a long inhale and exhaled. "Well, I guess I knew the allure of treasure is too tempting for any young man to pass up. Did you find it?"

"No," I said, shaking my head. "Either it was never there, I was wrong about where Frankie hid it, or someone beat me to it." I explained what had happened, telling him every detail.

"What do you think Detective Blunt would have done had the money been there, Shoe?" Phish asked.

"It's an awful lot of money for someone to pass up. Especially a public servant on the verge of retirement. It must be hard for Blunt to watch all those criminals living the good life."

"You could have been killed, William. If the money had been there, I don't think Ernie Blunt would have passed up taking it. But either McKinley or Conner also could have shot and killed you."

"You're right," I said. "And I realize no amount of money is worth that risk. Especially now that I'm about to have a wife and hopefully a family to support."

"You patched things up."

"With your help."

Phish smiled. "Mr. Giovacchini called to thank me. He said his daughter is very happy. How do you think she would have felt if instead of a proposal she received the news that you'd been shot?"

"It was selfish of me," I said.

Phish took another deep breath, removed his glasses, and cleaned the lenses. "What would you have done with the money, had you found it?"

I let out a sigh. "Blunt asked me a similar question. I'd like to believe I would have turned it over to the authorities, that I'm better than George Miller and Frankie Ray. But if I'm being honest, I don't know. I'm not going to lie and say I didn't think about how the money could help my family. But it's dirty money, Phish. Four people died for it. I would have always been looking over my shoulder."

"How is your father?"

"He's coming home soon, though I'm not sure how much longer they'll have a home. My mother downplays it, but I know they're in a bad situation. If I had found the money, I would have been hard pressed not to pay off their mortgage and my father's medical expenses."

"Anything else?"

I thought for a moment. "Oh, yeah. I would have bought Joan Daley a tombstone. It's not right, her being buried in an unmarked grave. She was kind to me."

"That's a nice sentiment. Is that it?"

I thought about the restaurant Amara wanted but knew we'd both rather do that on our own. "Yeah," I said.

"Nothing for yourself?"

"For me?" His question surprised me. I'd thought about new suits and a new car, but only in passing, a fantasy I'd never been serious about. I considered my worn shoes with the holes in the bottoms and cardboard on the insides. "I guess I'd get a new pair of shoes. Maybe not new. I can get a used pair from Goodwill now that you've given me a raise."

"That's it? You wouldn't want the money for anything else?"

Again, I gave it thought. "Money didn't do Jay Gatsby much good. Or Edmond Dantès," I said. "My mother always said, 'No good comes from bad money.'"

"She sounds like a wise woman, your mother."

"She is. I just wish I could help her more."

"Tell me, to whom would you have turned in the money?"

That was the problem. I honestly didn't know. I came to Seattle naïve. I'd learned a lot, not everything, but enough to know few could be fully trusted. "I don't know. Seems everyone in Seattle is on the take, from the shoeshine boys to the mayor. Even Judge Kincaid if the officer at the door was to be believed. I guess if I had found it, I would have anonymously given it to worthy charities. There are a lot of charitable organizations out there doing good work for people in need. Maybe that would have been the best thing—something good."

"Do you know why Chicago's Al Capone never bothered with Seattle?"

"No."

"People think it's because there was no money here, but of course you now know there is. What kept Capone away is any money to be made from the sale of illegal liquor, gambling, or prostitution lines the pockets of the mayor, the chief of police, some of his detectives and officers, and others, and they will fight to keep it. It's been said that Roy Olmstead, Seattle's most notorious and most beloved bootlegger, commanded more officers as a bootlegger than he ever did as a lieutenant on the Seattle Police force."

"I didn't know that," I said. "But I guess it doesn't surprise me. I thought Judge Kincaid was Seattle's Wyatt Earp, but in the end, he, too, was in on the take."

"Wyatt Earp came to Seattle at the turn of the century."

"He did?"

"He opened the Union Club, a gambling establishment. The club lasted less than a month. The police shut it down at the request of the city's already established gambling houses."

"I didn't know that either."

"That was well before your time. But I know this. I know that if you had found that money, you would have turned it in, William. Perhaps to Blunt, who may have been using you from the very start."

"I didn't want to admit it, but I think you might be right."

"He might have initially called you with the story because he knew about the tax cases and the missing money, and he knew you were hardworking and industrious and would pursue that lead. Winn and Greer never would have. He also knew you were honest."

"I think maybe I was also a bit naïve," I said.

"We're all a bit naïve, William, but it's not a bad thing to be, to be positive and to view the world that way. Here's the thing, though. You never would have seen that money or the detective again, had you given it to him."

"No. Probably not. I guess I could have turned it in to the tax assessor's office."

"And again, it would have disappeared and lined the pockets of other men whose pockets are already lined. They're not the ones who need it, as you said. It's the poor, the people struggling to get by. Your mother and father."

"I'm glad I didn't find the money," I said. "I'm glad I didn't have to make that decision. I'm not sure what I would have learned about myself, and I like who I am now."

"It would have been a difficult decision for any young man just starting out. I know this personally, from my own circumstances. Which is why I went to the Topsy Turvy and took the money."

For a moment I thought I had misheard him. Phish stared at me from across his desk, his gaze somehow compassionate. "You took the money?"

"Those nights I left the office early? I was digging up the concrete and digging through the dirt, then repouring the concrete. And let me tell you, it was a lot more work than I'm sure you encountered."

I almost didn't believe it. I was stunned. Then I recalled the few cuts and scrapes on Phish's hands and arms and him saying he'd been fixing the printer. And I recalled the dirt in the hole being looser than I had expected, easier to dig than I had anticipated. "Why did you put the dirt back and repour the concrete?"

"Because of the very thing that happened. I wanted whoever was following you to believe the money was never there. That you got it wrong. If they thought you took the money, your life would have for ever been in danger."

"Thank you," I said.

We sat in silence for a moment, then Phish said, "I know what you want to ask me, so let me just tell you why I took the money. I took the money because I didn't want you to have to make that decision, to face that moral dilemma. My wife is the granddaughter of one of Seattle's first timber barons. As such, she inherited a fortune. Far more than what was in that suitcase. It's how her father could afford to offer me the *Daily Star*. I didn't have the money to buy it. But I wouldn't take it. Not for free. I wanted to earn it, so it would be mine. I wanted to stand on my own two feet and build something on my own. He wanted stability for his daughter. So he let me pay him, one week at a time. And he gave me a good price," Phish said with a smile.

"You have all that money and yet . . ." I caught myself before I insulted him.

"And yet, I dress like a pauper and take the bus? I don't make upgrades to the offices?"

"Well, yes."

He smiled, and it was sincere. "That's because I decided money would not change who I was or my work ethic. Yes, it provided my wife and me with a nice but reasonably sized home on Capitol Hill, and it paid for the finest schools for my children. But I would not allow it to define me. I made sure of that. I was raised much like you, Shoe. My parents didn't have much, and I have four brothers and sisters. My mother always said, 'Waste not. Want not.' My wife and I have used her father's charitable foundation for good. We've given lavishly, but quietly, to charities, to the poor and to the homeless during these difficult times, to hospitals, and to orphanages."

"That's wonderful, Phish."

"You know the old saying—it is better to give than to receive. It's the truth. It's a wonderful feeling. I think it has made me a better person, having that responsibility and carrying it out. I know it will make you a better person as well."

"Wait . . . What?"

"I don't want the money, Shoe. I have more than I can spend. More than I can give away."

"You're giving it to me?"

"No. I'm going to absorb it into our foundation, and I want you to come up with the charities to whom the money will be given. I'm sorry to burden you with it, Shoe, but I know you and your wife will be good stewards."

"How can you do this without anyone knowing?"

"Another thing money buys is good attorneys. My wife's attorneys are working on the paperwork necessary for the money to be well insulated. But I did want you to know that money from the foundation—not the tax money—has been transferred to the bank holding the mortgage on your parents' home. It will be anonymously paid off. The same with your father's hospital expenses, and a small cushion will be placed in your parents' bank account until your father is back on his feet. Also anonymously."

"Phish, I can't let you do that."

"I told you before, you keep telling me what I can't do, and people will think I work for you. I'm the administrator of the foundation and I deem this a worthy cause."

I struggled to hold back tears. "Phish, I don't know what to say. I'll pay you back . . . over time."

"As I said, my wife and I get great pleasure helping those in need, and this was particularly satisfying given what I just witnessed these past months. There are no strings attached, but if you can't stomach it, pay it back to the foundation . . . or don't."

I sighed. I didn't know what to think or what to say. "I guess I need to find a place that makes tombstones."

"That would be a nice thing to do, William."

I blew out a breath. "What's next?"

"What's next?" Phish stood. "The news, my boy! The news stops for no man. There's always the next story for a good reporter to cover. I'm not paying you ten dollars a week to sit on your arse. Get out there and get me the next banner headline!"

I hustled out of Phish's office to my desk. As I did, my desk phone rang. I answered it. "William Shumacher, the *Daily Star*, police, fire, and courthouse beat."

And I listened to what would be my next story while fishing in my satchel for paper and a pencil.

Phish was right. The news did not stop for any man or for any reason.

And for that I was most grateful.

Author's Note

As set forth in my acknowledgments, much of this story comes from dozens of newspaper and magazine articles written about the arrest, investigation, and trial of George Moore in 1933. I changed some names but otherwise did my very best to be true to the era. I was so happy I didn't have to deal with iPhones and personal computers . . . a simpler time back then. However, some things I changed—or knew about but ignored—for storytelling purposes. For instance, long-distance phone calls in the 1930s were incredibly expensive, with a daytime call from New York City to Kansas City (a comparable distance of Seattle to Kansas City) costing $4 to $5 for the first three minutes—way too expensive for my protagonist, William Shumacher. Meals at boardinghouses also varied in price, depending on the boardinghouse. I changed or slightly altered restaurant names, but I had the help of Emily Grayson, a librarian at the Seattle Public Library who provided me with detailed street maps from 1933 with restaurant and bar names and locations as well as a list of motion pictures that were shown at the Green Parrot. I also had the help of a few biographies of everyday people who lived during that time, though those were few.

Alas, I'm sure I've made a few mistakes, but hopefully it won't detract from the exciting and largely unwritten-about city of Seattle, Washington, of that era. It was a time of bars and brothels and gambling houses, of sailors on leave looking for companionship, of newspapers sold on street corners, and of police officers paid to look the other way. It was a time of boardinghouses and churches, of women's organizations and exclusive men's clubs. It was the Depression, bootlegging, dinner clubs, and speakeasies. And in this instance, a gangster murder.

Acknowledgments

When my wife and I began dating, she spoke frequently of how much she loved and missed her grandfather. As his heart failed in his later years, he lived with her family, and she saw him and her grandmother daily. I envied her. My father's dad died of colon cancer when I was an infant, and but for family gatherings, I had no relationship with my mother's father. I was fortunate to get to know my wife's grandmother Betty and considered her a grand dame of a bygone era when supper clubs and dance halls pocked the Seattle landscape. I will always recall Mama answering her front door well into her nineties but impeccably dressed in a cashmere sweater, slacks, and gold-colored slippers no matter the time of day. She usually had a pearl of wisdom for me to take away.

"Life," she once said, "is just the blink of an eye."

I was fortunate to find one of those blinks in the attic of our home one afternoon. I was upstairs looking for something, I no longer recall what, when I came across large black books with red spines. When I opened them, I stepped into a time machine that took me back to Seattle in the 1930s. The scrapbook contained newspaper clippings of legal cases documented in the *Seattle Post-Intelligencer*, the *Seattle Daily Times*, and the *Seattle Daily Star*. A former journalist and attorney, I was mesmerized.

I sat down on the plywood floor in our attic and read of that bygone era of "bunco games" and "racing swindles," and of the defense of a woman "out of her mind" when she shot her husband after a lifetime of physical abuse. I read of the first use of the defense of a "crime of passion" in the killing of a spouse caught in bed with another man. I read of the case of the man passing spurious checks, and another man who filed for divorce because his mother didn't like his new bride. Articles documented gambling raids and rumrunners, dope rings and opium dens. An eighteen-year-old girl claimed she was forced to drink alcohol and to accept unwanted advances, ruining her reputation in the community. A doctor was accused of a fake holdup, and another accused in a girl's death after an "illegal operation."

Nothing fascinated me more than the story of George Moore and the "underworld" shooting of Frankie Ray in the barroom of Moore's colorful Pom Pom Club on Profanity Hill. If that headline doesn't shout potential story, then I have no business being a writer.

The articles documented the morning of the shooting until the day Moore was sentenced. The reporters quoted witnesses speaking what almost sounded like a foreign language, and they included all the hijinks and shenanigans of the attorneys for the State and for the defendant. Famed Seattle trial attorney John J. Sullivan and an attorney out of Portland would advance a relatively new defense seeking to acquit Moore, arguing Moore shot Ray because he had "feared for his own life" and therefore justifiably had defended himself.

The jury decided otherwise.

But not before a parade of underworld figures including the defendant, convicts, prostitutes, and "Negro" entertainers took the witness stand. The word "Negro" is offensive, an ethnic slur, and socially unacceptable in current times, but the articles were laced with the word, and I tried to be true to the period in which the story is being told.

From there I launched into this tale of underworld figures and dames working in disreputable houses, of double crosses, and suitcases of buried money. I researched and read of Seattle in the 1930s, well into both Prohibition and the Great Depression; of vice crimes like gambling, prostitution, and bootlegging flourishing; of corruption so rampant Seattle mayor Hiram Gil became the first US mayor to undergo a recall election. Unemployed men and their families lived in cardboard shacks in Hoovervilles and starved, while others built elaborate mansions and surreptitiously donned tuxedos and furs and slinked out into the night to supper clubs, gin joints, and speakeasies, leaving plates of food hardly touched and mounds of cigarette butts in ashtrays on craps tables and bars littered with alcohol glasses.

I changed some of the names, and I imagined dialogue based on the snippets I read in the dozens of articles. I followed the daily events of the trial closely, but I fictionalized the circumstances and, ultimately, the motivation for the shooting. In real life, it appears George Moore fancied Joan Day and shot Frankie Ray due to jealousy and an unpaid hospital bill.

Though I had decided to tell the story from the perspective of a young defense attorney, a nineteen-year-old journalist from Kansas City kept inserting himself into my story until I finally gave up and let William Shumacher explain why. I'm glad I did. I came to love "Shoe" and Amara Giovacchini; "Phish," his publisher; and Mrs. Alderbrook, his boardinghouse owner. I marveled at famed Seattle homicide detective Ernest Yoris (Ernie Blunt), the dapper and debonair George (Miller) Moore, who was so deaf he had to use an ear trumpet, and the "exotic" Joan (Daley) Day, as well as all the other colorful characters I either came across in the articles or who refused to remain silent in my head.

I hope you did too.

Thanks to Meg Ruley, Rebecca Scherer, and the team at the Jane Rotrosen Agency. We've been together for twenty-five novels now, and I'm hoping we can reach fifty together. It will be an adventure!

Thank you to Thomas & Mercer, Amazon Publishing. They are always open to my ideas, even those outside the box. This is my first historical novel, and they helped me immensely to make sure that the setting remained a character in the novel. I'm glad they did. The Great Depression and Prohibition was a fascinating period in American history and especially here in Seattle, which really was the Wild West located out of the limelight in the northwest corner of the country. It's true that Al Capone never ventured this far because he didn't see a way around the corruption he'd have to compete with. Seattle was close to Alaska and the gold rush, as well as the businesses formed to support that rush, and it seemed everyone from the mayor to the shoeshine boys had their hand out.

Amazon Publishing has sold and promoted my novels all over the world, and when they send me out to events, they do it first-rate, which makes my life easier. Thanks to Sarah Shaw, author relations. Thanks to Tamara Arellano, production manager; and Jarrod Taylor, art director. Thanks to Dennelle Catlett for taking care of me at home and on the road. I'm grateful for all the promotion and publicity provided by Andrew George and Erica Moriarty.

Thanks to Julia Sommerfeld, publisher of Amazon Publishing, for creating a team dedicated to their jobs and allowing me to be a part of it. I am sincerely grateful, and even more amazed with each additional million readers we reach.

I am especially grateful to Amazon Publishing's associate publisher, Gracie Doyle. Gracie is my first read and wants my books to be successful and enjoyable as much as I do. She pushed me on this one, for all the right reasons. I'm glad that she did. Mostly, I'm glad she was open to the idea and allowed me to plot it out and create, I hope, a compelling story.

Thank you to Charlotte Herscher, developmental editor. All of my books with Amazon Publishing have been edited by Charlotte—from police procedurals to legal thrillers, espionage thrillers, literary novels, and now a historical novel. She never ceases to amaze me how quickly she picks up the storyline and works to make it as good as it can possibly be. Thanks to Scott Calamar, copyeditor, whom I desperately need.

Thanks to Tami Taylor, who creates my newsletters. Thanks to Pam Binder and the Pacific Northwest Writers Association for their support. Thanks to my daughter, Catherine, who helps me with my social media pages.

Thanks to my mother, Patricia Dugoni, and my father, William Dugoni. Two better parents a young man could never have.

Thank you again to my wife, Cristina, for all her love and support and her willingness to allow me to tell this story. And thanks to my two children, who make me so very proud.

Thanks to all of you tireless and loyal readers for finding my novels and for your incredible support of my work all over the world. I hope you find Shoe a compelling character and enjoy *A Killing on the Hill.*

I couldn't do this without all of you, nor would I want to.

About the Author

Photo © Douglas Sonders

Robert Dugoni is a critically acclaimed *New York Times*, *Wall Street Journal*, *Washington Post*, and Amazon Charts bestselling author, reaching over ten million readers worldwide. He is best known for the Tracy Crosswhite police procedural series. He is also the author of the Charles Jenkins espionage series, the David Sloane legal thriller series, and several stand-alone novels, including *Her Deadly Game*, *The 7th Canon*, *Damage Control*, and *The World Played Chess*. His novel *The Extraordinary Life of Sam Hell* was named *Suspense Magazine*'s 2018 Book of the Year, and Dugoni's narration won an AudioFile Earphones Award. The *Washington Post* named his nonfiction exposé *The Cyanide Canary* a Best Book of the Year. Several of his novels have been optioned for movies and television series. Dugoni is the recipient of the Nancy Pearl Book Award for fiction and a three-time winner of the Friends of Mystery Spotted Owl Award for best novel set in the Pacific Northwest. He has been a finalist for many other awards. Dugoni's books are sold in more than twenty-five countries and have been translated into more than thirty languages. He lives in Seattle. Visit his website at www.robertdugonibooks.com.